# THE SUN GUARDIAN

A Novel

by

T.S. Cleveland

*The Sun Guardian*

is a work of fiction.

Names, characters, businesses, places, events,

organizations and incidents

are products of the author's imagination

or are used fictitiously.

Any resemblance to

actual events, locales, or persons,

living or dead,

is entirely coincidental.

# TABLE OF CONTENTS

## Part One: The Monk's Path

## Part Two: Assassins' Hollow

*For my marauders*

# Part One
# The Monk's Path

# The Apprentice
# 1

Before it began, Scorch knew he would win.

His steps were light, measured, and easy. His heartbeat was steady. The staff in his hand was a natural extension of his arm; its weight was comforting, his grip around it sure and solid.

She came at him with bared teeth and an aggressive thrust of her staff, and he could have evaded the incoming blow, could have ducked and twisted and rolled and attacked from behind, but instead he met her straight on, lifting his staff, matching her ferocity. Wood cracked together like thunder and she stumbled back.

"Almost knocked it out of my hands that time," he laughed.

The woman before him in the sparring ring blew an errant strand of sandy blonde hair from her eyes and steadied the staff defensively across her chest. "Liar," she huffed, and it sounded like an invitation. It had certainly been an invitation the night before. Most words directed toward Scorch were an invitation for something *other*, for his reputation as an insatiable bedfellow was challenged only by his reputation for pyromania, and it was safe to assume, when he was being spoken to, the speaker was either sizing him up for a toss or wondering whether something nearby was about to start smoldering.

"Come at me again," she demanded, and Scorch's small smile became a mischievous grin; she had also spoken those words the night before. As if sensing his debauched line of thought, she rolled her eyes and slammed her staff on the packed dirt in a prompt for further violence. "Come on, Scorch."

He sighed. "If you think you can handle it."

"Shut up and fight me," was her quick reply, followed by a jumping high kick to his chest.

He staggered back, spinning his staff in the air as she stalked forward, searching for another opening. She wouldn't find one unless he wanted her to, and he wasn't in the mood to lose. The sun was bright, the day was cool, but his fingers were hot where they wrapped around the smooth wood of the training staff, and his palms were already growing sticky with sweat. His sparring partner quirked her head at him and he threw her a wink, hoping his cheeks weren't red from a heat that had nothing to do with the mild temperature of the morning.

She returned his wink with a grimace. "You can't distract me."

"Oh, I'm sorry. Do you find me distracting?" he asked, punctuating his question with a sweep of his staff that nearly knocked her off her feet.

She was fast, leaping before she could be toppled. Without pause, she began riddling him with formidable blows, which he blocked easily but enjoyed immensely. It seemed the time for banter had concluded and the remainder of the sparring session would be the sweaty onslaught of strength against strength that he craved, apprentice against apprentice. He was glad for it, treasured the release of tension a good round of sparring allowed. It was the best way he knew how to alleviate his occasional fevers. As he dodged the staff swinging at his face, he could already feel the heat in his fingers dissipating. She really was an excellent partner, and for the life of him, he couldn't recall her name. He felt positive it probably started with an M. Or N?

The slip in memory was excusable, in Scorch's opinion, as the Guild was rich with apprentices new and old, as well as graduated guardians returning for more training, assignments, or merely because, for them, the stone walls were home. Scorch had been an apprentice within the Guardians' Guild for fifteen years, but he could hardly be expected to remember every single person's name, regardless of whether he'd slept with them the night before or not. It was just too many names and too many faces. The strangest thing was that, whether they had just arrived or had lived there forever, succumbed to Scorch's considerable charms or not, everyone within the Guild knew his name with an instantaneousness that set him ill at ease.

He did not strive for infamy, yet it was always finding him. But what was he to do? He would not smother his exceptional skills because it made the other apprentices envious gossips, nor would he deny himself the comfort of companionship because it earned him dirty looks. And the single facet of his reputation he would have made an effort to stop was the one he could never disprove. *Scorch*, they had dubbed him. *A fire starter.* His alleged proclivities had earned him the nickname, and he was powerless to correct the assumption that he, Scorch, enjoyed playing with fire in the literal sense. It wasn't true. He didn't enjoy it. But letting them think he did was better than the alternative.

The world narrowed down to Scorch and what's-her-name, the clanking wood of their staffs, and the practiced in and out of controlled breaths, one after the other, as every kick was careened and every offensive strike was defended. She jumped at him with a grunt of frustration and Scorch ducked, twisted, and grabbed her from behind, holding his staff beneath her chin. She choked and he released her. When she swung at him, he blocked her with an upraised forearm and jabbed at the backs of her knees with his staff. She buckled and landed with a thud before rolling into a crouch, which she swiftly unfurled from with a sidekick.

He let it connect and grabbed her ankle in retaliation, giving it a brutal yank and sending her to her back. The air was knocked from her lungs in the time it took him to knock the staff from her hands and straddle her waist. He let his own weapon fall and clutched her wrists, pulling them roughly above her head in the dirt, sending a puff of dust floating around them. She strained against him and he sat triumphantly atop her for a few moments before relinquishing his hold and sitting back on his heels.

"I wish they would stop assigning you as my sparring partner," she grumbled. "It'd be nice to win every once in a while."

Scorch offered her his hand and she took it without question, letting him lift them both to their feet. He didn't miss the way her fingers brushed the underside of his wrist, or the way her lashes batted with intent. He responded with a leisurely step closer, until their hips were a hairsbreadth from knocking together.

"If you'd like, we could have a rematch," he offered slyly.

"Only if I end up on top next time," was her slightly breathless response.

He laughed, a hearty kind of laugh that lifted his face to the sun. His hair fell back from his forehead, scruffy and blond and boyish, and he knew she was admiring the chiseled line of his jaw and comely shadow of beard. When he lowered his eyes back down to her, he wondered whether he truly wished for that manner of rematch. A fight like they'd just had? Definitely. But a repeat of their less clothed sparring from the previous night? He wasn't so sure. She was pretty in a way that left no room for debate, with an alluring hourglass figure beneath a layer of taut muscle. Her lips were full, her cheeks a healthy pink. With her blonde hair and tan skin, Scorch mused that she looked a bit like he would look, were he female. But was he interested in lying with her again?

"Hey!" hollered a third voice. Scorch and his sparring partner both responded, turning their heads toward the figure approaching the training grounds. "*Scorch*," the newcomer specified, and now that he had walked nearer, Scorch could see it was Merric, the only apprentice he knew who had been living at the Guild longer than himself, and that was only because he was the Master's son.

"Missing me already?" Scorch asked with a cocky flit of his eyebrow. They had seen one another an hour ago for archery practice.

Merric crooked a finger once he reached the wood-post fence that surrounded the melee ring. Tragically, the Guild Master's son belonged to the slim lot of people stubbornly un-beguiled by Scorch's flirtations. Generally, Scorch didn't care much for Merric, but it was still tragic, because the young man was gorgeous. Deep auburn hair and green eyes and milky skin, made all the more irresistible by the fact that Merric seemed to loathe Scorch. He was the one to first spread rumors that Scorch was a fire-lusted fiend that set the forest ablaze. Still, Scorch could have overlooked their disagreements for what would undoubtedly be a glorious tumble, but Merric remained unshakable in his distaste for all things Scorch.

"The Master wants to see you right away," grouched Merric.

Scorch scooped up the training staffs, tossing one into his partner's hands, and they crossed the ring together. He leaned against the fence, lowering his head so his hair fell messily across his brow, and looked up at Merric beneath pale lashes. "If you're trying to get me on my own, all you have to do is ask."

Merric pointedly ignored him, averting his eyes as though it hurt to look at him, but when his cruelly exquisite gaze landed on the woman at Scorch's side, his face softened at once.

"Mazzy," Merric sighed by way of greeting.

*Mazzy*, thought Scorch with a rush of satisfaction. So it *did* start with an M. He'd have gotten it eventually.

"Hi, Merric," Mazzy replied, but she was pressed closely against Scorch's side when she said it.

Merric's eyes darkened. He straightened his shoulders and turned his attention to something past the both of them; an incredibly fascinating fence post, Scorch presumed. "Don't keep him waiting."

"I'm on my way as we speak," Scorch said, vaulting his long body over the fence and leaning the staff against a post for the next apprentice due for melee. He stole a quick glance at Mazzy, who looked decidedly disappointed that their conversation had been temporarily stalled. He delivered her a flash of a broad smile and a wink. After seeing Merric, he was in the mood for less feminine affections, but he didn't want to be rude. She accepted his smile with a hand on her hip and a coy flip of her hair, and then he directed his amber gaze to Merric. "Care to walk with me?"

Merric's lips curled into a snarl and he turned on a pissy heel, stomping in the direction opposite the Guild House. Taking his abrupt exit as a sign that Merric did not actually care to walk with him, Scorch headed off on his own, nodding once at Mazzy before he left.

Normally, he would have sparring for a full hour, but if the Guild Master requested one's presence, one dropped everything one was doing to attend him. Scorch, in particular, felt an incessant need to please the leader of the guardians, and not solely because the man had saved his life as a child. It was more that the man demanded one's full respect and adoration, and Scorch thought he adored Master McClintock the most out of all his acquaintances. They weren't particularly close, they didn't know one another particularly well, but he was the only semblance of a father Scorch could remember, outside a handful of blurry memories, and with no real family to speak of, he clung to the idea of the Master of the Guild and hastened to attend him.

If his heart was racing as he walked toward the stone building that fell somewhere between a fortress and a schoolhouse, it was only because he'd not been summoned to the Master's presence for a long while, not since a few weeks prior, when there had been an incident involving his laundry duties and a few burnt underclothes. As he'd told the Master then, anything could have set those personables on fire.

He strove to keep his skin from heating up and stuck his default grin on his face as he crossed beneath the archway of the Guild House. Turning left and walking down the sunlit hall had him passing several guardians and apprentices and a fat grey cat, and Scorch nodded pleasantly to each of them. No one stopped to speak with him. No one said hello. The cat, however, yowled at him for a scratch behind the ear, which he was happy to deliver.

Minutes later, he stood at the door of the Master's chamber, which he knew to be filled with stained glass and the smell of pipe smoke, but he hesitated to knock. There was always a whisper of fear living deep inside him, counting softly down to the time it would all end, and every time he was called to see the Master, he worried that the time had come.

He inhaled and it was sharp in his chest, but he didn't think he was sweating too badly, so he shrugged the worry from his shoulders and opened the door with a confident sweep, entering like the room was his in which to saunter.

Master McClintock stood from his writing desk, looking for all the world like his son, albeit an older, less grumpy version. He had a thick beard and was stouter, more solidly built, but the resemblance was striking. His green eyes flashed at Scorch's arrival, and he came around his desk to pat his shoulder.

"Ah. I half expected Merric to conveniently forget about relaying my message."

Scorch was already smiling, but his cheeks dimpled at the Master's words. It was no secret the Master's son disliked him. He had, on multiple occasions, tried his damnedest to have Scorch kicked out of the Guild, and if not for the Master's intrinsic sense of charity, it might have worked. Scorch liked to think the man cared at least a small fraction for the boy he had taken in, even if he'd proved more trouble than he was worth over the years.

"Merric was delighted to see me," said Scorch, sitting down at the Master's behest. The chair was sturdy and uncomfortable. The Master remained standing, not necessarily looming, but observing from a superior height. "And I must say, it's a delight to see *you*, Master."

"Hopefully not the same delight Merric feels for you," Master McClintock laughed. The greatest difference between father and son was humor. The father had it. The son did not. "I am glad you came so quickly. The matter I'd like to discuss is unusual and possibly urgent."

"Possibly urgent?" Scorch asked, shifting to the edge of his seat. He wasn't ready. If it was all about to end, he wasn't ready. Through years of practice, his expression showed none of the horror boiling beneath his skin. He tilted his head curiously at the Guild Master, politeness masking his panic. "What is it?"

Master McClintock lifted his pipe, and Scorch noticed for the first time that it had been white-knuckled in his hand since he'd stepped through the door. Smoke hung like a dreamy canopy above them, and the Master was blinking more than usual, his eyes irritated. It appeared he had been worrying his pipe all morning and, judging by the dark circles beneath his eyes, probably all night. Such an observation tightened Scorch's already tight chest. Something had kept the man up, and he didn't want to know what it was.

"The Queen has written," Master McClintock said.

That was not what Scorch had been expecting. "Oh?"

"She's received troubling information and has honored the guardians by bringing that information to our attention."

"That's—nice of her." What little Scorch knew of Viridor's Queen was limited to her strict policy on elementals; it wasn't as if he was subjected to much politicking within the walls of the Guild. The Queen and other royals would sometimes enlist the Guild for assistance, but their correspondence was strictly between the Guild Master and his chosen guardians, and as Scorch was an apprentice, any details relayed to him were inadequate. He itched to ask what the Queen writing had to do with him, if it had anything to do with him at all, but he didn't. He waited patiently for the

Master to take another thick drag of his pipe and blow a tendril toward the ceiling.

"What I'm about to tell you is confidential," he said, streams of smoke escaping between his teeth.

Scorch sat up straighter. "Of course."

Master McClintock looked frayed around the edges and worry for the Guild Master started creeping in around Scorch's worry for himself. The man set his pipe aside in order to flex his hand, and then he leaned back on his desk, fixing Scorch with a frown.

"We have reason to believe an assassination attempt will be made on the High Priestess."

Scorch felt his eyebrows knit together. More illustrious than even the Queen, he knew who the High Priestess of Viridor was. She was worshipped across the country for her saintliness, her connection to the Gods, and she lived in a temple atop Viridor's highest mountain, surrounded by a team of deadly and devout warriors. The Priestess' Monks, they were called. He found the idea of her being assassinated difficult to swallow, not just because everyone loved her, but because she was almost impossible to reach and protected by the best fighters in the country, possibly the world.

"Who would want the High Priestess dead?" he asked the Master, who was watching him with a disconcerting level of scrutiny.

"It's unclear at this time," the Master began. "The Queen's spies discovered only inklings of rumors, but it was enough to raise alarm. So here we are with a grave task at hand."

The Guardians' Guild was orchestrated for missions such as these. Perhaps not every mission was as dire as the assassination of a Holy One, but guardians were regularly sent from the Guild with various jobs. They were protectors; it was why they trained. If someone needed an armed escort through a bandit-infested journey, they would contact the Guild. If someone felt their life was in danger and wished for a bodyguard, they would contact the Guild. In a land like Viridor, there was always a job for one of its guardians, always someone to protect and serve. Scorch had not yet been on such assignments, so he was still considered an apprentice. He wondered why he was being told of assassination plots when he wasn't even a full-fledged guardian.

"I want you for this," Master McClintock announced with a clap of his hands that had Scorch jumping in his seat.

"Want me for what, Master?"

"I want you for this task, Scorch," the Master said, because even he called Scorch by his nickname. Scorch wondered if anyone even remembered the name his parents had given him. "I want you to warn the High Priestess of the assassination and defend her life, if necessary."

Whatever Scorch had worried the Master was planning on saying, sending him on a task to save the High Priestess had not been it. The bewilderment must have shown on his face, because the Master lifted from his perch on the desk to touch his shoulder.

"You're untested, I know," said the Master. "But you're also one of the Guild's most skilled apprentices. I'd been planning to send you out for your first task soon, and when this fell in my lap . . . Scorch," he said, bending down to look him in the eye, "I cannot send a seasoned guardian on such a dire task, because I cannot risk them being recognized. You're the one I want for this. Will you do it?"

"I will do it," Scorch answered, because of course he would. He would never say no to the man who had plucked him from ashes and saved him from worthlessness.

Something changed at that moment, in the Master's eyes. The tension in his shoulders screamed, but when he spoke, it was with an air of renewed calm. He took his hand from Scorch's shoulder and returned to his place behind his desk, pipe sticking back into the corner of his mouth.

"I knew I could count on you."

"You can always count on me," Scorch said, trying not to fidget in his seat. "What must I do?"

Master McClintock laughed, and Scorch felt a twinge of pride that he'd caused the man a moment's amusement. "Always so eager. That's why I know you're perfect for this." He reached for his smoking box and lifted out a fresh pinch of purple moss, shoving it down into his pipe. "Normally, I would give you an official Guild missive, but not for something like this. It's too risky. We can't have anyone knowing where you're going or why."

Scorch nodded his understanding. His throat felt dry. "Makes sense."

"I'd like to say the bulk of the guardianship will be informing the High Priestess of the plot and remaining at her side until the threat has passed, but the fact of the matter is you have to reach her first. And reaching her is where the trouble begins."

Scorch did not have to think long to remember his geography lessons. The High Priestess lived in a temple, on the highest mountain in Viridor, at the very heart of the country, and that alone would be enough to deter most. But the mountain was the least troublesome trial of the path. Surrounding the mountain was a desert plane, and surrounding the desert was a lake so big it had more in common with a sea. The pilgrimage to the temple was notoriously dangerous and only the most stalwart in their desires dared pass through the terrain. It was said only fighters wishing to become one of the Priestess' Monks still traveled into the Heartlands. It was a test of their worthiness.

Why, Scorch had asked when he was little, did the High Priestess live in such an inhospitable place? The Master had answered, "So she can speak more easily with the Gods."

"You know the route to the temple," Master McClintock said.

"I know the gist of it."

"Then you know why it's not often we ask our guardians to cross into such lands," the Master continued, striking a match and puffing at his pipe.

Scorch watched the flames flicker at the end of the match and felt his fingertips grow warm. "You would not ask me if it were not important," he said, sounding braver than he felt. He did not relish the route to the temple, but he relished less the disappointment in the Master's eyes if he revealed his hesitance. "I can do it."

"I know you can." He smiled warmly at Scorch before his expression grew grim and his voice sank to a serious baritone. "You have done well here. I think back to the day we met and—I am glad for it. You are," he paused, as if collecting wayward thoughts, "a *special* young man."

Uncertainty gripped Scorch when he answered. "Thank you, Master." He was glad the Master had found him when he was a boy of five, stained with soot, but he was not glad he'd needed finding. He was not glad his life had forced him to run into the Guild Master's arms. He had love for the Guild, it was true, but that didn't change the fact that the price had been too high.

The Master looked down at the smoldering pipe, watching its embers glow orange. "I know you will make the guardians proud. You have already made me proud."

Scorch was afraid to speak, so he settled for nodding his head and averting his gaze when the Master blinked more rapidly than was normal for tearless eyes. After a moment of silence between the two men, the elder stood up, walked around his desk, and extended his hand. The younger accepted it.

"So begins your first guardianship."

And so ended his apprenticeship. With his first guardianship, Scorch was a guardian. He stood. "When do I leave, Master?"

A sad smile tugged at the Master's lips and he squeezed Scorch's hand within his own. "I'm afraid you must leave at once."

"Oh."

"Yes, well, you must report to Etheridge first for a medical check and supplies, but then . . ."

"Understood. Of course," was Scorch's static reply, and when the Master let go of his hand, he wiped sweaty palms against his jerkin. "Then I suppose I should go."

The Master bowed his head solemnly, the skin tight around his tired eyes. "Goodbye, Scorch."

Scorch bowed his head, smiled his brightest smile at Master McClintock, and then he took his leave.

As he was walking through the white flaps of the herbalist's tent, stationed by the banks of the river, Merric was walking out. Their shoulders grazed and, though Scorch had been prepared to be ignored, Merric stopped.

"Scorch," he said.

Scorch turned to face the Master's son. His face was utterly blank, and Scorch found he preferred the crinkle between Merric's eyebrows that was the usual accompaniment to his Scorch-related ire. "Yes, darling?"

Merric bit at his lip, a habit Scorch was always happy to observe, and then he said, simply, softly, "Be careful."

A hundred quips dashed through Scorch's brain, but what he ended up saying was nothing at all. Instead of speaking, his eyes roamed up and down Merric's body, taking in his lean figure and smooth skin, the luster of his auburn hair. When he had trailed back to green eyes, he stared for a moment and wondered morbidly whether he'd ever see them again. He wanted badly to lighten the weight of his gaze, but could think of no better solution than a coquettish wink. It was arguable that he winked entirely too much, but he feared it had become a nervous twitch, which only worsened when he tried to stifle it.

Merric's mouth wavered for a few seconds before settling on a sneer. "See you," he spat, without nearly as much venom as could usually be discerned. Then he turned abruptly and walked away, back toward the Guild House.

Scorch dutifully watched his backside until it disappeared into the shadows of the building. After an indulgent sigh, he entered the herbalist's tent.

"Oh, it's you," Etheridge said, her arms up to the elbows in a bag filled with manure.

"And *you*," Scorch smirked, leaning against the pole of the tent. "I had no idea you liked it so dirty."

Etheridge, resident Guild Herbalist and in no way influenced by Scorch's charisma, made a disgusted face as her hands rooted around in the brownish muck. "I'm looking for Luna seeds," she explained. "Excellent for detox potions. A single Luna seed can cure almost any poison. I've been trying to get my hands on some for years, but they're rare, the stubborn things." Her eyes got big and she pulled a fistful of manure from the bag. When she unclenched her fist and wiped away the unsavory remnants, a single spherical stone rested in her palm, shiny as a pearl. "There you are," she whispered and dropped it into a seashell. It made a dainty *ping* and she smiled. When Scorch cleared his throat, she pulled her other arm free of the manure and walked right past him and out of the tent.

Not knowing what else to do, he followed. "Master McClintock sent me to see you."

She knelt beside the river and dunked her arms beneath the water. "I know. That's what Merric was here for." She looked over her shoulder at him, her dark braid a severe cord swinging at her back. "First guardianship, huh? It'll be strange not having you around. Though I won't miss worrying about my garden going up in smoke, you scoundrel."

Scorch wasn't sure whether Etheridge was being insulting or nostalgic. He'd only burned a few of her herbs that one time, and he'd helped her replant new ones. If he recalled, ashes in the soil made the crop especially lush that year, and anyone with an upset stomach reaped the benefits.

"What do you think about giving me a proper sendoff?" he asked, offering his hand as she crouched by the water.

She stood up without his help and shook her arms. Little droplets of water landed across the bridge of Scorch's nose. "If by proper sendoff you mean a medical check, then absolutely. Get in the tent."

"Bossy," he laughed, picking up his pace when Etheridge kicked at his heels.

Once inside the tent, the herbalist dried her hands with a cloth and ordered him to take a seat. Her chair was much softer than the Master's and he sank into it gratefully, stretching his long legs and crossing his ankles languidly.

"Sit up straight," Etheridge said. "And wipe the smugness off your face before I smack it off. This is a checkup, not a seduction."

"Trust me," Scorch crooned, "if I was seducing you, you would know."

"*You* would know because my boot would be up your arse." She pushed her hand up beneath his jerkin and linen undershirt. "Don't get excited. I'm just going to listen to your chest."

Etheridge walked him through a series of checks, swatting his shallow advances with cold hands. His lungs sounded fine, his eyes were clear, and his heart was pumping blood through his veins at a healthy pace. When he jokingly bent over for a more intimate exam, Etheridge smacked him hard on the behind and told him to get his act together.

"I hope the Master knows you'll be spending half your time on your task and the other half on your back," she said, handing him a drawstring pouch.

"What's this?" he asked, already wrestling with the ties to get it open.

"A few things for the road. A salve for minor cuts, an ointment for your nethers."

Scorch cocked an eyebrow.

"Just in case," she said, a crafty smile beginning to bloom across her face. "It's better to have it and not need it than to need it and not have it. But to be on the safe side, try not to roll with too many bar wenches. Folks aren't as clean out there as they are in here."

Scorch held the pouch against his heart. "I love it. Thank you, Etheridge."

She sighed, shaking her head. "Don't get into trouble, Scorch." It was an order.

He tied the pouch to his belt and ran a hand over the scruff of his chin. Observing the herbalist with soft eyes, he teased, "You're the only trouble I want in my life. Will you wait for me?"

Etheridge responded by shoving her hands back into the sack of manure. "Don't set my tent on fire on your way out."

He glanced around the little tent, at the flowers hanging from every surface, at the woman he'd known for years who wouldn't hug his neck before he left. Before the heat could start building up beneath his skin, he patted the pouch at his side, nodded his head to her, and exited swiftly.

He had one more stop to make before he could leave, and he made it there on a wave of tired enthusiasm, avoiding populated halls so as not to exhaust his face with insincerity. When he finally reached his room, which was more of a closet tucked away on the highest floor of the Guild House, he was inexplicably tired. After trudging through the door, it was tempting to collapse onto his mattress, but he didn't dare. The Master had ordered him to leave immediately and he had no choice but to obey his wishes. Scorch had his guardianship, his medical check, and now all he needed was his handful of belongings.

He wouldn't take everything with him—not that he had much —but there were a few items that would be useful. He was already wearing his armor, since his morning had been spent in weapons training. It was more casual than the usual sort, made with rough leathers instead of metals. He disliked the weight of most armor, and the leather pieces allowed him valuable freedom of movement.

His sword rested in its scabbard, leaned against his windowsill, and he picked that up first, looping it to his belt. The weight of it was comfortable, hanging at his side. He cherished his sword. It had been a gift from the Master.

Everything else he packed into a satchel: a few extra shirts, underclothes, a flask of Guild-brewed whiskey, and a hefty coin purse given to him by Master McClintock for expenses. If he had anything of his parents, he might have tucked it safely away at the bottom of his pack, but he had nothing that hadn't burned fifteen years ago.

Scorch fastened a bedroll to the satchel, slung it over his shoulder, and stuck a dagger into his belt. He ran a hand through his mop of hair and realized there was nothing left for him to do. He had no friends to say goodbye to and no lover worth kissing for luck. He bid a silent farewell to the little room and left.

# *Flora*

# 2

The Guild looked different from the other side. Scorch found it quite ominous, with its high stone walls and intimidating towers. From the outside, one couldn't see the crystal blue river, or the gardens, or the acres of forest. From the outside, it didn't look like home, but then again, it had never really been home for Scorch. It was simply a place to live.

He did not linger forlornly outside the Guild, reminding himself he had a task, an important one that the Master thought only he could complete. He had to save the High Priestess, and since such a sacred charge would eventually require him to take a few steps away from the Guild, he tore his eyes from the old stones and began his solitary trek down the road.

The first five years of his life had been spent outside the walls, when he'd been with his parents, but he couldn't remember much of those early days, and once he'd joined the Guild, the opportunity to leave the grounds had been scarce. Several years after he'd begun his apprentice training, when he'd turned thirteen, he'd been sent into the surrounding woods for his hunting test. Given no more than a knife and a bow, he had to collect the hides of three rabbits, the feet of three birds, fill his canteen with the water of a fresh stream, and fill his pack with edible mushrooms and berries. He shivered to think of it. The test was supposed to last two days. He had been missing for two weeks.

But Scorch was older now, and the woods fascinated him more than they frightened him. It was refreshing to see new trees and rocks and sky after looking at the same surroundings for most of his life. And when a shadow in the trees startled him, and his palms became sweaty, he hummed a tune to calm himself. New as it all was, he was a guardian now, with no time to fear faceless shadows. The mantra in his head was steady and all-consuming as he walked down the path: *Save the High Priestess, save the High Priestess, save the High Priestess.*

By the time the woods began to thin and Scorch emerged from the Guild's corner of the world, the sky had grown dark and the stars had grown bright and his chest was puffed outward with self-assurance. His thoughts were less bothered by the journey ahead, and his ego was stroked by the certainty in his Master's voice. The memory of praise might have brought a blush to his cheeks, but the night hid it well.

But as high-spirited as he was, he was also road-worn and desperate for a meal, so when inviting lights twinkled in a village ahead, Scorch wasted no time in his search for the local tavern. He had never been in a village before, filled with ordinary people, and it was odd passing so many folks with no weapons strapped to their bodies. There weren't many out, because of the late hour, but those few roaming the dirt road seemed to be headed in the same direction. He followed, a drift of music catching in the wind. When a swinging sign with a mug emblazoned on its front caught his eye, he rushed forward, not even catching the name of the place before he opened the door and stepped inside.

It was wonderfully cozy, with a fireplace crackling on the far side of the room and the body heat of what looked like the entire village pressed together in barstools and dining tables. The source of the music was a feather-hatted flautist sitting on a modest stage. A few couples were dancing, but most everyone seemed to be there for the drinks and food. Scorch only had to stand in the doorway for a moment before a young lady linked arms with him and dragged him further into the tavern.

"Hi, handsome," she cooed. "I'm taking care of you tonight. Hungry? Thirsty?" She was a petite creature, with big doe eyes and bountiful freckles dusting her cheeks. She was fit and her skin was dark, and Scorch fancied her immediately.

He bent low to whisper in her ear. "Hungry and thirsty, yes. Among other things."

She laughed with a keen brightness in her eyes. "Well, follow me, sir, and I'll see what I can do for you."

The tables by the fire were full, so she led him to one near the bar, pushing him down into a chair and ignoring the whistles of a few drunken patrons.

"My name's Flora. Tell you what. I'm going to pop into the kitchens and have them fix you up a plate of something hot. But first, I'm going to pour you a mug of ale. You look like you need it." She kissed his cheek and smelled like freshly baked bread.

"Lovely. Then will you marry me?" he asked, tilting his head in a way he knew showcased the attractive jut of his cheekbones.

She snickered and shoved a playful hand into his shoulder before skittering off to the bar. He watched her appreciatively as she leaned over to exchange words with the barkeep, and he wasn't the only one watching; most of the men in the room, and a few women, were well occupied by the pleasant curve of Flora's body and the cheerfulness of her face. But there were a few patrons who seemed more interested in watching Scorch. As Flora bounced back to his table and set a frothy drink in front of him, he experienced the awkward moment of accidentally catching someone's eye. A strange man with roughly worn skin was studying him from the bar, and when Scorch met his gaze, the man held it like a dare. Never one to back down from a challenge (and still steamed up from thoughts of ravaging Merric earlier in the day), Scorch offered the stranger a wink, smiling at him and the two other men in his company. He held their slightly unnerving eye contact until Flora shifted her weight and created a barrier with her hips.

"Drink up, handsome, and I'll be right back with something for you to eat." She ran a hand through his hair and twirled off for the kitchens.

Scorch grinned into his mug as he took the first few sips. The ale was cool and he felt instantly revived. When he looked back up at the three men, they were no longer staring at Scorch, but speaking to one another with their heads huddled close. A spark of curiosity flared within him one moment and was smothered the next, when the flautist came over to his table and sat across from him.

"Sorry to bother you," said the flautist, a boy who looked no older than sixteen. "I couldn't help but notice you when you came in."

Pleased with himself, Scorch took another gulp of his ale. "And I noticed you," he confessed. The boy was too young to catch his genuine interest, but he had an interesting face and a pleasant voice, and after spending the day walking alone in the woods, Scorch was craving another human's company. "You're gifted," he said, nodding at the flute in the boy's hands.

"Oh, I'm nothing special. Not like you."

The words were said with such *knowing*, such *sureness* that Scorch froze, and for a few terrible seconds he couldn't breathe, but then the boy spoke again, oblivious to Scorch's momentary panic.

"I mean, I just play an instrument and tell stories, but you must be a real hero, right? You're a guardian, aren't you? We get some through here from time to time, but I've never gotten to speak with one before. You *are* a guardian, aren't you?"

Scorch drank deeply from his mug until nary a drop was left. He set it down and let it clunk loudly against the tabletop. His heart was beating fast and he laughed at himself for letting the kid give him such a jolt of adrenaline. *Special.* "You caught me," he answered. "I'm from the Guild."

"From the Guild?" Flora asked, appearing out of nowhere with a bowl of stew and a plate of bread and cheese. "Is that true? You're a guardian?" Scorch nodded and bit into a crusty piece of bread. "Oh! That's exciting, isn't it?" She scooped up his mug and nudged the flautist with her hip. "I'll be right back with a refill. Felix isn't bothering you, is he? He's awful nosy."

"No, Felix is divine," Scorch laughed, enjoying the flautist's widening eyes at a guardian's approval. "Maybe he'll play me a tune to keep me company in your absence."

But when Flora returned to the bar to refill Scorch's mug, Felix the Flautist stood up from the table. "I need to get back to work before I get in trouble," he said, fiddling with the flute in his fingers. "But I'd love to dedicate the next song to you." He was blushing fiercely now and not looking Scorch in the eye. "It's really such a pleasure to meet you."

Before Scorch could respond, Felix was half-running back to his little stage, the feather in his hat fluttering. A few patrons clapped for him, and he cleared his throat before speaking up. "Ladies and Gentlemen, t-tonight we have a special patron with us," he began, stuttering adorably and flourishing a hand toward Scorch's table. "It's always an honor to host a g-guardian, and this n-next song is for you."

When the music began, all eyes were on Scorch, including the three men at the bar, and when Flora returned with his ale, several men and women were flocking around his table. He could hardly hear Felix's flute with all the excited chatter surrounding him. As if staking her claim that she'd found him first, Flora set Scorch's mug down and then set herself down, right in his lap.

"You're too handsome to be a guardian," she declared. "Shouldn't you have grisly scars from fighting?"

"Not if I always win the fight," Scorch responded, and his audience laughed, charmed. He both enjoyed the attention and found it off-putting, but Flora's weight was warm and comfortable in his lap, and he let one hand rest on her thigh while his other hand fed himself dinner and finished off his second mug of ale.

Everyone at the table wanted to know more. Always more. So Scorch kept talking. Some of it was truth and some of it was what he knew they wanted to hear. For example, he really was an excellent swordsman, but he had never taken down a brigade of bandits before. He knew how to kill a man a dozen different ways, but he'd only ever practiced on straw-stuffed dummies. But since Scorch had never heard of a few fabrications causing anyone any harm, he saw no reason to feel guilty for his half-lies. Technically, he was a guardian. No one needed to know it was only his first day being one.

At one point, Flora whispered in his ear, "Have you ever fought an elemental?"

Scorch squeezed her thigh. He could feel her breath quicken. "No," he answered. "But I've met a few." And he told what truths he could.

When the night was headed fast toward morning and the last of the patrons were filtering out of the tavern, he had a stomach full of drink and a lapful of Flora, and when she wriggled playfully against him, he nuzzled her neck and gripped her side.

"I have a room," she said, "behind the tavern."

Scorch quickly scanned the bar for the men who'd caught his eye before, but they were long gone. After kissing the blushing flautist on the cheek, Scorch let the lovely barmaid take the lead.

*It started as a small flicker that warmed his heart, same as always. She touched his cheek and her fingers made his skin tingle. He watched her hand retreat and brush across the kindling.*

*He shivered on his bedroll. His father knelt beside him, pressed a large hand to his forehead, and he fell asleep in a summer fog.*

*Warmth, constant warmth.*

*Blood splattered his face, dripped in his eye, and it was hot. It burned his skin like the smoke burned his lungs. But he couldn't scream or they'd find him, they'd find him.*

*He cowered in a bush of thorns until their blood was cool and hard. Tears streamed more warmth down his cheek.*

*His flesh was splotched and feverish. He could see their bodies piled where he'd been sleeping so soundly.*

Scorch was gasping when he woke. He sat up in bed and grasped at his throat. It took him a few moments to regain his sense of reality. It always took a few moments, after he had a dream about his parents, to remember he was safe.

The room was dark, which was good. It meant nothing was burning. And once he put his hand down and felt the weight beside him, he remembered where he was and whom he was with. His eyes were slowly adjusting, and it was touch alone that guided his palm across the slope of Flora's hip, across her ribs, and over her curls.

Scorch wondered what time it was, but it could not have been too long since they'd collapsed into heavy sleep, because he could still feel traces of sweat dampening her skin. He half-heartedly wished to wake her. As used to nightmares as he was, they were easier to banish with the help of a physical distraction.

He trailed his fingers from her hair to trace the hollow of her neck, which had been sensitive to his attentions earlier. Her skin was slick with sweat, so he moved to adjust the blankets with thoughts that she must be too warm from all of Scorch's body heat. But when he gently pulled down the blankets, something wasn't right.

He couldn't yet make out her face in the dark, but he could make out her shape, and it jostled unnaturally when the bed bounced with his movement. He touched her shoulder.

"Flora?"

His fingers felt sticky as they lifted from her skin.

"We had to stop her from screaming, see."

Scorch's reaction was instant. He rolled from the bed and dropped to the floor. His hand reached out for his sword, which he'd leaned against the bedside table for the night, but his hands found nothing but empty air. He strained his eyes through the dark to find the man who had spoken. As soon as he spotted a dark mass moving by the window, hands seized him from behind and yanked him to his feet. He thrashed wildly, but whoever held him held him fast, their fingers like iron.

"She was a much lighter sleeper than you," the dark mass said, his shadow growing larger as he stepped closer. "Woke up right away."

He was right in front of him now, and Scorch's eyes were finally adjusted enough to make out a few details of his face. Gruff, leathery skin, a cold stare—it was the man who'd been staring at him from the bar.

"Now, I'd expect a guardian like you to possess about him certain habits. But you're shockingly green, aren't you? Weapon beside the bed, braggart in the tavern, not knowing the difference between being sized up for a brawl or a buggering." The man leaned in to whisper in Scorch's ear, and his breath was hot. "Led us straight to you."

Scorch bucked backward. The man at his back banged hard against the wall but didn't loosen his grip, and then a third man suddenly presented himself, stepping into Scorch's line of sight with a sword pointed at his belly—Scorch's sword—and he could see well enough now to see it was coated in blood.

His eyes flew desperately to Flora's limp form on the bed as the man hissed a cruel laugh.

"She's dead," he said.

"No," whispered Scorch, and now all three men were laughing, horrible laughs that made his skin crawl with fever.

He knew in the pit of his stomach she wasn't alive, but he didn't let himself think it until the man struck a match and lit the lantern beside her bed. There was no escaping her fate after that, because the man grabbed a fistful of Scorch's hair and forced him to look.

There was blood everywhere, soaking the sheets and the pillows, and pooling on the floor. And in the center of it all, there she was, throat gaping, not neatly slit, but gashed messily. Her eyes were open, grey and dead and staring at the ceiling.

A violent tremor took hold of him. A heave brought him to his knees and the man holding him let him drop. Scorch's fingernails scraped at the floorboards, and in the golden glow of the lantern, he could see his bloody hands. He looked down at his bare chest, and it was covered in blood. Flora's blood was all over him. He vomited. An agonizing groan stole from his throat.

"Ebbins, let's get out of here," said the man holding Scorch's sword.

Scorch was trembling; he couldn't stop. He tried to close his eyes and pretend he was back at the Guild, but all he saw was a neck hacked wide.

"Grab him and let's go," responded the man called Ebbins.

Fingers dug into his scalp and forced him up by the hair.

"He's naked," said the man with the iron grip, and Ebbins spat on the floor at Scorch's bare feet.

"Grab his clothes. Won't get paid if he freezes to death before we get there."

When Ebbins turned around, Scorch launched himself at his back. He could feel a chunk of his hair ripping free and nails scraping at his arms, but he kicked out desperately, landing a hit square in one man's stomach. He got his hands wrapped around Ebbins' throat, was choking, choking, but then he felt the tip of a sword at the back of his neck, and stilled.

Ebbins pried Scorch's fingers from his throat and turned slowly to face him. He gestured to the man with the sword to join his side, and the man circled around, keeping the tip of the blade against the soft skin of Scorch's throat, cutting a thin, shallow line that dribbled red.

Iron Grip returned behind him, locking onto his wrists. Scorch's breathing was ragged, and he could feel the heat rushing beneath his skin, could feel the control seeping slowly from his grasp.

"Fuck, it's hot in here," Ebbins muttered, wiping a trickle of sweat from his forehead.

He took Scorch's chin between his fingers and squeezed so hard, he thought he might be sick again. He was still shaking, sweat dampening his hair, and a sob was waiting in the back of his throat. All the while, Flora's dead eyes stared sightlessly.

Ebbins brought their faces close together. "I'd slice that pretty face right off if I didn't think it'd fetch me a higher price unmarred," he rasped.

Scorch surged forward with a desperate cry, bashing his head against Ebbins' nose. It crunched loudly as it broke. Heh had time to bark a laugh of triumph before he felt a sharp blow to the back of his head. He hit the floor and knew nothing else.

# The Circle

## 3

*H*is eyelids felt glued together and opening them was difficult, but the pain of searing daylight was worse. As soon as his eyes squinted open, he shut them again, a moan leaving his lips. He was no longer shaking, but the earth around him was. No, not earth. He flexed his fingers, hands bound behind his back, and felt the coarse texture of unfinished wood. He listened, heard the rumble and squeak of wheels. His nostrils flared and, beneath the heavy scent of blood and sweat and sick, he could smell horses. After a moment, he was able to pick up on the click of hooves, as well. So he knew he was in a wagon, but he didn't know where he was going.

Moving was useless. His feet were tied together, along with his hands, and a rope was fastened around his neck, tethered to something that resisted his pull when he tried rolling to his side. He struggled to open his eyes again, peering in a daze to his left. There was the rope leading from his neck, and at the end of the rope was Ebbins, holding on tight.

The night flashed behind Scorch's eyelids in horrific clarity.

He was almost glad when Ebbins stood in the moving wagon and delivered a swift kick to his stomach. The pain knocked him out again, and instead of red, he saw only black.

The next time he came to, it wasn't of his own volition, but at the insistence of the villainous grip on the other end of Scorch's rope. His eyes came open when Ebbins began dragging him from the wagon by the rope lead, his throat constricting beneath the pressure. He tried to scramble to his feet, but they were bound tightly together, so he had no choice but to let Ebbins drag him to the edge of the wagon. Thankfully, the man leapt down, and instead of pulling Scorch out by the neck, he drew out a dagger and cut the rope around his ankles. A moment later, the dagger was pressed against the corner of Scorch's eye.

"Try to run for it and I'll catch you. I catch you and I cut out your eyeball. Understand?"

Scorch understood and nodded weakly. If he'd been entertaining any grand plans of escape, they evaporated as soon as Ebbins hauled him from the wagon and he collapsed on numb, tingling feet. He couldn't have run away if his life depended on it. His life *did* depend on it, and there he was, a trained guardian, unable to even stand on his own.

Ebbins snorted and lifted him up. Scorch sputtered helplessly as his captor tugged him along. His neck was tender from the abuse of the rope and he was too nauseous to notice his surroundings. He only knew he was outside for several painful steps, and then he was inside, some place dark that smelled like spoiled meat.

His feet were asleep, stabbing him with a thousand needles, pain shooting up his legs every time he was forced to take another step. As Ebbins pulled him along a dank tunnel and commenced to lead him down a set of winding stairs, Scorch realized his feet were no longer bare. Sometime between being abducted from Flora's room and now, someone had done a haphazard job of dressing him. He wore his jerkin with no shirt beneath, and he had on his trousers but his belt was gone, along with Etheridge's pouch. His satchel was gone, too. His sword was fastened to Ebbins' hip. Rage curdled in his gut.

Ebbins shoved him ahead through a rickety door. Scorch fell forward, landing with a crack on his knees. He gritted his teeth and looked up at the room in which he'd been shoved. A sallow-faced man occupied it, and little else. Scorch could hear Ebbins breathing through his mouth while the man in front of him bowed down to get a good look, his eyes darting over Scorch's body in rude appraisal.

"Handsome," the sallow man remarked.

"You'll notice I took especial care not to mark his face," grunted Ebbins.

The man hummed his approval. "Stand him up."

Ebbins obeyed, lifting Scorch by the hair so the other man could direct his glare from head to toe. After several minutes of uncomfortable inspection, Ebbins spoke again. "He's a guardian. Was boasting something awful at a tavern, and me and my boys picked him up. He looks a little rough right now, but he's strong and he's Guild-trained."

The sallow man arched an eyebrow. "A guardian? We haven't had one here in years."

"I know."

The man stared at Scorch so hard he had to look away. He watched the floor for the remainder of the short exchange, which was mostly a stunted banter of unfamiliar jargon, followed by the clinking of coins passing from one hand to another. Then Scorch was being dragged again, Ebbins yanking him along by the rope.

In the back of Scorch's mind, he wondered how it was he was allowing himself to be led around like an animal. Why wasn't he putting up more of a fight? Why hadn't he tried to crawl away when he hadn't been able to run? To what level of disgrace had he sunk to have gotten an innocent woman killed and himself taken? Later, he would think back to his state of mind as he'd walked behind Ebbins down the torch-lit hall, his head concussed, and Flora's blood staining his skin, and he would recognize the sensations as shock. But in that moment, Scorch only knew he felt off-kilter, his senses dulled, like he was under water, and beyond the deep-seated shame permeating the forefront of his mind, Scorch's main focus was on the careful shuffle of his feet. The Guild felt a world away. He blinked and saw a neck split wide as a smile.

Ebbins pulled so hard on the lead, Scorch lurched forward, coughing as the rope dug into his skin. He was being taken through a maze of molding walls, the smell growing ranker the further they went, until, finally, Ebbins kicked him through a door that led to an open chamber. Scorch's heart thudded unnaturally in his chest. Every wall of the room was lined with grotesquely twisted wire cages, and in every cage was a human.

Ebbins dragged him toward the nearest cage, but Scorch was finally resisting. He wrenched his shoulders, trying to break free of the binding around his wrists, and the rope cut into his neck where he thrashed against its pull. He kicked with his free feet, but Ebbins drew him in close with the rope and grabbed him by the hair. Scorch gasped when he felt the blow to his kidneys, and before his eyes could refocus, Ebbins was ripping open the door to one of the cages and forcing Scorch inside.

He hit the ground hard, his head bouncing against the floor. He heard a soft intake of air and the slam of the cage, and then, for a long time, he just floated.

His vision was filled with clouds, and he was vaguely aware of cool hands cupping his cheek, a sweet voice, a gentle melody lulling the fever in his skin. His body ached in a thousand ways, but the voice was steady in his ears, until the clouds began to dissolve and his vision became clear once more.

The first thing he saw was the wire crisscrossing of ugly metal a few feet above him. He let his head fall heavily to the side and saw a young woman sitting cross-legged beside him in the cage. Her hair was shorn close to her scalp and she had a raw mark of a burn across her right cheekbone. She returned his gaze with piercing almond eyes, reminding Scorch of the grey cat that stalked the halls of the Guild.

He sat up and leaned against the wall of the cage. A sharp pain shot through the back of his skull and he lifted a hand to assess the damage. While prodding at the wound, he realized his hands were free from their binding.

"You did this," he said, and his voice was hoarse. He flexed his hand and could feel the blood pumping into his fingers.

The woman nodded, gesturing toward the pile of rope in the corner of the cage that used to be around his neck and wrists.

"I had a look at your injuries, too." Her speaking voice was as melodic as her hum. "They're not good, but they probably won't kill you."

Scorch's fingers were bloody where they'd touched his head, his fresh blood on top of Flora's dried blood. A wave of nausea rose in his throat and he coughed pathetically, turning away from the woman to look out through the cage.

With his mind no longer drowning in shock, he was better able to assess his bleak surroundings. He was in a large chamber, as he'd noted dazedly before, a dungeon, and the walls were lined with cages similar to the one he was in, most only holding one person. He stole a curious glance back at the woman. She wasn't watching him, but leaning casually against the side of the cage with her eyes closed.

He looked back out at the room, at the different people shoved into different cages. The ratio of men to women appeared to be equal, but they were all relatively young, relatively built, and plagued with the same body language of the defeated. Scorch unconsciously straightened his shoulders. He didn't want to look broken. He didn't want to believe he was broken.

In the cage beside his own, a man was rolled into a crumpled heap of bloodied rags and grime. He wasn't the worst off one in the room, but he was the only one close enough for Scorch to hear his low-pitched moan.

"That's Julian," the woman said. Her eyes were open again and she was staring unerringly at Scorch. "I'm Kio." To Scorch's surprise, she held her hand out. It seemed such a normal gesture for such a terrible place, but he took her hand without pause. She squeezed it once with a cool, strong grip before letting it go.

"I'm Scorch," he offered.

She narrowed her eyes at him for a moment before abruptly twisting around to bang on Julian's cage, which was flush against their own. Rattle their cage wall, rattle his. The man called Julian lifted his head from the floor, blinking confusedly.

"Hour's up," Kio told the man, and he groaned, unfurling from his cower on the ground. He stretched as much as he could in the cramped space allotted him, and when he scooted forward to get a look at Scorch, Scorch couldn't keep the shock from his face. Julian was black and blue with bruises, and one eye was swollen completely shut.

Kio shifted around and carefully maneuvered the gaps in the cages until the pads of her fingers touched the welt over Julian's eye. He whimpered beneath the touch.

"It's too soon to tell if you'll lose it," she whispered, and Julian nodded meekly. A tear rolled free from the swollen eye and Kio wiped it away.

"I can't see anything out of it." Julian's words sounded heavy in his throat, like he'd rather be screaming than speaking.

Kio kept the calm in her voice as she responded. "You only need to see out of one eye to win. Look at me." Julian's one good eye darted unsurely up to Kio as another tear traveled down his ruined face. "They're coming for you soon, Julian. Get yourself together. Cry when you come back, after you've won."

Scorch would have felt more awkward witnessing such an intimate moment if he'd been the only witness, but everyone in the room could hear Kio's words. In a way, it felt like she was speaking to every soul in every cage. More than a few were looking over, their own wounds gashed across their faces and chests and arms.

Julian wiped gingerly at the wetness on his face and turned away with a curt nod. He set his jaw firmly and sat as straight-backed in his cage as its height allowed. Kio placed her hands in her lap and turned away from Julian. The cage was so closed in that her knees were pushed up against Scorch's thigh, and he had to keep his head bowed or it scraped the wired ceiling.

He was on the verge of asking her where they were, what had happened to Julian, what had happened to her and everyone else in the dungeon, but before he could solidify his questions into sensible sentences, a heavy parade of steel footsteps sounded in the adjoining hallway.

At once, the atmosphere of the room shifted as dozens of panicked heads looked toward the source of the noise. In the cage beside them, Julian was moaning again.

"Don't hesitate, Julian," Kio commanded in a rushed whisper right before a team of masked men barreled into the room.

Cages banged and shook as the captives beat against them, but the men paid them no mind, walking straight ahead. For a frightening moment, Scorch thought they were coming for him, but no. They were coming for Julian. They stepped in front of his cage, and the biggest of the men, with a plain black mask, unlocked the cage door and reached in with leather-gloved hands.

Julian was fished from the cage, dragged out by his throat, and thrust into the arms of the accompanying guard. Scorch could do nothing but watch as he was led from the room with a sword at his back. Scorch turned to Kio, alarmed, but she lifted a hand, a quiet plea for his silence. He followed her gaze back out amongst the cages, where more masked men were opening a second cage and pulling out another man. This one looked slightly older than Julian did, and dirtier, and the masked men held most of his weight as they shuffled him from the room.

When they were gone and their footsteps could no longer be heard echoing off the walls, the others stopped beating at their cages and slowly grew muted, save for occasional murmurs, sobs, and tortured groans.

Kio touched Scorch's knee and he turned to look at her. The burn on her cheek looked angry.

"Kio?" he asked, suddenly uncertain whether he'd hallucinated her name or whether she'd told him. He waited for her to nod before continuing. "Where are we?"

Even scrunched up in a cage, Scorch could tell she was graceful; it was evident in the way she turned her head and shifted her shoulders. "The Circle," she answered.

He frowned, chipping flecks of dried blood from his forearm. "I don't know what that means. Where have they taken your friend?"

Kio answered with carefully measured words. "They took him upstairs, along with the other man. They'll fight until one of them is dead, and they'll bring the winner back here. Julian's last fight was two days ago, and now it's his turn again." Her eyes were sorrowful. "They'll come for you soon."

He shook his head, which still throbbed. "I don't," he began, searching wildly for a composed thought, "I don't understand. Why? What is this place?"

"I told you, it's the Circle."

"I don't know what that means," he replied, bitterness fighting his shock. "I'm a guardian. I've done nothing wrong. Why would I be taken here?"

"You're a guardian?" asked Kio. "That explains why you're here. Slavers, people like the man who brought you here, take the most skilled fighters when they can. You're worth more. Last longer. Put on a better show." Her eyes raked up and down his hunched body. "How were they able to take you?"

Scorch's breath rattled from his lungs as a vision of gored flesh flashed behind his eyes. He ran his hands over his face, as if he could wipe the memory away.

"I was caught off guard," he answered, and Kio accepted the explanation with a small hum. "What about you?"

"I was also caught off guard," Kio said casually, as though they weren't inches apart and stuffed in a cage. "I've been here eight days. I've been through three fights."

Scorch was worrying more dried blood from his arm when she answered, and his head shot up. "That means you've killed three people."

"Yes," she admitted.

"How? *Gods*, how?" He couldn't stop the horror of Flora's bed from flooding his mind. He stuffed his head between his knees, taking deep breaths and trying not to get sick.

Kio's cool hand rested on his shoulder. "Because I don't want to die," she soothed. Then, softer, "Do you want to die?"

Scorch didn't look at her, but he shook his head. He thought of Julian crying from his one good eye and shivered. "They can't force me to kill anyone. I won't kill an innocent."

Fingers hooked beneath his chin, lifting his head. Kio demanded his eyes. "It won't feel like killing. It will feel like surviving."

He pulled his knees to his chest and spent the next several minutes trying to even his breathing and tamper down his nausea, but there were too many points of pain on his body, too many rumblings of despair in his ears. His skin was hot and his fingertips dewed with sweat, but he swallowed it, pulled it deep down in his chest, where it bubbled and roiled and sent acid crawling up his throat.

All too soon, the sound of heavy boots infiltrated the room and every caged human looked up at the door to see who would be dragged back through it. Scorch saw a masked man first, and then, staggering behind him, splattered in bright, fresh blood, with gruesome scratches joining the bruises on his face, he saw Julian. He was marched back to his cage and thrown inside. Scorch made to speak to him but Kio gave a minute shake of her head. The masked men locked the cage and Julian was quick to gather himself into a ball on the floor, hiding his face. A sob burst from his throat, raw and ghastly, and Scorch reached for the cage siding.

Kio placed a hand on his wrist and looked him in the eyes. "Don't worry about Julian," she told him. "Worry about yourself."

He squinted at her in confusion the instant before their cage door opened. Kio released his wrist but maintained eye contact with him when the masked men reached in with grabbing, greedy hands and ripped him from the cage.

The others banged violently on their cages, filling the room with a symphony of rebelliously clinking metal. Scorch struggled against his handlers until he saw the sword pointed at his navel and felt the sting of a dagger against his tender throat. His hands and feet were unbound. All he needed to do was get his hands on a sword, and then—what? Even standing straight had his head spinning, and if not for the hands on his arms, he was sure he'd be on the floor. Water hadn't passed his lips in at least a day, and he was weak. If he managed to get his hands on a weapon, could he take on all of these guards by himself? He couldn't even take Ebbins and his men, and six had come to escort him from the cage.

A horrible feeling knotted in his gut. *Helplessness.* When the dagger pressed against his neck, he let the masked men walk him from the room.

He was taken a different route than when he'd first arrived with Ebbins, and he concentrated on the number of turns down the different, moldy halls, trying to memorize the way. There wasn't much to commit to memory—left, left, narrow stairwell, right— and then he was shuffled into a small room with black stains all over the floor and nothing else. One of the men locked the door while a second stalked to the door on the opposite side of the space. Scorch could see daylight streaming through its edges, and then it was unlocked and pulled open.

He hadn't been expecting an entire speech or anything, but a few words of direction would have been appreciated before the dagger left his throat and he was unceremoniously kicked out the door. He landed on his knees in the mud. It was raining and the air was cool enough that little clouds of breath puffed from his mouth. Beyond the steady patter of rain on his bare shoulders and the hastening beat of his heart, a roar was erupting all around him.

Scorch lifted his head, his hair already darkened by the rain and clinging to his forehead. He was in a mud-caked circle, slightly smaller than the training rings at the Guild, but he didn't have the mind to suss out an exact measurement. It was enough room for a proper scrimmage, and from the looks of it, it had been well used and poorly maintained. There were patches of mud stained a disconcerting reddish-brown.

All around were onlookers, sooty faced with scraggly clothes, packed together behind the high chain fence that surrounded the circle. They whooped and hollered a collection of obscenities and nonsensical chants, some shaking pouches of coin. Shoved in amongst the spectators were more men wearing black masks and carrying swords. The fence was made with a similar wire as the cages and stretched beyond the top of Scorch's head, but it wasn't so high it couldn't be scaled.

Scorch stood, his boots sliding in the mud, and that's when he noticed the two weapons lying in the center of the circle. His first steps forward were hesitant; he hadn't walked without being pulled or pushed in what felt like a lifetime. It was a pleasant surprise when his body carried him, without fail, all the way to the wooden staffs collecting raindrops on a heap of blood and mud. Scorch's boots squelched as he bent down to take a staff. He held it up for inspection, disbelieving it was really in his hands. It was nowhere near the quality of the Guild's practice staffs, but it was heavy and thick and his palms warmed beneath its weight.

He gave it a twirl with nimble fingers, testing his own balance as much as the staff's. His hands were shaking, but he didn't drop it. In fact, with a weapon in his hand, he almost felt normal. But that feeling faded fast when the crowd erupted in a renewed wave of jeers and whistles. Horror prickled his spine as he watched a second door open on the far side of the circle.

Scorch hadn't taken notice of another body being pulled from the cages before—he'd been too bleary-headed—but, of course, they had taken a second captive. There were two weapons in the circle. One for Scorch and one for the man he was expected to fight to the death, the man who had just been shoved through the door.

Like Scorch, he landed on his hands and knees. He scrambled to his feet at once, his eyes darting between Scorch and the staff still lying in the mud. Scorch stepped back several feet and held up a hand in peace. The rain was falling heavier now, and the dried blood on Scorch's skin was streaming pink rivers down his arms.

The man's body was tense, reminding Scorch of a hunting lesson, and the deer that heard a rustling of leaves and bent back its ears, preparing to bolt. When at last the man did move, it was a broken run toward the staff, so quick his feet slipped out before him and he landed on his side with an audible smack. The audience cheered and Scorch took several steps further away. The circle wasn't nearly large enough now that there were two of them within its walls.

The man rolled onto his knees and used the staff to haul himself up. His movements were clunky with the staff, but he brandished it in front of his gaunt body like a sword. Scorch kept one hand wrapped around his own staff, but the other he maintained before him, palm turned outward, trying to keep his body language as non-aggressive as possible.

But the man was a beast of aggression, wild and snarling. At Scorch's lifted hand, he growled and began inching slowly across the center of the circle.

Scorch shook his head, droplets of water flying free from the tips of his hair. "No. You don't have to," he pleaded, but his words were pounded out by the rowdiness of the crowd and a clap of thunder. The man continued pacing toward him, one wavering step at a time. The closer he came, the younger he began to look. Scorch had seen twenty years, hardly seasoned, but the man approaching him with clenched teeth was not a man at all. He was smooth-cheeked, scrawny-limbed, petrified, and looked no older than the flautist. And he was gaining ground across the circle, so close now that Scorch could hear his ragged breaths over the cacophonous onlookers and relentless storm.

"Wait," Scorch tried again. His voice sounded strange in his ears, like he was talking in a dream, everything about the moment an unreality. "Wait."

The boy did not wait. He swung his staff with a scream and finished the distance between them.

Scorch stumbled back as the boy collided into him, their chests slamming together.

"Stop!" he yelled, desperate, but the boy was clutching his staff with both hands and beating at Scorch's side.

Scorch let the boy shove him backward until he was pressed up against the wires of the circle wall. The boy tried slamming the blunt end of the staff under Scorch's chin, but Scorch grabbed his wrists, dropping his own staff in the mud at their feet. He held the boy with both hands, shaking him until he dropped the weapon. The boy was crying, his eyes huge and unseeing. As he writhed, Scorch kept him firm in his grip.

"Don't fight me," Scorch begged. "I won't hurt you."

The boy threw himself forward and kicked his legs, the toes of his boots connecting with Scorch's shins so hard he fell to his knees. He let go of the boy's wrists for one second and that was all it took for the boy to pin Scorch on his back and straddle his waist.

Scorch cried out as the boy clawed at his face. A sharp nail snagged on his skin and dragged a bloody scrape from his temple to his jaw.

"Please!" gasped Scorch, slapping at the hands that were now gathering around his neck.

But the boy was mad and no words would reach him. His fingers tightened around Scorch's throat and began to crush with all his strength. It was a strong grip, but Scorch was stronger, and he pried the boy's fingers off and flipped their positions. Now the boy's back was in the mud and Scorch was pressed down on top of him. New puddles were forming all around their struggle as the rain turned torrential, every drop feeling like ice against Scorch's hot skin. The boy lifted a knee to try and displace him, but Scorch could not be displaced. He held the boy's wrists until they flailed with such abandon that the boy let out a cry. Fearing he'd wrecked the boy's wrists, Scorch reflexively released them.

"I'm sorry," Scorch said, speaking loudly over the rain.

The boy had grown still beneath him, his hands dropping to his sides. Scorch smiled softly down at him.

"Yes," he sighed. "Good. See, they can't make us. They can't make us."

The crowd was booing and throwing rocks over the walls, and Scorch watched one sail far to his left. He laughed, a brief moment of levity before a sharp pain exploded in his thigh. He felt a tremendous, searing pressure and looked down to where the boy had stabbed him with a small blade.

Scorch cursed and dismounted his attacker, his hands sinking into pits of wet earth, but the boy followed, leaping to a crouch and wrapping a quick fist around the knife's handle. He pulled it free of Scorch's leg and brought it down again, aiming for his chest. Scorch blocked, but he was too slow, and the blade still went in, stabbing into his shoulder. Heat blossomed in his chest, and he grabbed the boy, giving him a shake before throwing him off. The audience's response was deafening, but Scorch could only hear the rushing in his ears, the thump of his blood racing through his veins. When the boy landed in a puddle, Scorch pulled the knife from his shoulder. It wasn't as deep a wound as it could have been if the boy had known how to fight at all, but it was enough to make his shoulder vibrate with pain. He cast a glance at the boy, who was already hastening back to his hands and knees.

Without bothering to fully stand, the boy launched himself on top of Scorch, his dirty fingernails digging into the skin of Scorch's neck as he rolled them. They stopped with Scorch's head in a dip of the ground, filled with mud and water, and the boy didn't hesitate to push down on Scorch's neck until his face was submerged in the muck.

*Caught off guard.* Why was Scorch always caught off guard? When he was plunged into the depth of the puddle, he gasped, and as easily as that, he was drowning. Panic shot through his system and he thrashed against the boy pinning him down, but couldn't throw him off, couldn't make his hands uncurl around his throat, couldn't lift his head the inch it needed to gulp fresh air. His vision was blackened and fuzzy, his lungs were sloshing with grime, and his hands were balling into desperate fists.

As the thunder rumbled, Scorch felt the smooth handle in his hand burning hot against his palm. Instinct drove his forearm up in a lethal curve. Adrenaline filled his tired muscles with strength and ignored the burning pain in his shoulder. Skill directed his aim when he sank the knife's blade into the boy's neck.

The hands around his throat slackened at once, and Scorch surged up, shoving the boy off and crawling away from the puddle as he hacked and heaved and struggled for breath. Dark fluid dripped from his mouth and Scorch wiped it away. He leaned back on his knees and lifted his face to the rain, inhaling slowly, easing the heat of his skin, and tucking it deep.

The spectators were yelling and rattling the walls with grubby, coin-clenching fists. Scorch spied one of the doors creaking open, masked men stepping through. Confused, he turned his head. Several feet away, sprawled in the mud, was the boy, the knife still lodged in his neck. Blood was sprayed all around him where Scorch had stabbed into his artery. Remnants of life oozed around the handle. He was dead.

Scorch stared at the body until hands grasped his arms. He let the masked men boss him to his feet, feeling once again like he was dreaming. The rain had washed away the bulk of Flora's dried blood, but now he was dirty with another's. It was nothing like he'd been trained for, nothing like he'd expected. He felt numb. It had happened so fast, been so easy. *It shouldn't be so easy.*

The crowd raged, their voices a sickening medley, and Scorch was glad when he was led back inside and the door shut behind him, blocking out all sound save the in and out of his breathing. He remained in a dissociative daze as the men herded him back to the dungeon, walking with his eyes trained to the floor until they were approaching the cage room, and then Ebbins appeared in front of him.

Scorch blinked. Ebbins poked a finger into the rope burns around Scorch's neck, a sleazy smile stretching his lips.

"Atta boy," he said, and Scorch's stomach rolled violently. Ebbins whispered in his ear. "Did you like the present I slipped in there for you?"

Scorch didn't understand until Ebbins made a rude gesture with his fist, a stabbing motion against his own neck. His teeth gleamed sharp in the pit of his smile. He had slipped the boy the knife.

Ebbins' laugh was too loud in the narrow hall, bouncing an ugly echo off the walls. Scorch felt sick as the masked men poked at his back with their swords and urged him onward. He was relieved to leave Ebbins in the hall until he realized the man was following their little procession. Scorch risked a glance over his shoulder and saw Ebbins strutting behind him, his two cronies from the tavern following with a limp body dragging between them.

The masked man with a fist in Scorch's hair gave his head a jerk and directed his eyes forward. Seconds later, he was being pushed back into the room full of cages. He could feel every eye on him but didn't have the strength to meet anyone's gaze, not even Kio's, whom he knew was watching calmly with her legs folded up beneath her. Instead, Scorch craned his neck to catch another look at Ebbins' new capture. He saw a shock of black hair before the masked men tore open Kio's cage and shoved Scorch inside, hurriedly locking the door.

Scorch was smashed up against Kio, and he quickly began disentangling himself from her stoic limbs. She tried to cup his cheek with her hand, but he shook his head from her gentle touch and pushed himself as far to the other side of the cage as he could. He didn't want her sympathy or advice or whatever it was she was about to offer him. He wiped the sweat from his forehead and stared out at an empty cage across the room, where Ebbins' men were tossing the unconscious body of their newest victim. Scorch wondered where the empty cage had come from, until he realized it must have been where the boy had been. The boy he had killed.

Scorch coughed, still bringing up flecks of mud from his lungs, and stared at the new body in the cage. He wished he could be unconscious, and then he could ignore the weight of Kio's eyes on his back. Without facing her, he spoke.

"I've never killed anyone before." It was barely a whisper, but it stung his eyes.

When Kio responded, her voice was equally soft. "You're a guardian."

He tensed at the title. He felt like a dirty thing. A murderer. An *assassin*. The thought jarred his brain and his Master's task surfaced like blood in the water. He'd let his guardianship sneak to the back of his consciousness since Ebbins had taken him. In the wake of his own trauma, he'd ignored his duty. Master McClintock had trusted Scorch with a sacred task and within twelve hours of leaving the Guild, he'd proven himself unworthy. If Scorch was a guardian, he was truly the worst the Guild had ever produced.

The shame of it was nearly enough to cloak the guilt of the boy's death, but not quite. Now, when Scorch shut his eyes, he saw more than a blood soaked bed and a mangled neck. He saw a dead-limbed boy twisted in the mud.

"We do what we have to do," said Kio after a pause. "We have no choice."

Scorch stared across the room at dark hair glimpsed through a wire cage. "I had a choice. I chose to save myself."

"Isn't that normal?"

Finally, Scorch looked at her. The burn on her cheekbone was blistered and pink, and her eyes were as sharp as ever, even in the dim light of the dungeon.

"Being a guardian isn't about killing. It's about protecting. That boy needed my protection and I—I killed him."

Again, Kio reached out and Scorch didn't stop her. She touched his hand. "You needed protection too, Scorch."

It was the first time someone had used his name since he'd left the Guild and he felt oddly disconnected from it, like it no longer belonged to him. He sat in silence for a long time, letting Kio tear strips from her cloth tunic and wrap the stab wounds at his shoulder and thigh. The gash down his face she dabbed with her sleeve. Masked men returned to the room and placed a bowl of water in each cage, along with hardened half loaves of bread. Kio tore the bread in two and made Scorch eat, but only after he had his fill of water.

After, Scorch grew dizzy and Kio settled him onto his side, keeping his head in her lap. Fatigue gripped him tight and soon he would be asleep. Before nightmares could claim him, Scorch's fingers fell closed around Kio's wrist.

"I won't do it again," he promised. "They can't make me do it again."

# *Aren't You Killing Me?*
# 4

*H*e slept for hours, a miraculous feat in a roomful of creaking cages and hapless moans. It was impossible to tell exactly how long he slept, but it felt like a long time. His dreams had certainly stretched on and on, relentlessly hammering his mind with one horror after another.

*His mother smiled at him until the fire caught her hair, and then her features were lost to a billow of smoke.*

*He started running, his feet sinking him deep in mud. When he screamed for help, water rushed into his mouth. A small hand reached for him. Flora. But when he leaned in to kiss her cheek, her head rolled back, and her neck split open. He tried to press his hands over her wounds and stop the bleeding, but ropes lashed around his neck and dragged him back.*

*Ebbins placed a knife in his hand and threw him in a cage, but not with Kio. A dark-haired figure was lying there, face in shadows, a smooth exposure of neck shimmering in moonlight. He fell to his knees beside the stranger and held the knife to his own throat instead.*

Scorch opened his eyes.

"You had bad dreams."

Kio was gone and Julian was watching him with a frown on his blue and black face. Scorch uncurled from his ball on the floor and ran a hand through his hair. It was tangled and stiff with filth, and his fingers brushed against the gash scabbing on the back of his head.

"Yeah," he answered. Despite his portion of water, his throat felt scratched and sore.

The other man nodded. The fear in Julian's eyes was less, and he was no longer a trembling heap of nerves. "They came for Kio a few minutes ago," he told Scorch, his whisper conspiratorial.

Scorch grimaced at the idea of her in the circle. But hadn't she confessed to him that she'd won three fights already? He was comforted by the thought that she could take care of herself, until he remembered taking care of herself meant someone else's death, and how could he be comforted by that?

Julian tried speaking to him a few more times, but Scorch filtered out his words. His shoulder and thigh were throbbing from his stab wounds and he was afraid to look beneath Kio's makeshift bandages to check for festering. He missed Etheridge, wished for her pouch of salves. Knowing her, she would have included something specifically for stabs. She probably had some sagely hunch that Scorch would end up being stabbed at least once. He positioned himself so no unnecessary pressure was on his injuries, and then leaned his good shoulder against the side of the cage, looking out into the room. The same dirty faces were in the same dirty cages with two exceptions: an empty cage on the far side of the room where Kio's current opponent had been taken and an unfamiliar set of eyes in the cage opposite Scorch's. It was the dark-haired newcomer Ebbins had dragged in. He was awake, and he looked furious. And he was a *he*. Scorch hadn't been sure when hair had been hiding his face, but it was obvious now.

He had the fairest shade of skin Scorch had ever seen, made all the lighter by the stark contrast of black hair and clothes. He looked small in the cage, but dangerous. Even sitting there on his knees, hands resting on his thighs, the man exuded lethality. Scorch wished he was close enough to make out more details, but he didn't need to be close to read the malice on the man's face when their eyes met. Scorch's cheeks heated and he turned away.

Julian was absently tapping his fingers against the wires of his cage and Scorch concentrated on that irregular rhythm until the sound of steps began echoing through the outer hall. The masked men were already returning. He exchanged a heavy look with Julian, and then they both directed their gazes toward the door.

The masked men stormed in, hauling a cooperative Kio behind them. Scorch had never seen her stand upright before, all stretched out. She was taller than he'd assumed, and her hips less narrow, but his idea of her gracefulness had been accurate. She slinked across the room, and when the men brought her to the cage, she bent down and crawled inside before they could shove her, and then she closed the door herself. The masked men grunted and locked the cage, then filed from the chamber without a second glance. When they'd cleared from the room, the relief was tangible. They weren't taking anyone else. Not yet.

Julian was the first to speak when they were gone, pressing his face against the side of the cage to get a good look at Kio.

"Are you okay?" he asked.

Kio smiled, a small thing that didn't quite reach her eyes. "I'm okay."

Her chin had a smear of blood across it, but she wasn't as muddy as Scorch had been. The sun must have come out and dried the grounds. She wiped at her face with her sleeve. Scorch couldn't help but stare at her, raking his eyes across her body in a search of injury, any injury. The only marring of her skin was the burn on her cheek.

"I'm okay," she repeated.

He wanted to ask her how. She was so gentle. How did she walk away with nothing but a streak of someone else's blood on her chin? But he didn't ask. He didn't want to hear how she killed another person, no more than she probably wanted to tell him. So he just nodded, hoping it conveyed his gladness that she was still alive, and scooted the inch over to the other corner of the cage.

Kio whispered with Julian, but Scorch fazed them out, not wanting to listen. Somehow, his eyes found their way back to the strange man in the cage across the room. He was glowering at his untouched bowl of water, his arms folded across his chest, and Scorch took the opportunity to drink his fill of the curious image. The man was clearly attired in some form of armor, but it was nothing like Scorch had seen at the Guild. It was black and sleek, but the material was impossible to pinpoint from Scorch's distance. It fit snugly against the man's body, covering high on his neck and down his arms. The only skin exposed was on his face and hands, white as the moon blossoms in Etheridge's garden.

Scorch passed an indeterminate amount of time watching the man exist within the cage, sneaking looks when he thought he wouldn't get caught. At one point, the man nudged the bowl of water with the tip of his boot. He picked it up, held it to his nose, and sniffed. Dark eyebrows cinched together, eyes closed. Then he took a tentative sip. He set the bowl down after that, but half an hour later, he returned to it and drank the rest of the water. Finished, he licked his lips and examined the empty bowl, smashing it against the floor several times to test its breakability. It didn't break, and the man returned to posing on his knees, his eyes surveying the dungeon.

When his scrutiny reached Scorch's cage, Scorch glanced away. But after a minute, when he was sure it was safe, Scorch looked back. He started slightly, because the man was still watching him, casting the same speculative glare at Scorch as he had the water bowl. Scorch idly wondered whether or not the man would try to sniff him next. He hoped not. After the few days he'd had, his odor could be nothing but disagreeable.

The longer the man stared at him—rudely—the longer Scorch kept his eyes likewise fixed, until a flare of heat in his chest made him gasp and he had to turn away. Kio and Julian looked at him askance as he clutched a hand to his heart and sucked in several strained lungfuls of air. Embarrassed, he resigned himself to focusing on the floor and steadying his pulse. When he was just on the verge of smothering the fever whirling around his insides, the relative quiet of the cages broke into a metallic maelstrom. Scorch's muscles seized as the heavy march of boots bounced malevolently off the dungeon walls. He found himself inching closer to Kio, who was shushing Julian, trying to calm him. Scorch needed some of that calmness, and when he pressed his shoulder against Kio, she said nothing, but reached out one of her hands and wrapped it loosely around his forearm.

Ten masked men bustled into the dungeon moments later, going straight for the newcomer. When they opened his cage, instead of simply yanking him out as they'd done the others, they tossed a rope inside that caught over the man's head on the second

attempt. Scorch watched it tighten around his neck and held a hand
to his own throat in sympathy as they hauled him from the cage.

As soon as the man was on his feet, he attacked, slamming the
heel of his hand into one of the masked men's faces, making blood
pour from beneath the mask. Then he jabbed with an elbow,
ramming it into a second guard's throat. He spun, kicked the sword
from another man's hand. Scorch was mesmerized. He moved so
quickly. But there was a reason so many guards had come, and
before too long, the prisoner received a blow to the temple that
knocked him dizzy. The masked men took the opportunity to shove
a bag over his head and tie up his wrists and ankles.

The man struggled, but he was manageable now, and one of the
masked men lifted him up and threw him over his shoulder. Scorch
was humiliated for him. And then the remainder of the men turned
to observe him in his cage.

Scorch shook his head and Kio tightened her grip on his arm,
but there was nothing to be done about it. They were coming
straight for their cage and Kio had just returned from her fight.
They wanted Scorch.

They ripped open the door of the cage and grabbed his ankles,
pulling him out carelessly. Scorch's head wound scraped against
the floor and he blinked away the tears in his eyes. They stood him
upright and held him at bay with a sword pointed between his
shoulder blades. Scorch looked back at Kio and Julian, possibly
for the last time, and then let the masked men march him from the
room.

He watched his destined opponent being carried off down a
separate hall, but the masked men led Scorch on the exact path as
last time. Soon, he was back in the small room, watching the

masked men open the door to the outside. They threw Scorch through before he could walk, and slammed it shut behind him.

Again, Scorch was on his hands and knees. The ground was damp beneath him, but the sun was drying up the remainder of puddles and flooding his vision with blinding light. Shielding his eyes with a hand, he stood. The crowd on the other side of the wiry walls was bigger than before—the weather encouraged more interest in the morbid entertainment, he supposed—and the number of armed, masked men at the perimeter was greater. He wondered if that had anything to do with the dark-haired man being hauled through the opposite door. A masked man entered the circle with him, quickly cutting the ropes from his legs and wrists, unlooping the rope from his throat, and ripping the sack from his head before running back through the door and pulling it closed with a thud.

The man stood leisurely. His skin was so pale, it practically glowed in the harsh sunshine. He took in Scorch's presence across the circle, and then they both seemed to notice the weapon waiting for them in the center of the ring. A staff. Not two staffs like last time. Just one.

Scorch imagined that if he bothered to look closely into the crowd, Ebbins would be there, grinning wickedly at his predicament, but he didn't dare take his eyes from the man stealthily stepping toward him. He braced himself, remembering the swift movements of the man in the dungeon, but he wouldn't be the one to try for the weapon, wouldn't tip the fairness of the fight in his own direction. He tried not to stagger back when the man reached the center of the circle.

Now that he was only a few feet away, Scorch admired him with the luxury of nearness. The stranger was slight and slim, with a narrow waist and cords of lean muscle visible through the snug material of his armor, which Scorch decided must be leather from the way it reflected the light. He wore his dark hair long enough to tuck behind his ears, but a thick strand had escaped and was hanging straight and smooth over one eye. Scorch squinted, trying to determine an eye color, but he couldn't; he was still too far away.

The man stood at the center of the circle, appraising Scorch with equal vehemence, and Scorch resisted the instinct to quaver under the stare. His hand flexed at his side, itching to run through his mess of hair, but he banished the thought from his mind. If he was about to be in a fight for his life, he didn't need to primp.

The man's lips were pursed in a severe line as he finally looked away from Scorch and down to the staff at his feet. He bent over, a fluid motion that Scorch would have enjoyed under different circumstances, and scooped it up. He threw the staff up in the air and caught it again with dexterous hands, testing its weight. Scorch could tell he was practiced by his stance and the way he gripped the wood, twirling it with ease.

The crowd grew restless watching Scorch's opponent waste their time. They wanted blood. They wanted screams. Scorch didn't flinch when the man met his eyes again, but he wanted to. There was an innate volatility about him. The mere act of being *looked* at by him seemed risky. When he finally drew the staff back over his shoulder, Scorch readied himself to dodge whatever was coming.

The man took several quick steps forward and launched the staff into the air. It whizzed high over Scorch's head. He threw a quizzical frown at the man before turning to watch the progression of the staff. It cleared the wall and commenced to sail downward until it collided with the surprised eye of a crude spectator.

The first reaction was stunned silence, everyone watching as the man fell to the ground, the staff firmly lodged in his skull. The second reaction was wild cheering. Soiled shoes kicked the dead man out of the way and greasy fingers shook the walls of the circle. Shocked, Scorch whipped around to face the other man and jumped; he'd closed the space between them and was standing right in front of him.

Scorch had time to notice his eyes were an eerie shade of amethyst before he had to duck the first attack. Since Scorch was taller, his reach was longer, but the other man was faster. He moved with impossible speed, sending an elbow flying at Scorch's face. He blocked it with his forearm and spun away from a flurry of fists. He backed up as the man tracked him across the dirt. It was nothing like his previous fight, when he had been pitted against a boy with no skill. The man stalking him was a trained fighter. Scorch thought back to what's-her-name in the sparring ring and almost smiled. Then the man rushed forward and there was no more room for thought.

Scorch had a reputation for being one of the best apprentices in the Guild for a reason. He'd mastered every level of training they'd thrown at him, and that included hand-to-hand combat. He utilized that expertly honed skill, sending silent thanks to his instructors every time he narrowly missed a flying knee or snuck a strike through the other man's scarily resilient defenses.

It soon became clear the fight was even, their skills a kismet match, and Scorch's heartbeat fell into the familiar rhythm associated with the give and take of a thoroughly enjoyable spar. A blur of white zoomed past his block and struck his neck. His head knocked back and he coughed, but recovered with adamant speed, letting lose a kick that hit the other man in the chest. The man grasped at Scorch's leg in retaliation, but Scorch snapped it out of his reach before he could complete the hold.

For a time, they were trapped in an endless volley, neither man getting past the other's guard. It was a storm of strength and speed, and they were both caught up in the wind of it. Until, of course, the inevitable happened and the scales tipped slightly in one man's favor. Scorch feinted a punch to his opponent's gut and threw a side-winding fist toward his head. When the man made to duck the hit, Scorch caught him with a brutal knee to the chin. The man went down and Scorch came down on top of him. The fight was in Scorch's hands. But then he made a mistake. It was a small mistake, but an integral one. He peered down at the man trapped between his thighs.

And he hesitated.

At the Guild, the fight would be over. But Scorch recalled, with a dark spoiling in his stomach, that he wasn't at the Guild, and it wasn't a sparring match, and he didn't know what to do. He wasn't being held down with his head under the water. There was no knife in his hand or earth shattering panic in his heart. He sat uselessly on top of his opponent for the shortest of seconds, hesitating, and then his world flipped over. Literally. The man rutted up and flipped him to his back, sinking on top of him, his knees pinning Scorch's shoulders. He bent low, one hand tightening in Scorch's hair while his forearm pushed against Scorch's windpipe. Their faces were intimately close. His eyes narrowed at Scorch, and his lips parted, breathing harder than he had the whole fight.

Scorch struggled but the smaller man was ridiculously strong. He choked in a gasp of air past the pressure on his throat, positive that, in a moment, it would become too much and he'd lose the fight in an irrevocable sort of way. But that moment didn't come. If anything, the pressure eased from his neck after his desperate gasp. Scorch's hands grappled at the man's waist, pinching and scratching in an attempt to make him move, but the man held utterly still, keeping his knees pinned ruthlessly against Scorch's shoulders.

Somewhere in the corner of his mind, he was aware the crowd was spurring them on, but he had no mind for anything but the stony expression of the man on top of him. Scorch was so focused on the curious bow of his mouth that he hardly understood that first rough whisper.

"What?" Scorch gasped stupidly, his voice straining and rasping beneath the abrasive forearm.

The man's eyes flashed with annoyance and he bent lower to speak in Scorch's ear. "Pretend I'm killing you." His voice was a deep, static rumble.

Bewildered, Scorch asked, "*Aren't* you killing me?"

Hair tickled Scorch's face as the man increased the pressure on his throat. "I'd rather kill everyone else. Shut up and make it believable. Then follow my lead."

The man sat back before Scorch could agree or disagree, and landed a hard smack across his jaw that sent the crowd into a frenzy. Then hands wrapped around his throat. The man maintained eye contact as he bore down, not on Scorch's windpipe, but against his own thumbs, pushing them together in a discreet hover above Scorch's skin, tensing his hands and creating the illusion of life-squeezing effort. Scorch played along, slapping at his wrists, trying to break his hold, and enjoying the smooth texture of—yes, he'd been right—leather beneath his fingers. He bucked, kicked, writhed, and wriggled until he received an irritated look from his murderer, and then he wrapped it up as best he could. He grew still, twitching sporadically. He closed his eyes and forced his limbs limp. Hands gave his throat a squeeze before letting go, and then the weight of the man disappeared.

Scorch remained sprawled and frozen in the darkness of his own eyelids, trying to make out the following events by sound alone. He heard light footsteps beside his head. He heard the crowd raving like vultures and shaking at the walls. He heard the creak of the far door opening and the familiar trudge of masked men crossing the grounds, making it vibrate against Scorch's supposedly dead body.

He was beginning to worry about what kind of lead, exactly, he was going to be given, when he heard a whoosh, followed by a crack, followed by a "Now!"

Scorch's eyes flew open and he sprang to his feet. A short storm of violence sped by, tumbling past one of the masked men, popping up behind him, and snapping his neck with a flick of his hands. He pried the man's sword from his hand and tossed it to Scorch. Scorch caught it and his hand warmed instantly around the grip. He turned with a sweep to meet the masked men attacking from behind and blade clanged against blade.

There were twelve men in the circle with them, Scorch counted. Ten meant to handle the difficult survivor and two meant to drag Scorch's dead body away, he guessed, but one of them was already down, and as Scorch looked beyond the swordsman in front of him, he spied the difficult survivor downing a second masked man, then a third, then a fourth. Somehow, he'd gotten his hand on two swords in the time it had taken Scorch to knock the blade from a single man's hand. The masked man scrambled for his fallen sword and Scorch brought his foot up in a swift kick to his face. The man fell onto his back, blood and bits of teeth spraying from his busted mouth, the mask lopsided and hanging from his face.

Scorch surveyed the result of his aggression and found he was hardly bothered by it, not when it was delivered onto such a deserving party. He turned to face the next masked men, two boxing him in on either side, and met their attacks with a flourish of his sword. It felt good to have a blade in his hand, and he smoothly unarmed them both.

Suddenly, a rope closed over his throat and Scorch spun—the friction burning his skin—to face the man pulling him in. Scorch sliced down with his sword, disconnecting himself from the rope lead, and brought the pommel down on his assailant's skull, adding him to the accumulating pile of bodies in the center of the circle.

There were four masked men left now, three of them surrounding Scorch's nameless comrade and one eyeing Scorch warily. Scorch held his sword before him and cocked a pale, inviting eyebrow. The masked man took a few steps back before spinning on his heel and flat-out running toward the door. He made it halfway there before a sword speared him through the chest. Scorch's eyes widened as he looked at the dark-haired man. He'd taken down one of the three remaining men and thrown his sword like he'd thrown the staff.

Scorch ran to help him with the final two men in the circle, and, together, they finished them off, one falling by Scorch's punishing knock to the head, and the other run through to the hilt by the merciless, yet brutally efficient nameless man.

They were the only ones left standing in the circle, but Scorch knew it was only a matter of time before more guards were sent to capture or kill them. His temporary companion didn't seem interested in waiting. He ran for the wall, Scorch following close behind, and they started climbing, the wired texture making for perfect handholds. People in the crowd screamed and finally began to disperse once they realized their own lives were in imminent danger.

They had crested the top of the wall when Scorch stopped. He watched as the other man threw a leg over the side, pausing long enough to fix Scorch with a put-upon glare.

"Hurry up," he said, a line forming between his eyebrows.

Scorch swallowed hard. He wanted to leave, wanted to keep climbing, but his body stopped him. He sighed, looking back toward the building. If he followed the man over the fence, he'd be protecting himself, but who would protect Kio, Julian, and the dozens of others below, still in cages?

"I have to get the others," Scorch heard himself say.

The man stared at him for a moment before swinging his other leg over the wall and descending at a rapid pace. Scorch climbed back down on the side of the circle grounds, his hand fastening over the hilt of his sword. He cast a final glance toward the stranger, already down on the opposite side of the wall and disappearing into the crowd.

Scorch took a deep breath. He had a sword and he was riding a burst of confidence. The masked men inside would know the fight had taken an unexpected turn. They would be coming for him, and he was sorely outnumbered, but he wouldn't be for long, not if he could make it to the dungeon before he was overpowered. It may have taken his lissome opponent to make him see it, but escape was possible. Scorch was a guardian with a weapon. Green or not, he was a superior fighter.

He steeled himself and headed through the door he'd entered by. A hush of silence enveloped the room as he closed the door. He cocked his head, listening for telltale sounds of trouble and hearing the faint echo of footsteps and muffled talking, but it was still a few hallways away. Scorch opened the second door and stepped into the maze of halls, recalling the path he'd been dragged along.

He walked as quietly as his boots allowed down the torch-lit hall and hoped the masked men were headed down the alternate route to the circle. He paused, listened, and made his first turn— *left*. The hall was empty, but Scorch could hear nearby yelling. He tightened his hold on the sword and quickened his pace. After heading down the stairwell, he reached the next turn—*right*—and then the next—*right*—and then the door to the dungeons was right there, at the end of the hall. Already, he could hear the cages banging.

Scorch ran.

The door to the dungeon was locked when he reached it, but he kicked it in with no trouble, busting into the room with a crash. If the masked men hadn't known his whereabouts before, they did now. There was no time to waste.

He went straight for Kio's cage first, heaving his sword through the lock. The cage door fell off its hinges and she crawled out. Scorch offered his hand. The rest of the room had grown silent. His heartbeat felt like the loudest thing in the room before he said, voice pitted, "Kio, help me." She nodded and he handed her the sword. Without direction, she began sweeping down one side of the room, hacking the locks off every cage, while Scorch started on the other side, kicking at rusted locks until they came free. In minutes, all the cages were open, and weary, injured, furious women and men were crawling from them and helping each other to their feet.

Scorch came to stand beside Kio, who was holding the sword in one hand and Julian's hand in the other. He glanced around at the bruised and bloody faces, smiling softly.

"We have to fight our way out of here, but we *will* get out," he said, putting as much conviction as he could muster into the words. For good measure, he winked. Then he felt like an ass for winking. Then he said, "I'll protect you," and headed through the broken door. He breathed a sigh of relief when he heard dozens of feet following.

"Scorch." Kio touched his arm, and he looked over his shoulder to where she walked behind him. She offered back the sword and he accepted it with a solemn nod.

The fastest route would be the one he'd just traveled, leading out to the circle, but a look at the others made him discount the option. Once outside, they would need to scale the walls to escape and most looked too haggard to climb. The best chance at leading everyone to safety was the way Ebbins brought him in, but Scorch had been in such a haze at the time, he wasn't sure he remembered the way. It had been a labyrinth in his concussed state. Unfortunately, it was the only solution he could think of, and so he turned down the hall he thought might be the right way and tried to walk confidently as he led the others.

They managed to maneuver through three hallways and up one set of stairs before they ran into the first team of masked men. They appeared around a corner, fully armed and breathless, a leader at their front shouting orders to "move faster." When they saw the escapees at the end of the hall, they paused for a moment, shocked, and then everything happened rather quickly.

Scorch raised his sword and ran toward them, an angry cry tearing from his lungs. He met the leader of the masked men with a crash of metal, meeting his blade once, twice, before he knocked it from his grip and it clattered to the floor. He kicked it back with his boot and punched the stunned guard in the throat before tossing him out of the way. He greeted the next man with a kick to the groin and a swift sweep of his foot that had him falling onto his back and smacking his head against the floor. Scorch picked up the abandoned sword and tossed it behind him before moving on to his next target.

He tried to keep the bulk of masked men trapped, but there were too many, and he couldn't stop a swarm from maneuvering past him in the narrow hall. He worried until he heard the sharp ringing of connecting blades. After slamming another assailant against the wall, he stole a glance behind him to check on how the others were faring. Kio had taken up one of the discarded swords and was slashing at the masked men approaching her. Her skill looked sloppy, but her swings were fierce. Julian circled around one man's back and pushed him off balance. The masked man fell forward as Kio heaved, and the blade pierced through his stomach.

That was when the others went wild. All that time starved and locked up and forced to kill one another, and now they wanted blood they could *choose*. They raised their voices to a fearsome howl and moved forward like a single unit of revenge, weaving around Scorch and throwing themselves on the remaining masked men in the hallway. They didn't need superior skill when they were running on pure adrenaline and savage reciprocity. A few picked up swords but most settled for their hands, strangling and scratching and biting and kicking, and when all the masked men were dead or dying on the floor, they moved on, a wave of destruction, not even waiting for Scorch.

He followed behind them as they ravaged corridor after corridor, beating down every guard they encountered. When he passed a splintered old door, he finally recognized where he was. He slowed, peering into the room where Ebbins had dragged him. The sallow man who had judged Scorch's worth was lying dead on his rug. Scorch felt a flutter of satisfaction and then hurried to catch up with the mob he'd created.

He found them storming the front door of the building, could make out Kio in the front, hacking at the chain lock with a sword until it busted. The escapees rushed outside, stomping on the final masked guards on their way out. Scorch followed them into the sun and watched as everyone scattered, running in different directions, some into the woods, and some down a dirt road.

He was gathering himself, trying to decide his next move, when he heard someone approach from behind. Before he could react, something sharp pressed into the small of his back.

"You're gonna pay for what you've done to this place, boy," Ebbins rasped. "You've just ripped the income out of my hands, so I'm gonna to need to rip something out of you. It's only fair."

Scorch felt his blood rushing hot. He spun, knocking Ebbins' sword clear and wrapping his hand around his throat before he could so much as breathe. As soon as Scorch's skin made contact around the leathery neck, Ebbins' face began to turn red. Sweat dripped down his brow and his eyes widened with surprise. Scorch detected a spark of understanding in the twist of his face before he reared back his sword and pushed it through the slaver's stomach.

He let him drop and stared at the red marks he'd left on his throat. Scorch wouldn't let himself feel anything but righteousness for his death, not after what he'd done to Flora, not after the work he'd been doing, enslaving men and women to the Circle for coin. He wiped the gore from his blade on Ebbins' trousers, and a familiar glint caught his attention. Lying beside Ebbins was the sword he'd taken from Scorch, the one from the Master, the one piece of the Guild he had left. He dropped the lesser blade and reclaimed his own, unbuckling Ebbins' belt and pulling it free to wind around his waist, along with the matching scabbard. He sheathed his sword and the weight was an instant comfort, as well as a reminder.

Scorch was beaten and bruised, bloody and filthy. The time he'd spent in the stone depths of the Circle, he hadn't been able to think clearly, but now he was free, and his responsibilities as a guardian weighed heavily on his thoughts. His mind was racing so fast he failed to notice the two people walking from the tree line until they were upon him.

He focused his eyes on Julian and Kio, who stood there, just as filthy as Scorch, watching him patiently but expectantly, clearly waiting for something.

Scorch didn't look back at Ebbins' slain body, but he saw Kio's eyes wander toward it. The daylight leant her olive skin an ethereal sheen. She looked like a goddess beside Julian, whose bruises were fading to a torrid green and yellow. His eye, at least, was less swollen.

"You're bleeding," Kio pointed out after averting her eyes from Ebbins.

Scorch lifted a hand to his face to feel for blood. He couldn't remembered being hurt in the escape, but there was a trickle of red slick easing from his nose.

"Come with us," Kio said. Scorch noticed her own face was relatively unscathed, only a small bruise forming on her jaw and the burn on her cheek.

"Where are you going?" he asked.

"We're taking the road until we hit the next village. I need supplies. You look like you," her eyes flickered over his body, "might need supplies, too."

Scorch began to refuse, but his voice faded after a struggling second of trying to drum up excuses. He had regained his sword, but he'd lost the medicinals Etheridge allotted him, along with his spare clothes and bedroll. But none of that mattered when he'd also lost his coin purse. "I have no means to refresh my supplies."

Kio smiled and stepped past him. He watched her kneel beside Ebbins' body. She reached a hand beneath his gore-stained vest, and, a moment later, her hand re-emerged with a leather pouch that, when shaken, betrayed a considerable clinking of coins inside. She tossed it at Scorch and he caught it with one hand. He fingered the pouch. It wasn't his, but there was a good chance a heft of the coin inside was. Still, he hesitated.

"Either you take it or leave it for scavengers. In this corner of the world," she said, gesturing at the building behind them, "that coin will probably do more good with a guardian than with anyone lingering around the Circle."

"*We're* lingering around the Circle," Scorch mentioned, but he stuffed the coin purse into the waist of his trousers and tied the strings around his belt. He smoothed the long trim of his jerkin over his stomach and gave Kio a shrug. She returned his shrug with a nod, stepping past him and taking up Julian's hand.

"Come with us," she repeated. "Let me take care of your injuries. I would see you well before parting ways with you. It's the least I can do after what you've done for me."

Scorch was about to open his mouth to argue when a searing pain in his thigh activated the searing pain in his shoulder, which spurred the dull ache in the back of his head. He couldn't deny he was in poor shape.

"Where I'm from, I was training to be an herbalist," Kio entreated. "Please allow me to help. It would be an honor to assist one from the Guild." Julian leaned in and whispered something in her ear. Kio made a face, and then added, "I'll buy you a drink."

Scorch smiled and the clawed mark down his face tugged tight at the expression. "Pull my leg, why don't you? Fine, yes, I will be happy to accompany you to the next village." He glanced down at his filthy state. "Maybe I can get a bath before that drink though."

"I'm glad you said it first," Kio agreed.

They started their way down the road. Scorch would get clean, get bandaged, and get his plan straight. The Circle was an unexpected hindrance, but he would not abandon his guardianship. He repeated his mantra as they walked: *save the High Priestess, save the High Priestess, save the High Priestess.*

# Vivid

## 5

Considering the volume of men and women loosed upon the countryside, Scorch expected to come across others from the Circle on the way to the village, but none emerged from the trees to join their trio. They walked in silence, which Scorch attributed to the wariness of his companions and the harried business of his own mind. He attempted to organize his thoughts, wondering whether he should write Master McClintock and tell him what happened, warn him about the slavers and the Circle. He felt like he'd been trapped in that cage for weeks, but he knew, rationally, that it had been nowhere near as long. He asked Kio, and she told him with a sad smile: "Two days."

Two days was all it had taken to unravel Scorch. True, he had summoned his wits in the end, but would he have pushed himself to do so if not for the dark-haired stranger's prompt? The gloom of such thoughts tried dragging him down, but Scorch twisted his mood brighter with the reminder that he'd only been delayed from his journey for two days. Hopefully, two days would not be the difference between assassins reaching the High Priestess and Scorch arriving in time.

He was still teetering between self-loathing and reluctant optimism when they entered the village hours later. It was simple and small. The blacksmith and tanner and seamstress shops were nestled beside one another on the main road, and an inn sat in the midst of several one-room homes. Set up at the edge of the village was an herbalist tent and Scorch felt a sudden pang for the Guild. After agreeing to meet back at the inn in an hour, Kio parted ways with Scorch and Julian, heading straight for the tent to restock her medicinals.

Scorch watched her retreat with an admiring eye. "Right," he announced. "I need fresh underclothes."

He walked with Julian to the seamstress and they handed over a hefty portion of their newly acquired coin in exchange for garments that weren't covered in blood and grime. Scorch left the shop with clean linen shirts, underclothes, and a spiffy new jerkin, as well as a fresh bedroll and a satchel in which to carry his new possessions.

Kio was waiting for them outside when they reached the inn, which was surprisingly large for a village so small. Either they entertained a great number of passers-by, or patrons came from nearby villages for drinks. Scorch couldn't care less as long as there was a tub. When Kio announced they did indeed have a tub, and that she had already procured them a room and requested hot water by the buckets, he felt satisfied. Kio put up hardly any complaint when Scorch and Julian insisted she bathe first, and they promised to let her poke and prod at their injuries afterward. In the meantime, they would eat.

The lighting was dim inside the inn and Scorch was instantly on alert. The hour wasn't terribly late—the sun had only recently started thinking about going down—but there were enough patrons that their arrival drew no one's attention. Kio nudged past Scorch and headed for the stairs. He watched her ascension and made a note of the room she entered—second door to the left—just in case. Julian harrumphed at his shoulder, making Scorch jump.

"Sorry," Julian apologized.

"No, I—" Scorch began, but what was he to say? *I'm feeling a tad jumpy because the last time I was in a place like this, I got a girl murdered and myself kidnapped?* It wasn't the way Scorch wished to start his evening, so he forced that old familiar smile onto his face and said, "Just a bit tired."

"I can't imagine why," was Julian's reply, delivered in such a dry tone that it took Scorch a moment to realize he was attempting humor. The fact that a man with that many bruises could still attempt mirth caused warmth to spread in Scorch's stomach, and he clapped Julian amicably on the back.

"Some food will help. I'm famished," Scorch announced, clicking his fingers playfully to catch the attention of the kitchen boy. One look at Scorch had him bustling over with a grin. Much to his credit, he didn't shy away when he got close enough to see their injuries and, most likely, smell their smell.

"Didn't see you boys come in. Here for a room?"

"Oh, we have one of those already," Scorch replied. "We could really do with a bite."

"Aye, we've got those, as well." The kitchen boy was tall and wore his hair pulled back with ribbon. "Sit wherever you like and I'll bring something for you to nibble."

"Obliged to you," said Scorch, waving Julian toward a table against the back wall. They took a seat, Scorch careful to angle himself in his chair so he could keep an eye on the inn rooms, the bar, and the front door. They sat in silence until the boy came back and set a tray of bread and cheese on their table, along with a few mugs of spiced wine. They thanked him and tucked in, both too hungry to try for conversation until they'd finished half the spread.

"So," Scorch ventured after a hearty sip of his drink, "how do you know Kio?"

Julian looked perplexed as he inhaled another bite of cheese. Scorch waited patiently for him to chew and swallow, and then he said, slowly, as if Scorch was simple minded, "Her cage was next to my cage."

Scorch shuddered involuntarily at the word "cage" as Julian shoved more food into his mouth. Only a few hours ago they'd been locked up in the Circle. It was weird to be sitting comfortably in an inn and sharing a meal when they might have been made to kill one another on the morrow. Scorch didn't want to think about it, so he pursued his curiosity from a different angle.

"You didn't know each other before? She's very affectionate with you." Scorch hadn't spared much thought to it at the time, but Kio and Julian had seemed familiar with one another from the beginning. He assumed they had met previously, but Julian shook his head.

"You don't have to know someone a long time to feel close to them."

Scorch felt a stitch in his chest at the statement. He'd known many people for a long time and never felt close to them. How was it Julian felt that way about Kio?

"So you two *are* close," he hunted. "Need me to get my own room tonight so you can be even closer?" He hadn't expected to see Julian's blush beneath all the layers of bruising, but scarlet crept up beneath the yellow mottling of his cheeks.

"It's not like that," Julian insisted, hiding his red face in his mug. "Kio kept me alive. I wouldn't have made it past my first fight if it hadn't been for her. But it's not like that. I'm not like that."

"Oh, I see," Scorch whispered good-humoredly. "What are you like?"

Julian let out an exasperated little sigh. "Devoutly abstinent."

"Is this an inappropriate time to mention my insatiable attraction to priests?" joked Scorch. Julian looked unimpressed and Scorch wondered if he would need to be added to the *Immune to Scorch's Charming Personality List.* "Sorry," he offered. "Afraid I'm a bit of a heathen."

"You saved my life today. And Kio's. I don't care if you're a heathen." Julian clanked his glass against Scorch's. "Besides, the only ones I've met who are truly unforgivable in this world are elementals. Luckily, they're few and far between."

Scorch's laugh burned in his lungs. "Luckily," he agreed with a hasty swig from his mug.

"They're the reason I was brought to the Circle, you know," Julian continued, his one good eye growing darker. "The slavers were in my town searching for elementals and they found me instead."

"Why would slavers want to bring an elemental to the Circle?" asked Scorch, mimicking his tablemate's body language and shifting forward.

"They wouldn't," answered Julian. "Too dangerous. But they would try to kill one and bring its corpse back to the Queen for a reward. It's been that way ever since she passed the ordinances. Best Queen we've had, if you ask me, and the reason the elemental population is so low these days. There's someone who understands how horrendous those creatures are. Not to mention she's a loyalist of the High Priestess."

"I see," laughed Scorch. "So you're hard for the Queen. Saving yourself for her?"

Julian leaned back in his chair and crossed his arms. If not for the bruising, Scorch would have sworn he wasn't sitting with the same man who'd been trapped in the neighboring cage. The person watching him was sharper somehow, now that he'd been freed from his wiry prison, and Scorch wondered if he even remembered curling into a ball and sobbing. Maybe he was just trying his best to forget, or, like Scorch, pretending he'd already forgotten. Regardless, Julian was appraising him with a smirk on his swollen face.

"Do you always bring everything back to sex?" he asked.

Scorch huffed, amused and disconcerted by the pious man's brazenness. "I try to give the people what they want," he replied with a shrug.

"*I* don't want you," Julian deadpanned.

"Of course not," Scorch allowed, "but everyone else in this room does."

"Are all guardians as cocky as you?"

"No," he said, considering. "But then, they're not all as good-looking as me either."

Julian blushed again and found solace in the bottom of his mug. "You really are a heathen. But I don't believe you."

"I look a lot better once I've cleaned up. You'll see," Scorch assured him.

"I meant not everyone in this room wants you," Julian corrected and Scorch frowned. "That man over there hasn't looked over here once."

Scorch followed Julian's squinty gaze across the room where a man was sitting at the bar.

A wave of warmth hit him fast and he chugged his spiced wine. "Excuse me," he mumbled, standing up and making a quick path to the bar. He slid onto the wobbly stool beside a slight man and let his eyes graze indulgently over the dark hair and moon-pale skin he thought he'd never see again. After waiting several heartbeats for the other man to recognize his existence, Scorch dove in with the cleverest of openers. "Hi."

The man ignored him, staring straight ahead, but Scorch could see his nostrils flare. He tried again, angling himself closer so, were the man to look, he would be treated with the enjoyable landscape of Scorch's broad shoulders, even though they were spattered with blood and dirt. "Fancy running into you again," he said, but his voice wasn't its usual smooth loll; it was laced with something else he couldn't quite identify. He cleared his throat valiantly. "Can I buy you a drink?"

The man's head turned, barely, and Scorch was met with cold, amethyst eyes. "No."

Scorch opened his mouth, but no sound came out, and the man returned to staring straight ahead. Scorch stole a glance back at Julian, who was watching the strange scene play out with some interest, and then he fidgeted on the barstool and looked back at the other man disbelievingly. He lowered his voice and affected his brand of surety that had led to the successful bedding of half the Guild's apprentice population. "Is there another way I can pay you back for saving my life?"

Scorch winced. His words had come out more desperate than debonair. He examined the man's profile—pleasant angles and lush curves—but failed to catch a single flinch or twitch save another minute flare of his nostrils. Finally, after what felt like years, the man answered. "No."

"Right. Well." Scorch clawed his mind for something, anything to coax the man's attention. "Sorry, but don't you recognize me? You straddled my face, pretended to choke me to death, and then fought by my side. That was you, wasn't it?"

There. The man turned his head, his eyes flashing. He stared at Scorch for a stretch of uncomfortable seconds before speaking in a bored drawl. "Your assistance was necessary for my escape. There's no imbalance of favors between us. But if you're bent on gratifying me, you can go away. I'd find your absence suitable repayment."

Scorch floundered beneath the man's glare and stood from the stool. He hovered there, uninvited, even as the other man reverted back to his natural state of ignoring him. Scorch's feet were stuck. He couldn't make them move. It was only when a hand came to rest on his shoulder that he was startled from his immobile befuddlement.

"Scorch?" Kio asked. She was clean and carried with her the scent of roses. "I've had the bath filled with fresh water." Her eyes fell on the dark-haired man for a moment, and Scorch knew she must recognize him from the cages, but she made no effort to speak to him. Instead, she gripped Scorch's arm and led him away. Scorch did his best not to look back at the bar as they climbed the stairs, Julian laughing smugly behind him.

The inn room was small but clean, and it may have boasted several amenities and charming furnishings, but the only thing Scorch had eyes for was the large, round tub in the corner, the water steaming hot. It lured him close and he dipped his fingers into the heat, closing his eyes.

"Since Scorch has the stab wounds, he should bathe first," Kio instructed, seating Julian at the edge of the bed and dumping a hefty sack onto the mattress. She pulled out a heap of bandages and creams and suspicious looking herbs. "Julian, how does your eye feel?"

Scorch zoned them out and stripped immodestly from his clothes, starting with his boots. His jerkin came off with little effort, only making him ache when the material brushed against the wound in his shoulder. The trousers were more difficult, as the blood from the stab wound in his thigh had sealed to the leather. He gritted his teeth as he pried them off his legs. The wound wasn't nearly as inflamed as he'd suspected, but there was horrific bruising surrounding the point where the knife had gouged. It looked much worse than the twin wound in his shoulder, but neither appeared infected. That was a mercy. It would be much harder saving the High Priestess if he had to hobble up the mountain one-legged.

He slid off his underclothes last, toeing them into the pile of bloodstained, dirt-cracked clothes. The water was scalding, but Scorch's skin acclimated easily as he lowered himself into the tub on shaky arms. He bit his lip to keep from crying out when the water hit the wound on his thigh, and then on his shoulder, but when it lapped up against the multiple burns and cuts on his neck, he couldn't contain the soft hiss of pain.

Kio and Julian were polite enough to pretend they hadn't heard, and Scorch took several deep breaths to collect himself. Everything hurt, but the hot water was soothing the aches in his muscles from being cowered in a cage for two days, and before too long, he was able to relax past the throbbing pain in his shoulders and thigh. He was resting his head against the rim of the tub when Kio reminded him to clean his face and hair, as well. He dunked his whole head beneath the water and scrubbed at his hair. When he breached the surface, his eyes were blurry with tears, the scratch down the side of his face lit with pain. He shut his eyes and saw the boy's manic eyes as he clawed desperately at Scorch's face. Kio summoning him from the bath a moment later was a welcome distraction.

She helped him from the tub, handing him a thin sheet to wrap around his waist. "You can get dressed after I see to your injuries," she said, and he snuck a wink to Julian.

The bath was left murky from Scorch's scrubbing, but fresh water was already on its way. In the meantime, Julian went to wait by the window, looking out at the village street below, and gifting Scorch all the privacy he could afford.

Kio sat Scorch on the bed and tucked her fingers gently beneath his chin. "That's a nasty scratch," she said, carefully directing his face left to right. "It will scar."

Scorch sighed. "Guardians are supposed to have grisly scars."

She didn't comment, only dabbed a minty-smelling cream over the scratch with the pad of her finger. She worked silently down his body, smoothing the cream over his various cuts and scrapes. He hissed in discomfort when her fingers glided over the rope burns on his neck. When she began poking at the stab wound in his shoulder, Scorch attempted an unsuccessful flirtation to distract himself.

"You have talented hands," he commented, voice husky with hurt.

"Thank you," she brisked, sticking a clean strip of bandage across the wound. "If you were my type at all, I'd put my talented hands to better use."

Julian didn't try to stifle his laughter from the window, and after an embarrassing moment, Scorch laughed, as well. Kio just kept working, and when she kneeled in front of Scorch and scrunched up the sheet to mend his thigh, he swallowed every joke, innuendo, and proposition that flitted through his brain. After his body was approved, Kio examined the back of his head.

"Head injuries are serious," she said softly at his ear. "Since you haven't died yet, this probably won't kill you. But I'd advise against getting hit in the head in the future." She applied a generous amount of minty cream to the back of his skull, and then ruffled a hand through his clean, damp hair.

"I'll be sure to ask future bad guys to be more considerate." Kio started digging around her pile of medicinals and putting aside fresh bandages for Julian. "Sorry to disappoint," he said, standing up with a stretch, "but I'm going to get dressed."

Julian and Kio looked elsewhere while Scorch slipped into his fresh clothing. He sighed enthusiastically and smoothed the soft undershirt over his chest. His newly tanned jerkin was next, falling shorter over his hips than his Guild initiated one, but Scorch wasn't terribly bothered by the way the cut accentuated his backside in his leather trousers. He wished he had a looking glass to check his hair, but a sweep around the room told him there was none. He pulled his boots on and settled for a quick comb with his fingers.

"Hoping he might be more responsive now that the smell is gone?" Julian asked.

Scorch was scraping together an appropriately nonchalant response when the innkeeper barged into the room with two buckets of water. He sidestepped the sloshing water and slinked through the doorway with a brief wave to Kio and Julian, and a promise he'd save them a table downstairs.

The atmosphere of the inn had changed. It seemed the length of his bath had carried the inn's business from late afternoon into thriving evening. Most of the tables were full and several people were placed at the bar. Scorch's eyes raked over the patrons in search of a surly, dark-haired man and quickly found him in the same place as before, stationed at the bar and nursing a mug in his hands. Adamantly ignoring him, Scorch cozied up to the end of the bar, several seats away and separated by five different patrons. He summoned the barkeep with a smile. If his fellow escapee didn't want Scorch to buy him a drink, Scorch would buy one for himself.

A few people wandered over to him while he sipped at his ale, but he politely declined each request for company. His hands shook around the handle of the mug as he remembered a barmaid's weight in his lap and her blood on his hands. He flexed his fingers and took a deep breath before wiping the sweat from his brow. When he took the next sip of his drink, it was warmer than room temperature, and he decided to stand up and stretch his legs. He paced to the back of the room, by the stairs, trying to calm himself, but he still saw them when he closed his eyes: a woman's neck destroyed and a boy's body sprawled in the rain. Scorch was so preoccupied with managing his nerves that he almost missed the conversation happening at the table beside him. Fortuitously, the men were speaking just loudly enough and their vocabulary was just crude enough to snare Scorch's attention.

"I don't mind a cock if he's got a nice mouth to go with it."

"And hair to pull on. Turn the little thing around and it's all the same."

Scorch's ears pricked up at the exchange and he leaned casually against the stair rails, glancing up as if waiting for someone to descend.

"Did you see him up close? Eyelashes like a girl and a plump ass."

Scorch scanned the group of men. Four of them. Late thirties. Muscular. Empty, cruel eyes. They reminded him of Ebbins and he clutched his stomach warily. They continued on in their vulgar prose until one among them stood, his chair screeching over the floor.

"Looky there," the man said. "I spy a serendipitous occurrence."

"Guv, I wish you'd stop teaching him new words. He's used that one five times today."

The other men stood from the table and Scorch followed their lecherous gazes toward the bar, where the dark-haired man was setting down his mug. Scorch watched him stride for the front door, and after he disappeared outside, the group of men went after him.

Scorch followed.

When he stepped outside, he saw no one, but that didn't deter him. He stepped away from the inn door and listened. Besides the anxious buzzing in his ears, he heard what might be construed as a grunt, so he followed that sound where it led him, to the mouth of an alley between the inn and the stables. He arrived just in time to see one of the four men flying through the air.

Scorch's sword was lying in its scabbard in the inn room, but he didn't need it. He rushed into the alley, ducking a second body as it was thrown in his path. Scorch dodged, rolled, and popped back to his feet behind the third man, who was reaching to get his hands around the smaller man's waist. Scorch grabbed the morally skewed patron by the collar and hauled him back, punching him in the jaw, then he let him take a swing, blocking it with his forearm and a smile. The heat was already subsiding and his skin felt cooler as his fist sailed through the air and into the man's nose.

They wrestled for a moment—the bar patron was tall and built, but no match for Scorch—and then he finished it, knocking the man against the alley wall until his eyes slid shut. Scorch released him, letting the unconscious body collapse to the ground. Before he could even turn around, he heard a thump and a crack, followed by another, heavier thump, and then the dark-haired man was standing in front of Scorch. His hair was mussed, a thick strand falling over his eye, and his face was stormy, his stance a threat.

"Who are you?" he asked in that deep voice that sounded more thunderstorm than human.

"Who *am* I?" Scorch held a hand to his chest indignantly. "Other than the man who leapt into battle to protect your virtue?"

The man was on him impossibly fast, pushing Scorch against the wall with a hand pressed to his wounded shoulder. Scorch cried out.

"Are you following me?" his aggressor asked, pushing harder into his shoulder bandage.

"What? No," Scorch stammered, his vision prickling white around the edges from the pain. "I was trying to help you. Gods, please stop doing that."

The man let him go and stepped away, crossing his arms over his chest. Night had fallen at last and the brightest thing in the alley was the white glow of his skin. Scorch bent over when the pressure eased off his shoulder, trying not to vomit.

"Let's try this again," Scorch breathed. "I'm Scorch. I saw those men following you and I wanted to help."

"I don't need your help."

"Evidently," Scorch replied, straightening his back and wincing.

The man stared at him unblinkingly for a time before asking, "What kind of name is Scorch?"

Scorch puffed out a breath of laughter. "A nickname. What kind of name is yours?"

That earned another beat of silence as the man considered him. "Vivid."

Scorch looked at Vivid and decided the name was entirely fitting. "Vivid," he said, testing the shape of it in his mouth. "Hi."

Vivid was a statue of stillness until, abruptly, he wasn't. He turned away and began a brisk walk down the alley. Scorch didn't hesitate to walk after him, tripping over the bodies splayed on the ground.

"Wait," he said, his long legs bringing him to Vivid's side in a few strides. They rounded the corner, returning to the front of the inn, but when Vivid walked past the front door, Scorch's forehead scrunched in confusion. "You're not staying the night?" he asked, jogging to catch up with Vivid as he continued down the road.

"I shouldn't have stopped here at all," was Vivid's prickly response. After Scorch walked at his side for several more steps, Vivid stopped, shooting Scorch an irritated look. "Go away."

Scorch held his striking glower as long as he dared before taking a step back. Vivid's shoulders were flexed with tension and his mouth was severely straight. Scorch had made him look that way, and the realization made him ill. Why was he following someone who didn't wish to be followed? "Right," he said stupidly. "Sorry. Happy travels."

Vivid watched his retreat, he was sure of it, but Scorch made himself not look back until he reached the inn door, and by then, the other man was already swallowed by shadow.

Kio and Julian were there when he came in from the night, and they gathered around the one free table by the stairs. Scorch assured them its former occupants wouldn't be an issue. He did *not* say that was because they were in a pummeled pile outside. They ordered more food and drinks and enjoyed their mutual cleanliness. Julian was in high spirits because Kio told him his eye was looking much better, and if either of them noticed that Scorch's mood had darkened, neither of them mentioned it.

Scorch scratched at the scruff of beard thickening on his jaw and pondered his next move. He would remain at the inn with Kio and Julian for the night, but in the morning, he would need to part from their company and continue with his task. There could be no more dallying at taverns or being taken prisoner or dark-haired distractions. He would head east, find the path to the temple, warn the High Priestess, and finally be worthy of the Guild. The difficulty of said path he would worry about later. First, he needed to reach Viridor's Heartlands. If he kept to the main road and didn't take any unnecessary breaks, he could be there in a few—

"Oh no," Julian gasped.

Kio touched Julian's hand, and then Scorch's. "We need to get upstairs. Now."

Scorch could hear the dread in her tone, even beneath its usual calming hum. She and Julian were both staring at something behind Scorch's back, and he twisted in his seat to look. He shouldn't have done it, because the sudden movement drew the attention of those whose attention he did not want: five men around the bar, with masks hanging loose around their necks. As Scorch saw them, they saw him, and it took no time at all for them to place why he looked so familiar.

He turned back in his seat with wide eyes. "Oh, *fuck*."

Kio made the first move, standing from her chair slowly, but as soon as she was up, the masked men charged forward, tossing their drinks on the floor and hollering obscenities. Scorch yanked Julian out of his chair and the three of them took to the stairs, running as fast as they could to their room. As soon as Kio slammed the door shut, an onslaught of bangs started shaking the cheap wood in its frame. Julian helped her keep the door closed, throwing himself up against it.

"Scorch, quick," Kio pleaded, and he didn't need her to explain. He flew to the bed, where she still had her medicinal supplies spread out, and gathered them hastily into her pack. Next, he picked up his sword and buckled it onto his belt. His new satchel was already packed and he swung it over his shoulder, along with Kio's and Julian's.

There was shouting on the other side of the door, and then a booted foot kicked clear through, making Kio and Julian scatter. Scorch ran for the window and knocked its flimsy shutters open with an elbow. In the next moment, the door was kicked again and the men bottlenecked into the room. Their faces weren't roughed up, but they were furious. They must have been the guards outside the Circle that ran when Scorch and Vivid started scaling the wall.

"Go!" Scorch yelled, shoving Julian and Kio out of the way. He unsheathed his sword and steadied it at the intruders. Behind him, he could hear Julian and Kio scrambling out the window. When the masked men rushed him, Scorch was ready. He kicked the first man, making him stumble back into the others, and since that was the only chance Scorch might have had, he took it, sheathing his sword and jumping out the window.

He landed hard. Kio and Julian were right there, scooping him up by the arms, and then they were all running. Seconds later, they heard the inn door slam open.

"They're chasing us!" Scorch warned, but they were already running as fast as they could. The road ahead was dark and the masked men's voices were loud, their footsteps louder as they gained more ground.

They ran down the road, the trees obscuring even the tiny bit of light from the moon. Scorch could hardly see a few feet in front of him, and he definitely didn't see the rock that tripped him and sent him falling face-first into the dirt.

He groaned and pushed himself to his feet, but before he could run, a hand grabbed him by the neck.

"I got one," the masked man cackled. "I'm gonna bleed you dry," he hissed in Scorch's ear, pressing a knife to his throat.

Scorch tried to reach for his sword, but before he could manage a grip, the man at his back moaned and spasmed against him. A moment later, he fell. A dagger was sticking out of his head. Vivid, who had appeared out of nowhere, pulled the dagger free and leapt past Scorch, double blades whirring as he cut through the second man's offensive sword strikes and shoved one of the blades deep between his ribs.

Suddenly, Kio and Julian were at his side and Scorch regained the sense to draw his sword, but Vivid didn't need his help, and he didn't allow it. Scorch's stunned eyes followed his slim body as he danced violent circles around the remaining masked men, jabbing, slicing, ruining with his twin daggers until all five men were irrefutably dead. When he was done, he stood in the middle of the corpses and wiped a splatter of blood from his cheek.

"I thought I told you to go away," Vivid said flatly.

"Where did you learn to fight like that?" Kio asked. Her voice was smooth but her eyes were narrowed at Vivid, like she was figuring out a puzzle.

Vivid ignored her and sheathed his blades—one in each long sleeve of his arm—and the look he gave Scorch was murderous. Scorch would have feared a look like that if Vivid hadn't just saved his life. Again.

"That's twice in one day, you know," Scorch said, and Vivid's black eyebrows furrowed. "If you're so against my existence, you might want to try *not* prolonging it."

Julian made a tiny noise of confusion, but Kio was still studying Vivid. She took a step closer, ignoring his scowl. "Where did you learn to fight like that?" she asked again. She was taller by several inches, but Vivid's presence was a looming, perilous thing, unbound by trivialities such as height.

"Just be thankful I did or else you'd be soaking your shoes in your useless friend's blood." Vivid shoved past her and came to stand directly in front of Scorch. "This is the last time I tell you to stop following me," he growled, and then he turned and started down the road.

Scorch exchanged glances with Kio and Julian before calling after him. "Can I walk in front of you, then? Because it seems we're headed in the same direction."

Scorch counted to ten before Vivid stopped walking. He ran to catch up and Vivid cast him a frustrated glance.

"I need to take this road east," Scorch explained.

"Take another road," Vivid snapped.

"There is no other road to the Heartlands," Scorch argued.

"Why are you going to the Heartlands?"

Scorch was surprised by the spark of interest in the other man's voice. He straightened his shoulders. "I have a guardianship to attend in the mountain temple."

The night became silent except for the wind; it howled and whistled and pushed the hair back from Scorch's forehead. He patted it down and raised a questioning eyebrow at Vivid, who looked like he'd been slapped across the face. "What?"

"You're a guardian," Vivid said, and it wasn't a question.

"Yes," Scorch answered, tugging at his jerkin, as if his clothing made his duty obvious. "I've a task of the utmost importance concerning the High Priestess and I cannot be stalled because you refuse to share the road with me. Travel behind me, if you want, and you'll be rid of my backside soon enough. How far will this road take you?"

"As far as the Heartlands," Vivid answered sharply. "I am also headed to the temple, to train with the Priestess' Monks."

They stared at one another.

"This is good news," Kio said, her voice a melody fighting against the wind. "The Monk's Path is said to be the most dangerous land in Viridor. Our chances of survival should be improved if we travel together."

Scorch processed her words slowly, but when they finally sank in, he looked at her curiously. "Kio," he started, but she took his hand and squeezed it gently.

"If you're going down the Monk's Path, I want to go with you," she said.

"Like you said, it's dangerous."

"Which is why I should go with you," she countered. "Your wounds need looking after or they'll fester."

"Guardians don't usually walk around with personal helpers."

"Are you a trained herbalist?"

Scorch looked at Julian for help, but he was looking at the ground. "No," he answered.

"Do you know what a Peggotty Lush-fern looks like?"

A long pause. "No."

"Then I'm coming with you. Unless you want to accidentally touch one and die of boiling fever blisters before you reach the mountainside." She still held Scorch's hand. "Please," she said. "You need someone protecting you."

Scorch thought of her cool hands and soothing voice, the care she'd taken wrapping his wounds, and the sincerity in her request. He glanced at Vivid, but he was staring straight ahead, ignoring all of them.

"I won't send you away," Scorch said at last. He didn't like it, but it wasn't his decision.

Kio gave his hand a final squeeze before dropping it, a pleased smile on her face. "Julian?" She walked to him and placed her fingers beneath his chin, raising his eyes to hers.

"I have nowhere else to go," he said softly, and Scorch saw another glimpse of that broken, caged person. "When the slavers took me, they killed my . . ." he paused, choking on his words. "I have nowhere else to go."

"Okay," Scorch said, and his voice sounded too loud for the quiet forest road. He knew well enough what it was like to have nothing and no one. "Okay." There was nothing left to do but turn to Vivid, who retuned Scorch's gaze reluctantly. "I would offer to stay behind and let you gain ground ahead of us, but I can't delay."

The hair had fallen back over Vivid's eye, but he didn't bother to push it behind his ear, not in the gusting wind that would rustle it right back. "Neither can I."

"Well, then," said Scorch, not entirely sure what had just been agreed upon, or if anything *had* been agreed upon. He handed Kio and Julian their packs, which were slung around his shoulder from their close escape, and then he adjusted the strap of his own satchel, busying his anxious hands. When everything was tightened and tidied and he could think of no more diversions, Scorch gave an awkward sort of nod and began walking down the road. Kio and Julian fell in step at his side.

Scorch held his breath until he heard a fourth set of footsteps taking off after them.

# Dream Moss

# 6

That first night, they did not travel far before stopping, for they were all exhausted. Veering a safe distance from the main road, Scorch resisted checking over his shoulder too often to see if the fourth person sharing the road with them intended on sharing a camp, as well. Miraculously, when Scorch finally set down his pack in a fit clearing and looked up, he saw that Vivid had not only followed, but was currently making quick work of collecting kindling for a fire.

Scorch was practically itching with interest, but he refrained from indulging in the deluge of questions whirring about in his head. It was clear from the stern lines on Vivid's face that he would not take kindly to questions, nor any conversation at all, and so Scorch steered clear of him, trying his damnedest to avoid eye contact when he knelt beside the kindling to set it ablaze. The act brought to mind the image of his mother, her elegant hand arching over smoking wood. Scorch, instead, used a flint, and his heart beat a mournful rhythm in his chest.

Since they'd already dined at the inn, there was little for four strangers to do but go to sleep, and now that Scorch was finally readying for rest, he could feel the trauma of the past few days settling heavily in his body. He vowed to ignore it, and when everyone else claimed their respective spots around the fire, so did he. The ground was hard, but it wasn't a cage, and so sleep came quickly.

For a time, he was peaceful. But in a mind like Scorch's, it was never long before the peace sizzled and smoldered and was replaced with the thick, suffocating nature of nightmares.

*Flames licked his skin. He was choking on acrid, black smoke. But it was the tangy smell of blood that twisted his insides.*

*He grabbed her as her skin finally began to burn. A sob tore from his throat.*

*Behind him, his father lay in pieces.*

Scorch jolted awake and his eyes opened to the glow of fire. Gagging at the phantom stink of crackling skin, he pressed a hand over his mouth and shuffled clumsily to his feet, stumbling from their little camp until the fire was only a flicker in the darkness. He grabbed at the nearest tree, his fingers scraping against the bark as he doubled over with dry heaves.

He was no stranger to nightmares, but it had been a long time since he'd woken so violently. Tears leaked from his bloodshot eyes and he remained hunched and heaving for several torturous minutes while a slew of unbidden thoughts haunted the backs of his eyelids: the boy in the rain, the girl in the bed, his parents on the forest floor. Scorch shook, clammy-skinned, gasping great bouts of breath, until finally, blessedly, his tremors ceased, and the bile in his throat subsided. He wiped the tears from his face and walked back to the camp.

Kio and Julian had not stirred, but Vivid was awake and leaning against a tree. Had Scorch woken him with his nightmare? Had he witnessed his graceless retreat from the camp? Embarrassed, he worried for a moment that Vivid would inquire after his whereabouts, maybe ask what he had dreamed, but when Scorch walked past him and resettled on the ground, Vivid said nothing.

Scorch lay on his back, listening to the calm sounds of the night: Kio and Julian breathing steadily, the leaves whispering in the soft breeze, the fire hissing and cracking. But he didn't sleep again. He kept his eyes shut, feigning rest in case Vivid was watching, and when the sun finally began to rise and he could stop pretending, he was thankful.

The next day was warm and the sunshine fell in brilliant stripes through the treetops. Scorch set a hastened pace down the road with the intent of reaching the Heartlands in a week's time. Eventually, the main road would split in two, to the north and to the south. They would keep going east, off the road and into the inhospitable lands of Viridor's center. But until then, Scorch could do nothing but walk one step at a time. Kio and Julian walked next to him and Vivid remained several paces behind, ghostlike. But for someone who was barely there, Scorch was hyper-aware of his presence, constantly finding reasons to turn around, even if it meant falling victim to Vivid's glower.

Scorch's body was sore from his days cramped in the cage, and his multiple wounds ached with every step, but he was young and strong, and the exercise was soothing, the air refreshing. In the sunlight, his black dreams felt far away, and he wished he could sleep in the glimmers of sun, like the fat grey cat from the Guild. A yawn escaped him and he gave his head a shake. Kio was speaking softly about a wild flower that grew on the temple mountain when the first scream came.

Scorch stopped in his tracks and looked around anxiously. "Did you hear that?" he asked the others. Kio and Julian nodded, looking around with wide eyes. Vivid had unsheathed his daggers.

When Scorch heard the second scream, he took off, not even checking to see if the others were following. He ran as fast as he could down the road, taking the turn so sharply, he nearly toppled himself, and then, straight ahead, was a village in discord. Scorch stopped to catch his breath and observe the tumultuous herd of villagers as they streamed from their homes and gathered around the obvious site of destruction. It was a collapsed house, a heap of ruined planks and split bricks, with a thick cloud of smoke hovering overhead. And standing in front of the house was the source of the screaming: a young boy, twelve or thirteen, covered in dust.

The boy screamed again, and Scorch began weaving through the crowd for him, but the villagers were densely packed and had no interest in yielding to a newcomer. Peering over the heads of several, Scorch saw a large man sweep the boy up in his arms. The boy's screams intensified and he began beating wildly at the man's chest. The villagers were yelling something, but Scorch couldn't understand. An older woman was standing in front of him and he tapped her on the shoulder. "What's going on here?"

The woman was startled by Scorch's sudden appearance, her eyes darting down to the sword at his hip and then up to the scar on his face.

"I'm a guardian," Scorch said as confidently as he could. "I can help."

That calmed her and she nodded toward the pile of debris. "The miller's house fell down," she said.

Scorch frowned. "How?"

"The ground started shaking, just in that spot, mind you, and then it stopped standing upright. Made an awful sound. The dust is only now starting to clear." She coughed, not bothering to cover her mouth.

"Was anyone hurt?"

"There's no one could've survived all that rubble crashing down."

Scorch moved toward the destroyed house but the woman caught his arm and said, "It's for the best they're dead."

He stared at her. "What do you mean by that?" The villagers' yelling was growing louder, clearer, and he was beginning to understand what, exactly, was being chanted.

The woman had to speak loudly for Scorch to hear. "We've never had a quake here before. They're saying the child who lived there is an elemental, brought the whole house down on top of his parents. And if he's one, chances are his parents were, so it's best for us all, lucky even, that they're dead. The High Priestess has smiled on us today."

Scorch's face was white. He tore his eyes from the woman and cast a nervous glance around. "Where's the boy?" He shouldn't have let him out of his sight. Neither he nor the man who'd picked him up were visible in the crowd, but now Scorch knew perfectly well what the people around him were yelling: "Kill it, kill it, kill it!"

"They took it away to deal with," the woman answered. Her eyes shone greedily. "The money for its body will get the whole village through the winter."

A second later, Scorch heard the scream again, and then it came to an abrupt end. He spun around, looking for the boy, but he still couldn't see him, couldn't see where that man had taken him. A surge of adrenaline turned him in a circle, eyes searching. He wanted to yell after the boy, wanted to shake the merciless woman and the other villagers, their eyes darkened by bloodlust, their voices loud and noxious. His hand fell to his sword hilt, his palms sweaty.

A door slammed in the distance and Scorch veered around in time to see the man emerge from a house down the street, dragging a large sack behind him. The villagers clapped and cheered, making a path for him to walk through. When he passed Scorch, it was clear what he had inside the sack, and Scorch's jaw clenched against a wave of nausea. The world was suddenly scarlet-edged.

They had killed him. They had killed him yards from where Scorch stood. He cried out in frustrated pain, but his was only a drop in a sea of bellows. He wanted to brandish his sword. He wanted to cut the sack open and pull the boy out and see that he was breathing. He wanted to tear down the monstrous man who had thrown a boy over his shoulders and—

A hand grabbed his wrist and Scorch was too fever-headed to resist. He let himself be pulled through the crowd and away from the village, keeping his eyes fastened on the man dragging the sack. When his feet hit the main road, the hand around his wrist yanked hard, forcing Scorch's attention. He looked up, expecting to see Kio's concerned face, but it was Vivid.

"They killed that boy," Scorch whispered. He knew what was done to elementals—it was considered common practice in Viridor—but it still made him sick to witness it firsthand.

"You were reaching for your sword."

Scorch nodded, dazed and queasy. "They killed him."

"Since when is it a guardian's job to protect elementals?" asked Vivid. It was the first time he had spoken all day.

"It's not," Scorch answered, and it wasn't. The Guild upheld Viridorian law, and the law did nothing to protect elementals, not even if the elemental in question was a child. Scorch knew better. He did. But he had also been raised on the instinct to protect, and that boy had needed his protection. "I—I wanted to," he tried, his words sticking in his throat.

Vivid glared. "It doesn't matter what you wanted. Hurry up or I'll leave you behind." He stormed down the road, where Kio and Julian were waiting, and Scorch, after sparing a final glance at the village, hurried after him.

All day, the image remained with him. All day, he watched the sack slide by. All day, he strained to breathe in and out as if it was no bother. But that night, when they stopped again for camp, Julian's take on the day had his stomach turning worse than ever.

"That's part of what makes them so dangerous," he said, warming his hands by the fire. "They're sneaky. You could live in a village with one for years and never know until it was too late."

Scorch had caught rabbits for dinner with one of his Guild-learned traps and was rotating the skewer over the flames. Kio crouched beside him, replacing his shoulder bandage. Vivid wasn't there; he had left to find fresh water for their canteens.

"Those poor people," Julian continued. Kio's remedies had already improved the swelling around his eye and, apparently, the less bruised he became, the more confidence he gained. "I guess it must have been an Earth, to bring that house down. At least they'll be compensated by the Queen."

Scorch struggled to swallow his dinner that night and, later, he fought to stay awake, not because he wasn't tired, but because he feared the horror that sleep would bring. Ultimately, though, despite his stubborn resistance, he couldn't keep from slipping. Darkness grasped him, wrapping around his sleeping brain and replaying the boy's screams again and again.

When Scorch woke, it was the middle of the night. Kio and Julian were asleep and Vivid was yet to return from his quest for fresh water. Like the night before, Scorch stumbled from the camp and found a quiet piece of forest in which to panic silently. He did not get sick, but his body curled with tension and he dropped to his knees, his breathing strained and shallow. Sweat spotted the ground where it dripped from his face. He stayed that way for a while, until his skin didn't feel so hot and his lungs didn't feel so tight. He rubbed at his neck, his throat dry, wincing when his fingers brushed against the rope burns. So deep was he in the aftermath of his panic, he didn't hear the nearing footsteps until they stopped beside him. A canteen dropped next to his head, and Scorch picked it up, taking an eager sip. The water was cool and comforting, and a single sip turned into several, thirsty gulps. When he looked up, sated, he saw nothing but a dark figure stalking back toward camp.

Once Scorch mustered the strength to return, he set the canteen back down beside Vivid, who was sitting away from the fire and staring idly into the distance. "Thank you," Scorch whispered, but Vivid had no words for him that night, nor did he have words for him the following day. But on their third night of camp, after another long stretch of traveling, when Scorch bolted up from another nightmare, Vivid was sitting right beside him.

Scorch gasped and blinked the morbid images from his eyes. It was a shock, seeing him there, not only close, but staring directly at him, and when Vivid stood, so did Scorch, following him into the trees. He watched, fascinated as Vivid navigated through the underbrush with steps so light they hardly disturbed the leaves. Meanwhile, Scorch's boots crunched loudly over every twig and leaf.

"Your nightmares are a problem," Vivid declared when they finally stopped walking.

Embarrassment crept up his cheeks. "I'm fine," he lied.

"I don't care whether or not you're fine, but when you have a bad dream, it keeps you up all night, and you don't get enough rest. And if you don't get enough rest, your reaction time becomes sloppy."

Scorch snorted indignantly. "I'm not sloppy."

Vivid's foot shot out, linking behind Scorch's knee and knocking him flat on his back before he could even register Vivid had moved. He leaned over Scorch, a pale face taunting him from above. "Sloppy," he repeated. "And when you're sloppy, you put the people traveling with you in danger. I won't let you be a risk."

Scorch swallowed. Suddenly, the man above him seemed even more threatening than usual. "Are you going to . . . kill me for being sloppy?"

The stare he received made his heart race. Vivid reached into a compartment of his tight leather trousers that Scorch had never noticed before—not that he spent much time examining Vivid's trousers—and produced a small bag. He dropped it onto Scorch's chest.

"Dream Moss," he explained. "Chew on the stem before you sleep and it keeps your mind restful."

"I know what it is," said Scorch, sitting up and looking into the bag full of thick, ivory stems. Etheridge grew Dream Moss in her garden.

"Then you have no excuses," Vivid grumbled. "Don't keep me up again."

With that, Vivid left. Scorch pulled a stem from the bag and popped it into his mouth. When he made his way back to camp, Vivid ignored him and Scorch ignored Vivid, irritation fuzzing his brain. *Sloppy.* Scorch was not *sloppy.* He was thinking over examples to prove his extreme non-sloppiness when he fell back to sleep.

The following day came easier for Scorch, and they made excellent time. The wounds in his thigh and shoulder ached considerably less after several days of Kio's salves, and the good night's sleep had granted his frantic mind a reprieve. He felt better than he had since leaving the Guild, and it was that foolish high of contentedness that made Scorch slow his steps. Kio and Julian passed him on the road and Scorch aligned his pace with Vivid's, who committed promptly to ignoring him. But Scorch was not deterred.

"I slept well," he provided brightly.

Vivid stared straight ahead, and Scorch used the opportunity to study him. His hair was straight and black and his eyelashes were long and thick. The day was overcast, making his white skin even whiter. He looked like he was carved from marble, straight-faced and sternly beautiful. And though he was much smaller than Scorch, shorter and less muscular, the way he moved spoke to the discreet prowess of his strength, and Scorch would bet that, beneath the yards of leather coverings, Vivid's muscles were lean and taut. Every movement of his body promised violence, and Scorch couldn't fathom how the men at the inn had thought to take advantage. Couldn't anyone with eyes see he was dangerous? Scorch could see it. But it wasn't all he could see.

"You could be a guardian," he said.

Vivid didn't respond, apart from a twitch of his eyebrow.

"You're clearly a talented fighter," Scorch continued. "And you're still young. How old are you?"

Twitch.

"You're also compassionate, and that's an important quality to the Guild."

Twitch.

"You'd like it there. It's beautiful inside the walls, and the Master is—"

"Be quiet," Vivid said, cutting him off. "I don't care."

Scorch laughed at his bluntness, earning another quality eyebrow twitch. "You care about some things," he kept on. "I've never known anyone to take the Monk's Path. All so you can train with the High Priestess' Monks. Are you hoping to become one of them or do you just want to learn what they know?"

The sound of Vivid's voice caught Scorch by surprise, as he hadn't been expecting an answer. "They're the best."

"That's the rumor, but who's seen them in a fight? They're secluded on a mountain in the middle of the Heartlands. I'd take training with the Guild any day."

"The Guardians' Guild is for cowards and fools," Vivid hissed. "It's a joke."

And like that, Scorch's pleasant mood faltered. "I grew up there," he said. "They took me in when I had nowhere else to go. I won't listen to your insults."

"Then I guess you better shut up and leave me alone."

Scorch stopped trying to engage Vivid in conversation, but he didn't increase his pace to get ahead of him. He kept his stride even with Vivid's and hoped the annoyance of his presence would be fair enough payback.

That evening, Scorch chewed on a Dream Moss stem while Kio freshened his bandages, and then he walked to find fresh water. The stream's distorted reflection was the only clue he had of the other man's arrival.

"How are you so quiet?" Scorch asked as Vivid knelt down to fill his canteen.

"I just seem quiet because you never stop talking."

They remained crouched by the water for several minutes, but when the wind began to whip in threat of a coming storm, Scorch stood. Vivid remained low, staring at the water as it rippled around the lip of his canteen.

Scorch was turning to leave when Vivid said, quite unexpectedly, "You're not a coward." He was looking up at Scorch expectantly, the wind pulling and pushing at his hair.

After a long time—because it took a long time for Scorch to manage a response—he asked, "Just a fool, then?"

"Yes," Vivid answered without pause.

Scorch felt he should be offended, but Vivid's words rang with a cadence of regret that incited curiosity instead of anger. He considered the accusation, thumbing at a droplet of water running down the side of the canteen. "Maybe I am," he conceded with a shrug.

Vivid's eyes traveled over Scorch's face, and he tried not to fidget, but it was a challenge. "There are worse things to be," Vivid said, and then he stood from the stream and headed back for camp.

Scorch watched him go.

Their journey on the main road ended midday on the sixth day, when the road split. Scorch halted at the edge of the forged path and reached out his foot to touch the wild grasses growing where the Heartlands began. The week of traveling had numbed his mind, but now that his task was blatantly before him, it all felt too real. The Master believed in him, but Scorch knew himself, and he knew there was a good chance he wouldn't be coming back.

"Kio, Julian," he said to the companions at his side. "You should turn back."

"No, thank you," said Kio.

Julian looked at Scorch with dedicated eyes—both finally of equal size and seeing ability—and shook his head. "I want to meet the High Priestess. I'd like her blessing. Maybe I can train to be one of her monks, too."

Scorch couldn't resist cutting a glance at Vivid. Sure enough, one eyebrow was raised slightly, but he didn't comment, and if his incredulity had been audible, he was too far back from the others to be heard. For Scorch's part, he tried to keep the doubt from betraying his own expression as he faced Julian and Kio.

"I can't keep you from something you want to do," he began. "But I want you to understand how dangerous the path truly is. The Guild hardly ever sends guardians through the Heartlands. I don't know if I'll be able to protect you."

"Do *you* know what lies ahead?" Vivid asked, walking up to Scorch. He looked out over the high grasses. "Did your Master tell you?"

Scorch's temperature rose. "There is scant knowledge available of the Heartlands," he answered. "No one really knows what lies between here and the mountain temple."

"I do," Vivid said.

Kio's eyes narrowed. "How?"

Vivid just stared at her.

Scorch ran an anxious hand through his hair. "What do you know, Vivid?"

"The path is a test," Vivid rumbled, "to separate the worthy from the useless." He glanced at Scorch before looking back at the grasses. "Only those most deserving will reach the temple."

"A test?" Kio asked.

Vivid paused before answering, as if weighing whether or not he wished to speak to her at all. Finally, he did, but it was more like he was speaking aloud than answering Kio. "Serenity, Focus, Fortitude. If you don't possess these qualities, don't expect to live through this."

Scorch sighed. "Why can the tests never be great hair, a tight ass, and stamina for days?"

"Like that would help you," Julian mumbled, and Kio laughed.

Vivid wasn't amused. He turned heated eyes to Scorch, staring up at him through a lock of dark hair. "If you don't take these tests seriously, you will die, and I will let you."

Scorch nodded, but fear coursed through his body. He tried to ignore it. Being afraid would do him no good. "Last chance," he told the others. "I have to go."

"I want to go," answered Kio.

Julian bit his lip, but after a moment said, "Me, too."

Scorch took a deep breath and stepped from the main road, into the Heartlands. Vivid stood at his side, tense and sharp-eyed.

"Let's not waste any more time, then," Scorch said.

He repeated his mantra in his head to cool his nerves: *Save the High Priestess, Save the High Priestess, Save the High Priestess.* For the first time since leaving the Guild, he felt as though his guardianship had truly begun. Now he just had to stay alive long enough to complete it.

# *Serenity*

# 7

The grasses grazed Scorch's hip as they trudged through the marshy Heartlands. The sudden change of geography from firm, well-traveled road to soggy, un-trodden earth was disconcerting, but after walking for an hour, Scorch could see in the distance where the grasses calmed around a copse of trees. All were quiet as they traveled and Scorch wondered if the others were as nervous as he was, except Vivid, of course. Vivid had the air of someone whose nerves never trumped their resolve. He walked stoically, the only sign of his concern the unnaturally straight line of his shoulders. Scorch let his hand rest on the pommel of his sword, its smooth surface familiar and comforting.

When they reached the trees, Vivid held up a hand. Scorch stopped. He watched Vivid tilt his head to the side and close his eyes. A gust of wind ruffled his hair.

"The lake is through the trees," he announced, and his voice was deep, careful, and quiet. "We build here."

Scorch thought he heard wrong. "Build? Build what?"

"A raft," Vivid replied. "Unless you want to swim."

Scorch may not have known about specific tests, but he was well aware of the lake they needed to cross. He could remember studying the Viridor map as a child, and it was nearly as big as a sea. Definitely not swimmable.

"Shouldn't we build at the shore?" he asked, waving at the thick cropping of ash-white trees. "This is cramped quarters for raft building."

"We can make no noise on the shore," was Vivid's short answer before delving deeper into the white trees.

"The first test is serenity," Kio said, and Scorch glanced at her. The burn on her face was nearly healed; only a shiny pink blur remained. The rest of her was bright and airy, and she was lovelier than ever, graceful lines and delicate hands, warm skin in a forest of white bark. He was suddenly very glad she'd come. Scorch couldn't imagine being left in the Heartlands with only Vivid to keep him company. He was rather less thankful for Julian's presence, however. Scorch didn't dislike him, not excessively anyway, but he couldn't understand him either. And when he looked at Julian, the sight of him left a sour feeling in his stomach.

A loud crack broke Scorch from his introspection and he turned wide eyes in the direction Vivid had headed.

"I think," Kio said, "we're meant to be cutting up lumber for a raft."

The echo of something heavy falling made Scorch raise his eyebrows in disbelief. "Did he just cut down a tree?"

Kio smiled. "How tough is your sword?"

Tough enough, it turned out. They used his sword to chop at thin tree trunks, Scorch grimacing with every blow. His sword wasn't made for chopping down trees, but they were spindly things, and the bark was soft enough to sear through without breaking his blade, though it took a dozen swings at the neck of each tree to down it. Julian and Kio had blades, as well, picked up during their escape from the Circle, and one by one, they collected a modest mountain of logs for building.

The day was growing late and Scorch was sweating profusely by the time Vivid reappeared, dragging a litter of timber behind him. Scorch allowed himself a moment to be amazed by his strength, to admire the concentration knitting his brow, the bead of perspiration trailing over snowy skin, until Vivid glanced up and their eyes met. Scorch turned away and rubbed at the beard making his chin itch; he needed a shave.

They worked in tandem setting the logs together, and then Vivid presented a bundle of thick, malleable roots. He pressed a heap into Scorch's arms and, while Kio and Julian held the logs in place, Scorch and Vivid wound the vine-like roots around the wood, weaving them together. Scorch tried his best to sneak discreet glances at Vivid's fingers as they deftly manipulated the bindings—they had not covered raft assembly at the Guild—but Vivid caught him at it more than once. Scorch was squinting as they began to lose the light, struggling to see the knots in front of his eyes, but Vivid appeared to have no trouble. When Scorch fumbled with the final ties of the raft, Vivid wordlessly took the roots from his hands and finished it himself, then commenced to attach a crudely made rudder, which consisted of a thick branch tied to the back of the raft so they could steer.

As the sun disappeared beneath the ashen trees, their raft was completed. It was small, would be a tight squeeze for four passengers, but it would have to do, and Scorch smiled as he inspected their creation. Contrarily, Vivid's face revealed nothing but displeasure. He sniffed at the air, the wind whipping his hair in one direction, and then another. He looked at Scorch.

"Give me your shirts," he demanded.

"Trying to get me naked? All you have to do is ask," was Scorch's automatic response, which he immediately regretted. "I mean," he huffed awkwardly, "w-why do you need my shirts?" He pressed his hand protectively over his satchel, feeling the lump of brand new clothes he'd purchased only a week prior.

Vivid didn't answer, just crossed his arms and waited. It didn't take long to crumple beneath that indifference. Scorch succumbed haughtily, reaching into his satchel and pulling out his collection of clean linen shirts. He handed them to Vivid, who fingered the fabric, stretching it and holding it up to the sky before he ripped one down the middle.

"Hey!" cried Scorch. He hadn't even gotten to wear the blue one yet.

Vivid rolled his eyes at Scorch's distress and ripped another, placing the shreds of cloth across the body of the raft and stepping back to inspect them. He ripped the third and final shirt and added it to his collection, but a miniscule frown still bothered his lips. He whipped his head around and stared at Scorch so hard that Scorch's palms began to sweat.

"Will you take off that shirt?" Vivid asked casually.

Crassness built swiftly on Scorch's tongue, but he dared not speak it. Instead, he shifted uncomfortably, crossing and uncrossing his arms, tugging a restless hand through his hair.

Vivid scowled. "You said all I had to do was ask. Give me your shirt."

Scorch felt a compulsion to mention that Kio and Julian both had clothes, too, which certainly looked capable of ripping, but he kept his mouth shut and removed his jerkin. His shoulder throbbed a bit when he lifted the leather piece over his head, and his grunt of pain echoed in the quiet of the trees. Kio held the jerkin while Scorch stripped the undershirt from his back. It was damp with sweat, but when Vivid held out his hand, Scorch handed it over.

Vivid ripped it up and set it with the others before giving Kio his full attention. Scorch was mildly offended that Vivid didn't give his bare chest even the most fleeting of once-overs.

"You have needles?" asked Vivid.

Kio gave Scorch back his jerkin and began to dig through her pack. She handed him the flint and asked him to light a fire. He hurried to torch one of their leftover branches and held it over their heads while Vivid and Kio bent over the ripped shirts. They were making a sail. It was logical, he supposed, but he still lamented the loss of his clothes. At least, he thought to himself, Vivid hadn't demanded his underclothes, as well.

Once the sewing was done, Vivid rigged the patchwork sail to the final tree limb and secured it to the raft with the last of the roots.

"Lovely," Scorch said. "I've always wanted to build a boat in the middle of a forest. It's so useful here, so majestic, the way it floats on the underbrush."

Julian snorted, apparently in the upswing of a good mood. Scorch preferred it to his religious-ranting mood and his trembling-victim mood.

When no one spoke, Scorch continued. "Was building the raft supposed to be the serene part of the test? Because I don't feel serene, just really sore, from, you know, cutting down trees with a *sword*." He could practically hear Vivid's eyebrow twitch.

"The test begins when we leave the safety of the trees," Vivid said with a threatening lilt in his voice that made the hair stand up on Scorch's bare arms. "There must be utter silence as we approach the lake, while we are on the lake, and as long as we remain on the shore of the opposite bank." He glared at Scorch as he spoke. "Do not speak, do not cough, do not splash the water. We set the raft down gently and let the sail guide us across in silence. Absolute silence. If you make a sound, we die."

Kio, Julian, and Scorch all stared, standing with a touch of shock at the harsh warning. Scorch eyed Vivid's hands. His fingers were caressing the wrists of his sleeves, where his twin daggers dwelled.

"Absolute silence," Vivid repeated gravely. "I will not die because of you." He waited for nods of agreement, and once he received them, he moved for an edge of the raft.

Scorch snuffed out their fire and hurried to the opposing corner of the raft, while Kio and Julian took up the back. Together, they lifted, heaving the weight onto their shoulders. Scorch was taller than Vivid by a good seven inches, and the raft's weight tilted back and forth between them as Scorch tried to lower his side and Vivid tried to lift his higher. The struggle remained a voiceless argument between them as they made their way through the winding trees. They were all breathing too hard beneath the weight of the raft to converse, but right before they stepped through the final row of trees and onto the bank, Vivid delivered unto their party a final reminder: "Quiet." Then they stepped onto the shore.

The moon was waxing and meager in the sky, but Scorch could still make out the vague glitter of rippling water as the lake lapped against the bank. In a way, he was thankful for the darkness, not overly eager to see the vastness of the water they were about to cross.

Vivid led them to the edge, and the others copied his motions of bending to one knee and slowly, carefully, placing the raft on the dewy grass of the bank. The slope was slight and slick with mud, and as they positioned their bodies onto the raft, it slipped into the water with little more than a slap of sound. Vivid touched Scorch's shoulder, snaring his attention, and they set to work spreading and fastening the sail, until it stretched wide across their tiny raft. Scorch's repurposed shirts caught the wind with gusto and coaxed them from the bank.

For a while, fortune favored them. The wind was strong and easterly and the raft floated with surprising speed across the lake's black surface. Kio and Julian sat on one side of the raft, and, to evenly distribute the weight, Scorch was stuck sitting next to Vivid on the other side. The space was so limited, he couldn't keep his long legs from brushing against Vivid's thigh, but—much to Scorch's amusement—Vivid could say nothing about it.

They sailed through the darkest hours of the night, Vivid steering them, and the only noise was the soft rhythm of water brushing against the wood of the raft. Scorch watched the sliver of moon cross the sky and tried to keep track of the time. Hours inched by, but no one tried to sleep. Everyone stayed stiff with alertness. No one spoke. No one breathed loudly enough to be heard. They were the perfect picture of silence, and as the sun finally began to rise, Scorch did feel serenity coursing through him. It calmed him, watching the sky leisurely fill with the scarlet and gold light of dawn, while the water glimmered with pinks and oranges. Soon, he could make out the opposite shore, but it was hazy and blurred.

The wind maintained its strength and continued to push them steadily forward. Scorch was loath to imagine the length of such a journey with no favorable breeze. He thought of what might have happened if circumstances had led him to cross the lake on his own. He probably would have lacked the foresight of a sail, and he certainly would have made noise, not that he knew the penalty yet of such a discrepancy. Hardly for the first time since leaving land, Scorch turned his eyes to Vivid, but the other man was distracted by something, his focus zeroed in on the water, so Scorch looked at the water, too.

A shadow passed beneath their raft and Scorch glanced up at the sky to check for rainclouds. He saw only clear, pink sky melting into blue. There were no clouds. He looked back down at the water, waiting for another shadow but seeing none. When he returned his gaze to Vivid, Vivid was watching him. The flash of warning in his eyes told Scorch that he had seen the shadow, as well.

Scorch swallowed down the anxiety forming in his chest, but now that he'd opened his mind to it, dark thoughts began to swarm his imagination. He felt a not entirely irrational fear that the raft would burst into flames, and he almost dipped his fingers into the water to cool them before he remembered Vivid's warning. He sucked in a large inhale of cool air and raided his surroundings frantically for something to distract him, settling on the slender knuckles of Vivid's fingers as they tapped silently against his leather-clad knee. Tap, tap, tap they went, long and powder-white. Tap, tap, tap. Scorch concentrated on those fingers and kept breathing in and out. He did not look at the water or the distance to the opposite shore, just those fingers tap, tap, tapping. Relentless and elegant and ceaselessly distracting.

When Scorch had regained a sense of calmness, he spared a look at the others. Kio was sitting peacefully, her legs crossed and her eyes heavily lidded. She was meditating, Scorch decided. Then he looked at Julian and his heart clenched, because Julian was watching the water with a panic-stricken face. Scorch's own panic re-surfaced as he saw Vivid tense beside him. Sensing something was amiss, Kio came out of her dazed state and looked worriedly at Julian, who was leaning further over the water. Kio took Julian's hand in hers and, for a moment, Scorch thought she would hum softly to him, but she couldn't. She could do nothing to comfort him but squeeze his hand.

It wasn't enough.

Scorch saw it when it passed beneath their raft again: a titanic shadow. It darted beneath them, lightning-fast. Now they were all watching the water except for Vivid, who was staring at Julian.

Julian was shaking with fear. The shadow circled them, racing back and forth beneath their raft. Kio rubbed at Julian's arm, lifted his chin, and pressed a single finger to her lips. His breathing was clearly labored from the strain of panic, but he was doing a fine job of keeping himself quiet. If the shadow hadn't scraped the bottom of the raft, Julian might have held it in until they reached the shore.

But the shadow scraped the bottom of the raft, and Julian's mouth fell open to form a scream.

Vivid was quick. Before the sound could rip from Julian's throat, he was there, clasping his hand over Julian's mouth. The raft rocked, and Kio scrambled to sit beside Scorch and keep it balanced. The moment was so fueled with energy that it was impossible to tell what was happening at first. Scorch watched Julian claw at Vivid's arm, but Vivid kept his hand clamped firmly over his mouth. Julian struggled, and Vivid turned them, angling their bodies until Scorch could no longer see their faces. They struggled silently, and then, moments later, the struggle ended. Vivid laid Julian down on the raft. His eyes and mouth were open and his face was purple.

Scorch didn't understand why he looked so strange at first, not realizing, not *wanting* to realize, that Vivid had just killed him.

Julian was dead. Julian's corpse was lying on the raft, a foot away. Julian was dead.

Vivid had killed him. Smothered him? Strangled him? Scorch couldn't concentrate. Julian's lifeless eyes were staring at him and it took all of Scorch's strength not to throw up. How many dead eyes would he have to see in his life? How many people would he have to see murdered in front of him? He raged. His heart pounded and lungs burned as he looked between Julian's dead body and Vivid's live one.

He shouldn't have looked at Vivid at all, because the look on his face said, quite clearly, that he would kill Kio, and he would kill Scorch, if either of them even thought about making a noise. Julian had never even managed to scream before Vivid fell upon him to stop it. The mere anticipation of a scream had killed him.

Kio took Scorch's hand, and he looked up at her. She had taken over Vivid's steering, but he could tell she was in shock. The raft rocked again as the gigantic shadow zoomed beneath. Had it been following their raft the whole time? Had they only now noticed it because the sun was up? Had Vivid really just killed Julian right in front of him? Had Scorch just watched it happen?

Julian was lying beside Vivid and Vivid was staring straight past Scorch and Kio to the shore. It was too far away. Much too far when sharing a raft with a corpse and a murderer. Scorch's terror rose as thoughts of flame engulfed him. His face felt red-hot. He wanted to scream. He wanted to shake Vivid. But he could do nothing but sit and watch the shoreline. And wait.

When the sun was cruelly bright, the shadow was gone and the shore was yards away. Julian's body was stiff with rigamortis.

The closer they came to the shore, the less steady Scorch felt. Never had he wanted to escape from a place more than he wanted to escape the raft, not even the Circle dungeon. When the raft finally pressed against land, Scorch ignored Kio's comforting hand and stood up on wavering legs. He lifted Julian's body beneath the elbows with plans to drag him, but Vivid lifted Julian by the ankles and they toted him together, off the raft and onto the shore. Kio watched with her hands steepled over her mouth in silent prayer. They carried the body until they'd reached the beginning of the high grass and then they set it down gently.

Scorch launched himself at Vivid.

He didn't draw his sword—he wasn't suicidal—but he knocked Vivid to the ground and climbed on top of him.

"YOU KILLED HIM!" Scorch yelled, all the rage that had been bubbling up inside him escaping in that single cry.

Vivid's hand flew up to Scorch's mouth. Fingers pressed roughly against his lips and Scorch's senses were overwhelmed with the scent of tree sap. His world was amethyst and black hair and a gravelly whisper telling him to shut his mouth. Vivid breathed and Scorch moved with the rise and fall of his chest.

Somewhere nearby, Kio was on her knees. Somewhere nearby, Julian was on his back. But even nearer, slithering from the surface of the water and creeping up the bank, was something else.

Scorch sat back slowly until Vivid's hand fell away from his mouth, his thighs fitted snugly around the smaller man's waist. He felt breathless and foolish. But he didn't feel like getting up yet.

A moment later, Vivid's hand gripped his ankle. Scorch looked down at him questioningly, only to see both of Vivid's hands resting against his chest. Scorch furrowed his brow and Vivid mimicked the expression, and that was all the time they had before Scorch was snatched backward with incredible force.

Vivid's figure became smaller and smaller as Scorch was lifted higher and higher in the air. He was upside down, hanging by the ankle, but could see nothing of what held him, only Vivid and Kio moving on the shore and Julian lying there, and then, as quickly as he'd ascended, he was falling. He slammed into the ground, felt Vivid's hands grabbing at his arm, his shoulder, his hair, and then the thing wrapped around Scorch's ankle pulled him into the water.

He held his breath, submerged, but the thing kept dragging him deeper and deeper. Scorch forced his eyes open. They burned beneath the water, but he was mindless of that particular discomfort. There was something about the enormous, tentacled monster that really demanded his full attention.

The details of the creature were murky in the dark depths of the lake, but Scorch could make out more than enough to terrify. The tentacle wrapped around Scorch's ankle was only one of many, and though its skin was rubbery and slick, he could feel tiny, needle-sharp spikes puckered into the flesh of his ankle to keep him from slipping from its grip. He couldn't make out a face, but there was a central point where needled tentacles merged into a lumpy, grotesque mass with a giant hole that plunged the water, sucking and spitting. Scorch had no doubt that the tentacle dragging him was dragging him straight for that hole.

The lungful of air he had the wherewithal to breathe was shortly spent, and the sensation he'd felt when the boy pushed his head in the puddle came roaring back. He was deep beneath the lake's surface now, with two choices before him. He could open his mouth, let his lungs fill with water, and drown. Or he could try to hold on and find out what happened when the creature fed him into that hole.

A mad, third choice popped into his mind, but the water flooded him with wet chills and the brief hope burned out alongside the heat beneath his skin. Drown or Be Eaten. Drown or Be Eaten. Scorch closed his eyes and tried to think of something pleasant, a final memory to replay before he died, but he couldn't think of one. He couldn't even picture his parents' faces. Or Merric's. Or Etheridge's. Or Master McClintock's. All he could see were sparkling amethyst eyes, as though they were right in front of him.

In an instant, the tentacle around his ankle loosened its grip and Scorch was floating free. He blinked and the amethyst didn't disappear, only faded as spots of light began pricking the edges of his vision. Something gripped his shoulders and shoved him away, and Scorch was filled with an unexplainable second wind. He moved his arms violently, kicking his feet, struggling and fighting until he could see the light rippling above the surface of the water, and then he burst free, his face breaching the surface of the lake. He gulped in sweet air, over and over, treading water and wondering how he was still alive.

He couldn't think clearly, but he could see, and the water around him was clouded with red. Seconds later, a second head broke the surface and Scorch yelped. Hair was plastered across Vivid's face, and he gasped, spitting up water before setting one of his daggers between his teeth, fisting Scorch's collar, and urging him to follow, urging him to swim. Scorch could hardly doggy paddle, but Vivid kicked at him beneath the water. When Scorch's exhausted head began to sink, Vivid pulled him back up, muttering curses and pulling him along until their feet touched the ground. Scorch stumbled in the mud and Vivid used both hands to haul him onto the bank.

He was dizzy and his mind was muddled, but he was aware of Vivid's cross face as he slid an arm around him and lifted him to his feet. A soft voice sounded in the ear of his other side, where Kio had taken up his other arm. They marched Scorch across the tall grass for several laborious minutes before Vivid dropped him.

Kio collapsed beneath Scorch's weight and they both went down.

"Scorch. Scorch." She held his face in her hands. Adrenaline still pumped through his veins and made his muscles tingle, and for a few minutes, all he could do was blink at her and breathe. He could faintly hear Vivid's voice storming in the background, could see his slim silhouette pacing frantically. Kio kept humming calming melodies until Scorch's body could move again, and then she helped him stand.

"Can you walk?" Kio asked.

His heartbeat was in his ankle, throbbing, but he nodded, grimacing at the pain. The whole right side of his body ached where he'd been slammed into the ground. "Julian," he whispered. "We have to go back for his body. We have to bury him."

"We can't," she said, and before Scorch could ask why, Vivid's voice cut at him through the air.

"It took his body, after it took you."

Scorch stumbled on his weakened limbs as he faced Vivid. He was soaking wet and furious, but so was Scorch. He limped over to Vivid, his hands in fists at his sides.

"You killed him." Scorch meant the words to sound angry, but they came out breathless.

"Scorch," Kio said, touching his shoulder.

Scorch seethed, wanting nothing more than to take him to the ground again, but Vivid's anger closed on his face like a curtain, and he turned, disinterested in Scorch's aggression.

"Kio," said Vivid. "We need to make camp, but we shouldn't do it here." He was speaking past Scorch, like he didn't even exist.

Kio agreed. "Lead the way."

Scorch wanted to ask Kio why she wasn't screaming at Vivid for murdering her friend, but he didn't have the energy. When Vivid started walking, and Kio started after him, Scorch followed. What other choice did he have?

# *Focus, Damn It*

# *8*

They walked, by Scorch's hazy estimation, another mile before Vivid stopped. Tall, green grasses made way for sparse clumps of dying blades and dirt. The desert was ahead of them, Scorch recalled, thinking back to the Guild maps, but they wouldn't be crossing it yet.

Kio threw her pack down and directed Scorch to sit, so he sat. While Kio searched through her pack, Vivid walked the perimeter of their camp clearing. It was still daylight, but he started collecting pieces of kindling for the evening. Scorch felt useless sitting there and watching, but he didn't want to look at Vivid, let alone help him. Instead, he tried to focus on Kio as she pulled one of her ointments out of her pack.

Scorch's ankle felt swollen now that he was sitting, and Kio had to take off his boot, cut his trouser leg open, and peel the leather back to expose his skin. He bent over to watch her work. His ankle was puffy and bruised, with a ring of puncture holes where the tentacle had worked its needle-like suction spikes into his flesh. A pinkish fluid oozed from the holes. It hurt, but at least his ankle wasn't broken. Scorch gave his foot a timid twist, and

Kio was satisfied with its mobility. She cleaned the wound before wrapping it in bandages. Considering he'd been pinioned by a lake monster, Scorch's ankle was tolerable. It was the bruising down his side that had him squirming uncomfortably.

Kio trailed over his skin with a careful finger. "You have bruising on your jaw and shoulder," she said. "Could you remove your clothes so I can check the rest of you?"

Scorch's eyes sought Vivid's, but he was already stalking away, back toward the tall grass. "You might have to help me with this," Scorch mumbled as he lifted the hem of his jerkin. After an awkward struggle with the wet leather, Scorch was laid out on the ground in nothing but his underclothes while Kio placed her cool hands over his skin. His entire side was splotched with bruises where he'd collided with the ground. She prodded at his ribs, and though he cringed and his eyes watered, Kio deemed his bones unbroken.

"You're lucky," she said as she rubbed a cool cream into his side. "You could have broken your neck."

"I'm built pretty solid," Scorch told her, mostly as a joke, but she nodded her head in agreement.

"You are."

Even with the sun still out, Kio and Scorch started the campfire so his clothes could dry. In the meantime, Scorch remained nearly naked, perched beside the fire at Kio's behest, and he wasn't about to tell her that he didn't get chilled easily. She took the opportunity to redress his stab wounds and apply an ointment to the last of the rope burn around his neck. The gash at the back of his head was healing nicely, as was everything else. A week with Kio had done him wonders, and he felt a warmth in his heart for her presence.

He started to thank her several times as they sat together by the fire, but he couldn't get out the words.

It was Kio who started talking first.

"Some people are weak," she said. She had a strong jaw and a long neck, and her skin was glistening with a light sheen of sweat. She was beautiful, and the words coming from her lips were harsh. "Julian was weak. He clung to things he hoped would be strong *for* him. The High Priestess. Me." Kio's eyes were shining, but not with tears. "Vivid killed him because it was either Julian or all of us."

Scorch shook his head.

"Scorch," Kio continued, "he did what he had to do. And then he did what he didn't have to do. When you were pulled into the water, he didn't hesitate. He jumped in after you before I'd even realized."

It had just happened, but the memory of being underwater felt a lifetime away. Julian's dead eyes felt a lifetime away. "Does saving my life make up for taking Julian's?"

"You're strong. Maybe Vivid thinks your life is worth more."

Scorch frowned at her. He had expected tears and sadness from her, not insensitive logic. But that wasn't fair. He didn't know Kio, after all. She was still unpredictable, so early in their friendship. And it did feel like friendship, the relationship budding between them. Scorch hardly knew what to do with the idea of it, except hold it close to his heart and make no mention of it. Friendships were too rare to ruin with the title.

"My life's worth no more than anyone else's," he said.

Kio hummed softly to herself, and Scorch thought she hadn't heard him, but then she said, "Just because you feel that way, doesn't mean everyone does."

She made him remain stripped until the ointment dried on his skin, and by that time, his clothes had dried enough by the fire to put back on. He wished for his clean, crisp shirts as the damp jerkin settled against his chest, but he tried to be thankful that not everything he owned was ruined. He hadn't been holding his satchel when he'd been dragged into the water, and his sword had remained fastened to his belt for the excursion. Of course, that made him curse himself an idiot for not remembering the weapon at his side when his life had been at stake. He was supposed to be a Guardian of the Guild, and more and more it seemed that if he made it through his guardianship at all, it would be a miracle. What would he say to Master McClintock when he asked for his report of events? "Well, I almost died every other day, and I forgot how to use a sword. It's the pointy end, right?"

He tried to drown his pathetic thoughts in his canteen, but the water only made him hydrated. Scorch didn't want to be hydrated. He wanted whiskey. He hated Ebbins for taking his pack with the flask of Guild-brewed whiskey inside, the insidious bastard. If he had a drink of whiskey, maybe he would be able to stop thinking about dead eyes, and worse, amethyst ones.

Vivid didn't reappear until nightfall. Scorch didn't ask him where he'd been, because he knew he wouldn't get an answer, and besides, it was obvious. Three rabbits swung from Vivid's fist, already skinned. He ignored Scorch and Kio, skewering the rabbits and setting them out to roast over the fire.

"Excuse me," Kio said, standing up and stretching her arms over her head. "I need to freshen up." She grabbed a few things from her pack, but left the medicinals lying on the rock beside Scorch. He tried to catch her eye and silently plead with her not to leave, but she only smiled kindly at him and trotted off into the grass. Scorch tried not to begrudge her for it, but it was difficult, because now he was left all alone with Vivid.

There were amazingly few things to look at now that night had cloaked their campsite. Scorch didn't like staring at the fire for too long, and he had already studied his hands to death. He'd cleaned his sword, looked at the stars, and watched the rabbits cook. Really, there was nowhere left to look but at Vivid. But one did not just *look* at someone like Vivid. Scorch set his head in his hands and stole glances when he thought Vivid wouldn't notice.

Vivid's hair had dried a little wildly after the dip in the lake, and he was having a harder time than usual keeping that thick strand tucked behind his ear. It kept escaping to hang over his face, and so Scorch could tell every time he exhaled because the hair floated away from his lips with every puff of air, and then he would tuck it back behind his ear with his right hand. When Vivid moved to turn the skewers over the fire, he did so with his right hand. When he reached for his canteen, which sat to the left of him, he reached for it with his right hand. Vivid was ignoring his left arm almost as much as he was ignoring Scorch, and once Scorch realized that, it took him no time to figure out why. He picked up the ointment Kio had used on his wounds earlier, which she kept gathered inside a small wooden box with a latched lid, and journeyed around the fire.

Unsurprisingly, Vivid acted as though Scorch wasn't there, even when he sat down right beside him.

"You're hurt."

Vivid was unresponsive. In a horrendous example of self-preservation, Scorch reached out his hand and pressed it against Vivid's left shoulder. Scorch thought his hand would instantly be knocked away, or that he would be punched in the face, but instead, Vivid's body shuddered before becoming completely still. Scorch could feel the tension buzzing beneath his palm. Feeling slightly entranced, like he was being allowed the privilege to touch a wild animal, Scorch let his hand remain for a few seconds, and when he took it away, he did it slowly. His hand was bloody. He cocked an eyebrow at Vivid, holding up his palm.

"Why didn't you let Kio take a look at that?" he asked.

Vivid's body was stiff from the touch, and it took him a long time to answer, but after turning over the skewers again and tapping his fingers against his knee one or twenty times, he turned to face Scorch. The firelight cast half of him in gold, while the other half was blanketed in shadow.

"I don't need your sympathy," spat Vivid.

Scorch laughed. "You don't have it. But you do have a wound. And if you're injured, you could get sloppy. And if you're sloppy, you're putting me at risk." He tossed the ointment in the air between them and caught it with a wink. "Now take off your leathers so I can help you or I'll have Kio do it when she gets back."

Vivid's eyes narrowed, but after glaring at Scorch for several heated seconds, he moved his hand to his back and began unbuckling the straps to his cuirass. Scorch watched his finger skirting across the metal buckles, half a dozen down his spine. As each one came undone, the leather of his top fell open. It seemed an inconvenient process, having to unbuckle oneself from behind, but Vivid had no trouble, even one-handed, and soon the garment was hanging loosely across his back. Unfortunately, his back was away from the fire, so Scorch couldn't make out much more than a strip of pale skin and a knobby spine. Vivid eased the leather from his wounded shoulder, keeping his other arm entirely in its sleeve. Only the necessary expanse of skin was revealed to Scorch in the firelight. He stared. He couldn't stop himself.

Vivid's shoulder was angular and sharp and corded with lean, finely sculpted muscle, just as Scorch had imagined. There was a puncture wound, which had stained the skin red and was still leaking blood, but that wasn't what made Scorch's jaw drop. The wound Vivid had sustained in the water was not the only wound on his body. Down his elegant neck and prominent collarbone, across his sharp shoulder and along his preview of pectorals, Vivid's skin was riddled with scars. They were silver with age, some raised in gruesome ridges, some smooth and barely there, but they were many, and Scorch was sure that if Vivid's back was turned to the light, he would see them there, as well. He wanted to peel off the rest of Vivid's clothes and search for more secrets, but he refrained, for he had already come close to death once that day.

Vivid's body was rigid. It was clear he was uncomfortable being so exposed. Scorch gave his head a little shake and tried to ignore all the conflicting signals his body was sending him. He shifted a bit, cleared his throat, and opened the ointment box. Vivid caught his eye—demanded it really—and glared at him, as if daring him to mention the scars, but Scorch had decided the moment he saw them that he would say nothing and ask nothing. Being revealed that small portion of flesh already felt like an extravagant gift.

He dipped his finger into the little wooden box. "This will make it feel better," Scorch said, before dabbing the ointment on the wound. It looked identical to the punctures in Scorch's ankle, but bigger. "I have to rub it in," he warned.

"I don't need you to talk me through it," Vivid grumbled edgily. Scorch glanced up at him. He was watching Scorch's finger closely.

"Right," Scorch said. He began spreading the ointment over the wound and in the reddened flesh around it in slow, careful circles. The campfire was far too hot, but Vivid's skin was cold, probably from walking around in soaking wet clothes all day. Scorch tried to stay focused on his task, dipping his finger for more ointment and continuing his thorough circles. The pads of his fingers traced over a raised, silver scar and Vivid inhaled sharply. Both Vivid and Scorch pretended like he hadn't.

"What happened under the water?" Scorch asked. He had to get up to hunt for a fresh bandage in Kio's pack, and when he turned back to Vivid, the image struck him: Vivid's cuirass hanging off one shoulder, his hair falling rebelliously over one eye. Scorch hurried back to his side with the wrappings.

"I killed it," Vivid answered.

Scorch wiped the excess ointment on his trousers and brought the bandage up to Vivid's shoulder. He pressed it gently against the wound. "How?"

Vivid kept his eyes trained on Scorch as he began wrapping the bandage in place. To secure it, Scorch had to reach his arm around Vivid's back, winding the wrappings under the arm of his wounded shoulder and over his neck. He did the best he could, trying not to touch more of Vivid than he absolutely had to, but it still felt like an awful lot of touching to Scorch.

"That's three times now, you know," he pointed out.

"Three mistakes," Vivid corrected.

Scorch tied off the wrapping and sat back to appraise his work. Scarlet dots were already presenting through the clean bandage, but not a lot, not enough to worry about. "You could dry your clothes by the fire," Scorch offered nonchalantly, but when Vivid's eyebrow twitched, he shrugged his shoulders and added, "Or not."

He watched Vivid slip the cuirass back on, wanting to help but knowing that help would be unwelcome. Vivid handled the buckles up his back with ease and soon he was completely covered once again. Only now, Scorch knew what his naked shoulder looked like. He knew what was hidden beneath that tight leather, that there was a wound still bleeding because of Scorch. *For* Scorch.

When Vivid moved to turn the rabbits, Scorch beat him to it. "I understand why you had to kill him," he said as he watched the rabbits rotating slowly over the flames. They would be done soon.

Vivid didn't answer, but Scorch hadn't expected him to. They sat in silence until a rustling of grass cued them to Kio's reappearance.

"Don't forget to chew your Dream Moss," Vivid said before Kio was close enough to hear. "I don't feel like dealing with you tonight."

Scorch vigorously chewed an ivory stem that night with a full stomach and an aching side, and though his nerves felt shot, and his mind was willing his thoughts to race in a thousand directions, eventually he drifted to sleep.

He dreamed, and his dream made his pulse race, but he didn't wake up gasping in terror. It wasn't that kind of dream.

Vivid woke Scorch before the sun had risen and he sat up with a groan. Kio was already awake. He thought about complaining, but there was just enough light to interpret the look on Vivid's face, and it was not a look to be greeted with anything but patience.

So he waited, and after a stretch of silent brooding, Vivid used his words. His voice sounded raspy with exhaustion and Scorch wondered how much sleep he had gotten, if any.

"We need to reach the desert at sunrise," he explained. He eyed Scorch's foot, where the bandage was peeking through the tear in his trouser leg. "Can you walk?"

Scorch nodded, and when Vivid kept staring at him, he sighed and got to his feet. There was soreness in his ankle, but it was only flesh deep. He did not, as a whole, feel his best, but he tested his weight, walking the span of their tiny campsite, and determined, "I can walk."

"Good. We won't be stopping," Vivid said. "Our priority will be reaching the edge of the desert before the sun sets."

"I'm all for making good time," Scorch said, stretching his tender, sleep-stiff body, "but why can't we be in the desert at night? Wouldn't it be cooler to travel when the sun goes down?"

"When the sun goes down, we don't want to be anywhere near the desert." Vivid rolled his left shoulder, testing its mobility, and Scorch watched his face closely for signs of pain. He saw none. *Of course, he saw none.* Vivid's entire body was a closed-off, intangible entity. Scorch couldn't believe he'd touched his skin only hours before. It didn't feel like something real. Maybe it hadn't been.

"It might be helpful to know what unspeakable dangers we'll be facing this time," Scorch said softly. He wasn't trying to antagonize. Julian was dead and Vivid had killed him, but Vivid had also saved Scorch. After last night, Scorch was wrestling with a multitude of feelings, but none of them was an urge to blame, not anymore. Scorch probably still should have been angry at Vivid for what he'd done. He just wasn't. But he did want answers. "What's the next test, Vivid?" he asked.

"Focus."

"Focus," Scorch repeated.

Vivid might have rolled his eyes; it was still too dark to tell. "If you're going to bombard me with questions, do it while we're walking." He lifted his head to the sky, where a few stars were still shining, and started a path to the east.

Scorch glanced at Kio, who shrugged, and they set off behind Vivid. The ground beneath their feet was dusty, the grass brown and dry. It wouldn't be long before they reached the beginning of the desert.

Vivid crossed the terrain the same way he'd crossed through high grasses or village roads, with polished steps and a severe posture. His trim figure was a black silhouette, and the only color Scorch could see was the stark white of his hands as they swung lightly at his sides.

"What's in the desert?" Scorch asked after they had set their pace.

"There are creatures in the desert that fear the light. They'll leave us alone if we cross during the day," said Vivid.

"And if we don't make it across in time?"

"They don't fear the dark."

"Care to be less vague?" Scorch pressed.

For a moment, the only sound was of boots crunching over desolate earth, and then Vivid spoke. "Cannibals dwell beneath the ground. They come out at night to hunt. They are fast and they are monstrous, and if they catch us, they will eat us alive."

"Ah." Scorch glanced over at Kio, who reflected his look of dread while also maintaining her usual air of calm. It was quite spectacular, those dual expressions, and he wondered how she managed it.

"So we cross the desert before the next sunset," Kio said pleasantly, adding to the conversation for the first time that morning.

"Well, I certainly hope so," Scorch muttered beneath his breath.

Their pace was brisk and their timing was immaculate. As the sky began its somersault of colors, Vivid stopped. Scorch walked up beside him and examined the toes of their boots, which skirted the precipice of sand. Beyond, the desert waited.

Scorch squinted, but he definitely did not see any cannibals running around out there. The sun was barely up; they must have been extremely light-sensitive monsters. What he did see was an array of strange plant life: spiky, waxy flowers and dry bushes that looked to be made up entirely of thorns and bleached bones. He had expected rolling hills of sand, dunes, like in his geography studies at the Guild, but everything was astoundingly flat.

"Before sunset," Vivid cautioned, and then he took the first step forward, from dirt to sand.

Scorch had never seen where a desert started and stopped, but he certainly hadn't pictured its beginning being so abrupt. It was not what he'd been expecting, but he supposed he should have expected that.

Vivid walked quickly, having to take twice as many steps as Scorch to stay ahead of him, and Kio kept diligently at their side. There was a feeling of foreboding in the air. Scorch could sense it keenly. It made his fingertips burn with anticipation.

They walked for hours as the sun rode high overhead. The day was unapologetically blue and cloudless and so warm that if

Scorch had been wearing one of his undershirts, he might have taken it off. Instead, he sipped thirstily at his canteen and spoke little. Kio hummed a tune at his side and Vivid said nothing at all, just stared straight ahead and kept his feet jetting across the sand. Focused.

Kio pointed out the Peggotty Lush-fern as they walked by, a fat, shrubbish plant with black and white nettles and pink pistols. "I would stop and clip some of its roots if we had the time," she sighed. But they didn't have the time.

She fussed a bit over Scorch's ankle, trying to look at it while he walked, and he had to assure her it was feeling fine. His bruised side was hurting, and his stab wounds were still sore—he wondered if they would always be a bother—but he was okay, considering. She eventually stopped trying to change his bandages en route, but her concern only brought Vivid's injury to the front of Scorch's mind.

Vivid walked smoothly, but he was still avoiding the use of his left arm, and as Scorch stared at his back, he could picture the moon-white skin beneath all that black leather, the silver scars etched into every inch, the puncture in his shoulder. He wished they had time to stop, only for a moment, only so Scorch could check beneath the bandage and see if Vivid was still bleeding, only so he could make sure it didn't need more ointment. But they didn't have the time.

They kept walking.

Every quarter mile or so, Scorch would see a divot in the sand. Once, as they passed one, he peered down to examine it closer and saw the slender black opening of a tunnel. He swallowed the lump of fear in his throat and doubled his speed for a few minutes, trying to ignore Vivid's silent protest when he walked ahead of him. He slowed down marginally after a time, but not by much. He didn't want to see what dwelled inside that tunnel. Every time he saw another divot nearby, he held his breath until they passed it. Scorch did not like the desert.

He didn't think Julian would have liked it either. Scorch tried to imagine him walking beside them, but he couldn't. Kio's words pierced him, making him question whether Julian would have been strong enough, focused enough to keep up. For her part, Kio didn't appear to be having any trouble. She was neither winded nor wary. It helped that she was absent of injury. Scorch didn't feel especially worn out yet either, even though the sun was getting to be a bit much, even for his naturally tan skin. It was less of a problem for Kio for the same reason. But Vivid? Scorch kept an eye on him. The other man's skin was diamond-bright with the reflection of the sun. His face, usually a static spread of white, was reddening around the cheeks and brow. He was burning.

As Scorch studied the pink, sweat-dewed skin, something strange began to happen. Beneath Vivid's eye, over the sharp slope of his cheekbone, the skin began to move. Scorch watched, wide-eyed, as a blister bubbled up from the flesh, and then another beside it, and another. Smoke was rising from the burning plane of Vivid's face. Scorch grabbed Vivid's hand, stopping them in the middle of the desert to pull him close.

"Don't touch me," Vivid snapped.

Scorch blinked and Vivid's skin was smooth and untouched once more. "But, I saw—" Scorch began weakly.

Vivid shoved him away. "Focus," he said before he continued walking.

Scorch tried, but it became increasingly difficult when more and more images coming into focus were things that couldn't possibly be real. Vivid's face didn't burn anymore, but there was fire. Scorch saw it in the distance, a bluster of flames, and inside the flames were shapes, two bodies, trapped. Scorch could almost smell the burning flesh.

"Mom," he whispered.

Kio took hold of his hand and forced him to keep walking. Scorch kept his eyes on the fire and his parents burning inside it, but he knew it wasn't real. He knew he had to stay focused. His parents were already dead. They had already burned. The fire coloring the edge of his vision was a trick. Scorch made himself look away. He focused on the backside of the man walking in front of him. It wasn't the worst distraction in the world.

He was trying so hard not to be drawn in by the crackling fire in his periphery that when Vivid stopped walking, Scorch ran right into him.

"Sorry," he apologized.

Vivid spun around and looked up at Scorch with huge eyes. His pupils were blown, and the amethyst was a thin ring around a pool of black. That should not have been possible, not with the sun beaming down on them.

"Vivid," Scorch breathed. "Are you okay?"

Kio let go of Scorch's hand and reached out to touch Vivid's shoulder. Scorch didn't have time to warn her against it before Vivid's fist lashed out and caught the side of Kio's jaw. Her head snapped back and she stumbled.

"Vivid!" Scorch yelled, torn between gawking at Vivid, and seeing if Kio was okay, but then Vivid started screaming and that made Scorch's choice much easier.

He forgot about Kio. Vivid's skin was clammy with sweat and his eyes were wild. He was facing Scorch, but it was as if he was looking straight through him, seeing something horrible. He screamed again, a terrible, pathetic sound, and his hands scratched at the collar of his cuirass, his fingers grappling desperately at his neck.

"Vivid," Scorch said again in his most commanding tone. "Vivid, focus." But Vivid wasn't comprehending him, wasn't hearing him. His body was trembling and another scream ripped free as he stared at an invisible terror. "Kio, what do we do? What do we do?"

But before Kio could tell Scorch what they could do, Vivid ran.

"*Gods*!" Scorch yelled, darting after him.

Kio ran behind him, calling to him in a voice as close to panic as he'd ever heard from her. "Scorch, stop! We'll lose the light! Scorch! Let him go!"

Scorch blocked her out. He blocked out everything in the desert that wasn't Vivid's body racing away. Vivid was fast, and Scorch thanked the Gods for making him tall, because his superior leg span was the only reason why he was able to catch up. Even then, it took longer than it should have.

He was huffing exhaustedly by the time Vivid was close enough to reach out and grab, and Scorch clutched at a tuft of hair and yanked him off his feet. Vivid crashed to the ground with a cry, and Scorch scooped him off the ground, holding him tight so he couldn't struggle free and escape. Vivid's whole body bucked, and his feet kicked off the ground. His eyes were squeezed shut, like he couldn't bear to have them open any longer.

Scorch heard Kio padding up to his side. "He can't focus," she said, not sounding nearly as out of breath as Scorch. "He doesn't know what's real."

Vivid thrashed so ferociously that his entire weight was supported in Scorch's arms. "Vivid," Scorch said.

Vivid sobbed and a tear rolled down his sunburnt cheek. It was terrible, and it startled Scorch into more forceful action. He pressed his thumb into Vivid's left shoulder, right in the puncture wound.

Vivid's eyes flew open.

"Come back," Scorch demanded, digging in his thumb.

Vivid's eyes were still hazed and dilated, but his lips reacted to the pain, parting on a tortured groan.

"That's it," Scorch whispered. He let his thumbnail dig into the wound and held a gasping Vivid in his arms. "Come back. *Vivid*." Kio was pacing behind him. "Come on." He let go of one of Vivid's shoulders long enough to backhand him across the face. It made his chest tighten, but when he saw the pupils shrinking in Vivid's eyes, he did it again. He pressed and prodded at the shoulder wound as much as he dared without causing serious damage. "Vivid," he whispered, licking his lips. "It's Scorch. Come back to me."

Vivid's eyes fluttered shut and he collapsed, no longer struggling. Scorch lowered him to the ground.

"We can't stay here," Kio said, casting a nervous glance at the sky.

"I'll carry him," said Scorch, lifting Vivid's body in his arms like a ragdoll.

"He'll slow us down," she said, and Scorch scowled at her. He didn't usually scowl, but Kio's cool adamancy had wrenched it from him. He held Vivid's limp body against his chest.

"He won't slow *me* down," Scorch said. He turned in a circle, looking up at the sky, and then back at Kio with a frown. "Which way is east?"

"This way," she answered, pointing behind them. "I think."

Scorch looked up at the sky again, looking for the sun, but his eyes felt blurry. He blinked several times, trying to clear his vision. He could see Kio fine, and Vivid's face was crystal clear, but every time he tried to find the sun, he couldn't. Kio was having the same problem.

"We lost the sun when we lost our focus," she said. "The desert's playing tricks on us."

"Well, we can't stand here and do nothing. Pick your favorite direction and we'll start walking."

Chasing Vivid had taken them off course and they couldn't even trace their footprints back to where they'd started because the wind had blown them away. Kio ended up seeing an interesting plant in the distance and led them in that direction, whatever direction that might have been.

Scorch walked behind her, navigating the tunnel divots underfoot, which seemed to be multiplying the farther they ventured. He hoped that was a good sign. He hoped it meant they were making progress.

Vivid was no trouble to carry, and, in fact, it made Scorch feel more useful than he had in days. Perhaps, he mused, when his guardianship was over and the High Priestess was safe, Scorch could specialize in person-toting, though he didn't imagine most other people would be as pleasant to tote as Vivid. He was thinking how much more amiable Vivid was when he was unconscious, when Vivid's eyes opened.

"Oh." Scorch stopped walking. "Kio, he's awake."

Vivid's eyes were clear at last, his pupils tiny dots beneath the glare of the un-findable sun, but it still took him a moment to figure out his strange surroundings. Scorch knew it the second he did, because he could feel Vivid's body tense against his chest.

"Put. Me. Down," Vivid growled.

Scorch put him down, but he kept a hand on Vivid's back until he was sure he could stand on his own, or until Vivid slapped him away. As pleasant as an unconscious Vivid was, it was impossible not to prefer him now, awake and fierce, with murder in his eyes. Scorch was considering whether to ask Vivid how he was feeling, when Vivid looked up at the sky.

"You shouldn't have run after me," he said.

Scorch wiped the sweat from his forehead. "You remember all of that?"

"We won't make it," Vivid said, dutifully pretending he hadn't heard Scorch's question. "We lost the sun when we lost our focus."

"That's what Kio said."

Vivid wasn't studying Scorch or Kio, but the long-away horizon. "The desert won't let us cross in time."

Scorch shot Kio a worried glance. "But we haven't been lost for that long."

"Your perception can't be trusted," Vivid said. "Chances are you were wandering aimlessly for hours."

"How is that possible?" Scorch asked. It had been less than ten minutes since he'd picked Vivid up in his arms.

"Because you lost your focus," Vivid hissed. "Look." He pointed to the horizon. "The sky is already growing darker."

Scorch could feel the rapid pulse in his fingertips as he surveyed the distant sky. Sure enough, light blue was already making way for a deep, velvety sapphire. "It was not that dark a second ago," he argued.

"It will only get darker." Vivid unsheathed the daggers from his wrists. "They'll come when the last light has gone. I'd get out that sword."

Scorch and Kio both readied their weapons. Vivid appraised them warily. "Do you have anything flammable in that pack?" he asked, glaring at Kio.

"Just the flint," she answered, turning hopelessly toward Scorch.

"I don't have anything flammable except underclothes," he insisted.

"Then we outrun them until they catch us, and then we fight them until we can't."

Scorch's head felt sick with fever. His hand was moist around the grip of his sword and he had to wipe his palms against his trousers. He looked at the sky and still couldn't see the sun, but he could see the colors deepening, and he could see the sorry splinter of moon hanging low, waiting for its turn.

"How fast are they?" Scorch asked quietly. "Can we outrun them?"

A high-pitched wail sounded in the distance and Vivid sneered. "Let's find out."

Vivid cut a clear path through the sand, which Scorch and Kio zealously followed. They were already losing the last of the light, and Scorch was running as fast as he could. His ankle was swelling up, he could feel the ooze seeping through his bandage, and he worried his feet might snap off at the ankles, but he kept running. When only a faint, balmy blue light lit the sand, the divots scattered across the desert began echoing with more high-pitched wails. The black holes, the mouths of the tunnels, looked ominous and awful in the almost-darkness.

And then all the sunlight was gone.

The worst thing about it was that Scorch's eyes had already adjusted to the lack of light, so when the pale fingers crept from the divots, Scorch could see them perfectly, wriggling like worms. The wails became louder and more frequent as they ran. Vivid tried to lead them as far away from the divots as he could, but there were too many. As they ran past one, an entire hand shot out, reaching for Scorch's ankle. He leapt away from its touch and pushed his speed even faster, but his heart was heavy with the impossibility. They were directionless.

Ahead of him, he could already tell that Vivid was losing steam. Whatever the desert had made him see had weakened him. Scorch made a decision as they ran. He wouldn't leave Vivid if he fell. He wouldn't leave Kio either. Either they made it out of the desert together, or they all died. The latter seemed the likelier of outcomes when he felt the vibrations beneath his feet.

He threw a glance over his shoulder. "Faster!" he yelled. "Run faster!"

Behind them, a hundred fleshy, humanoid creatures bolted after them, and more were crawling from tunnels and joining in the chase. Scorch watched one pop out of its hole and grab for Vivid, only missing by an inch. Their wails filled the air as more and more crawled from the earth. They were gathering ahead of them, their heads reared back, their mouths gaping. Vivid changed directions, but the longer they ran, no matter the path, the more creatures were freed from their holes. The room to run was shrinking quickly. They would be surrounded in seconds.

Vivid stopped, falling into a defensive stance, his twin daggers gleaming in the scant light of the stars. Scorch skidded on his heels and stopped beside him, their shoulders pressing together. Kio was at their backs, her sword held aloft. Scorch looked down at Vivid, breathing hard. A gust of wind sent his dark hair flying back from his face.

"This isn't how I thought I would die," Scorch panted. "Tell me, do I at least look ruggedly handsome and brave?"

Vivid spared him a heated glance. "You look like a fool who's wasting his time looking at me when he should be sizing up his enemies."

"I don't know if I would call looking at you a waste of time."

The creatures were crowding around them, pushing up against each other, their fleshy white hands reaching with gnarled fingernails. They were snapping their mouths with stained, jagged teeth, so close that their ravenous wails pounded against Scorch's eardrums. He could see their faces clearly, and where eyes should have been, there was only lumpy flesh.

Scorch's skin was burning hot, heating the grip of his sword all the way up to the blade. It roiled inside him, flames sloshing up the cavity of his chest, reddening his vision. The creatures were a finished circle around them now, and they lifted their blind heads to the night sky and wailed in unison, one piercing, terrible sound. Then they attacked.

Scorch slashed his sword to keep them back. He could hear Kio's grunt as she did the same. He could see Vivid in the corner of his eye, daggers flying in front of him, slashing and hacking and fighting to keep the monstrous things away. But they were too many and they were too hungry. They were a wave of flesh and teeth, surging forward and smashing Scorch against Kio. Vivid was pulled away from them. Scorch watched, horrified as deadly white arms wrapped around Vivid's chest. He screamed as the sight of Vivid's dark hair was swallowed up by a gyrating mass of cannibals.

Then, it was happening.

Scorch felt the heat melt through his fingertips, sluicing through his veins. His body bent, burning so hot that the creatures clawing at his flesh scampered back. His marrow was molten fire, molding his muscles and stretching his shoulder blades until barbs of searing bone burst through his skin. Scorch screamed, but instead of sound, smoke billowed from his lungs, choking him with white-hot ash. Fire churned inside of him, hardening his flesh into crimson scales. His amber eyes glowed like liquid gold and his jaw thrust forward, teeth extending, everything roughening and sharpening and sparking. His fingers curled into slicing, ebony talons. His pulse pounded a fire dance through his heart, and the bones sprouting from his shoulder blades stretched up and up, leathery skin spreading and splaying like so many ripped shirts in a sail. It had been such a long time inside him, years and years since it had been released, but it burst free of him now, and he beat his wings against the cool night air and lifted onto his haunches. He slammed down, shaking the desert, and the cannibals wailed in confusion, smelling smoke but hearing no fire. Not yet.

Scorch turned his long, spiked neck, seeking out two small figures in the dark. He stepped over them, his belly hanging protectively above their heads. The fire was inside of him. All he had to do was let it out.

He screamed and it was a roar, deafening and powerful and full of fire. Flames blazed from his throat, drowning the cannibals in an inferno of scorching yellows and reds and oranges. They burned, their bodies melting and falling, and the light of the fire sent the others running. Scorch let the heat build up again, could feel his entire body tingling with it, and then he released another bellow of fire, turning in a great circle as it streamed from his mouth, until they were surrounded by a ring of light.

Beneath him, he felt hands rubbing at his scaled stomach. Tendrils of smoke curled from his nostrils as he ducked his head to watch. Vivid was pushing Kio up, holding her until she grabbed onto the spiked ridges of Scorch's spine, and then he leapt up, climbing shiny crimson scales until he swung his leg over Scorch's back and grabbed hold of another spike, as easy as if mounting a saddled horse. Vivid's face was lit up by flames and his eyes were wondrous, long lashes casting thick shadows across his cheekbones. He leaned forward, one hand gripping a stone-smooth spike while the other pressed against Scorch's scaly skin.

The need was burning Scorch. He couldn't wait any longer. As a great gust of wind caught the fire and carried it further across the sea of burning monsters, Scorch lifted from the ground, wings pounding the air like drums, sending him high above the burning desert. He could feel Vivid's hand pressed against him, feel his thighs squeezing tight, feel his fist around the spike of his back, and he could feel Kio, too, her body cool and balanced against the heat of his scales.

Soaring high above the disorder of the desert, Scorch could focus. He didn't need to find the moon or look at the stars, because his body knew the way. He pivoted his great wings in the air and flew east.

He had almost forgotten the feeling of wind beneath his wings. He had only felt it once before in his life, and it had been so long ago. The sand below was a blur, and the sky above was sparkling with stars. And most spectacularly, the heat inside him, the heat that always threatened to explode, was satisfied. It fueled him for the length of the desert before it began to taper out.

Scorch stalled his wings when the time came and descended in a controlled spiral until his clawed feet landed on prickly grass. He was vaguely aware of the bodies clamoring down from his back, and then of a cooling sensation rushing through him. He curled into himself, lying down on his side. His wings shriveled up into his back, his talons shrank into calloused fingers, and his teeth receded into his shortening jaw. He sighed, nuzzling his face into the grass, and a pillow of smoke puffed from his lips, followed by an exhausted moan.

He heard whispers in his ear and a hand against his cheek, but he was too tired to open his eyes, too tired for anything but oblivion. Fingers combed gently through his hair and Scorch began to drift, falling into a sleep so deep, not even his nightmares could reach him.

# *Forts*
# 9

Scorch's throat was dry and he was naked; those were the first two things he noticed upon waking. He was lying beneath the shade of giant, star-leaved tree. A hodgepodge of clothes, consisting of Scorch's own underclothes and a handful of soft things he recognized as Kio's, were thrown over his vulnerably bare bits. A full canteen of water sat at his side, and by the time Scorch had guzzled down most of its contents, he finally remembered.

A panicked glance around told him that Kio and Vivid weren't there, so they had either left him—which would have been a mercy—or they were preparing for their second option. But why would they not have done it while he was sleeping? Maybe they just weren't coming back, had gone ahead without him, hoping the Heartlands would finish the job.

He groaned miserably and sat up, every muscle in his body protesting. He didn't remember it hurting so much, but then, he had tried to forget everything about the first time. His clothes must have been ripped to shreds, he surmised, looking down at his bare chest. Even his boots were gone.

His hands raked through his hair and flakes of ash sprinkled free. He reeked of smoke, and his beard, he noted after speculative prodding, was singed. Never had he felt like such a wreck. He slumped back down beneath the tree and sighed.

A moment later, there was a rustling in the brush and Scorch reached for his sword, but it was gone. They had taken his weapon. He picked up a rock instead, but then set it back down. He wouldn't try to hurt them. They were just doing what everyone did. They were just upholding Viridorian law and protecting themselves. From Scorch.

Kio emerged from a wall of foliage. She held a bundle of fresh flowers and herbs in her arms and her face was sooty. She studied him a moment before stepping closer. He shrank away.

"Scorch?" she asked, kneeling cautiously at his side. She set the bundle on the ground between them and extended her hand. Scorch flinched from her touch.

"He thinks we're going to kill him," came a voice from around the star-leaved tree. Scorch looked up as Vivid stepped around the thick trunk, his arms crossed casually. He had been there the whole time.

Scorch tried to glare at him, but he didn't have the strength. He could only watch helplessly as Vivid sat beside Kio on the ground, his legs folding up beneath him. Scorch was sure only Kio and Vivid could manage to look elegant perched on the ground, filthy, in the middle of the Heartlands. Vivid's face was darkened by soot like Kio's, but beneath the black, his cheeks were pink from the desert sun.

"I found some useful plant life," Kio said, her voice gentle and melodic. "This one can be made into a balm to encourage recuperation." She held up a fluffy brown bushel of weeds. When she gave it a shake, gold, shimmery dust floated to the ground. "I don't have any experience with . . . but I think it might help you feel better." She scooted back a bit and started digging around in her pack. After a moment's searching, she came out with a mortar and pestle.

Scorch studied her as she began breaking up pieces of the plant and grinding it with a meticulous hand. For once, Vivid seemed interested, but not in Kio's ministrations. He was looking at Scorch as if he'd never seen him before. Scorch thrummed beneath the attention, thoroughly confused. Why had they not killed him yet? Had they somehow missed what happened in the desert? Had they hit their heads and forgotten?

Scorch cleared his throat and shifted, extremely aware of the scant clothing hiding his nakedness and trying his best not to uncover anything best left covered. He forced himself to look Vivid in the eye and said, with a voice that trembled, "I'm an elemental."

Scorch had never spoken the words aloud. He had tried to not even think them. Kio didn't look up from her mortar, but Vivid continued to stare at Scorch. His lips, usually drawn thin and straight, were slightly swollen from biting, and Scorch watched him suck his lower lip between his teeth before releasing it again, pink and shining.

"Fire," Scorch added, and one of Vivid's black eyebrows arched high on his forehead. It was the most expressive Vivid—or Vivid's eyebrows—had ever looked.

Vivid remained sitting in silence across from Scorch, tucking and re-tucking the hair behind his ear. The daggers at his wrists were firmly inside their sheaths. Vivid wasn't attacking, and his body didn't look primed for attack, didn't look primed for any action besides staring. The idea crossed Scorch's mind that Vivid might be in shock. After all, it wasn't every day one stumbled upon an elemental. Maybe, once the initial surprise wore off, Vivid would remember himself and do what was always done. Scorch thought of the man from the village dragging the sack.

Maybe the balm Kio was concocting wasn't a remedy at all, but a poison.

Scorch clutched a hand to his tired heart. He couldn't handle Vivid's stare any longer, so he closed his eyes, leaned his head against the tree, and let himself think about his parents.

He remembered that morning with murky detail, how his father had woken him from sleep and shoved him into the bushes. Scorch had closed his eyes, but he heard everything. They'd put up a fight, but they hadn't won. When Scorch had sensed the fire, he opened his eyes and peered through the dense leaves of the bush, twigs scratching at his face. His parents were in a pile in the center of their forest camp, and their tents were on fire, the flames creeping closer and closer to their bodies. When their flesh began to burn, Scorch knew they were dead. It was the only way the fire would have hurt them. He ran, trying to escape the smell. He ran and ran, until someone stopped him. Master McClintock.

Scorch had been five.

Now he was twenty. Fifteen years he'd gone undiscovered, and it had only taken a few seconds to throw it all away.

"It's ready." Scorch opened his eyes. Kio had scooted closer to him, and her fingers were dipping into the mortar's gold cream. "I need to rub this on your pulse points. May I?" she asked.

Scorch nodded. If she was about to poison him, at least she was being polite about it. Her fingers came forward and she dabbed the balm at his temples, his throat, and his wrists. It was cold against his skin. He waited for its toxicity to sink into his bloodstream, paralyze him, or stop his heart, but nothing happened. Well, that wasn't necessarily true. The instant the balm touched his skin, Scorch's muscles released a great tension, and his shoulders slumped with a pop. He still ached all over, but it was a quieter ache that was steadily growing smaller as he sucked in deep, slow breaths. Maybe the poison would make him fall into such a state of comfort that he'd be too relaxed to breathe, and too calm to care if he was dying.

"Better?" Kio asked and Scorch nodded, slinking further down the tree. The bare skin of his back scratched against the bark and his head lolled.

"Lie down before you hurt yourself again," Vivid ordered. Scorch looked up at him, and his face was like stone. "You've slowed us down enough as it is."

Scorch's head felt heavy, not in an overstuffed, throbbing way, but in a warm, sweet way. He pried his back from the tree trunk and lowered himself to the grass with a sigh. His hand roamed down his body in a halfhearted attempt to keep his coverings in place, but he was suddenly too tired to care.

"Go to sleep, Scorch," Kio hummed. "You'll feel better when you wake up."

He felt sure he would never wake up, but he was thankful to her for making it so painless. "I wish," he muttered, voice drunk with exhaustion, "my parents had died so well."

The last thing Scorch saw was a glint of amethyst, and then his eyes fell shut.

"The mountains will be cold. These will have to do."

"Leave him naked. What bother is it of mine?"

"You don't have any other clothes he could wear?"

"You think he could fit in them if I did?"

"If you hadn't torn up all of his shirts—"

"In retrospect, I suppose I should have killed Julian sooner. We could have used his clothes for our sail and I would have been spared his whining."

Scorch cracked his eyelids. He was lying beneath the tree, it was daytime, and Vivid and Kio were standing a few feet away.

"I'm not dead?" he asked, sitting up. He didn't feel dead. Actually, he felt pretty good, beside the smidgeon of embarrassment when he noticed his coverings had slipped off him as he slept. He put them back in place and looked entreatingly up at his companions. Kio was holding a bundle in her arms that looked like furs. Vivid raked his eyes up and down Scorch's body, unimpressed.

"Are you always this useless afterward?" Vivid asked.

Scorch blinked the remaining sleepiness from his eyes and tried to suss out what Vivid was talking about. He paused when he saw the streak of black soot at Vivid's hairline, like he'd tried to wash away the evidence but left a trace behind, and then it all came rushing back. The sated feeling Scorch had experienced when he'd been flying was gone, and he could feel the familiar fever smoldering beneath his skin in panic. "I don't know," Scorch answered at last, a bit breathless. "I've only ever changed like that once before, and it was a long time ago."

Kio nodded, intrinsically tranquil. "Will you tell us what happened?"

Scorch still wasn't sure why he was alive. The urge to stand up and pace was strong, but he'd not forgotten that he was burdensomely naked. "I'll tell you what I remember," he agreed, "if I can get dressed first." He nodded at the bundle in Kio's arms. "Are those for me?"

She smiled and handed him the furs. "It's all we could do. The land is sparse of wildlife."

Scorch couldn't help but focus on the usage of *we* as he accepted the bundle, but one glance at Vivid told him not to mention it. At close inspection, they seemed to have hunted and skinned a white-furred creature, though the texture felt unfamiliar to any animal Scorch had ever seen. The fur was long and silky and he stroked his fingers through it. Soft as it was, there wasn't necessarily much of it, and he wasn't entirely sure how to go about putting it on.

After a few minutes of blushing and unsuccessfully trying to wrap it around himself like a cloak, Kio took his hand and led him around the tree. Scorch could hear Vivid sharpening his blades on the other side while Kio manipulated the furs with a knife and needles from her pack. They fashioned him a piece of clothing similar to his usual leather jerkin. It rather looked like he was wearing a thigh-length, sleeveless, furry dress until she handed him his belt and sword. His eyes glistened at the sight of his Guild weapon, and he buckled it around his waist immediately. In the end, he probably looked more ridiculous than he'd have liked, but the good news was that he had his sword, and really, what else did he need? Shoes might have been nice, but he wasn't about to complain. But, of course, because she was Kio, a moment later she presented him with white leather strips from the animal's hide, and commenced wrapping his feet, tying them up with a strong cord that looked suspiciously like the roots from the lakeside trees.

Scorch looked down at himself, at the clothes she had made for him, and felt an overwhelming abundance of affection. She led him back around the tree where Vivid was glowering at nothing in particular. His eyes cut to Scorch's furs for only a second before casting their severity elsewhere. Kio crossed to the star tree and sat down beneath its shade.

They were waiting for him to start talking.

"The last time this happened was the first time," Scorch began. He felt exposed and stupid, so he started pacing while he talked. Vivid was standing, watching him with his arms crossed. Scorch tried not to look at him too often as he spoke. "I was thirteen and had just left the Guild walls for my hunter's test. We train in the Guild forest, but for our test, we have to go into unfamiliar territory. Everything was going well until a boar charged me. It came out of nowhere, scared me. Before I knew what was happening, I had—changed. I guess instinct took over and I flew. But I ran out of energy fast, and when I landed back in the forest, I was lost.

"I didn't want to be found. I didn't understand what had happened to me. My parents told me they were different, but I'd never seen them become—that." He thumbed the hilt of his sword nervously. "They found me eventually, two weeks later. They thought I might have died in the forest, because, you see, it had caught on fire." He remembered Merric's face when he'd returned, the way he'd sneered and accused Scorch of trying to burn down the forest. "That's when everyone started calling me Scorch."

Vivid's lips parted on the beginning of a question and Scorch paused to let him ask, but no words came. Vivid gritted his teeth and ducked his head. Scorch continued.

"After that, I was aware of every flare of heat, every burning candle. I realized I was the same thing everyone feared, an elemental, and that my parents were, too. I was scared to death it would happen again, that I'd be overwhelmed and change in the middle of the Guild. But it didn't happen again, and I learned to shut those feelings down. They still come out in bursts here and there. Sparks, fevers. The threat's always here," he placed a hand over his abdomen, "but I've kept it down for so long. I knew if anyone at the Guild found me out I'd be killed, like my parents, so I hid it as deep as I could. What happened in the desert was an accident."

"You saved our lives," Kio said.

"I lost control," insisted Scorch with a shake of his head.

"Your Guild Master doesn't know your true nature," Vivid said slowly, like he was sorting through the sentence for something that made sense.

"No," Scorch said. "He would never have sent me on such an important task if he did. I wouldn't be alive if he did." He sighed.

"Stop feeling sorry for yourself. It's exhausting to watch." Scorch scoffed, and Vivid ignored him. "Julian might have thrown your body in a sack and dragged you to the Queen, but he's dead, and I have more important concerns than whether or not you're going to set yourself on fire." Vivid gestured at the vast mountain stretching above their heads. "I'm going that way."

"I'm going that way," Scorch declared.

"I don't care what you do." Vivid turned and started walking without a second glance.

Scorch rushed after him. He didn't need to check if Kio was following. He knew she was.

The maps Scorch had studied as a boy never mentioned an exact height of the mountain. It had only ever been, to Scorch, a triangle inked onto a piece of parchment. He tilted his head back and couldn't even begin to see the top of that triangle. The tip of the mountain was cloaked in clouds, and Scorch wondered what kind of woman the High Priestess must be for her to live so far away from everyone and everything. And what kind of person would want her dead so badly they'd cross such hell to reach her? He decided that everyone was mad, and left it at that.

His thin-hide shoes didn't boast much of a grip on the rocks of the mountain trail, especially when their mountain trail was nothing more than a succession of rocks that looked the least likely to crumble beneath their weight when they climbed over them. Vivid was in front, his lithe body scaling rocks like he was raised among mountain goats. Scorch supposed he could have been—it wasn't as if he knew anything about him to assuage the possibility. Vivid's shoulder seemed to be better, because even though he still favored his right arm, his left was quite mobile and capable, and Scorch watched him stretching those capable muscles as he lifted and climbed, rock after rock.

But the mountain trail wasn't all rocks and climbing. Occasionally, the ground would even out and they would be able to walk without fear of falling to their deaths. Scorch liked that time the best, mostly because he wasn't as worried about exposing his bottom to the others when he had to lunge across a difficult rock face, a trying feat when one was attired in a thigh-high sheath of fur. Vivid had gotten an eyeful about a mile back and had refused to look anywhere but straight ahead ever since.

It was during one of their smooth sections of mountain climbing when Kio turned to Scorch and asked, "Couldn't you fly us to the top of the mountain?"

"I don't think it works that way," he answered with a mixture of surprise and apology. He still couldn't believe Kio and Vivid hadn't killed him, and now she was *asking* him if he could use his elemental powers. "I think it might be an only-if-my-life-is-in-danger kind of thing."

"Or Vivid's life," she said, softly enough so only Scorch could hear.

"What?"

"You could have changed any time we were being chased by the cannibals," Kio ventured lightly, "but you didn't change until they grabbed Vivid."

"Erm," Scorch stammered, "I don't think that was a factor."

"Hmm," was Kio's sole response.

He was relieved when, shortly after, they had to start climbing again, because everyone was concentrating too hard on not falling to say anything else embarrassing. They didn't have to climb far before the air began to change. The temperature was dropping and the air was thinning, and though the cold didn't bother Scorch's overheated skin, he knew it would become difficult for Vivid and Kio to handle. They wouldn't be able to travel come nightfall, and they wouldn't be reaching the top before then. Scorch started looking around worriedly, wondering where they were going to rest for the night. They would need shelter. Scorch found comfort in the fact that they still had hours of daylight left before shelter would become a necessity. But then, well before the first sign of sunset, the snow arrived.

At first, it spiraled daintily down in crystalline flakes, pretty and feather-light. But in minutes, delicate snowflakes made way for dense, fat drops of icy gloom, soaking their clothes and masking their view with a white, impenetrable veil.

Scorch hollered ahead at Vivid, whose dark form he could barely see. "What did you say the final test was?"

Vivid turned on the rock, his hair whipping around his face. His nose was red. "Fortitude."

"Right," Scorch mumbled. "Fortitude." He glanced around them. It was already nearly impossible to see. He reached a hand out in front of him, groping for a firmer purchase on the rocks. His fingers brushed up against something round and firm, but decidedly not rock-like enough to avoid getting swatted at by Vivid. "*Gods*! Sorry!"

"If I could see you, I'd throw you off the mountain," Vivid growled, and then, a moment later, "Take my hand. My *hand*, not my ass."

Fingers slid against his palm and Scorch clutched at them. Vivid's hand was frozen and he squeezed with his heated fingers. With his other hand, he reached behind him. "Kio?" She found his hand and grabbed it. Her face was a teeth-clattering blur. Scorch followed Vivid's tugs, keening to the left of the rocks. Kio slipped, and fell into the snow, but Scorch's hold kept her close and she ambled back to her feet.

"Where are we going?" Scorch asked Vivid as they slowly traversed their way across a plateau of jagged rocks. They weren't vertical anymore, but he still couldn't see through the onslaught of snow farther than a few inches. Scorch would have felt extremely disconcerted by their predicament if Vivid weren't leading him with a stalwart grip.

A blast of strong wind cleared the snow long enough to illuminate a dark depth in the mountainside, and Vivid was leading them right to it.

"Can't spell fortitude without a fort," Scorch mused.

"It's a cave, not a fort."

When they stumbled into the cave, Vivid dropped Scorch's hand like it was on fire—it wasn't, he checked—but Kio kept hold of Scorch, shivering fiercely. He turned to face the mouth of the cave and the raging blizzard outside.

"Is it going to be like this the whole way up?" he asked. He gave himself a shake and his furs released a spray of water.

"I hope not," said Kio. "I'm freezing." Her eyelashes were fringed with snow. Behind them, Scorch could hear Vivid rummaging through the cave. His grumbles of disapproval echoed.

"I'm assuming you can't help light a fire, since you're basically useless," Vivid said after a moment.

Scorch wondered if he would ever get used to the casual mention of his powers. It was odd to hear, especially coming from Vivid. "I don't have that kind of control. I think it only works when I'm feeling threatened."

"What if I threw you off the side of the mountain?"

Scorch gulped.

"I have the flint in my pack," Kio said. "Is there anything to burn?"

Vivid was bent over, scrounging through a pile of debris that had come from Gods knew where. With their luck, they were probably in the murder den of some foul mountain beast that only preyed on fools who came looking for the High Priestess.

"Something nested here a while ago," Vivid said. "Whether it's too damp to catch fire, we'll have to see."

Kio dropped Scorch's hand and approached Vivid with the flint. Vivid took it from her and threw Scorch a pointed glance before kneeling. Scorch crept closer to watch him ignite the heap of shriveled leaves and twigs and matted feathers. He flexed his fingers as the sparks caught the kindling. He should be able to wave his hand in front of anything and make it burn, like his mother did when he was small, like she still did in his dreams. She would hold her hand over the kindling and it would catch the perfect flame. Perhaps if she had lived, if his father had lived, Scorch would have learned. The fire inside him spit jealously as Vivid worked the sparks over more of the kindling, and soon the pile was smoking and crackling, tiny flames leaping to action.

"This won't burn long," Vivid said. He sat down in front of the fire and held out his hands. They were purpling at the fingertips.

Scorch felt guilty for his preternaturally high temperature. He wished he could share his heat. And then, with a smirk, he decided he could. He sat between Kio and Vivid in front of the small fire and stretched his long limbs. His side smarted, but the balm Kio gave him had worked wonders on his long list of maladies.

Vivid was a shivering wall of apprehension, and he glared at Scorch's brazen proximity. "Don't touch me," he hissed when Scorch's arm bumped into his damp hair.

"I have to dry my fur," Scorch insisted, nestling in as closely as he dared. He'd been told by his tosses in the Guild that his body was akin to a furnace, and it must have been true, because despite Vivid's brutal gaze, he wasn't moving away.

Kio had no qualms indulging in Scorch's heat. She pressed up against his side as she held her hands to the fire. Her clothes were the wettest out of all of them after her slip, and she was shaking worse than Vivid.

"You know what would make this cozier?" Scorch asked.

"You being quiet," Vivid supplied.

"No. Whiskey. Guild-brewed whiskey. I had some with me when I started out, but—"

"I can't imagine how much more intolerable you would have been if you'd been drinking this whole time."

"If you were nice to me, I'd share with you."

"*Your furs are touching me.*"

"I might have something in here," Kio cut in, digging through her pack. "There's a flower that grows on the mountainside. It's said to imbibe one with inner warmth." She presented a tiny blue flower in the palm of her hand. "I picked it from the base of the mountain. We can make our own whiskey."

"Mountain Flower Whiskey," Scorch laughed.

Kio popped the top of her canteen open and dropped the tiny flower inside. She gave the canteen a shake and handed it to Scorch.

"I think I already have inner warmth," Scorch said, giving the flower water a sniff. It smelled like musky cave, but he sipped it all the same. It was cool going down his throat, but when it hit his stomach, he felt his heat rise. Not in a disastrous way, but in a flushed face way. He smiled broadly and handed the canteen to Vivid.

Vivid held it up to his nose and gave it a sniff, the way he'd smelled the bowl of water in the Circle cage. Kio's brew must have passed whatever aromatic tests he had, or maybe he was just that cold, because a second later he took a small sip. Scorch watched his face, looking for the moment when the heat reached Vivid's stomach, knowing it had once his lips curved into the barest bones of a smirk. He tried to pass it back to Scorch, but Scorch wouldn't take it until Vivid had taken a larger sip.

"A little more inner warmth won't kill you," Scorch told him, and Vivid indulged in a hearty gulp. He wiped his mouth with the back of his hand and passed the canteen off to Scorch, who passed it to Kio.

They took turns finishing off the Mountain Flower Whiskey, which turned out to be a surprisingly enjoyable beverage despite having no alcohol and no flavor. But Kio's words proved true; Scorch was practically beaming with inner warmth. The cave had transformed before his eyes into the coziest place in Viridor, though nothing had changed except his perception of it. He laughed until his abs were sore, and when his knee brushed against Vivid's leg, Vivid didn't jerk away. Scorch appraised him unabashedly and was pleased to see that Vivid was no longer shivering, and a normal color had returned to his fingertips. He was staring into the fire, the muscles in his face relaxed. That thick lock of hair fell over his eye and Vivid blinked at it but made no effort to move it. Scorch, resonating goodwill and lacking good sense, reached out and brushed the hair from Vivid's face, tucking it behind his ear.

Vivid turned his head from the fire and stared at Scorch.

"You're lucky I'm filled with inner warmth right now or I'd kill you," he said. His voice crashed like thunder in the echoing cave, but it was the kind of thunder at the tail end of a storm, whose menace had moved so far away that you no longer feared its lightning.

"I've been having a pretty lucky few weeks," Scorch answered with a grin.

On his other side, Kio rested her head against his shoulder and he could feel an odd vibration.

"Are you *giggling*?" he asked her.

Her breath was a warm puff against his bare shoulder. "You're a Fire," she wheezed, "who can't even light a fire."

He joined her in her laughter, because it was pathetically hilarious. Kio clung to his side, and when she splayed out on the floor, Scorch went with her, stretching out on his back. It was one of the more unexpected moments of his life when he tugged at Vivid's back buckles and Vivid sprawled out beside him with no more than a grunt of complaint.

Scorch sighed contentedly, because for the moment, he was content. He was lying between the only two people in the entire world who knew who he really was. They had known for a whole day and hadn't tried to kill him. Instead, they had helped him, hunting him down new clothes, tending his wounds, and holding his hand when he couldn't see through a blizzard. A word floated up from the warmth of his belly and he mulled it over in the increasing fuzziness of his head: friends. Well, Vivid hated him, so it was more like friend, singular, but still. He felt warmth from every angle, inward and outward.

He also felt sleepy.

"I'm sleepy," he informed the ceiling.

"Then shut up and go to sleep," Vivid grumbled. Scorch made his head roll to the side so he could look at the grumpy man lying beside him. Vivid's eyes were already shut. His eyelashes were long and curled.

"Pretty," Scorch whispered. He felt Kio snuggling up to his side. He smiled, and then let his own heavy eyelids surrender to the irresistible beckoning of happy sleep.

# The High Priestess
# 10

$\mathcal{S}$corch could count the number of times he had gone to sleep with the world one way, only to wake up and find it in shatters. People came to kill his parents, to kill Flora, and now, as the Mountain Flower Whiskey swam in his head, they came again.

He did not stir quickly, didn't jolt abruptly into wakefulness, gasping and crying out. Rather, he slipped into consciousness, one foggy thought at a time. His neck hurt and his head was draped heavily between his shoulders. Awareness was a slow fight. His feet were moving beneath him, but he wasn't walking. He heard voices in his head, but it wasn't his voice, or Kio's melodic hum, or Vivid's thundering growl. Heat nestled in his stomach, but the air around him was cold and wet.

When Scorch did finally find the strength to open his eyes, he did so gradually, groggily. The sudden light was too much and he shut them again. Shouldn't he be lying on the floor of a cave, with Kio and Vivid at his side? Shouldn't he be dry and sleeping?

He tried to lift his head, and his hair stuck to his forehead. Drops of ice dotted his lips and he wetted them with his tongue, tasting snow. He couldn't remember leaving the cave. He grasped out with his hand, feeling for Vivid. If Scorch was in the snow, Vivid should be beside him. But he couldn't find him. He was reaching blindly.

Scorch forced his eyes open, squinting against the light, made brighter by the harsh reflection of snow on the mountainside. His first look was at the sodden ground, and though the muscles in his neck creaked painfully, he made himself lift his head, made himself take in his surroundings. They were not as they had been before he slept.

He was no longer in the cave, that much was evident, but neither was he scaling the sharp rocks. He was on a narrow, winding path, and he wasn't alone. Robed men stood on either side of him, holding him up by the arms, and dragging him down a frosty road. His sword was gone.

"Vivid," Scorch groaned. His voice was scratchy. He coughed and tried again, louder. "Kio?"

The robed men at his side said nothing, but Scorch heard a weak rumbling behind him.

"Vivid?" He tried to make his feet stick to the ground, but the men just kept dragging him and dragging him and he couldn't get a foothold. He twisted his head back, desperate to see. There were more robed men walking behind him, but in one of their arms, Scorch saw a dark-haired man, cradled and unconscious. "Vivid!"

A whimper fell from Vivid's lips, but he didn't wake. Scorch pulled down his arms until his knees hit the snowy path, bringing the robed men down with him. They were up a mere second later, but now Scorch had regained his footing, and he walked instead of being dragged. Their grips were strong and Scorch's muscles felt weak. He thought quickly. Even if he could escape the two robed men holding onto him, he wasn't sure about the others, and he wasn't sure he would be able to carry Vivid far, light as he was. And he wasn't leaving Vivid.

He searched for Kio, but she was nowhere to be seen. There were more robed men walking behind Vivid, but Scorch couldn't see well enough to make out if she was with them. He tried calling out her name again, but his voice was lost on the wind.

"My friend," he said, turning to one of the men holding him and realizing he was, in fact, a woman. Her hood cast a dense shadow over her face. "Kio. My friend. Where is she? Is she okay? Please. Please, tell me," he begged, but the robed woman was immovable. She stared straight ahead with no expression. It reminded him of Vivid's brand of indifference. And then a thought struck him. "Are you the Priestess' Monks?" he asked.

She didn't answer, but that didn't keep his hope from flaring.

"You're the Priestess' Monks! You must be!" He turned his head to look at the robed man on his other side, who was, in fact, a man. "I'm a Guardian of the Guild. Master McClintock sent me on a task of the utmost importance involving the High Priestess. I must speak with her at once. He's with me," Scorch said, nodding his head back to Vivid. "He's my friend. We don't mean you any harm."

They responded only with silence.

"There was someone else with us," Scorch continued, so excited his thoughts were running over each other. "A woman. Kio. I can't see her. She was in the cave with us. Is she alright?"

No one responded. They hardly acknowledged his presence. With all of his questions left unanswered, Scorch stopped trying to ask them. He let the monks lead him up the mountain path. Concern was eating at him for Kio and Vivid, but he felt positive their quiet captors were the Priestess' Monks, which meant the path they were ascending would lead to the temple. Scorch took a deep breath. The High Priestess was finally close. It wouldn't be long until he was able to fulfill his guardianship.

By the end of it all, Scorch was thankful the monks had found them in the cave and taken them along the secret path, because even with the hidden route, the journey took the rest of the day. Scorch couldn't imagine trying to reach the top the way they'd been climbing. It would have taken days.

When they finally reached the end of the path, Scorch caught only a glimpse of the temple's golden columns before the monks led him around the back of the structure, where dilapidated stone steps descended deep into the earth. They nudged him lightly and he took to the steps, letting the monks escort him into the dark, underground chamber.

Scorch's hope had been that the monks were leading him to bathe, maybe change into something other than a fur dress before he went to see the High Priestess, but the only thing in the chamber was a cell.

He stopped, digging in his heels. "No, I don't think you understand," Scorch blustered as they continued to haul him forward. "I'm a guardian. I need to see the High Priestess." He begged them, but his pleas did nothing to halt one monk from opening the cell door and another monk from tossing Scorch inside. Vivid was thrown in a moment later, and then the door was shut and locked.

Scorch rose to his knees and shook the bars. They were ice cold, but warmed instantly beneath Scorch's touch. "Listen to me! My name is Scorch. I am a Guardian of the Guild. It is paramount that I see the High Priestess immediately. Please!"

The monks turned away and began their march up the staircase, disappearing into the darkness. Scorch slammed his hand against the bars in frustration before attending the unconscious man in the cell with him.

"Vivid? Vivid, wake up." Scorch shook him gently and his eyes fluttered open.

Vivid licked his lips and groaned, but his eyes were unfocused. Scorch looked down at his shivering body. He was so cold.

"You're probably going to kill me," Scorch whispered, and then he lifted Vivid off the cold floor and settled him in his lap, letting his head rest against his shoulder. "I'm not being weird," Scorch assured him, though he doubted Vivid could hear him in his state. "I'm just really hot. I mean temperature-hot." He tried to concentrate on letting his body heat radiate freely through his skin, but since he had no idea how any of that worked, all he could do was hope that Vivid was getting warmer. He rubbed Vivid's hands between his hands and tried to think warm thoughts.

Vivid grumbled something nonsensical and Scorch froze.

"Vivid?"

"Kio," Vivid rasped.

"I don't know where they've taken her. Did you see? Are you alright?"

Vivid coughed, and then his eyes closed and his head fell back against Scorch's shoulder, unconscious.

"*Gods*," Scorch sighed in frustration.

It was difficult to say how long he sat in the cell holding Vivid against him, but when the echo of footsteps brought him back to the present, he realized he'd been spacing out. He carefully removed Vivid from his lap and set him on the floor right before two robed men appeared before the cell.

"The High Priestess will see you now," one of them announced.

"Oh, good," said Scorch, relieved. "Look, can you see about my friend? He needs a hot bath and food. Some dry clothes. He's freezing. And Kio. Can you tell me where she is?"

"Come with us," said the other monk, unlocking the cell.

Scorch clambered to his feet, glancing back worriedly at Vivid. He looked like his shivering had calmed down, at least a little. Scorch felt a pang in his chest to leave him, but he had a guardianship to complete. He squared his shoulders and exited the cell, and the monks led the way up the steps.

It was night, and more robed bodies were waiting at the top of the steps with lit torches. Scorch eyed the flames and felt a flicker of heat inside his stomach. The monks surrounded him, ushering him forward to the front of the temple, where, finally, Scorch was treated to its splendor. Even by the scant illumination of the torches, the sight of it was magical. The gold columns he had caught sight of before were taller and more extravagant than anything he'd ever seen. The steps were gold, as well, and intricately carved with interlinking vines and animals. Scorch wondered if one of the depicted animals had white, silky fur, but the monks led him up the steps too quickly for him to investigate.

He was walked down a daunting hallway, where torches on the walls blanketed everything in a yellow wash. Everything about the temple's insides felt warm and strangely expensive for a religious temple at the top of Viridor's highest peak. But for all its grandeur, Scorch didn't have far to walk before the monks paused outside an especially ornate door, broad and intimidating, with a bronze knocker the size of Scorch's head. One of the monks stepped forward and knocked it once, twice, three times, then released it and stepped back.

As they waited, Scorch became uncomfortably aware that he was dressed in what basically amounted to a damp, furry dress, and he vainly hoped the specifics of his first guardianship would remain veiled in mystery. He made a mental note to pack loads of spare clothing for future endeavors and was in the process of finger-combing his scruffy hair when the door creaked open.

Another monk peered through the crack at Scorch. "Her Holiness will see you."

Scorch nodded. "Great. Good. Thank you."

The monk opened the door and, after a moment to rally his nerves, Scorch entered the room. The door clicked behind him and the monk put his back against it, waving Scorch toward the archway in the center of the room. Scorch followed the silent direction and walked beneath the archway, where silken scarves were draped in a purple and gold curtain. On the other side, a woman was perched on a settee. Her hair was a silver-white cascade down her back.

"Guardian," she said, fixing him with sky blue eyes. Her face was porcelain. She was pretty, in a surreal way, and the longer Scorch looked at her, the harder it was to guess her age. She'd been around too long to be young, but her skin was as smooth as the marble floors beneath her bare feet.

"High Priestess," he said with a bow. It might have been a good idea to school himself on how to interact with the Holiest figure of Viridor before he was standing in her chambers like a bumbling fool. Hopefully, she was too distracted by his ridiculous attire to notice any discrepancies in his greeting.

"Come. Sit." She crooked a finger and he obliged with haste, congratulating himself when he reached the cushions opposite of Her Holiness without tripping over his own feet. He settled down on the plump satin pillows and tried not to feel awkward that the Priestess was looking down at him from her settee. "You have journeyed far," she said, her voice like wind chimes. "It has been so long. I barely recall the last time a guardian passed my tests." Her head tilted. "Do you believe you are worthy to sit before me?"

Scorch fought to remain reverential, but something about the High Priestess consternated him. She was so smooth, but her eyes were sharp. "I don't know if I'm worthy of the trials it took to get here," Scorch told her, deciding honesty was the best route when confronting Holy types. "I know I never would have made it here without the aid of my companions." He sat up straighter on his little mountain of pillows. "Your Holiness, there was a woman with me, but your people won't tell me where she is or if she's okay. And the man in the holding cell needs blankets or—"

The High Priestess lifted a single finger and Scorch quieted. "Do not worry for your companions," she soothed. "You are a guardian who has traveled far to implore my ear. Is all you wish to speak of your friend's lack of blankets?"

"No," Scorch said. "I come to you with dire word from the Guild Master."

"Is that so?"

He strained his memory for his interaction with Master McClintock, which now seemed as if it happened eons ago. "The Queen has reason to believe there is a plot against your life," he told her in a speech gravely low. "I am here to warn you of an assassin plot and aid you in whatever way you wish. I realize you're in good company, surrounded by the monks, but I offer you my blade, as well." His hand automatically fell to his hip, where he felt nothing but damp fur. "I mean, my blade is missing at the moment, but give me a weapon, any weapon at all, and I will protect you with my life."

She held a delicate, bejeweled hand over her chest, the porcelain matte of her skin hardly a contrast against the pale shade of her satin robes. "Assassins?" she asked, worry finally gathering between her silvery, finely plucked eyebrows. "That *is* dire. Would you come with me? I think I would feel much safer in my adjacent chambers."

"Whatever you wish, your Holiness." He stood when she stood. She was willowy and tall, nearly Scorch's height.

"This way," she said, and she led them across the marble floor, past ivory sculptures of twisting flames and cresting waves, until they stood before a massive, floor to ceiling painting. Scorch gazed up at it in awe. It was a portrait of the High Priestess. In all honesty, he found it garish to have such an extreme portrait of oneself on display in one's quarters, but he supposed he was no judge for decorations. The only decorating decisions he'd made in his room at the Guild consisted of where to lean his sword and in what corner to throw his dirty laundry.

"Lovely," he told the High Priestess, who watched him with an eerie sheen in her light blue eyes. He was pondering whether to compliment how the artist had successfully captured the elegant bow of her lips when she held out her hand and pushed against her oil-painted bosom. The painting swung open, because it was also a secret door, and the High Priestess invited Scorch to enter in front of her. He did, though the way was too dark to step with a sure foot. Once inside the lightless chamber, Scorch felt a cool hand on his arm and heard the High Priestess enter behind him.

"Now we can speak more freely," she said. "Please, sit."

The hand on Scorch's arm led him forward and then pushed him into a chair. A moment later, he felt metal bands slap across his wrists and ankles.

"Wait," he began, and the room was filled with light as a torch was lit. The monk who had fastened him to the chair turned to face Scorch, standing beside the High Priestess. Scorch couldn't see the monk's face; it was lost to the hood's shadow.

The room was surprisingly large and stone and not entirely unlike the Circle dungeon. The most troublesome thing by far was the fact that Scorch's chair seemed to be on a pedestal surrounded by a pool of water, excepting the narrow footpath that had led him across. It was incredible he'd not fallen in when the room was in darkness.

"I apologize for the poor hospitality on my part," the High Priestess chimed, "but you must understand. Assassins? Guardians? You have brought troubling news to a sacred place, to my home, and I would be remiss not to take every precaution available to me."

"I'm no threat to you," Scorch said, trying to figure out the best way to struggle against his bonds without appearing rude.

The High Priestess laughed. It was a high-octave noise that called to mind the wails of the desert. "Such sweet words to come from the dirty mouth of an elemental."

Scorch's heart seized in his chest and his pulse galloped.

"You look caught off guard," commented the High Priestess.

"He looks like that a lot," said Kio, lowering the hood from her head. She stood beside the High Priestess, adorned in monk robes, and smiled kindly at Scorch. "I'm touched you were so concerned for my safety," she said, "but as you can see, I am perfectly well."

"Kio," he gasped. "What happened to you after the cave? What are you doing here?" His first thought was that she had gone ahead for help, and the monks had given her their clothes to wear, and she had made friends with the High Priestess while awaiting Scorch and Vivid's arrival. But in the back of his mind, he knew it was preposterous. He knew it had not been that way. "The Mountain Flower Whiskey. You drugged us?"

"Scorch," Kio said, calm and cool and looking at him like nothing extraordinary was happening. "This is my home."

The High Priestess placed her hand on Kio's robed shoulder and smiled at her adoringly. "Kio has done very well and made me extremely pleased." She snapped her eyes back to Scorch. "Do you know how long it has been since an elemental was in my temple? Alive?" She twirled a long strand of silver hair around her fingers. "Kio was only a small babe then."

"But I remember the joy it brought to your eyes," Kio hummed peacefully.

"And now you have brought me another." The Priestess looked at Scorch hungrily.

"Kio," Scorch cried. "I don't understand. You said you were an herbalist. You're a Priestess' Monk?"

Kio was unerringly serene. "Am I not allowed to be both?"

"You lied to me." He felt a sob welling up in his throat and choked it down.

"Did I?" she asked. "I told you I had been training as an herbalist, and I have been, here, under the High Priestess' tutelage. I told you it would be an honor to keep you properly mended during your journey through the Heartlands, and it was. There is no greater honor than delivering unto the Holiest One a rare gift."

He couldn't believe what he was hearing. It was impossible. "Am I to take it that I'm the rare gift?"

"Of course you are," Kio said with an approving nod. "You know as well as I do how rare elementals are. When you were thrown into the cage with me, it was a blessing from the Gods."

He balked. "You couldn't have known what I was as early as the Circle."

Kio put a finger to the faded burn across her cheekbone. "When you were delirious with concussion, you touched me here and called me mom." The High Priestess laughed and Kio cast her a happy smile. "Normally, I would have killed you. It's my duty. I had planned to do it the night we escaped. I was going to let Julian help me—I thought he might make a decent monk—but when I found out where you were headed, it changed everything."

"No," Scorch whispered, shaking his head, denying the words being poured into his ears. "No. You were my friend."

"I was doing what I had to do," Kio said. "It's been over a decade since a live elemental was brought to the temple. Your kind is usually too volatile to bring in breathing. But you were headed here on your own. There was no forcing you."

Scorch had no words. He felt insane. How could he have been fooled so horrendously? How had he let himself trust her, when he had known next to nothing about her? Why had he accepted all the coincidences that continued to stack higher and higher around him? Because she had been kind to him. Because he'd thought she was his friend. He let his head fall back against the chair with a thud.

"So what now?" he asked. "You have an elemental strapped to a chair. Am I right in assuming there's more to your plan than light bondage?"

The High Priestess shrugged her hair behind her shoulder and caressed a hand down Kio's back. "You are dismissed for now," she told her. "Go rest. I am so proud of your accomplishments."

Kio bowed to her before exiting through the secret door. The High Priestess watched the door until it clicked closed, and then she returned her attention to Scorch.

They were alone.

"Kio is a special girl," she said.

"Yeah. The best."

"But you are special, too, aren't you?" she coaxed.

He snorted. "I've been told I have nice hair."

The High Priestess narrowed her eyes at him. "Through my research on one of your fellow abominations, I discovered something." Her hand danced across a metal wheel jutting from the wall. "When overcome by an opposing force, your powers are rendered obsolete. Kio tells me you changed into something quite formidable during your trek through the desert. I wonder whether my discoveries hold true for a creature as powerful as you. Shall we test it?"

"You're making me seriously reconsider my priest kink."

She appraised him passionlessly. "It is too bad your parents were slaughtered before they could teach you any manners," she countered, pulling a long ceremonial dagger from an inner pocket of her robe.

"*What?*" he asked, his cheeks reddening from the flare of heat beneath his skin.

Her bare feet slapped against the floor as she crossed the narrow pathway to his pedestal. "Does that make you angry?" she asked him. "Kio tells me you are plagued with nightmares, and that, for a vile, monstrous thing, you're sensitive. Soft." She held the knife's edge to his mouth, pressing it against his lips until blood sprang forward. Scorch tensed against his bindings as she dragged the knife down, splitting his lip with a thin red line. "You do have nice hair," she continued. "But you need a shave." She swiped the blade along his jaw with a laugh. "Oh, I can feel your heat from here. Spectacular." Her knife whispered down his throat until it reached the collar of his furs. The smile on her face was smug as she cut the furs open, down to his navel.

Scorch took deep breaths. When her blade sliced across his chest, a spark escaped from his fingertips.

"Yes," she crooned in delight, cutting more clean lines across each pectoral. Blood seeped from the wounds and rolled down his stomach, soaking his furs.

"Just to save us both some time," Scorch said, grateful for the steadiness of his voice, "I've had a lifetime of practice with this. Nothing exciting is going to happen for either of us unless my life is threatened, and right now, all you're doing is giving me paper cuts."

She sliced a deeper line over his bellybutton before pulling away, tapping the blood-tipped knife against her chin. "That could be a problem." Her eyes were crazy. Had Scorch thought they were crazy when he first saw her? Gods, he was a poor judge of character. "Tell me," she said. "If I have no intention of killing you any time soon, how could I possibly incite your body into changing?"

He glared at her.

"What about your companion in need of blankets?"

Scorch's fingertips sparked again. "Don't touch Vivid."

"Vivid?" the High Priestess asked. "Fascinating." She leaned in, bringing her face close to his. "What if I told you my monks were with Vivid right now, beating him to within an inch of his life?"

Scorch bucked against the restraints of his chair, sweat streaming down his face. The High Priestess laughed and left him alone on his pedestal. She returned to the wheel sticking from the wall and turned it. His chair began to lower and the water pooled around his ankles, his shins, his waist. It reached the cuts on his stomach and he winced in pain.

"Do you not like the thought of me bringing your friend in here with us? I could torture him while you watch. Would that make you angry?"

Her words made him burn. His skin felt red-hot. He wished he could control it, that he could look at her and make her insides boil. "Vivid has nothing to do with me," he seethed, the water around him beginning to steam. "He came here to train with your monks and nothing more. Don't touch him."

She turned the wheel and his chair was submerged even further beneath the water, up to his shoulders. "Your face is so red. Let's cool you off." She gave the wheel a final crank and Scorch's head disappeared beneath the pool.

Water *again*? Was he being drowned *again*?!

He thrashed his head, his body struggling despite knowing he couldn't escape the bindings of the chair. As his lungs began to scream, his skin sizzled, but like the time he'd been in the lake monster's clutches, he could affect no change to free himself. The High Priestess was right; his powers were useless beneath the water, no matter how threatened his life became, and it felt pretty threatened at present. Scorch strained his eyes and could barely make out the High Priestess' figure above the water, leaning beside the wheel with her hands clasped before her like an excited child.

Just when his vision began to swarm black, she turned the
wheel and his chair rose from the pool. His body dripped water
everywhere, splattering all around the pedestal. He shook the
soaked hair from his eyes and gasped greedily for air.

"That's better," she sang. "I think I will keep you alive for a
long time. I've yearned for another elemental to run my tests on.
You could be the key," she said, coming toward him again, "to
exterminating your kind for good."

Scorch coughed, glaring at her with red eyes. "Why do you hate
elementals?"

"You say it like you aren't one of them. Your kind is unnatural
in this world. The Gods have spoken to me and told me so. I have
made it my life's work to rid Viridor of your blasphemous stain."

Scorch groaned. She was absolutely insane and that never
boded well. "I'm starting to realize why someone sent an assassin
after you."

She brandished her knife again and stuck the tip over Scorch's
throat. "Assassins are no threat to me, you filthy creature. Your
entire mission was a joke. A waste."

"Mine wasn't," a voice rumbled.

Scorch's breath hitched. Out of the shadows, Vivid stepped,
and he wasn't the groggy-eyed, shivering man from the cell. His
presence filled the room. The air felt charged and dangerous.

"Vivid," the High Priestess greeted. She turned slowly to face
him. "Here to save your friend?"

"No." Vivid's eyes were a torrent of menace. Scorch stared at
him breathlessly.

The space between Vivid and the High Priestess was heavy
with silence for several seconds. Scorch could see the expression
on Vivid's face. It was too calm.

The High Priestess' back went rigid and she threw her knife, which Vivid dodged easily. She tried to run past him, but he caught her. His hands moved like lightning and a sickening crunch echoed through the chamber as he snapped her neck.

Scorch gaped, speechless, as Vivid let her dead body drop to the floor.

A thousand questions beat at Scorch's brain, but the only one he asked, the only one that mattered, was, "You're the assassin!?"

Vivid's face was blank and pale as his eyes flashed between the body on the floor and Scorch strapped to the chair. "Yes," he said, unsheathing his twin daggers.

Scorch sighed dejectedly and let his head hang. "Of course you are." He felt a hysterical bubble of laughter rise up and pour from his mouth. "Of course you're the assassin I was meant to stop." He laughed so hard it hurt his chest and tears fell down his cheeks. "Did you know Kio is a Priestess' Monk? Did you know this whole thing has been a game to get me here and tie me to this torture chair? And now you're going to kill me, like I knew you would, and I'm going to die in this stupid dress."

Vivid stared at him. "Kio is a Priestess' Monk?" he asked, his black brows stitching together furiously.

"Like you didn't know."

"I didn't know," Vivid growled. "I knew I didn't like her, but I didn't know why."

Scorch huffed, pulling against his restraints and eyeing the shiny blades in Vivid's hands. "So. How are you going to do it?"

"Shut you up? I have no idea."

"You're an assassin. Aren't you going to kill me?"

Vivid looked, as usual, unimpressed. "I had a job to do," he said. "Same as you. Killing you wasn't a part of it."

Muffled yells could be heard beyond the chamber and Vivid took a step toward the exit. A moment of choice passed, as Vivid stood with his daggers unsheathed, and Scorch could see them at the top of the Circle wall: Vivid's legs straddling the wire, Scorch telling him he had to go back for the others, and Vivid leaving him behind without question. He had probably expected Scorch to die, to never see him again, but now, there they were, and Vivid stood on another fence. If he had made it out of the cell and past the monks to the secret chamber undetected, Scorch wagered he could make his way back out unscathed. All he had to do was leave Scorch strapped to the chair.

Vivid moved toward him.

A loud bang sounded in the adjacent room and Vivid spun on his heels, standing between Scorch and the portrait door. It swung open, revealing Kio in a rectangle of light, a throng of monks standing with her. It only took her a moment to find the satin, silvery crumple on the floor at Vivid's feet.

"No! What have you done?" she cried, and for a second she sounded like a real person, broken and disbelieving. But then her composure snapped back into place and she said to a monk at her side, "Sound the bells. We're under attack."

The monk fled. Scorch could hear the hurried pace of their feet on the marble, and moments later bells began to ring a deafening alarm. Scorch wished his hands were free, if only so he could cover his ears.

Kio assessed Vivid coldly. "Assassin," she whispered. "I should have figured it out sooner."

Vivid's fingers tightened around his daggers. "Likewise."

Scorch watched helplessly, waiting for Vivid to vault from the scene, to magically disappear himself and leave Scorch behind to face the vengeance of the monks.

That's not what happened.

The Priestess' Monks were rumored to be the best fighters in Viridor. Scorch had heard it his whole life. They had to be tough, didn't they? To pass the tests of the Heartlands? To travel the Monk's Path and live to serve the High Priestess in her temple atop the mountain? They had to be the best. And as the fight unfolded before his eyes, Scorch couldn't deny the monks were supremely skilled. But they weren't the best. They weren't as good as Vivid. He was a storm of swirling knives and black leather, lashing out in acrobatic kicks and jabs, elbows flying and knees crushing, with a face grim and purposeful. Kio, however, was an element of her own as she pitted her skills against Vivid's. The assassin verses the Priestess' Monk.

Scorch understood at last how Kio survived all her fights in the Circle. All the times he'd seen her clumsy with a sword had been a lie, like everything else about her. She moved fluidly with her blade against Vivid's daggers, putting Scorch's esteemed swordwork to shame. If only the Guild could see him now, tied up, his guardianship failed, history's best melee competition happening right in front of him, while he watched on, uselessly strapped to a chair. He longed to be free of his bindings so he could grab a blade and help fight their way to freedom.

Vivid excelled on his own for a while, which was an incredible feat when surrounded by a dozen monks with their hearts filled with fury for their Holy One's murder. Vivid held back their advances, blocked every killing blow, and met their quick attacks with even quicker defenses. It was hypnotizing to watch, but Scorch could tell the second Vivid's strength began to dwindle.

It happened fast. Kio's high kick connected with Vivid's bad shoulder, and he was thrown off balance and into the arms of the surrounding monks. Scorch felt the panic surge in his bones. Kio positioned her sword while Vivid struggled to break free of the monks holding him down. In seconds, her blade would run him through. Scorch's skin burned so hot that the metal bands around his wrists began to melt and his fingertips sparked weak bolts of fire that landed uselessly in the pool surrounding him. He felt the beginnings of his flesh hardening, but he would be too late. He yelled, watching helplessly as Kio's sword plunged toward Vivid's heart.

Suddenly, Kio, her sword, and the monks surrounding Vivid flew backward. Their bodies crashed into the walls and ceiling, then came falling back to the ground with bone-breaking thuds. A fierce wind ruffled Scorch's hair.

The monks groaned on the ground, but Kio was already getting to her feet again, her blade held out before her, blood running freely from a gash on her forehead. "*You*," she whispered, and then Kio's hands flew to her throat.

Scorch didn't know what was happening. "Vivid?" he asked.

Vivid said nothing, but his stare was murderous. Kio's eyes were huge and terrified and her face began to turn purple.

"Vivid!" Scorch yelled, and when Vivid turned his head, a gale of wind encircled him, making his raven hair stream out around his face. His amethyst eyes were a tempest. *An actual tempest.*

Kio fell to her knees, her eyelids spasming, her nails gouging gruesome marks down her neck. She was suffocating. And Vivid was making it happen.

"Vivid, stop!" Scorch cried.

At once, the whirlwind surrounding Vivid ceased and Kio fell forward, coughing and gasping for air. Vivid twirled his blades a moment before sheathing them, and just when Scorch thought he could never be surprised by anything ever again, Vivid ran toward him and dropped to one knee. He pulled a lock pick out of nowhere—seriously, Scorch couldn't see any pockets on that skintight leather—and began fiddling with the bindings at his wrists and ankles. It only took a handful of bated breaths before he was free.

Vivid pulled him out of the chair by the furs and they stood uncomfortably for a moment, the sound of seriously injured monks groaning all around them. The alarm bells were still ringing in earnest.

"I can't believe it," Scorch whispered.

Vivid's nostrils flared in irritation. "That won't be the last of the monks, and I can't fight them all by myself. I need you to not be useless. Can you do that?"

"Yes!"

Vivid's eyebrow twitched in a way that made Scorch think he didn't believe him. "Come on." He grabbed Scorch's hand and they ran from the secret chamber, leaping over the array of robed bodies. Scorch stole a final glimpse of Kio lying on the floor, breath strained, but alive. He could afford her no more sympathy, because more monks were blocking their path as they passed through the High Priestess' archway. Scorch readied himself to attack, but Vivid lifted his hand and the monks were blown backward, cracking their heads against the marble.

Scorch stared at Vivid as they continued to run. "*Gods,*" he whispered in amazement.

Vivid only paused long enough to tear the robes from one of the fallen monks' backs and throw it over his leathers, then he led them out into the long hallway, where the sound of ringing bells was even louder and more monks were spilling in from the outside, charging up the golden steps.

"I can help you fight them," Scorch insisted as Vivid pulled him through the nearest doorway.

"Save your energy," Vivid said, maneuvering them through a dark room filled with pews and a statue of the High Priestess.

"She's a bit conceited, isn't she?" Scorch asked as he brushed up against her marble-carved hips.

"*Was*," Vivid corrected before shoving Scorch toward a slit of a window. "Climb."

Scorch heaved himself up onto the sill, and when his feet kicked, trying to gain purchase, he felt a swell of air lift him up and nudge him the rest of the way out the window. He fell in a thorny bush outside, prickly on any occasion, but made even pricklier on account of Scorch's bare legs and arms. Vivid tumbled through the window after him, landing gracefully beside the bush.

Scorch only had time for a harrumph before Vivid was grasping his hand and hauling him up. They dashed toward the trees—the temple was surrounded by snow-capped, star-leaved trees—but Scorch could hear they were being followed. The cries of angry monks pierced the thin mountain air. Vivid's grip was a vice as he cut a path. It was almost as if he knew exactly where he was going, as if he had been there before. When they hit the edge of the tree line, they ran out of mountaintop.

Vivid released Scorch's hand only to grab his face. Scorch tried to reel back, surprised by the intimate contact, but Vivid's hold was foolproof. In his peripheral, Scorch could make out the bobbing light of traveling torches. It wouldn't be long before the monks caught up to them. He gulped, his eyes darting to their feet. They were skirted beside a precipice, the sheer drop of the mountain only steps away.

"Scorch," Vivid commanded, digging his fingers into Scorch's hair and tugging his head down for a more intimidating angle. Scorch had to slouch for their faces to be even, but he was still damn intimidated. Vivid was a fearsome creature to behold at the edge of a cliff. Wind lifted the fallen snow from the ground and it whipped around them.

"You're an elemental," Scorch breathed, mesmerized anew by the man squeezing his face.

"Yes," Vivid said, "but only one of us can fly." Scorch tried to shake his head, but Vivid's hold was unbreakable. Vivid glared at him, their noses almost touching. He was too much to take at such close proximity. Scorch feared he might catch Vivid on fire if he didn't let go of him. "You're hot," Vivid said, giving Scorch's hair another yank. "I can feel your power. You have to use it now and fly us down the mountain. It's the only way we can escape."

"I can't!" Scorch said. "You know I can't! I told you I can't control it."

"You *can* control it, you're just afraid to," Vivid growled. "I thought you weren't a coward."

"I'm not!"

"Prove it."

"I can't. I don't know how!"

Vivid's stare was more electric than any lightning in any storm, and his words were absolute. "I thought you wanted to pay me back for saving your life. This is how you can pay me back."

The noise from the trees was growing louder. The lights from the torches were growing brighter. Vivid was growing more impatient.

"Scorch," he growled. "We don't have time for this." He pushed Scorch away and leapt off the edge of the mountain.

The change was immediate. One second, Scorch was gaping at the empty space Vivid had just occupied, and the next, he was scaled and winged and diving off the mountain after him. He plummeted headfirst until he sailed past Vivid's falling body, and then he cut to a ninety-degree angle and thrust forward. He felt Vivid's hands grappling onto one of the spikes of his spine and his legs hooking over his back. An upsurge of wind caught beneath Scorch's wings as he extended them fully, and they rode the current of air away from the mountainside.

Scorch's heart was beating impossibly fast and his chest was full of fire. He let it burn inside of him and fuel his flight. Beneath them, the desert appeared, but from their height, Scorch couldn't make out the cannibals prowling the sands for a meal. He beat his wings and urged them faster, and when he began to feel drained halfway across the desert, Vivid's hand smoothed across his scales and fresh air filled his lungs, making the heat inside him burn brighter. Vivid was using his air to spur Scorch's fire.

Eventually, the desert disappeared, but Scorch pushed onward. The lake glistened, black and perilous, but Scorch kept flying. He'd never flown so far, or felt so empowered, and whenever he waned, Vivid rubbed at his scales and the wind took up his slack. His massive wings kept them in the air and Vivid's currents boosted them further and further, until the sun became a pinkish inkling, and the sky began to fill with vibrant shades of red. The sunrise was on fire as the lake turned into a copse of ash-white trees, and only then did Scorch begin to spiral slowly to the ground.

It was a rough landing.

Scorch's wings tangled in the dense trees and Vivid was thrown from his back as they crashed. Scorch felt his scales morphing into human skin, his wings snapping back into his shoulder blades, and his snout reverting to a handsomely sculpted nose. In moments, he was Scorch-shaped again. And naked, naturally.

He was also exhausted. He panted, hands on his knees, fighting to remain conscious. He couldn't pass out like he had last time. He had to find Vivid and make sure he was okay. He lifted his head with a groan and scanned the nearby trees for the assassin. When Vivid kneeled beside him a second later, Scorch jumped, emitting a truly embarrassing yelp.

"You're too easy to sneak up on," Vivid said, easing the monk robe from his shoulders and settling it over Scorch's bare back. "The assassins will fix that."

Scorch slipped his arms through the sleeves of the robe. It smelled pleasant, probably because Vivid had been bundled up in it all night. He struggled to keep his eyes open. "Are you hurt?" he asked Vivid. And then, a little more awake than before: "What do you mean *the assassins will fix that*?"

Vivid slipped him his canteen and Scorch was perplexed, once again, by the many secret compartments of Vivid's clothes. "You're coming back with me to the Assassins' Hollow."

"No," Scorch said after a grateful drink of water. "I have to go back to the Guardians' Guild and tell them what happened. The Master will be expecting me."

"Don't be a fool," Vivid chastised, taking the canteen back for a sip. "Your guardians don't want you back."

Scorch rubbed at his face. He was too tired for this conversation. "Yes, they do."

"Look at me," Vivid said, and Scorch couldn't help but look. His bleary, tired eyes focused on Vivid. "Do you truly think your Guild Master didn't know exactly what he was doing when he sent you to the Heartlands? He knows what you are. Your guardianship to save the High Priestess was a suicide mission."

"The Master would never do that to me," Scorch said, but even as the words left him, he wondered. He remembered the troubled look in Master McClintock's eyes when he gave him the mission, how tired he had been, like he'd been up all night with worry. Scorch frowned. Could he truly say he trusted the Master when he had proved to be terrible at reading people, recently and repeatedly?

"Why else would a Guild Master assign an untested apprentice to such a task?" Vivid asked.

"How do you know I was only an apprentice?" asked Scorch, and Vivid arched his brow. "Was it that obvious?"

"One way or another," Vivid continued, "your Master discovered what you are. He might not have had the heart to kill you himself, but he sent you away knowing you would die. If you return to the Guild, do you think he'll be happy to see you?"

Scorch pulled the robe tighter around his shoulders. He wasn't cold, but he wanted desperately to disappear inside the soft cloth.

"Come with me to the Assassins' Hollow," Vivid said.

Scorch shook his head. "Even if the guardians want me dead, why would I become an assassin? I want to protect people, not kill them."

"You need to learn to harness your power."

Everything was still. The air. The trees. Vivid.

"What do assassins have to do with being an elemental?" Scorch asked. He was so tired.

"Where do you think I learned?" Vivid asked.

A breeze stirred and Vivid's lips quirked up at the edges. It was almost a smile. Almost.

"Talk to me again once I've slept for a year," Scorch mumbled, letting his body curl up on the forest floor.

Before he nodded off, he heard Vivid's disapproving sigh and a soft rumbling voice. "Useless."

# Part Two
# Assassins' Hollow

# How to Steal and Look Your Best

## 11

*H*e was lying in the grass, the rush of the river babbling over sun-drenched pebbles. His eyes were closed and a breeze drifted over him. Easy warmth tingled beneath his skin and a fire crackled in the pit of his chest.

Far away, in a distant corner of his sleeping mind, he wondered where the horror had gone. He wondered when the scent of burning flesh had been replaced with the fresh air of Etheridge's garden, when sprays of blood across his cheek became a beam of sun. He opened his eyes, and instead of murdered girls in bloody beds, he saw clear blue sky.

He stretched his arms, arching his back from the grass, and felt an unfamiliar heat pressed against his side. His hand found a trail of skin, textured with scars, and he traced his name until soft hair threaded between his fingers.

Without turning his head, without looking, he knew what had happened to the nightmares.

The wind had blown them away.

When Scorch roused from his sleep, Vivid was glaring at him. "I'll obtain more Dream Moss when we reach the next village," he said.

Scorch sat up with a sigh, raking fingers through his tousle of hair. Vivid's words confused him, for he had not woken from a bad dream. Why would Vivid bring up the—*oh*. Scorch ducked his head to hide the blood rushing to his cheeks, and he lifted his knees to his chest to cover the blood rushing elsewhere.

"Did I," he began with feigned nonchalance, "make any noise? Like I was having a nightmare?"

"You were moaning like you were in pain."

"Pain," Scorch repeated, utterly red-faced. "Yes. Gods, yes. Awful pain. Terrible dream." He stole a glance at Vivid, prepared to explain his flush away as a lingering symptom of his elemental power, but Vivid wasn't looking at Scorch, wasn't even facing him. He was seated yards away with one of his twin daggers over his knee, sharpening the blade.

"More Dream Moss will shut you up," Vivid said. "Just while you're asleep, unfortunately."

"Okay," Scorch responded cautiously. He waited a moment for Vivid to continue, to say something else on the matter, or broach a secondary topic, but he didn't, and Scorch was relieved. It gave him time to organize his thoughts and discreetly rearrange his robes, because it had not been a nightmare that pulled the moans from his throat.

Scorch got to his feet, which were bare, and tested his strength with a bounce. After flying miles nonstop and sporting an array of fresh injuries, compliments of the late High Priestess, Scorch didn't feel as terrible as would be expected. The strongest emotion battering inconveniently against his insides was shame, sprinkled with, if he was being honest, arousal. He was familiar with the former as much as the latter and he buried both feelings with a laugh as he recalled their brief conversation before his hibernation.

"I have no shoes," he announced. Vivid was concentrating on sharpening his blade and didn't respond, so Scorch moved to stand in front of him. "I was just wondering if the assassins have a no shoes, no service policy."

Vivid ignored him.

"Since you claim to be taking me to them, I figure it would be nice to have some idea whether I'm walking into my doom. With or without shoes."

"If I wanted you to die, I would have left you strapped to that chair."

Scorch's mouth worked open, silently and stupidly, for several seconds before he found his voice. "Kio said she wanted to help me, and then she handed me over to be experimented on." He felt her absence keenly. Had Kio been with them, she would have already soothed his cuts and wrapped his feet in leathers. But she was gone, over treacherous miles of Heartland, mourning within a golden temple.

Vivid slipped the dagger back into his sleeve and stood. He only came up to Scorch's chin. "Have I told you I would help you?" he asked.

Scorch's first instinct was to say yes, but his instincts were frayed as of late, so he took a pause to consider the man in front of him. Vivid had saved his life over and over, from the Circle and onward, but had he ever vowed to protect him or even seemed relieved when Scorch lived? Had he ever presented himself as anything but annoyed and inconvenienced by Scorch's mere existence?

"Why are you taking me to the assassins, Vivid?"

"I've been instructed to collect stray elementals when the opportunity presents," he answered, tucking his unruly strand of hair behind his ear.

"Right," Scorch said, irked by the twisting in his stomach at Vivid's reveal. "You're not helping me. You're only following orders."

"Should I lie to you? Tell you I want to help you become your best self?"

"No."

Vivid glared up at him, his lips a thin line of displeasure. "I'm not her."

Scorch nodded, the shame creeping back. "I know."

"In the next village, we'll get you shoes and something else to wear. I won't be bringing a haggard brute to the Hollow."

Scorch scratched his beard self-consciously. He had trusted Kio and that had been a mistake. Vivid had obfuscated the truth, but he was standing before him now, stony-faced and sincere. Scorch had questions, and if going with Vivid to the Assassins' Hollow could answer even a few of them, it was a risk he had to take, a trust he had to extend.

"Fine," he said with a sigh of finality.

Vivid's eyebrow twitched.

"Fine," Scorch elaborated. "I'll go with you to the assassins."

"It wasn't up for debate." Vivid passed him their shared canteen and started walking. "Before you start complaining, you only have a few more miles to walk barefoot," he called over his shoulder.

"A few more miles?" Scorch asked, the naked soles of his feet trying to avoid the pointiest sections of terrain as he walked. "After we find the main road, it's forever until we reach the next village."

"True, but we won't be walking by then," Vivid stated matter-of-factly, as if it was the most obvious thing in the world.

"I'm not flying us anywhere anytime soon." Even if Scorch had the energy for another change, he didn't think he would be able to accomplish it.

"You won't need to," Vivid said. "We're going to steal a horse."

Scorch was lying in the middle of the road. He could feel the wagon's vibrations rattling his bones. As the sound of hooves and wheels drew closer, he fought the instinct to roll out of the way. If this was all an elaborate scheme to get Scorch run over, he would only have himself to blame, and on the long list of different ways he'd recently nearly died, death by lying in the middle of the road was the dumbest. But it was Vivid's idea, and so he tried his best to go along with it.

The afternoon had grown blustery and Scorch hoped his monk robe would not blow open. He doubted the wagon would stop if he were obscenely exposed; it would diminish the likelihood, at the very least. He could not help but wonder if Vivid was making the wind tease at the hems of his robe, but that line of thought threatened to redden his cheeks again, so he banished it and did his best to pretend he was a beaten up monk who needed help. Hopefully, the folks driving the wagon cared about monks in the road. Scorch thought that was a pretty big gamble, but Vivid had insisted grimly that it would work.

Sure enough, the squeak of the wheels slowed to a stop before Scorch was crushed to death. Through his shut eyes, he heard a troubled gasp and then more squeaking as a body lumbered out of the wagon seat. Footsteps came closer until they halted by his head, and then there was a crack of tired knees bending.

"Oh my Gods. Are you alive?" someone whispered over Scorch's body.

He let his eyes flutter open and groaned. The groan was real because he was on top of a rock and it was digging into his spine. "I-I was robbed," he rattled.

The man above him had a handlebar mustache and kind eyes. "What kind of monster would rob a monk? They took your shoes, too! Here," he said, gently grasping Scorch's shoulders, "let's get you standing up."

Scorch laid on the theatrics as he hobbled to his feet. "Do you have any water?" he asked faintly.

The man linked his arm with Scorch and helped him walk to the back of the wagon. "Should have a fresh jug back here somewhere."

"Oh, bless you," said Scorch before bending over with a roaring cough. He braced his hand against the wagon's side, his eyes watering.

"Wait right here," said the man, and he scrambled through the canvas flaps. "I know I have some back here. Just got fresh from the river this morning," he hollered, voice muffled.

Scorch coughed again, louder, to cover the snort of the horse. "Take your time," he wheezed as he peeked around the front of the wagon. The man began to emerge from the canvas with a large jug cradled in his elbow and Scorch steepled his hands together in prayer. "A bite of something to eat might soothe my harassed nerves, if you have any to spare, my child." For a second, he was convinced saying "my child" to a man easily thirty years his senior was a mistake, but the man only nodded enthusiastically and ducked again into the depths of the wagon.

Scorch hacked another loud cough to mask the clip-clop of hooves. Vivid was sitting atop the horse with the reins in his hands, looking absurdly casual to be in the midst of thievery. Scorch couldn't help but lift a dubious brow at the inferred seating arrangement, but Vivid showed no sign of scooting back in the saddle, only cocked his head in silent assignment, and Scorch had no choice but to lift himself onto the horse. He nestled in behind Vivid. There was some intimate pressing, but it was, regrettably, unavoidable. Vivid leaned forward to whisper something in the horse's ear and then she was off, galloping at such a pace that Scorch was forced to either wrap his arms around Vivid's torso or fall off.

They dashed down the road, and Scorch could hear the poor man calling after them. He felt guilty for the deception, but he could hardly be worried about it at the moment, not with the leather beneath his fingertips and the hard muscle tensing beneath his touch.

They rode in silence—because Vivid never spoke and hated when Scorch did—so Scorch spent his time organizing his thoughts and trying not to grind against Vivid's back. It was a difficult task, but Scorch thought he made a valiant effort. Organizing his thoughts was undoubtedly the more trying task, and he was relieved when, after not too long a time, they came upon a dusty little village; Scorch remembered passing it on their way to the Heartlands, but they'd not stopped there for supplies, not after what happened to the boy in the other village.

Vivid dismounted and Scorch could finally breathe again. He slid to the ground, his bare feet finding the only sharp rock on the entire road. He whimpered in pain and gingerly lifted his foot to inspect the damage: a small cut on his heel. When he looked up, Vivid was just turning his head away from him.

"Shoes," he stated, taking the horse by the lead and walking down the village road.

The village was a humble clump of houses, but it had the essentials to suit their needs. Vivid tied the horse to a post outside the seamstress's hut and they wandered inside. It was a single-room shop, its walls lined floor to ceiling with shelves of fabrics, shoes, and hats. Racks were pushed into every corner, laden with vests and trousers and jackets of formal and casual make. At first, Scorch thought the shop was absent of its keeper, but then a ruffled blouse and feathered hat began to move and a wiry young man was shoving his way out from behind a pile of clothes.

"What can I do you gentlemen for?" the shopkeeper asked, eyes sizing up the men in front of him. "Or can I just do you gentlemen?" He laughed, throwing back his head and clapping his hands together. "I'm sorry! Ha! Kidding, kidding. How can I help you?"

Vivid threw Scorch a pouch of coin. Scorch made a mental note to ask him where he sequestered so many bulky items in his tight leathers.

"He needs everything," Vivid said, turning to leave. "I'm going to find the herbalist tent." That was just for Scorch, spoken in a deep pitch that made something flutter in Scorch's stomach.

Vivid walked out, leaving him alone with the tailor. He shuffled his feet awkwardly. "I need everything," he sighed.

The tailor smiled. "I'll say. Slip off that robe and we can get you measured up."

Scorch lowered his voice to a whisper. "I don't have anything on under this." He tugged at the robe.

"Trust me," the tailor replied with a smirk, "that's perfectly alright with me."

An hour later, Scorch walked out of the shop with a sack full of tailored garments. Because he still needed to tend to his injuries, he had insisted on keeping the monk robe a while longer, but he did have new boots on his feet, in supple, red leather. For some reason, the tailor kept pushing the color red. "It suits you," he insisted. "He'll love it on you," he also insisted, and Scorch had frowned in confusion.

Now, dressed as a monk with fancy new boots, he looked up and down the street, but Vivid was nowhere to be seen.

"I procured us a room."

Scorch jumped, startled, then turned around to find Vivid standing directly behind him with a cloth sack in his hand. They walked together down the road until they reached a tiny inn. There was a bar stationed in the corner and a dining room, but Vivid waltzed right through the downstairs and they winded their way up a creaky staircase. On the upper floor, there were only four doors, and Vivid already had the key for their room.

The quarters were modest and dusty, but to Scorch's delight, there was a tub filled with water, and a tray of food sitting on the bed.

"Food or bath?" Vivid asked, shutting the door and locking it.

"What?"

"Are you hungrier or dirtier?"

Scorch checked in on his bodily desires. "Hungrier," he decided.

Vivid unsheathed his daggers. "Eat while I take the first bath." He set the twin blades on the stand beside the tub. "Do not touch my weapons."

Scorch scoffed, but he made a wide berth as he passed the daggers and headed for the bed. His mouth watered at the sight of freshly baked bread and roast beef. There were two plates on the tray and he picked one up greedily, sitting on the bed and balancing the plate in his lap. He stuffed a bite of meat and bread into his mouth and glanced up at Vivid, who was lingering beside the tub uncertainly.

Scorch shifted so he was facing the window. "I won't look," he promised.

"I don't care what you do," he heard Vivid snarl. Scorch remembered the silver scars peppered across the skin of his shoulder, and how stiff he'd been when Scorch had applied the ointment to his wound. The memory nearly made him choke on his meal, but he managed to swallow. He listened to the sounds of Vivid unbuckling his cuirass, the rustle of leather dropping to the floor, and then there was a splash of water as he slipped into the tub.

"How is your shoulder?" Scorch asked around a mouthful of food.

"It feels better when you're not talking."

So Scorch stopped talking and concentrated on eating. It was difficult, however, to completely shut out the subtle sounds of bathing happening only a few feet away. But it turned out, and Scorch should not have been surprised, that Vivid's bath regimen was as promptly executed as any of his other regimens, and after a few minutes of submersion, he heard the disturbance of water as Vivid stepped from the tub. Scorch squeezed his eyes shut, fearing that if he did not, the urge to dart his eyes toward a sopping wet, naked assassin would be too great, and he would have survived all his recent hardships only to be murdered in a dusty inn room.

When Vivid strutted into his line of sight in nothing but his tight leather trousers, Scorch shoved the last of the bread into his mouth to avoid saying something he shouldn't, though the possibilities abounded in his mind, insufferably knocking against one another. For example, "Wow!", "Gods, help me!", and "Please put your clothes back on before I die" were a few exclamations fighting to get out. He must have made a distressed sound around his bread, because Vivid shot him a contemptuous look as he searched through the herbalist sack.

Scorch looked down at his empty plate, but the image of a fair, lean chest was seared into his eyes, and he could still see it amongst the crumbs. Vivid's left shoulder was bruised purple around the wound, and the wound itself, a blackish circle, was in the middle of scabbing over. Without the coverings of his leather gear, the expanse of his scarring was evident: a constellation of silver markings across the hard planes of his body. But it was hardly the wounds, new or old, that jarred Scorch's senses. It was the oddity of seeing so much bare skin at one time.

He dared another glance as Vivid pulled an ointment box from the sack and sat down on the bed, thus allowing Scorch to examine his back freely. At such a close distance, Scorch could have reached out and traced the scars. Vivid's back was not as silvered as his front, but the scars were still there, and they were still excessive in their number. Also excessive were the muscles beneath the scarred skin, flexing as Vivid lifted his hand to rub the ointment into his shoulder.

"Still hot," Vivid said.

"*What?*"

"The water."

Scorch had to stand from the bed and physically turn away to remove his eyes from Vivid's back. The tub was steaming slightly, and it appeared clean, as if it had never been used. At the Guild, Scorch had always enjoyed fresh baths, and only rarely had he rinsed in water someone else had used, but for some reason the idea of sharing bathwater with Vivid didn't bother him. He checked to see whether Vivid was watching—he wasn't—and then stripped the road-weary robe from his shoulders. He had to bend over to unlace his boots before tugging them off, and then he eased himself into the tub, wincing as the hot water touched the cuts on his body. Strangely enough, though his chest and torso had been sliced up by the High Priestess' dagger, it was the minor cut on his foot that ailed him the most. Once he was fully seated, however, Scorch was able to push the pain away and relax into the warmth of the water. He leaned his head against the rim and stole another glance at Vivid. He was wrapping his shoulder, a less than easy task for one person. Scorch was debating whether or not to leap from the tub and offer his assistance when a flash of yellow caught his eye.

Propped on the stand beside the tub was a small looking glass. It had been weeks since he'd seen himself, and he scooted forward in the water, drawing nearer to his reflection. His beard had filled in and his hair was a scruffy tangle on his head, not entirely different from its usual state, but his face—his face was someone else's. Amber eyes glinted amidst a map of hardships. Scorch turned his cheek and touched the side of his face, from temple to jaw, where the boy in the Circle had marked him. His lip was split and swollen from the High Priestess' knife. His neck was bruised. A smudge of soot streaked across his brow. He would scar and look hard forever, and for a moment, he missed the untested image that used to look back at him from the Guild looking glass. *Either you scar*, he told himself, *or you die*. At least he finally looked like a proper guardian, even if he didn't feel like one.

Sitting beside the glass was a razor, and whether it was complimentary or left behind by a previous patron, Scorch picked it up and turned it over in his fingers. He dunked his head beneath the water and resurfaced with a splash. Then he got to work.

When he finally stepped from the tub, he was clean and fresh shaven. He ran a hand over his smooth cheek and sighed contentedly, wrapping a towel around his waist.

"What happened to your face?"

Scorch had walked to the bed, toward the medicinals, and Vivid was still sitting there bare chested, only now, instead of staring daggers at his own shoulder wound, he was staring daggers at Scorch.

"You said you couldn't bring a—what did you call me?—a haggard brute back to the Assassins," Scorch answered with a smug smile. "So I shaved." He felt along the clean jut of his chin, watching Vivid watch him. The man looked personally affronted. "What is it?"

As if slapped, Vivid recoiled, standing abruptly from the bed and stalking past Scorch to reach the second half of his leather ensemble, which still lay on the floor. He picked up the cuirass with a curious hostility, his lips thinning as he pulled it over his hurt shoulder.

"Flummoxed by my good looks?" Scorch asked with a grin, keeping his eyes on the ointments and bandages instead of the other man agilely buckling his shirt.

Vivid picked up his daggers from the table and knocked them back into their sheaths with a threatening ring of steel. "Hardly," he said, his voice like stone, quite the contrast to his face, which was tension personified.

Scorch let it drop, because he didn't care for the stiffness of Vivid's shoulders when he was the cause. Assuming he was the cause. Wasn't he usually? He couldn't even shave without perturbing the man, and that grated on his carefully construed confidence, but he couldn't allow it to distract him overly much.

He toyed with the ointment box and contemplated where to start first. A shift of his weight reminded him of the cut on the sole of his foot, and that seemed as good a place as any to begin. He sat on the bed and folded up his leg to assess the damage. It was a smallish cut, but it stung. He swiped a glob of ointment onto it and wrapped it up, then moved on to his stomach. His time strapped to the High Priestess' chair had been brief, but not brief enough. He wondered how many more cuts he would have if Vivid had not appeared when he did. His body would have been covered in scars.

Scorch looked at Vivid, who was crossing back toward the bed for his plate of food. His hands and face were the only pieces of skin exposed to Scorch's scrutiny, and he studied the long fingers carefully. He saw no scars there, nor on the deceptively soft curves of his face.

Vivid sat with his legs crossed on the bed, the plate balanced pristinely on one knee. He must have been hungry, because he was eating quickly, with tidy, neat bites. Scorch rubbed ointment on the cuts across his chest as his mind quested. He wanted to ask

Vivid how he got those scars. It would be so simple if he could simply ask, and Vivid could simply answer, and then he would know. But nothing felt simple, and he knew Vivid's reaction to questioning would be met with disapproval. Clearly, the man had secrets, and that, at least, was something Scorch understood well. If they were to have nothing else in common, it could be that single thing. And Scorch would respect it. He would try, anyway.

When he finished tending himself—the stab wounds at his thigh and shoulder were well on their way to being healed and no longer required bandaging—he lingered in his towel a while longer, but after several minutes of Vivid pointedly looking everywhere but at Scorch, he decided to don his clothes.

The tailor had been leisurely in the way he'd taken Scorch's measurements, especially his inseam, but it paid off in the end as Scorch tugged on the richly brown trousers. The soft leather was snug against his backside, and he moved about, trying to get a look. Next, he slid on a cream-colored undershirt that was kind to the array of injuries on his skin. Finally, his jerkin. Blood red to match his boots. It was a bit flashier than he was used to, but the feather-hatted tailor had been adamant. Besides, Scorch was never one to disappoint, and the way the man had swooned when he saw Scorch in his new gear led Scorch to believe he definitely did not disappoint.

He combed fingers through his still-damp hair and resisted a return to the looking glass, opting instead to glance at Vivid to gauge his reaction, but Vivid had returned to pretending like Scorch didn't exist, and the last thing Scorch would ever do was twirl in front of the assassin and ask him if he liked his new outfit.

Scorch paced back and forth across the length of the room while Vivid finished his meal. After a few minutes, Vivid stood, plate in hand, and crossed in front of Scorch to set it on the table. Then he fixed him with a glare, one of his eyebrows quirking slightly.

Scorch smiled. "Presentable?" he asked, feeling instantly idiotic.

Vivid scowled, his eyes searching for something as they roamed from the top of Scorch's sunny hair to the tip of his crimson boots. "They will wonder why a guardian has no sword."

Scorch's hand flew instinctively to his belt, where the scabbard of his Guild sword should have been, but it was gone. It had been gone since the monks kidnapped them on the mountain.

Before Scorch could speak—not that he knew what to say—Vivid tossed him another purse, jingling and heavy with coin. "I'm going to sleep," he announced, turning toward the bed. "Go to the blacksmith and arm yourself, since you didn't think to do it before."

"Where did you get all of this coin?" Scorch asked.

"Unlike you, I'm good at the jobs I'm assigned," was Vivid's terse response.

Scorch felt a flare of anger heat his face. "I'm a guardian," he argued. "I'm not assigned jobs, I'm assigned missions."

Vivid remained perpetually unimpressed. "You're not a guardian, Scorch," he said. "No more than I am. Go and find a sword." He tossed Scorch the key to their room and lay down on his back.

Scorch was frozen, watching his lean body stretch across the bed, until frustrated eyes found his.

"*Go*," Vivid ordered.

Scorch went.

He found the blacksmith, and though her collection of swords was small, Scorch settled on one that would work well enough in the interim: a sleek, long blade with a sturdy grip and pleasing heft. After testing its balance with a few practice jousts that made the blacksmith take several disgruntled steps back, he purchased it, emptying half the purse Vivid had thrown at him. The man seemed to have purses hidden all over his person, maybe even in his thick hair. Scorch bid the blacksmith good evening and walked back toward the sleepy inn.

Vivid was an assassin, which was surprising enough on its own, but he was also an elemental. Scorch couldn't help but wonder how many "jobs" he had completed, how many people he had killed, either with his twin daggers or air manipulations. Vivid looked young, too young to have such a bloody history, and yet the scars on his body told a different story. Scorch wanted to know *more*. Perhaps he would be able to unearth a portion of Vivid's past when they were with the assassins.

Since he had coin left over, when he passed through the dining room, he stopped for a drink. The barmaid was small-village pretty, with strawberry blonde braids and a beauty mark on her dimpled cheek. She was quick with Scorch's order and stared a little too long at the cut on his lip, and in another world, Scorch would have flirted with her and tried to coax her into his lap. But in this world, at this time, Scorch was unmoved. He smiled and thanked her politely and enjoyed his ale, but when she batted her lashes and asked if she could do anything else for him, he laid her tip on the table, said no thank you, and headed back up the stairs.

He found himself carefully inserting the key to their room and quietly edging inside, locking the door as quietly as possible. Vivid's eyes were shut and he was lying flat on his back, but

Scorch didn't believe he was asleep. He set his sword in its scabbard and leaned it against the wall, grabbing a pillow from the bed, which suddenly appeared incredibly narrow. It only took him a second's debate before he decided the floor would suit him fine. He stole a brief look at Vivid before he curled up on the floor, between the door and the bed. Then he got up, fetched his sword, and cozied up again, this time with the weapon held firmly in his hand.

A few moments later, he felt something hit him on the head. He pushed up on his elbow and looked over his shoulder. Vivid was still lying with his eyes closed.

Scorch's hand found what had been pelted at him. A small linen pouch with a drawstring. He opened it and took a grateful whiff of its contents: silvery leaves and ivory stems. He took out one of the stems and popped it into his mouth.

"Thanks," he whispered to the quiet room.

Vivid said nothing.

# *Assassins*
# **12**

The next morning, karma had miraculously spared Scorch and Vivid, and their stolen horse was waiting for their return in the inn's stable.

"Don't you think I should ride in front?" Scorch asked as Vivid hoisted himself into the saddle. "Unless you like me behind you." To anyone else, his words might have been smooth, but when delivered to Vivid they came out jumbled and cheesy and more lecherous than Scorch had intended. With flushed cheeks, he mounted the horse, his groin pressing traitorously against Vivid's back.

"Feels like you don't mind all that much," Vivid mumbled grumpily, and Scorch's surprised huff was lost to the wind as Vivid commanded their horse forward. She whinnied agreeably as they trotted out of the village.

When they returned to the main road, Vivid opened the horse to a gallop, and they made quick time. Scorch could admit that riding was much more pleasant than a weeklong walk, even if he had to keep his hands firmly clasped around Vivid's hips to keep his seat.

They stopped only to rest the horse and relieve themselves, and then they were off again, Vivid at the reins and Scorch pressed up against his back. During that time, he couldn't help but take note of a few facts: Vivid's hair smelled like the forest in wintertime; when seated, the top of Vivid's head came up to just above Scorch's chin; Vivid's part zigzagged at the crown.

Ultimately, a journey that lasted a week by foot, took only three days on horseback, and on the evening of the third day, Vivid slowed the horse to a lazy trot and led her off road, into the dark forest. The day before, they had turned off the western road and taken a route to the north. Scorch had never ventured into that part of the country before, and he took in their surroundings with hungry eyes. The air was colder and the trees had thicker trunks and greener leaves.

"Is this where the assassins live?" Scorch asked softly.

"We're close now."

They clopped along, the horse's steps subdued against the forest floor, until Scorch detected an odd sound, like a roar that never ended. Vivid slid from the saddle and began leading the horse by the reins.

"Let me get off first," Scorch insisted, feeling ridiculous still mounted while Vivid walked. Vivid stopped the horse and let Scorch ease off her back, a bit clumsily, and then they walked together toward the roar. It didn't take long for Scorch to peg the sound, and when they turned the corner around a steep, mossy boulder, there it was. A waterfall.

Vivid whispered something to the horse. Her ears twitched, she snorted happily, and then she trotted off.

"You like animals," Scorch accused, amused.

Vivid dusted off his leathers and mindlessly tucked the strand of hair behind his ear. "Of course."

*Of course,* Scorch thought with a roll of his eyes.

They watched the horse disappear into the dense foliage of the forest, and then Vivid started leading them toward the waterfall. It was the first real waterfall Scorch had ever seen, though he'd glimpsed several drawings in books at the Guild. Books, he was learning, could never quite compare to real life. He craned his head up at the cascade of crystal blue water.

"It's beautiful," he told Vivid.

"It's not as beautiful on the inside," Vivid retorted, jumping nimbly onto the rocks at the base of the falls.

"The inside?" Scorch scrambled after him, slipping on the slick rocks. His knee fell hard against the stone and he gritted his teeth. Vivid turned back to him, his eyes heavy with judgment. "Don't help me up or anything," Scorch spat with an unbidden gush of anger, or something like it.

"If you insist," was Vivid's answer, and he turned away from Scorch to continue scaling the rocks.

Scorch pulled himself up. Thankfully, he'd not ripped open the knee of his new trousers, though he could already tell he would have a nasty bruise to contend with for the next several days. He took a deep breath and swallowed his uncharacteristic bout of anger. Vivid liked animals, but he did not like Scorch. Scorch knew it, he just hadn't known it thoroughly enough. He followed after Vivid on careful feet and avoided falling again. Vivid awaited him at the cleft of the rocks, and then they walked behind the waterfall.

It was loud and magical, and Scorch walked slowly to keep from slipping as he stared at the water. He was mid-bask when he felt a sharp point at the small of his back.

"I could make a joke, but I'm a little too terrified," Scorch breathed.

One of Vivid's daggers was pushed against his back, but the tip wasn't digging in. It was only a graze. "It's tradition," Vivid said.

"For me to be terrified?"

"For any newcomer to the Hollow to be escorted by a dagger's point," Vivid explained. He was standing close and whispering his words against Scorch's neck, because he couldn't quite reach his ear. "When we enter, speak to no one. Don't even *think* about touching your sword."

Vivid grabbed Scorch's shoulder that was absent of a stab wound—very considerate of him—but the blade at his back was still disconcerting. Plus, there was the fact that Scorch was being led into a den of assassins, behind a *waterfall*. The whole situation was alarming. Nonetheless, he supposed he had experienced worse days, much worse, and despite himself, he trusted Vivid not to kill him, or at least trusted him to be honest about killing him. Vivid gave him another shove and kicked at a black stone lodged in the wall. The whole waterfall groaned as a passageway opened up before Scorch's eyes.

"Earth elementals," Vivid whispered as explanation. He nudged the back of Scorch's heels with his foot. "Remember what I said. Move."

Scorch kept his eyes trained on his new boots and stepped into the passageway. It was a cave tunnel, but it wasn't long, and at the end of it, Vivid revealed a slip of cloth from somewhere in the mystery folds of his clothes. It was a blindfold. Scorch snorted and

Vivid narrowed his eyes. A charged few seconds later, Scorch bent his head in acquiescence and Vivid tied the material around his eyes.

It sounded like Vivid kicked against something, and then there was only silence. For about two minutes, they stood in the pitch-black darkness of the tunnel, waiting. Vivid's fingers flexed against Scorch's shoulder and the dagger remained a whisper against the small of his back. They were standing very close and Scorch could hear Vivid breathing. They were steady breaths, like Scorch's used to be, back when he still had some semblance of control over his life.

When the door opened, light bled through Scorch's blindfold and he bent his head. The hand at his shoulder gripped him roughly.

"Vivid. You were expected back two days ago," came a woman's voice, pleasingly tarnished, like she smoked too much pipe weed. "But now I see you had some extra weight to carry. Who's the lug? I know, I know. Not for me to know before Axum. He's in his rooms." She spoke as if she knew Vivid didn't want to speak, playing the conversation out for them both. "Find me later, would you? I've been forced to practice with Elias."

Vivid remained silent at Scorch's back for a moment before commenting. "You need the practice. Your eyebrows are singed again."

The woman faked a laugh, and then she must have stepped to the side, because Vivid pushed Scorch forward.

Scorch felt vulnerable walking blindfolded through the Assassin's Hollow, but the hand leading him was firm and didn't seem to be aiming to walk him into any fireplaces or holes in the ground. All around him, he could hear voices, some whispering about Vivid and his "lug" and some speaking normally about something else entirely. No one tried to stop them as they threaded through, room after room. At least, it felt like multiple rooms, or multiple cavern chambers. Were they still inside a cave? The air didn't feel damp. It was quite comfortable, wherever they were, and it smelled nice, like cedar.

When Vivid finally stopped, he removed his hand from Scorch's shoulder to rap curtly against a door, and then returned his hand, squeezing gently. The gesture, if it was a gesture at all, made Scorch wish he could see Vivid's face. The dagger at his back eased slightly, and the hand squeezed once more, and then the sound of a door opening made him straighten with renewed alertness. He could sense Vivid's body doing the same.

"Vivid," said a voice, a tad high-pitched, but prosperous with authority. *The man in charge.* "Come in."

Scorch was instructed forward, and he felt the air change as he entered through a doorway. The light beneath the blindfold diminished. Vivid guided him to a chair, but unlike Kio, who had shoved him down into his seat, Vivid waited for Scorch to feel the chair at the backs of his knees, and then he pressed lightly against Scorch's shoulder for him to sit, which he did, though he did it with a begrudging frown. He waited for chains or ropes to bind him, but none came. He heard Vivid sheath his dagger, and then felt his hand reappear at his shoulder.

"You are two days off schedule," said the man. He did not sound angry or worried. He was simply stating a fact.

"There were circumstances which led me off course," Vivid replied.

"But not off job?"

"I'm never led off job, Axum."

It was beyond strange to hear Vivid speaking to an authority, because for Scorch, it was impossible to imagine anyone being in charge of the small assassin. He wondered if Vivid even considered Axum to be in charge, or if he was just another annoyance in his life that must be managed with forced patience. It was impossible to tell by the tone of Vivid's voice, which sounded as thunderously bored as ever.

"You never go off job?" Axum asked. "Is that why you've brought me a gift?"

Scorch flinched at the word *gift*. That was what Kio had called him when she handed him over to the High Priestess. Vivid's hand tightened on his shoulder, his fingers digging into the muscle, not enough to hurt, but enough to remind. *I'm not her*, the fingers said. Scorch breathed deeply and resisted the urge to reach for his sword.

"I completed the job," Vivid said. "Successfully."

"Good," replied Axum. Scorch heard footsteps traveling in a wide circle around his chair. "And was this man a circumstance of your lateness?"

"Yes."

"Explain."

"He's an elemental," answered Vivid. "Unstudied. Unpracticed. He has no control over his power."

"His power being?" asked Axum. Scorch detected an iota of interest in his voice.

"Fire."

"That would make him the first Fire since Elias," Axum whispered. "Untrained, you said?"

"Utterly."

Scorch shifted in his chair, the epitome of awkwardness.

"How has he survived on his own all this time?"

"He was raised in the Guardians' Guild," answered Vivid, and Scorch could sense the caution in his speech. A moment later, the slide of metal releasing from its scabbard rang throughout the room and he felt a cold blade press beneath his chin.

"You brought a *guardian* to the Hollow?" growled Axum.

"He is barely more than an apprentice," Vivid noted with disinterest. If Scorch could see him, he would probably be idly checking beneath his nails for dirt. "Imagine his strength, to have survived so long undetected beneath the Guild's roof. His willpower is impeccable, only he's applied it to suppress instead of express. With the right guidance, he could be a powerful asset. Unless you would rather send him back to the guardians?"

"I have a sword at your throat, boy, and you haven't reached for your own," Axum snapped, addressing Scorch at last. "Why?"

Scorch cleared his throat. "That is an excellent question."

The blade disappeared from his throat. "*That voice,*" Axum whispered before hands ripped the blindfold from Scorch's eyes.

He blinked rapidly, adjusting to the firelight of the room. He couldn't see Vivid, because he was still at his back, but he could see Axum standing right in front of him, his eyes so dark a brown they might have been black. He was tall and thin, with gaunt cheeks and thin eyebrows, and he wore his graying hair slicked back.

"What's your name?" Axum demanded in a manner so forceful that Vivid started squeezing Scorch's shoulder again.

"Scorch," he answered.

Axum stared at him. "That's not your real name."

"It's real enough."

"Where are you from?"

The question made him dizzy as he groped his mind for memories he no longer recalled. "I don't know."

Axum's face was wrought with disbelief. It was a face made for meanness. Severe and humorless. "Your parents. What were their names?"

Scorch felt like he'd been hit in the chest. He looked over his shoulder at Vivid.

"Do you remember?" Vivid asked quietly.

He didn't remember much about his parents, but he remembered their names. He nodded and turned back to Axum, swallowing the lump in his throat. Their names tasted like ashes on his tongue. "Nahla," he said. "And Rosen."

"Gods, it can't be true," Axum whispered, taking a step back. "You look just like her. You sound just like him."

Scorch was silent with shock, but Vivid was not. He released his hold on Scorch's shoulder and stepped up to Axum. "What is this?" he demanded.

"Your complication is no ordinary elemental, Vivid," Axum said. "This is the son of Nahla and Rosen Cole."

"H-how do you know who my parents were?" Scorch asked, dumbfounded.

"Because they were assassins, once upon a time, before the High Priestess had them killed." He strode past Vivid and bent over, putting his face in Scorch's. "You were supposed to be dead. We thought you had burned with them."

Scorch's lips were parted in astonishment. He couldn't speak. The room whirled as Axum's eyes bore into his.

"You should not be alive," Axum whispered.

"Axum," Vivid said, and the air crackled. When the older man did not seem to hear, Vivid repeated himself, this time with such strength that Axum straightened his back to glance at the assassin beside him. "This conversation can be continued at another time, when Scorch has rested. It's been a strenuous journey."

"Yes," Axum said, but his eyes said differently. His eyes said he wanted nothing more than to bludgeon Scorch with thousands of questions he doubtlessly had no answers to. But, at least for the time being, he was willing to suspend his desire. He waved his hand at Vivid. "Set him up with a bed and the like," he directed.

Vivid touched Scorch's shoulder, and just as Scorch had known to sit before, he now knew to stand, though he did so on wavering feet. He must have looked as out of sorts as he felt, because Vivid kept a guiding hand on his elbow as they walked together toward the door.

"Vivid," called Axum, before they could depart his company. "Bring him back to me in the morning. We're not done here."

Vivid nodded once before opening the door and nudging Scorch through.

Scorch followed Vivid in a daze. Now that the blindfold was off, he could finally see the inside of the Hollow, but his head could hardly grasp its incredible architecture. It was a cave, with stone walls, ceilings, and floors, and tunnels leading from one chamber to the next, but it was vast, its edges smoothed, its corners well lit, with colorful tapestries adorning the walls, depicting the elements. It was a cave, but it didn't feel like a cave. It didn't feel like the Guild either.

And Scorch didn't feel like anything. Axum's words numbed him. He'd not spoken the names of his parents aloud in fifteen years, had never known more about them than what a five-year-old child can know, and now, to learn they were assassins? It was too much. He couldn't think about it.

Vivid was leading him to an offset of rooms, neither of them speaking, when his grip tightened inexplicably around Scorch's elbow. A young man was walking toward them with narrow, swaggering hips. He had white-blond hair and a friendly face, but the way Vivid gripped his elbow put Scorch on alert.

"Viv," the man greeted. Vivid tried to walk past him, but they were in a tunnel, and the blond moved to block their passage with a smile on his face. "Gone so long and no hello?"

"Get out of my way," Vivid growled.

"Not until you introduce me to your friend," the blond cooed, casting sparkling blue eyes on Scorch and letting his gaze sweep lazily across his body. "I'm Elias." He extended his hand.

Scorch didn't know what to do, so he did what came naturally. He reached out his hand to shake Elias'. "Scorch," he said, trying his best to sound amiable in spite of his current foggy-headedness. He concentrated on Elias' blue eyes and fair skin. He was good-looking, no doubt about it, and Elias seemed well aware of the fact.

They shook hands, and Elias didn't let him go immediately. He kept Scorch's hand firmly in his own and caressed his wrist with his thumb. His hands were hot, even against Scorch's skin.

"You're a Fire," Scorch breathed.

"I am," Elias replied with another brilliant smile. "I bet you and I have a lot in common, Scorch." His eyes strayed casually to Vivid, who had stopped holding Scorch's elbow and was now poised with readied hands. He looked to be on the verge of unsheathing his daggers. Scorch shot him an incredulous look.

"Let go of him," Vivid rumbled.

Elias gave Scorch's hand a final caress before he released his hold. "Good luck keeping this one to yourself, Viv."

"Scorch, move," Vivid spat, pushing at his back. Scorch brushed shoulders with Elias and the blond winked at him. After all the winking Scorch had done in his life, he'd never been the recipient. He stared after the Fire until Vivid pushed him again, and then he had to turn away to keep from falling over his own feet.

"What was that about?" Scorch asked, the encounter having knocked some of the shock from his head, albeit not entirely.

Vivid refrained from answering and just kept walking until they'd cleared the tunnel. They entered a chamber, empty save for rows and rows of cots. There was no one in the room at the moment, and Scorch wondered if it was a room for guests, or possibly a medical wing, until Vivid plopped down on the cot in the farthest corner. He looked exhausted, an uncanny sight since Vivid never looked anything but unsatisfied and occasionally homicidal.

Scorch lingered in the doorway until Vivid motioned him forward with a tip of his head. He hovered beside a cot, the one next to Vivid's, and when he was met with no disdainful glares or vehement words that he shouldn't pick *that* one, he sat down. It was a cot of efficiency, not comfort, but it felt glorious on his backside, which was raw after days of ceaseless riding. Scorch's thoughts began trailing off to the state of Vivid's backside before he realized that was a bad idea. He raked his fingers through his hair with a troubled sigh. It would be so nice to think of backsides instead of his life, but the information Axum had throttled him with was buzzing mercilessly between his ears. He rested his elbows on his knees and looked up to find Vivid watching him.

"So," Scorch said, "home sweet home?"

"Not home," Vivid corrected. "Just a place to live." Scorch started at the familiar sentiment, but Vivid sailed on with his peculiar brand of detachment. "This is where you will sleep. I'll show you the training rooms tomorrow. We bathe in the falls. There's a food larder, but we don't dine together."

"Cozy."

"Like I said, it's just a place to live. Are you hungry?"

"Ravenous."

"Come on," Vivid said, lifting off the cot.

They walked back through the tunnels, passing several curious assassins on their way to the larder, which was a room lined with shelves, stocked with foodstuffs. Vivid dug his hand in a barrel, resurfacing with two apples. He threw one to Scorch and took a bite out of his own. Juice dribbled down his chin until he wiped it away with the back of his hand. Scorch blushed and studied his boots. He was becoming quite familiar with the stitching around the toes.

"There aren't a lot of people here," Scorch said, rolling the apple between his hands.

"Most are out on assignments," Vivid responded absently, filling two mugs with water from a pitcher.

"Assassin assignments?" he asked with a snort. Vivid nodded solemnly, and Scorch took a sip of the water offered him. "What's it like?"

Vivid was chewing on another bite of apple, his lithe body leaning against a shelf. It wasn't hard to imagine him killing for a living. Even the way he ate his apple looked menacing. When Vivid swallowed, he licked his lips. "You know what it's like."

"I don't."

"You've killed," said Vivid with a heated stare.

Scorch's skin tingled as bloody memories played a loop in his head. "In self-defense, yes," he admitted. It was mostly true. He threw his apple in the air and caught it. "Vivid, did you know who my parents were before you brought me here?"

"No." There was a long silence as they both stared at their apples, and then, quite unexpectedly, Vivid asked Scorch a question. "Do you feel different, now that you know what they were?"

The question was so genuine, so surprising, that Scorch couldn't answer at first, not until he recovered from the shock of Vivid actually asking about Scorch's *feelings*. It was unprecedented and required time to suss out a proper response. Only Scorch had no proper response. He shrugged sadly. "I don't know."

Vivid finished his water. "You should sleep. I'll be waking you early."

Scorch clutched his uneaten apple to his chest, finished his mug of water, and followed Vivid from the larder. When they reached the room of cots, Scorch sat down and toed off his boots.

"Eat," Vivid ordered gruffly, "and then sleep."

"What are you going to do?" Scorch asked, since the other man was still lingering in the entryway.

"That's my business."

Vivid disappeared from view and Scorch collapsed onto the thin mattress. He ached all over, but the ache in his heart was the worst. He mulled over Axum's words and thought of his parents. He knew they had been elementals, but assassins? What had they been doing, living out in the woods all those years? If Scorch's mom and dad had frequented the Hollow, why did Scorch have no memories of it? If they were assassins, how had they let themselves be killed?

He ignored his tears and bit angrily into his apple. He'd hoped to find answers with the assassins. He'd not expected to find more questions.

# *Fires*
# *13*

Scorch couldn't sleep. He tossed fitfully on the cot. Several times, he reached for the Dream Moss, but before he could fit the stem between his lips, more burdensome thoughts would weigh him down, thoughts he couldn't ignore, so he lay awake, dwelling.

Hours later, as he turned to his side, his sword beside him on the creaking cot, a single figure appeared in the doorway, slim and shadowed. At first, he thought it was Vivid, but as the figure moved closer with sauntering feet and swaggering hips, the candlelight illuminated white hair and teeth, and Elias came to kneel beside Scorch's bedside.

Scorch blinked at him.

"Can't sleep?" Elias asked. His eyes blazed in the candlelight, blue as the hottest fire.

"I have a lot on my mind."

Elias observed him with a tilt of his head that sent his silken hair sparkling across his forehead. "Need a distraction?"

Scorch was at a momentary loss, too tired to interpret the sly quirk of Elias' full mouth and the heavy lids of his eyes, but when

Elias placed a hot hand on Scorch's hip, he understood quite clearly.

"No," Scorch said at once. "Thanks."

If Elias was disappointed, he masked it well. "Suit yourself." He stood sleekly from his bended knee and slinked to a cot not far from Scorch's. He must have assumed he was being watched, because he readied himself for bed like a man on display, slowly removing his shirt and leaning down with his backside to Scorch to unlace his shiny black boots. Scorch watched—of course, he watched—but he felt removed from the exhibition of skin.

When Elias finally settled down on his cot, Scorch rolled onto his back and stared at the ceiling. Maybe he should have taken Elias up on his offer, but he felt too full to spend himself on such a shallow toss. Scorch of the Guild would have bedded him already. Distracted himself. Fallen to sleep sated.

He didn't fall asleep that night until much later, when a second figure ghosted into the room and found the cot beside Scorch. He didn't undress, take off his boots, or make any noise at all, but he waited a long time before blowing out the candle between their mattresses. Scorch's eyes were shut, but he could sense a heavy glare pressing against him. Vivid was watching him sleep.

Only when the candle was blown out with a gust of summoned air did Scorch dare open his eyes. Vivid, on the cot beside him, lifted something to his lips, taking it into his mouth to chew. Scorch reached into his pocket for an ivory stem and did the same, and after the rise and fall of Vivid's chest became deep and rhythmical, Scorch was finally able to close his eyes and sleep.

*Wind whirled around them, a cyclone of star leaves and snow. Fingers were fisting his hair. Palms were squeezing his temples.*

*He was roiling, smoldering fire on the inside, but outside was amethyst and the night sky.*

*"I thought you weren't a coward," the thunder rumbled in his ear.*

*"I'm not."*

*"Prove it," challenged the thunder, and the fingers twining through his hair pulled him forward.*

*He set his hands on a trim waist, could feel heat seeping through leather, filling them both. The air grew warm, hot, high on the mountain. He leaned forward and pressed his lips to black, shining hair.*

*"I don't have time for this."*

*He caught the wind in his hands and held it close to his chest. "Stay." He kissed a pale throat. "Stay."*

*"Scorch." His name came like a summons from soft, bitten lips. "Scorch."*

"Scorch, wake up."

He woke, rubbing at his eyes and groaning. When he could focus, he found Vivid standing over him, arms crossed, looking displeased, with a sprinkling of concern. Only a sprinkling, mind, and it only revealed itself in the faint line between severe eyebrows.

"You've neglected your Dream Moss," Vivid said sternly.

"No, I didn't," Scorch insisted, but the sudden awareness of tightness in the snug confines of his trousers silenced him. He bundled his blanket over himself.

"Don't lie. I heard you."

And for some reason, some inexplicable reason, probably from a desire to instill trust—with an assassin of all people—Scorch said, "I took the Dream Moss."

"You were moaning. You sounded troubled."

Scorch couldn't fight the blush. "It . . . wasn't a bad dream."

"Then why—" Vivid's eyes widened, and he turned away from Scorch to straighten the blankets on his cot that were already straightened. "Get up. Axum is expecting you."

Scorch shifted on the cot. "Right. Just, erm, give me a second."

Vivid mumbled something unintelligible and headed out of the room, leaving Scorch alone. He sighed, willing away the evidence of his dream. He could see Vivid's shadow in the tunnel outside the sleeping chamber, waiting for him. He could also see the cot where Elias had slept; he had left his covers unmade.

When the danger had passed, Scorch stood from the cot and straightened his blankets, copying the way Vivid had folded down the corners, and then he belted his sword around his waist and met him in the doorway. Vivid avoided eye contact and headed down the tunnel as soon as Scorch reached his side.

The Assassins' Hollow was livelier than it had been the night before, or maybe Scorch's head was merely clear enough to notice the smattering of surly, stealthy men and women roaming the vast chambers, all of them in black leathers similar to Vivid's. They passed a woman with an eye patch and honey brown hair. Her top was sleeveless, exposing lean muscles and inked skin.

"Vivid. Thought I saw a handsome man sleeping in the cot next to you," she said, falling in line at Vivid's side as they walked. Her voice was smoky and deep, and Scorch knew she was the woman he'd heard the day before.

Vivid didn't acknowledge her past the twitch of an eyebrow, but neither did he tell her to go away, which might as well have been an invitation to join them.

"Axum decided not to kill you, I see," she continued, looking at Scorch with her one eye. It was dark blue.

"I didn't realize that was on the table," said Scorch, glancing at Vivid.

"There's only one reason why Axum would let you stay," she said.

"You're right. It was because of my good looks."

"Elemental?"

He looked at her, not knowing if there would ever come a time in his life when the casual mention of his elemental powers didn't make his forehead bead with sweat.

Vivid spoke, filling the void of Scorch's pause. "Fire."

Her face lit up. "Fire? No wonder Elias was pissed off this morning."

They stopped at the threshold of the tunnel that led, if Scorch's shoddy memory served, to Axum's chamber. Vivid had a hardness to him, even more than usual, and when he addressed the woman, it was with a strained voice. "We have a meeting."

"Say no more." She strutted in the opposite direction, pulling a dagger from her thigh holster and twirling it in her hand.

"Who was that?" Scorch asked, his eyes following her retreat with fascination.

"Audrey," Vivid growled, already continuing down the tunnel. They stopped outside Axum's chamber. Vivid turned to Scorch, looked to be on the verge of speaking, and then Axum opened the door.

"Good," the assassin leader said. "Come in."

He stood aside as Scorch entered, but before Vivid could pass, he moved his body to impede his path. If Vivid had any respect for the man who was, theoretically, in charge, it didn't show in his eyes as he glared up at him.

"You are needed in the southern training room," Axum informed Vivid with a cold stare.

Scorch watched Vivid's expression darken over Axum's shoulder. His shoulders tensed and his eyes flashed to Scorch's for an instant, and then he nodded and turned away. Axum shut the door, and Scorch felt very much out of his element. It had been a long time since he'd been separated from Vivid and it gnawed at his nerves more than it rightfully should have.

"Fire," said Axum, turning from the closed door and leaning his back against it.

"I prefer Scorch, actually."

"But that's not your real name."

"No."

Axum's grey-speckled hair was slicked back, neater and cleaner than it had looked the night before, and he wore the same obscenely tight leather the other assassins were fond of. Everything about the man warned that he cut like glass.

"You have questions, I imagine."

"I imagine you have questions for me, too," said Scorch.

"I do." Axum waved his hand to the space at the center of the dim chamber. Two overstuffed chairs sat across from one another on a fur rug. Scorch wrinkled his nose at the sight of the rug. It was a white, silky animal skin. "Sit with me and we will see if we cannot satisfy one another's curiosity."

Scorch sat, squishing deep into the lush cushion. It was dangerously comfortable, but he strove to keep his back straight and his shoulders squared and his chin aloft. Axum graced the chair opposite him, crossing his legs so that his foot came to an idle suspension, inches away from Scorch's knee.

"Did you sleep well?" Axum asked.

"What is this place?" Scorch blustered, his hands moving before him, indicating absolutely everything.

Axum settled his own hands on the armrests of his chair, his pointer finger creating small circles in the velvety upholstery. The rest of him was still. Even his blinks were used sparingly. He was a sinister composition of a man. After a moment, he said, "Vivid doesn't like people."

"He likes animals."

"Maybe that is why he likes you." Scorch's heart thumped harder. "Elementals are rare. Fire elementals are the rarest. Do you know why?"

Scorch was too busy reeling over the fact that Axum said Vivid *liked* him to comment, but Axum didn't wait long before filling in his own blanks.

"Fires are the hardest to contain. Their powers are the most volatile. Makes it more likely they will be found out, more likely they will be killed. When the Queen passed her ordinances and the High Priestess started sending out her monks to hunt us down, it was the Fires' numbers that dwindled the fastest. That you remained hidden amongst the guardians for so long makes you special, but then, your parents were skilled at going unseen, as well."

The mention of his parents stirred his blood. "My parents, the assassins," he said. It didn't sound right and he felt his brow scrunch unhappily. "What can you tell me about them?"

"Quite a lot. Rosen and Nahla helped form this Hollow," Axum began. "After the ordinances, elementals were being murdered en masse. It was no longer safe for us out there, so we made our own place in here, remained hidden in an environment where we could hone our powers."

"But you're assassins."

"Even monsters have to make a living," answered Axum. "What better way to do that than by killing humans who would just as quickly kill us? Your mother was raised by a crew of assassins, knew the workings, knew the circuit, the higher ups. So we formed our own faction, taking in elementals when we could, taking out humans when the price was right."

"You say 'humans' like it's a dirty word," Scorch said. "I'm human."

"You are an elemental," Axum corrected. "And a powerful one at that, if I had to wager."

Scorch shook his head. "You keep saying that, but it's not true. I have no control."

"You need a harness to learn, like any other wild thing," Axum said. "The assassins can be your harness."

"Why? So you can use me to hurt other people?"

"So I can use your powers to help *our* people. The majority of our assignments deal in the eradication of those trying to eradicate us. I assume it did not escape your notice that Vivid was on such an assignment when you . . . *complicated* things."

In sharp bursts of color, Scorch saw the High Priestess' body going limp as Vivid snapped her neck, and the way he'd looked at Scorch after, as if he wasn't sure whether to kill him or free him.

"He killed the High Priestess," Scorch whispered. He wondered if the rest of Viridor knew of her death yet. They had heard no tale of it during their trek to the Hollow, but they had steered clear of the bulk of civilization and hadn't exactly chatted up the few locals they did encounter.

"He did. And the world will be a better place for us now that she is dead," Axum said.

Scorch wasn't sure if he could argue that one. He certainly harbored no love for her, her temple, or her monks. The thought of Kio made his insides churn, but he knew that soon her memory would be just another scar, tender if he poked at it, but easy to ignore if he left it alone.

"Scorch," Axum said. "I'd like for you to join us here. Train, learn who you are and what you can do."

"I won't kill people," Scorch said. "I don't want to. I want to protect them."

Axum held up a hand, the biggest gesture he'd made since sitting. "When the time comes for an assignment of your own, we can discuss it then, but for now, take advantage of what I am offering you. If we had known you were alive, we would have come for you fifteen years ago." He leaned forward in his chair. "This is where you have always belonged, Scorch, where you were meant to be raised."

*Then why did my parents take me away? Why did we live in the woods?*

Scorch sighed, feeling helpless. Maybe his parents would have wanted him to be an assassin, but it was Vivid's insistence he come to the Hollow that made him nod his head in agreement.

"That is the right choice," Axum assured as they stood from their chairs, though neither his tone nor presence lent any feelings of assurance. "Report to Elias to begin your training."

"Elias?"

"He is the only other Fire here," Axum retorted. "Who better to teach you? I assume you've met?"

"He introduced himself last night."

"Then you should have no trouble locating him." When Scorch stalled, Axum crossed the length of the floor and opened the door for him. "Now."

Scorch decided he didn't care much for Axum as he exited his chambers. He could feel black-brown eyes following his descent down the tunnel and he exhaled only when he heard the door finally close. He'd hoped Vivid would be waiting for him, but he was absent in the cavernous rooms as Scorch searched halfheartedly for white-blond hair.

Axum had told Vivid to report to a southern training room, and after a befuddling few minutes of trying to find it on his own, Scorch tapped on the shoulder of the first assassin he saw without a knife in their hand.

"Southern training room?" he asked politely, and the woman jerked her head to the left, toward a tunnel where the torches were all blown out. "Of course it's down the dark tunnel. Thanks." He was turning for the tunnel when someone, in turn, tapped him on the shoulder. He spun around and was met with a wide smile.

"Good morning," Elias said. He wore his hair stylishly mussed and had the sort of face that looked incapable of growing facial hair, perfectly clear and smooth. He wore the black leather garb of the other assassins, but there was considerably less of it today than there had been last night. His vest was snug, with no tunic beneath, and his trousers hung too low on his hips, exposing a strip of skin around his middle. His boots were a shiny obsidian-black, and his eyes twinkled an impish blue. "Looking for me?"

"Looking for Vivid," Scorch answered.

"Why would you do a thing like that?" Elias leaned in a touch too close. "Axum said I was to train you. Be a good boy and follow me."

Miffed, but at a loss of how to finagle an escape, Scorch found himself trekking after Elias' swaying hips. They passed Audrey on their journey, who glared at them both, and then they came to a stop in a wide-berthed room that Elias explained was the eastern training room. It was a circular, domed space with carvings on the walls of dancing flames. The room was sparsely filled, but there were a handful of items, such as a standing torch, a row of small white candles, and a great tub of water.

"Don't worry, I'm not planning on giving you a bath," Elias laughed. "Not right now, anyway. It's a safety precaution. In case it gets too hot."

Scorch walked slowly around the space, stopping to examine the flames carved into the cave wall. He could feel Elias step up behind him, felt his heat signature seeping into his own.

"So, Scorch, word is you're repressed."

"I had to be," Scorch defended, turning around to face the other elemental. "I would have died otherwise."

"Hmm. What *can* you do?"

Scorch considered the extent of his powers. "Well, I get overheated and sweat a lot."

"Those aren't powers. Those are symptoms of you denying yourself."

"Sometimes," Scorch admitted hesitantly, "my fingers spark. Things I touch can burst into flame. Or melt."

"Charming." Elias sauntered toward the standing torch. "Could you light this?"

"No," Scorch said with a shake of his head. "I can't control it."

"I wonder. Do you know what happens to Fires with pent up power?"

"I do," he replied, imagining a broad span of leathery wings and fire ripping from his throat.

Elias stared into his eyes, and his lips quirked into a grin, as if he could see the images playing in Scorch's mind. "We change. Become beasts, slaves to the fire."

Scorch frowned. He'd not felt like a slave when he'd changed in the desert or on the mountaintop. Rather, he had felt free for the first time in his life. It felt good, exhilarating, to let the fire take hold of him from the inside out.

"I bet your beast is beautiful," Elias sighed, his gaze shamelessly drinking in Scorch's frame from tip to toe. "But until you choose when to release him, it's still a beast, and that puts not only you, but those around you in danger." He gestured to the torch. "Light this."

"I told you," Scorch said with a frustrated sigh. "I can't."

Elias held out his hand. "Come." Scorch looked doubtfully at his offered hand before reluctantly accepting it. Elias tugged him close and whispered in his ear. "What if I told you what Vivid was up to last night when you were tossing and turning in bed?"

Scorch tried to move away, but Elias held him tight. "That's his business, not mine," he argued, his wrist trapped in Elias' hot grip.

"He was with me. It doesn't make your blood boil, thinking of sweet Vivid on his back?"

Scorch was disgusted by Elias' crudeness. "That's not true."

"No? Can't you picture all that pretty pale skin laid out beneath me? He makes the sweetest sounds."

Scorch felt his skin sizzle beneath Elias' touch. A pinprick of sweat dripped from his hairline and he sucked in a lungful of burning air. "I know what you're trying to do. Make me angry so I'll lose control."

"And look at you, fighting it so well. I guess jealousy isn't a strong enough trigger."

"Because I'm not jealous," Scorch claimed, but Elias only laughed and increased the pressure on his wrist. Scorch tried to wrench himself free, but the other man was ready for the attempt, sliding up his arm and rotating it with a quick heave. Scorch cried out and dropped to his knees.

Elias smirked, standing over him with his arm twisted behind his back. "Is it rage that breaks you? Do you think your parents were angry when they were chopped into bits?" He pulled back on Scorch's arm.

Scorch sobbed in pain. He saw his parents through the leaves. "Elias, stop, please."

"Did you know a Fire can't burn unless we're already dead?" asked Elias casually. "Then we melt and spit and cook just like any ordinary human. Ever smell roasted human flesh? Is that how mom and dad smelled when their bodies burned?"

Scorch's insides were boiling and his fingertips were as hot as the tears leaking down his face. "Please stop," he begged.

"ELIAS," a voice roared, and a second later, the hold on Scorch's arm released, and he fell to the floor with a grunt. He rolled over, clutching at his sore arm, and saw Vivid standing over him, his dark hair blowing back from his face with an invisible wind.

"I don't appreciate you interrupting our training session," Elias said right before he was backhanded across the face.

"Get out," Vivid snarled. His voice was two thunderclouds colliding.

From his position on the floor, Scorch's vision was filled with lethal forces. And leather. To his right was Vivid, eyes storming and fingers itching to release the twin daggers from his forearms. To his left was Elias, the air around him hazy with heat.

"Axum asked *me* to train him," Elias sneered.

"Let me worry about Axum," said Vivid. "Get out before I remove you myself."

Elias licked his lips and Scorch realized his lower lip had split from Vivid's blow. It was shiny with blood. "Oh, Viv," he whispered. "Please get rough with me."

Scorch felt foolish lying on his back while all of this unfolded, but he was also worried that if he made a sudden movement, either Elias or Vivid would strike at him on instinct, so he remained on his back, breathing hard as the two elementals stared at each other with pure venom.

After thirty seconds of competitive glowering, Elias barked a laugh that reminded Scorch—with a rush of nausea—of Ebbins. "Fine, fine. But I'm telling Axum."

"Good," said Vivid. "Save me the trip."

Elias stepped back, glancing down at Scorch with a wink. "I got you on your back," he laughed, and then he left the training room.

The temperature decreased immediately at his departure and Scorch took several deep breaths to steady his racing heartbeat and cool the too-hot blood swimming through his veins. A cool breeze swept the damp hair from his forehead and he looked up at Vivid.

"Awful drafty in here."

Predictably, Vivid said nothing, but he was staring down at Scorch with huge eyes. Scorch exhaled slowly and sat up. He rolled his hurt arm and was relieved to find it fine, except for the mild ache. He did not wait for Vivid to offer him a hand, and he did not ask for one. He stood up on his own.

"He wanted me to light the torch."

"He wanted to humiliate you."

"He thought if he upset me, I would be able to light it." Scorch looked down at his boots. They really were a comely shade of red.

"Look at me."

Scorch made himself meet Vivid's eyes. They were standing closer than he'd realized, and despite Vivid's shorter stature, his presence was strong and solid and sure. Vivid held up his hand, palm up, and for a baffling moment, Scorch thought he wanted him to take it. But before he had the chance to humiliate himself, Vivid lifted his hand, curling his fingers into a fist, and a strong wind made Scorch stagger back. Before he could fall, another buffer of wind came at him from behind. An updraft made his hair puff out around his face and, for a moment, his feet didn't touch the ground.

"Gods," Scorch whispered. The wind set him gently back on the ground before it died.

The wind had rustled Vivid's hair, and his eyes were intense, lending him a vaguely feral appearance. "Torture doesn't compel one to do their best work. Neither does bottling everything up and waiting for it to explode. You will learn to summon your power without the aid of distress, and I will teach you. Do you understand?"

*I don't understand any of this.* "But shouldn't I be taught by another Fire?"

"What happens to a fire that's been caught by the wind?"

Scorch pictured the desert, when he'd blown a stream of flame from his belly and the wind had spread it far across the sand. A small smile spread his lips. "Air makes fire stronger," he said. *You make me stronger.*

"I'll teach you," Vivid repeated.

"What about Axum?" Scorch wondered whether Elias was already with the assassin leader. "He was adamant Elias be the one."

"Because Elias requested you last night," said Vivid, his voice dipping dangerously low. "And like an idiot, Axum agreed, despite my arguments."

"Is that where you were all night?" asked Scorch, his heart adopting a quicker rhythm. "Fighting over me?"

Vivid looked bemused by the inquiry. "I doubted Elias' methods would be conducive to higher learning, considering your extreme ignorance and over-sensitivity."

"Right. So you were fighting over me?" Scorch was smiling and Vivid was surly, but wasn't that always the way of it? "You're going to teach me how to be a big bad elemental, Vivid?" Vivid's name felt pleasant in his mouth, and he vowed to find more opportunity to use it.

Vivid's nostrils flared in annoyance. "Yes."

"Great," said Scorch. "When do we start?"

"Now, if you ever stop talking."

In the wake of Elias quitting the room, Vivid tried to teach Scorch how to use his elemental powers. It was so unsuccessful that, by the end of the day, Scorch felt near to tears with exhaustive failure and Vivid's eyebrows were ragged from an intensive workout of furrowing in dismay at Scorch's lack of anything pertaining to skill. Without imminent danger or mind-boggling rage, he couldn't rummage even the smallest of sparks.

When they left the training room, Vivid saw that Scorch ate dinner, and then he marched him to his cot, watching like a hawk until Scorch had chewed his Dream Moss.

Scorch dreamt again, not of mountaintop embraces, but of an unlit wick, desperate to be ignited.

# *A Study in Wind*
# *14*

The next day was not an improvement.

Scorch and Vivid returned to the eastern training room, passing Elias on the way. He wore a wicked smile on his face and winked at Scorch, but said nothing. Vivid had disappeared again the night before, when he thought Scorch was sleeping, and Scorch could only assume he'd gone to see Axum. Since Vivid didn't mention the particulars, Scorch assumed he had gotten his way. By the look on Elias' face, Elias had *not*.

"Sit," Vivid instructed when they entered the training room.

Scorch took a seat on the hard floor and watched as Vivid gathered a single white candle and placed it between them. He sat across from Scorch, his face a mask of sternness, and Scorch wondered what it would have been like if Vivid had been one of his instructors at the Guild. He probably would have been an apprentice forever, if only because Vivid was so distracting that he'd never absorb his lessons. At present, he tried not to be too distracted by the assassin, but it was hard, because Vivid kept biting at his lower lip and glowering behind a rascally strand of hair.

"Elemental abilities don't usually present until one has reached pubescence," Vivid lectured, already sounding bored. "When you presented for the first time, you changed, as is normal, and became Fire in its purest physical form."

"During my hunting test," Scorch confirmed.

"A lucky coincidence that you were isolated when it happened," said Vivid. "After that, how did your powers progress?"

He thought back to that shaky, frightening time, when he had been so afraid of changing back into that thing that he cut himself off from everyone. On the inside, at least. On the outside, he formed his happy, boastful shell. "Slowly," he told Vivid. "I would feel it swelling up in me, re-gathering, and then it would burst out in tiny, unexpected moments. I set our herbalist's garden on fire, the Master's laundry. The occasional spark would set the occasional fire. People thought I was a fire starter." He laughed and it was bitter. "I guess I was. Am."

"Yet you managed to refrain from experiencing another outburst blatant enough to get you caught. Difficult for any untrained elemental to do, especially a Fire. How did you do it?"

Scorch couldn't look at Vivid's open stare any longer, so he lowered his gaze to the unlit candle between them. "I don't know," he answered honestly. "I take deep breaths when I feel it happening, try to cool down." He could see Vivid's fingers tapping against his knee.

"How do you feel now?" Vivid asked.

"Well, my life hasn't been in danger."

"That you're aware of," said Vivid. "How did you feel when you were hunting?"

Scorch was unused to Vivid asking him so many questions, and he couldn't deny the entire situation had him flustered. "My hunting test?" he asked, trying to think. "I felt a little nervous. But I was confident, the best of my age with a bow. I had no idea what was going to happen."

"And yet it happened, all the same." Vivid slid the candle an inch toward Scorch. "Your life wasn't in danger and it still happened, because one is not linked to the other. You can summon your power just as well right now as you could if I held a dagger to your throat."

"Yeah," Scorch laughed anxiously, "because I know you wouldn't kill me."

Vivid glared at him. "You're confident in all the wrong ways."

Scorch shrugged.

"You can light that candle as easily as I can steal the breath from your lungs," Vivid said. "The only difference between us is that I have the confidence to do it and you don't."

"Bit of a height difference, too, I think."

Scorch didn't light the candle that day, nor the day after that, and the only confidence he gained was in his ability to get a cramp in his leg from sitting all day, staring at a candle. But on the fourth day of his training, Vivid walked right past the tunnel leading to the eastern training room. He led them outside instead, and Audrey went with them, a bow slung over her shoulder.

Scorch gulped the fresh air with a smile and a relaxed roll of his shoulders. He had gone far too long without sunlight. The waterfall's mist made his hair go damp as they navigated down the rocks, Audrey and Vivid on dainty assassin feet, and Scorch slipping only the once, of which he was embarrassingly proud.

"Think the fresh air might improve my confidence?" Scorch asked, enjoying the sights of the forest.

"I think it will improve your smell," Vivid said. "You've not bathed since we arrived."

Scorch's face flashed hot. "It's not like I've had time. We've been staring at candles all day, every day."

Vivid swept the hair from his eyes with a hoity huff. "Our schedules have been identical and I have found time every day to clean myself." Scorch's mouth hung open stupidly as he imagined Vivid sneaking off to bathe beneath the waterfall, his skin glowing in the moonlight, shimmering with beads of water.

Audrey, who had, up until that point, been listening patiently, lifted her hands in the air and water from the pool began to rise. Scorch watched the mass of droplets float over their heads, and then, before he knew it was happening, she released them in a downpour. Scorch was soaked, Vivid was soaked, and Audrey was soaked.

"Audrey is a Water, by the way," mumbled Vivid as he shook out his wet hair.

"And she is capable of speaking for herself when the two of you aren't bickering," Audrey sniped. "Scorch, since you're already wet, why don't you get clean while Vivid dries our clothes. The water's nice, in case you didn't notice."

Scorch frowned, looking at Vivid. "You can air-dry clothes?"

Vivid's stare was impenetrable.

"There were a few times in the Heartlands when I could have used some air-drying, you know," Scorch said testily.

"It was tempting to reveal my greatest secret to a perfect stranger but somehow I resisted."

"So you thought I was perfect?" Scorch asked before stripping off his clothing, which had Vivid turning around to speak with Audrey about something direly important. Scorch smirked, dipping his toe into the pool, and then he jumped in with what he hoped was an obnoxious splash.

The water was crisp and cool and he really should have thought to bathe days ago. What was wrong with him? Had he grown so used to Vivid telling him what to do that, without specific instructions, he'd let himself ruminate in his own musk for a substantial amount of time? He dunked his head and scrubbed at his hair, then let himself bob along the surface, watching Vivid and Audrey conversing in the distance. Scorch squinted. Were they already dry?

He floated around for several enjoyable minutes before getting out, hesitating at the water's edge as he looked around for his wet clothes. Audrey murmured something to Vivid, whose back was still turned, and, without looking, he tossed Scorch's clothes over his shoulder. They landed at his feet, dry. Did Vivid have to touch his clothing to dry it? Did he have his hands all over his *underthings*? Scorch banished the thought and piled his clothes on in a hurry, which proved mildly uncomfortable, considering his skin was still damp.

"Okay, I'm as clean as I'm going to get," Scorch announced.

Vivid nodded and began walking away from the waterfall. Scorch hurried to catch up, walking in stride beside Audrey. He snuck a look at her; she was staring straight ahead, as Vivid was wont to do. Real personable, these assassins.

"Not that I mind the ravishing company," Scorch said to her, "but Vivid and I have always done this alone."

Audrey didn't turn her head as she walked. "I'm here in case you set anything on fire you're not supposed to."

"That's optimistic."

After walking for about ten minutes, Vivid stopped and turned to him. "You're going to catch us our dinner." He motioned to Audrey, who handed Scorch the bow. He took it, running his fingers along the smooth yew wood.

"Am I meant to shoot flaming arrows or something?" Scorch asked wryly as Audrey passed him the quiver.

"You're meant to do as I say," Vivid retorted. "Go. Hunt. But keep within a one mile radius."

"You're not coming with me?"

"No," was Vivid's answer. "Off you go."

Scorch secured the quiver to his back and headed into the forest, where streaks of sunlight dappled through the branches and cast an enchanting glow. It had been a while since he wandered on his own, and the bow in his grip lent him courage, confidence. He was far removed from that boy of thirteen.

Scorch did as Vivid instructed and kept within a mile of the great oak they'd stopped beneath. At first, he merely enjoyed the green perfume of the air and the scenery of giant, vine covered trees, and then he began to hush his steps and perk up his ears for animals. He spotted a furry red squirrel in a branch overhead and shot it a smile. It made a chirpy little squirrel sound and threw an acorn at his head. He frowned at the furry creature but moved on. He would not kill for petty revenge, and besides, who wanted to eat squirrel for dinner? Scorch remembered that Vivid was fond of rabbit, so he began searching the forest floor. Within half an hour, he had three hares.

When he returned to the oak, Vivid and Audrey had a fire going. Scorch sat down beside Vivid and handed him his bounty.

"I thought you would want me to start the cooking fire with my powers," Scorch said, nodding at the flames.

"Maybe, if I had no intention of eating," Vivid replied, "but I'm hungry." He took up the hares and walked away from the fire to skin them, a skill at which he was unsurprisingly proficient.

Audrey accepted the skinned hares, skewering them with sharpened sticks and settling them over the fire to roast. Vivid returned to sitting beside him and Scorch was reminded of the night they spent in the cave, with their little fire and the Mountain Flower Whiskey. He felt that same warmth in his stomach, too, only now it wasn't manufactured by Kio's deviousness.

The fire crackled as their dinner cooked, and though the three elementals spoke rarely, the silence was not uncomfortable; it was peaceful. After they ate, Scorch was pleasantly full and a little sleepy. It was an unexpected turn of events when Vivid took his hand and pressed something into his palm.

He examined the silver leaves against his skin, the leaves of Dream Moss. "I thought you chewed the stems."

"The leaves are also edible," Vivid explained.

"And you want me to eat this?" asked Scorch.

"I do," Vivid said, "but you should know that it's a mild hallucinogenic. It will make your mind bend in new ways."

Scorch held the silver leaf up to his lips. "I'm not going to wake up surrounded by monks, am I?"

Vivid's expression was blank, but Scorch thought he could detect a minute tensing of his shoulders, and he didn't like that, so without further questioning, he popped the leaf into his mouth. It tasted sweet and musky, and he let it sit on his tongue for a moment before giving it a brief chew and swallowing it down.

"So," he said, leaning back on his hands, "what's a hallucinogenic?"

The realization came upon him gradually, like a sunrise, while he was staring at the fire. A hand moved in front of the flames, and he thought it was his mother's hand. He smiled and turned to look at her, but Vivid was there instead.

"Vivid," he whispered. "Vivid." He liked to say that name, but he liked looking into the fire even more, so he returned his eyes to the flickering orange blaze. The hand passed over it again, but when he traced it down from wrist to forearm to soul, he saw it was his own. "She made it look so easy," he said to no one. "She would just," he waved his hand before the fire, "and the kindling would ignite."

Vivid moved closer. "You can do that, too," he told him. His voice was a whisper, but it felt to Scorch as if it echoed off all the trees of the forest, just to end up brushing against his ears.

"I can?"

"Lift your hand," Vivid said, and Scorch lifted his hand, fingers relaxed, palm facing the fire. He waved it back and forth. Nothing happened. A moment later, his other hand was holding something and his entire body felt light as a breeze. He waved his hand and the flame jumped, surging high in the air before returning to its normal height.

"*Gods*!" Scorch squeezed the object in his other hand, but when he looked down, he discovered it was not an object at all, but Vivid's hand. "Can we do it again?" he asked, glancing up at Vivid with pupil-blown eyes.

Vivid nodded and Scorch held his hand tight. He lifted his other hand and waved it confidently in front of the flames. They leapt into the air, higher than before. He laughed raucously, deliriously, and jumped to his feet, pulling Vivid with him. Vivid freed himself from his grip.

"Try again, without my help," he ordered, crossing his arms across his chest to keep his hands hidden.

Scorch felt a twinge of disappointment, but did as Vivid asked, giving the fire another sweep with his hand. The flames leapt, but not as high. He turned to Vivid, swelling with pride, but Vivid wasn't smiling, and he wanted him to smile. Scorch knew he had to light something else on fire, something that wasn't already burning, and then Vivid would smile. He gave a dramatic wave to a nearby bush and it burst into flames.

"Audrey," Vivid sighed, and the Water lifted both her hands in the air. One moment, Scorch was watching the fire spread from the bush to the brush beside it, and the next, it was pouring rain. The fire went out beneath the torrent, both on the bush and their campfire, and Vivid sulked like a wet cat. "You could have just doused it," he said.

Audrey gave Vivid a look with her one eye and said, unapologetically, "He likes to start fires, *I* like to get wet." She lifted her face to the rain and Scorch laughed.

Vivid looked up at Scorch and took his hand. They ran through the forest, the rain following them, and Vivid cursed at Audrey as she made it fall even harder. By the time they reached the shelter of rocks behind the waterfall, they were drenched to the bone. Scorch leaned breathlessly against the stones and Vivid dropped his hand. A whirl of wind kicked up around them, blowing them dry, and then Vivid grabbed Scorch's chin and directed his gaze.

"Your pupils are huge," he noted.

"Yours are big, too," Scorch sighed, staring unabashedly into Vivid's eyes. It was true; his pupils were large and black as he looked up at Scorch, but Scorch hadn't seen him take any of the Dream Moss leaf.

"I'm freezing," Audrey announced, opening the door of the tunnel. "Can you stare at each other inside, where it's warmer?"

Vivid dropped his hand from Scorch's face immediately and followed her inside. Scorch, still dazed, floated behind them. The torches lighting the cave chambers flickered with potential, and Scorch fancied it looked like they were waving to him. The trip to the cots was blurry, but he thought they might have passed Elias on the way there. He remembered blue eyes swimming in his vision, followed by a tug on his wrist as he was led quickly down a tunnel.

When he finally sat on his cot, he collapsed onto his back with a sigh. The ceiling was fuzzy, but in a wonderful, soft, happy way, and then he saw Vivid's face leaning over him, and that was soft and wonderful, too. Vivid held out an ivory stem and Scorch parted his lips for it. Vivid's eyebrows knitted together disapprovingly, but after a few second's hesitation, he placed it between Scorch's lips, carefully avoiding any physical touch. Scorched chewed at the stem with a smug grin.

"Go to sleep, Scorch," Vivid said, and then his face disappeared from view. Scorch could hear the cot beside his creaking. He shut his eyes, his fingers flexing excitedly.

A wall in his chest had been beaten until it crumbled, and now he could walk over the wreckage and see beyond. He fell asleep thinking about the fire leaping, and the way, when Scorch had squeezed Vivid's hand, Vivid had squeezed back.

The next day, Vivid herded Scorch to the eastern training room and wasted no time directing him in front of the tiny white candles. Scorch lifted his hand before he could second-guess himself, and the middle candle flickered to life, a small flame dancing on the wick. Vivid caught his eye, and though he didn't smile, his lips quirked. By the end of the day, the entire row of candles was lit, as well as the standing torch. Scorch was proud of himself, and he thought Vivid was proud too, at least a little.

The following day was considerably less pleasant. It began when Scorch woke to fingers brushing the hair off his forehead. He stretched languidly, opening his eyes. When he saw Elias sitting on his cot, he nearly threw himself off the mattress.

"Don't be scared," Elias breezed. "I only wanted to say hi. I can't do that when your watchdog is constantly sniffing around." He crossed his hands in his lap. "How is training coming along?"

Scorch wanted to leap from the cot, but he also didn't want to give Elias the satisfaction of perturbing him out of his bed. He braced himself and tried to appear relaxed. "It's going well, thanks."

"Good, good," said Elias, gratified. "And how do you find working beneath our dear Viv? Is he gentle with you? Does he take it slow?"

Scorch felt his fingertips growing hot. "You're obsessed with him," he hissed. There went acting unperturbed.

"Ouch." Elias held a hand to his chest in artificial upset. "Am I obsessed? I'm not sure. *You* are the one who calls out his name at night." At Scorch's widening eyes, Elias laughed. "And before you ask, yes," he leaned in close, his lips scraping Scorch's ear, "he's heard you."

Scorch blanched, pulling back to study Elias' face, but it was impossible to tell if he was lying. Vivid had already heard Scorch moaning in his sleep. It wasn't outside the realm of possibility that he overheard something else, was it?

"Let me give you some advice," Elias said. "Vivid is pretty, but he's hardly worth the effort." His fingers grazed Scorch's jaw, which was prickled anew with blond shadow, and Scorch wrenched back his head and caught his wrist. It only made Elias' smile widen. "I know you, Scorch," he whispered, "and he won't be able to give you what you need."

Scorch threw his wrist away and sprang from the cot with fire in his step. "You don't know me. And I don't think you know Vivid, either."

Elias made himself comfortable on the thin mattress, folding his arms behind his head and leaning back on the pillow. "I bet I know him better than you do," he said with a wink.

Scorch disliked him immensely in that moment, not only because of his rude words about Vivid, but because, in a warped, terrible way, Elias reminded him of himself, a gnarled version of who he might have become. Cocky and lewd and offensive. Was that the way people at the Guild saw him? Had Merric thought Scorch an arrogant, conceited ass, like Elias? The idea turned his stomach.

"Your face is red," Elias teased. "I'm not making you angry, am I?"

Scorch's fingers curled into fists, his nails denting the flesh of his sweaty palm.

"It enrages you to think of him with someone else, doesn't it?" the Fire continued with a sneer. "Do you think it's because we're both blond? Maybe he has a thing."

"It's your crassness that enrages me," Scorch said, realizing a second too late the idiocy in revealing his vulnerabilities to someone like Elias.

"That's phenomenal. Don't like me talking about Vivid that way? Then you probably don't want to hear about how easy he was to—"

Scorch grabbed Elias and ripped him bodily from the cot. His skin was prickling all over and his brow was sweaty. "Stop talking," he snarled.

Elias looked delighted. "Curious how overprotective you are for someone you don't even know. Is that what your beast responds to?"

Scorch clenched his fingers into a fist hard enough to make his joints pop.

"If I told you," said Elias, slinking into his personal space like he owned it, "that I was going to *kill* Vivid, slit his throat while he slept beside you—"

Scorch erupted, his fingernails bursting into talons and stabbing into his palms. He cried out, unfurled his bloody fists, and wrapped a hand around Elias' throat. His shoulder blades shifted beneath his skin, and the beginning of wings began to sprout, crunching and jutting his bones. He was going to change right there, he was going to lose control.

"Scorch," a voice said softly behind him, and Scorch exhaled a puff of smoke that parted Elias' hair. "If you do that in here, Axum will send you right back to Elias for training."

Vivid's voice echoed in his ears and his body shook in response. Elias smirked when Scorch released him, tossing his hair back from his self-satisfied face. Still burning on the inside, Scorch collapsed to his knees, trying to fight the rows of scales inching their way up his forearms.

He heard Vivid step beside him, felt his hand touch the top of his head. "Calm down." A cool breeze cooled the sweat on his body.

"How did you train him to respond to you so quickly?" Elias asked, and Scorch lifted his eyes to find the fiery blond squaring his shoulders.

For the time being, Vivid ignored Elias, opting to clasp his fingers in Scorch's hair and tug. Scorch's head bent back, and Vivid leaned down to speak in his ear. "You *can* control it."

He focused his eyes on Vivid. He sucked in a breath that burned his lungs, and his exhale steamed through his nostrils. But when he breathed again, the heat lessened, and with two more labored sighs, it was gone. His leathery sprouts of wings collapsed into his shoulder blades with a click. He ran a bloody hand across his wrist and the scales smoothed back to vulnerable flesh. Blood smeared his skin where his talons had pierced his palms. When Vivid's fingers loosened in his hair, gently tickling his scalp upon their departure, Scorch lamented their loss.

"What a good boy," Elias spat, and in the blink of an eye, he was on the ground with Vivid's boot pressed against his windpipe.

"Your company is unwanted," Vivid growled, pushing his heel into Elias' straining throat.

Scorch stood on shaky legs and watched as Elias coughed beneath the pressure of Vivid's boot. "Don't be so sure yours is welcome," he managed to choke out with an arrogant grin.

Scorch barely had time to process the sentence before Vivid was taking his blood-slick hand and leading him from the training room with a pace so efficient, they were practically running. In a minute, Vivid was opening the stone door that led to the waterfall.

The roar of the water seemed louder to Scorch than usual, his body sensitive after the almost-change, and Vivid released his hand as they began the slippy descent, taking his elbow in a firm grip instead. Scorch followed obediently, but not unquestioningly.

"Where are we going?" he asked.

Shockingly, Vivid responded. "Someplace private."

"*Oh*."

Vivid looked up at him, grimacing, and let go of Scorch's elbow once they'd made it down the rocks. He walked on, leading instead of taking, and Scorch kept an easy stride beside him, a smolder of energy still roiling inside with no way of releasing itself.

When they had walked a worn path of pale underbrush and low-hanging branches, Vivid stopped in a wide clearing. It was not, Scorch noted, a natural forest meadow. Rather, it took on the appearance of having once been filled with trees. Roots curled upward and drove back into the earth, befuddled, as if the trees had been ripped away. Or blown away. Scorch side-eyed Vivid.

"Have you taken me out here to kill me?"

"Unnecessary. If I wanted you dead, all I would need to do is leave you on your own for ten minutes. Now shut up and don't move."

Scorch settled his arms across his chest, trying to compress the rough-tempered beating of his heart. "Just stand here?"

"And watch me." Vivid turned from him, and Scorch had no trouble at all watching his body walk across the meadow until he stood at its most central point.

Upon viewing Vivid from such a distance, the memory of the Circle returned like a dream. Vivid had stared at him then like he stared at him now, but while Scorch once wondered the hue of those piercing eyes, he was now familiar with their shade and lashes and lids. He knew the touch of the leather that gleamed in the dappled sunshine, and the scars that hid beneath. Vivid remained a mysterious force before him, but Scorch felt he knew him, just a little.

A flowery smelling breeze wrapped itself around Vivid. It raised the dark strands of hair from his face and floated them about his head. It whipped the dead leaves from the forest floor and sent them on a voyage around his hips. The breeze became a wind as he lifted his palms, and when he tightened them into fists, the wind became a gale. The air swirled around his body, pulling up shreds of grass and clumps of dirt and leaves from the edges of the meadow, thickening Vivid's cyclone until Scorch could no longer see him within.

Scorch stood, mesmerized, as the vortex swirled and spun in tiny, threatening circles, stretching high in the sky. He was pulled forward by the sheer force of it, his feet scuddering along the ground until he planted his backside in the grass and anchored his fingers. As instructed, he watched, staring at the place Vivid had been, replaced now by a lethal confluence of air.

But Vivid had not been replaced; he had changed.

When the wind finally settled, the debris left a scattered mess about the meadow and Vivid reemerged from his elemental cocoon. He strode for Scorch, who remained seated in the grass, and as he neared, Scorch saw his eyes were a pigment lighter than usual.

Scorch watched his approach with awe stitched into his brow. His pulse was fast and his breath was coming quick.

"You were too easy to knock over," Vivid complained, and his voice sounded light. He looked down at Scorch and didn't need to put the request into words before Scorch pulled himself back to his feet.

He longed to say things he shouldn't, to tell Vivid his elemental form was beautiful, but he just stared dumbly and waited.

Vivid stood before him in a stony silence before reaching out his hand. He plucked something from Scorch's hair and came away with a small twig, which he let fall between them. "It is possible to be in control," he said, and Scorch wondered if the lightness in his voice was an effect of the change. If Scorch felt a constant wildfire in his chest, then Vivid must be full of wild gales, pounding against his insides for release. It must be a relief to let it out, to spin and whirl until he was spent. "I summoned the change without the fuel of angst. You can do the same."

Scorch scratched at his head and a leaf fluttered free, floating down until it landed in a precarious perch atop Vivid's shoulder.

"How?" he asked, his gaze entranced by the leather-bound slope.

"By not letting outside forces force out your insides," Vivid replied.

Tentatively, afraid every inch he would be swatted away, Scorch brought his hand to Vivid's shoulder and picked the leaf up by its delicate stem.

Vivid—who'd remained silent during the leaf retrieval—glared, and when he spoke again, it was with a deep rumble of irritation. "Don't let Elias burn you."

Scorch felt his temperature rise from the name alone. "I don't like him."

"Prove to Axum I'm training you well, and you'll never need to deal with him." His disapproval intensified. "Nearly lose control again in the middle of the Hollow, and Elias will be your new teacher."

"I would leave if that happened. I'm only here because of you."

Vivid's lips fell open on an exhale, and Scorch's eyes were drawn to them, like leaves caught up in the wind. The unbidden attention did not go unnoticed, and in the aftermath of a pregnant silence, Vivid took a measured step away and averted his eyes to the trees beyond.

"You're here to train, and you will begin more vigorous studies when we return to the Hollow."

Vivid walked past in a hurry, and Scorch followed suit, shaking the image of pink lips from his head. Another leaf fell from his hair.

"Vigorous studies? More vigorous than this?"

"The Guardians' Guild did you no favors in the teachings of grace and stealth. Those skills must be honed to bear the black of the assassins."

"I get to wear all that fancy leather, you mean?" Scorch asked, tripping over an upended root a second later.

He heard Vivid sigh and saw his head give a nominal shake. "Not for a while yet."

Vivid never complained that his hand was sticky with Scorch's blood, and when they returned to the Hollow, he silently helped him wash the wounds clean.

# Bruises and Honey
## 15

A new routine began for Scorch, and no longer was training in the eastern room the sole occupancy of his time. Upon first waking, Vivid would thrust breakfast of some sort into his hands and watch impatiently until he'd eaten it all. Then they would commence to the forest for what Vivid liked to call "stealth training" and Scorch liked to call "torture."

The dubious practice consisted of a number of activities, one of which involved Scorch trying his best to move silently through the trees while Vivid stalked him. Other times, it was Scorch's turn to attempt stalking Vivid without detection. Both scenarios always met the same end, with Vivid sneaking up behind him and proving how easy it would be to kill him, usually with a hand on his neck or his blades pressed against Scorch's back.

"You are hopelessly loud," Vivid scorned, and again, he would show Scorch the right way of placing his feet on the ground, and the proper way to breathe, of which Scorch had never known there was an improper way. The Guild had taught him how to swing his sword and nock a bow, but the guardians did not practice their skills in the shadows, so the only need for delicacy had been in hunting. But apparently, even that brand of silence was not enough to satisfy Vivid.

"Imagine your life depends on your stealth," Vivid instructed before beginning training one day. "Imagine my life depends on it."

Scorch groaned. "Gods, I'll kill us both."

"Not if you heed what I've taught you. Go."

Scorch nodded and walked ahead into the forest. Whoever was to be stalked began at the big oak tree. He arrived there with a nervous stomach; the idea of Vivid spying through the trees made it hard to relax.

The goal was to travel *stealthily* back to the waterfall without being heard. If Vivid detected a single twig snap or leaf crunch beneath brutish feet, he would appear moments later to pretend-kill Scorch. As of yet, Scorch had never made it to the waterfall and Vivid had killed him about thirty times. It was both terrifying and exhausting, but he could admit to himself that it was also thrilling, in its own way. When hands gripped his hair and slit his throat with an imaginary knife, or a swift foot swept his legs from under him and lethal thighs straddled his chest, his body would delight at Vivid's touch. It was always a shock when he was caught, and the takedowns were never gentle, but Scorch was never displeased to find Vivid upon him.

Still, he kept Vivid's words in the forefront of his mind and forced himself to imagine the penalty for being caught. If his light steps meant their survival, meant Vivid's survival, surely he could manage it. Maybe. He would try his best, at least.

He cleared his mind of loud thoughts. He forced his heartbeat to calm, and it was similar to holding back the change. If he could make himself relax, he would be less inclined to take a faulty, rushed step, gasp at a swooping bird, or get himself killed by an assassin. When he was calm, Scorch narrowed his eyes at the path before him and made a silent vow for success. He would hate for hypothetical Vivid to die, and he would hate more for actual Vivid to be disappointed in his being caught again. With that in mind, he set out for the waterfall.

Because of the late season and the northern climate, the terrain was difficult to trek, with fallen leaves aplenty strewn across the ground. Not only did they give away his location when stepped on carelessly, they hid even noisier items beneath, like twigs waiting to be snapped and rocks waiting to be kicked. Scorch, so used to walking with what Vivid referred to as a "bullheaded strut," found it difficult to move among the leaves soundlessly, but he kept his breathing steady and kept his mind still, and with one careful foot stepping after the other, he navigated the forest.

When he wasn't searching the ground for detritus, he was searching between the trees for Vivid. It was a fruitless endeavor; Vivid would never reveal himself until he wished to be revealed, but Scorch couldn't help himself from looking.

It was a clear-blue day and the forest was peaceful, with few sounds save trilling birds, and squirrels making the branches shake. Scorch finessed himself over a mossy log and tiptoed around a tricky root, adding no chorus of his own to the song of his surroundings. He crept slowly across a broad stretch of decaying leaves, and when they made no crunch, he smiled. But as silent as he sounded to his relatively untrained ears, he still expected, with every step, the suddenness of dangerous hands.

When he'd travelled halfway to his mark and still not been stopped by Vivid, his confidence surged. He'd never made it beyond halfway before. The certainty in his poise moved his feet faster and leant him the nerve to leap across a puddle of rainwater. He landed on the other side in a crouch, and his hand stole out for balance, too enthused. What he thought to be solid ground was muddy, and his hand slid. He lurched forward and caught himself on his elbows, holding his breath.

Quietly, he exhaled and lifted his head, bracing himself for impact. Though he tried to fall with minimal noise, he knew the thud of his elbows splattering the mud had found Vivid's ears and the assassin would be on him any moment.

He waited, but nothing happened. He stood, but nothing happened.

After several anxious minutes of waiting, he decided he must have been stealthier in his fall than he'd thought. With a triumphant smirk, he stepped around the mud and continued. He made it three whole steps before a blunt force shoved him forward and pinned him to the trunk of a tree.

"Argh!" he yelled.

"You've killed us both," Vivid announced. One of Vivid's hands was wrapped around the base of his neck and the other was pushing against his lower back.

A laugh was forced from Scorch's lungs as Vivid pressed harder. The bark scratched his face. "I can't imagine a scenario where I save your life through the power of divine stealth."

"Let us hope for both our sakes it never comes to that. We would die for sure."

Scorch closed his eyes and focused indulgently on the points of contact between them. Vivid's grip was not lessening, and the sustained touching was making him tingle. "I made it halfway this time," he boasted, struggling half-heartedly.

Vivid's hand slid from his neck into his hair, which he yanked before forcing Scorch's face back into the rough scrape of tree bark. "Stop talking. You'll try once more and then report to Audrey."

Scorch groaned in complaint when Vivid released him, and groaned in defeat when, several minutes later, he was caught again. That time, it was because he sneezed. Vivid entangled him in the crook of his elbow and sent him to his knees, looking down at him with impenetrable eyes. He kept him there, a captive at his feet, for several seconds before letting him go and sending him on his way, because Scorch had begun training with Audrey, as well, and she did not take kindly to late-arriving pupils.

With the Water elemental, Scorch sparred. He thought, naively, since he was one of the best among the apprentices, he would be able to handle her enough to keep himself from total embarrassment. As was the usual run of things, he was wrong.

While the Guild had cultivated strength, speed was the way of assassins, and for every blow Scorch attempted, Audrey landed five. She was ruthless and quick and spun about in an attractive manner Scorch likened to Vivid. He tried to keep up, but their styles were ill suited, and hers, proven time and time again, was superior.

At the end of a rigorous bout of getting his ass kicked, she threw him to his back and jabbed her elbow into his chest. "No wonder he bested you in the Circle." She offered him her hand and picked him up from the floor.

He rubbed at the back of his head where a lump was forming. He had been thrown down a lot. "Vivid told you about that?"

She poured them each a cup of water and sipped thirstily, although Scorch could see she was barely sweating and had never lost her breath. "He also told me you gave up your chance to escape, like a fool."

Scorch remembered cramped bodies in cages and uneasiness prickled the hairs on his neck. He shrugged it off and gulped down his water. "Sometimes the right thing to do is the foolish thing."

Despite Audrey's stare being restricted to one eye, it was as striking as a full set, and he felt exposed beneath it. But more disquieting was her accompanying smile. "We don't suffer fools in the Hollow."

"Are you sure? Some might call packing a bunch of murderers in a cave together foolish."

She laughed, not at his words, but at him. "Do you know what Vivid told me about your fight in the Circle?"

"I assume he told you he won and I lost."

"He told me you beat him, but that you lacked the nerve to kill him." She moved closer to Scorch, her single eye scrutinizing him, reading every tick of his expression.

Scorch recalled the moment with extraordinary clarity. "I refused to kill for the slavers' sport. If Vivid recounted the rest of the story, you know he refused, too."

"For his own gain," Audrey said, and it almost sounded like a question, so Scorch treated it as such.

"I've since seen Vivid take on enemies higher in volume and skill than the barbarians at the Circle," he said. "His survival didn't hinge on my help, but he spared me anyway."

"We all make mistakes."

After sparring with Audrey, Scorch's day returned him to the eastern training room, where Vivid waited among the unlit candles. Scorch would light the candles one at a time, put them out, light them all at once, and put them out again. Vivid made him flex his powers until sweat ran down his face from effort, but after weeks of harnessing his fire, he could feel the shift beginning.

When Vivid pointed out an unlit torch on their way to the food larder, Scorch brought it to flame with minimal effort. Lighting the row of candles grew simple, extinguishing them even more so. On those accidental occasions when Scorch found himself alone with Elias, the troublesome blond's jibes angered him, yes, but never made him lose control. The heat was always there, packed away, but for the most part, it only unfurled when asked, and with its every day routine of release, Scorch began to reap the benefits.

Calling to name the exact results was trying, but Scorch understood himself to feel an overall betterment of self and spirit. The same way Vivid's voice was lighter after changing into the vortex, Scorch felt lighter, too. Without the constant stress of suppressing his power, tension he'd forgotten did not belong in his body faded. And though Vivid never went out of his way to compliment his improvement, the shadow of a smile hinted on his face whenever Scorch mastered a new task. Years and years after his first burst into scales and wings and set the Guild forest ablaze, he was finally gaining control.

His sparring improved, as well. He still ended almost every training session with Audrey on his back, but that was only because she was perpetually better than he was.

Scorch's true rub, the greatest source of his vexation, was the damn waterfall, and making his way to it undetected. Weeks of creeping through the forest had brought him yards past the halfway point but nowhere near close enough to the waterfall to be counted as a victory, and he had the bruises to prove it. Vivid ambushed him mercilessly at the slightest sound, and Scorch's skin was abundantly marked. In the evenings, he would poke at the bruises while he bathed. His wrists were red from being held behind his back, and his chest revealed yellowing circles where knees had pinned him to the ground. He disliked the bruises for representing his failures, but the idea of Vivid marking him, oddly enough, was pleasing.

But Vivid was not pleased when Scorch failed the waterfall test for the fifth time in one morning. Instead of keeping Scorch bent at his knee or pressed into a tree as punishment, he pushed him away with a snort of disgust.

"This isn't working," he growled.

"I'm trying."

"Not hard enough."

Scorch went through the rest of his day with Vivid's disappointment hanging over his head, and in the evening, as he washed in the pool beneath the waterfall, Vivid appeared behind him on the rocks and scared him half to death when he said, "Axum likes honey cakes." It was the most startling delivery of "honey cakes" Scorch had ever heard.

After recovering from a gasp that made him swallow a mouthful of water, Scorch coughed and said, "I like honey cakes, too."

Vivid held up a hand for silence and Scorch bit his tongue. "He keeps them in his chamber, hidden on a shelf behind his hanging maps. You will fetch one and bring it to me without being caught."

Scorch resisted the very strong desire to splash him. "You want me to *stealth* my way into the Leader of Assassins' honey cake stash?"

"Perhaps the threat of Axum's punishment will better stimulate your ability to be quiet. Apparently, I no longer resemble enough of a threat to you." He eyed the newest bruise on Scorch's torso where he had kicked him earlier.

Scorch sank deeper into the water to hide his blush. Had Vivid seen him pondering his bruises? He was so frustratingly stealthy that he could have watched Scorch's entire bathing ritual without Scorch noticing. And, Gods, he certainly hoped *that* was not the case.

"Axum isn't in his chambers this time of night," said Vivid, prying his eyes from Scorch's body to deliver him a steely glare. "In case that interests you." He toed pointedly at Scorch's pile of clothes, scowled, and then left him to his bath, not that he could enjoy it now that the countdown had begun.

He rushed from the water and dried off before pulling on his clothes with impressive speed. His jerkin may have been inside out, but there were honey cakes on the line.

The Hollow was never at capacity, assassins coming and going with a regularity Scorch found distressing. The guardians were always coming and going, but their missions were to protect. The assassins returning to the Hollow were fresh from a new kill, and the ones leaving were about to kill again. Whether it was for the good of elementals or not, it didn't sit well with Scorch. It did however, leave the bulk of the Hollow unpopulated, especially in the evening hours, and that made his winding journey through the torch-lit tunnels unproblematic, and his path to Axum's door unhindered.

He checked over his shoulder for the tenth time and saw no one. When he put his hand on the door, his pulse quickened, but he breathed through his nose and out his mouth and made himself be calm. If Axum wasn't inside and no one was around to sneak past, Vivid's stealth assignment was going to be easy.

It should have been easy.

With a final glance to make sure no one was coming down the tunnel, he pushed open the door. He found it curious that there was no lock, but maybe Axum assumed no one would be stupid enough to sneak into his chambers. Scorch was stupid enough though, and he sneaked with weightless steps into the room. It was just as he remembered, but now that Scorch was free to examine it, he couldn't help but compare it to the Master's quarters at the Guild.

Master McClintock's space had been full of cloying pipe smoke and streaming lights from the stained glass window. It was all warmth and knowledge, with trinkets strewn across his desk and his sword mounted proudly on the wall. Axum's space was contrarily drab, the only décor being the maps of Viridor hanging on the far wall. That being the alleged hiding place of the honey cakes, Scorch made his stealthy way toward it.

The map clearly marked the Hollow's location, and it was much where Scorch had placed it in his head, almost due north of the Guardians' Guild, which was also specially marked. With the way he'd heard assassins react to mention of guardians, Scorch was not surprised; Master McClintock held similar ideas about assassins.

He set thumb and finger to the map's edge and lifted it from the wall, revealing an alcove. With a smile, he snaked his hand inside until he felt a spongy texture beneath his fingers. He grabbed the cake and smoothed the map back down. The cake was fragrant and fresh, and he wondered where Axum procured cakes with such regularity, since he'd not seen an actual kitchen within the Hollow, only the larder where pre-made foodstuffs were kept. Resisting the urge to sink his teeth into the sweet treat, he tucked it away beneath his jerkin, hoping it wouldn't crumble too terribly against his skin before he could get it back to Vivid.

He was still meditating on the marvels of baked goods when he heard voices, several of them, coming from the tunnel outside, and, judging by the rapid rise of volume, they were headed straight for Axum's chamber. In lieu of cursing, Scorch clenched his teeth, his eyes darting speedily about the room, searching for a place to hide. Anywhere, anywhere would do! Short of hiding beneath Axum's desk, which Scorch would have done if he thought he could reach it in time, the only object large enough to mask his presence was a chair angled in the corner by the hanging maps. It was a terrible place to hide, but when he heard the shuffling of boots directly outside the door, he knew it was his only option. Trying to keep a calm head, he leapt for the chair and shoved himself behind it in a ridiculous huddle, his head tucked into his chest, and his arms wrapped around himself, trying to make his body as small as possible. His knees pressed into the chair's back and his back pressed into the wall. As the door opened, he shut his eyes and prayed it would be enough.

"Come in, come in. Shut the door."

Scorch recognized Axum's voice, and he could hear him walking straight to his desk to take a seat. Lucky, then, that Scorch was not beneath it.

"Here, let's have some wine. Elias, pour the wine, please."

Scorch's heartbeat ticked at the confirmation of Elias' presence, but he shoved down the panic. He may not have been able to achieve full stealth mode in a forest full of obstacles, but he could keep quiet behind a chair when the thought of being found out by Elias was at stake. It was a blessing the room was so dimly lit and that the corners were relatively dark, or else, as more bodies spread out across the room, Scorch would have surely been discovered.

The gurgle of wine flowing from a jug repeated six times and Scorch wondered who the four assassins were besides Axum and Elias.

"Good, thank you," Axum said. "If everyone is ready." There was a wave of agreeable murmurs followed by the clinking of several glasses. "Elias, what do you have?"

"Their base has moved, as we suspected" Elias reported, in a far more formal tone than Scorch had ever heard from him, "and their numbers remain a problem."

"Location?"

"Twenty miles east of here, in an abandoned fortress."

"And the new leadership?"

"Unknown."

"*Elias*," Axum sighed.

"After three days of scouting, no apparent leader was seen, and the base was too closely guarded to infiltrate on my own."

"I can think of someone who would have tried regardless."

"And they would be too dead to report to you, as I do now."

An awkward silence fell upon the room and Scorch wished it would stop, because it made his breathing sound dramatically loud in his head. Thankfully, after a lengthy gurgle of pouring wine, the conversation continued.

"You will go back," Axum ordered. "Bring Umbren and Finn and do not return until you can tell me the name of their leader."

"Yes, Axum," Elias returned, sounding properly scolded.

"And what news of the Queen?"

Scorch's knees curled tighter into his chest and spongy crumbles smashed against his abdomen.

"She seemed neutral to the High Priestess' death," said a female voice Scorch didn't recognize. "I believe it's possible she may be swayed to our plight, and if not, it would be an easy enough task to eliminate her."

"That's good news," Axum said. His chair creaked and Scorch could picture him walking around his desk, could hear his feet as they paced leisurely across the room. All else was silent. "If she is malleable, let us try to keep her for the transition. Her voice of support could help tame the masses. If not, she can be replaced with one of our own. It must be done eventually, anyway. Elementals cannot rule Viridor with human royalty."

"Why not kill her right away?" Elias asked. "Why not kill all the humans?"

"Because death is too kind for those who have hunted us and dwindled our numbers down to scraps. Better to bend and break the humans as slaves. Better to make them the dirt beneath our feet so that we may step on them the way they have stepped on us." Glasses clinked in a toast. "Though our domain is now but a single Hollow, soon it will be all of Viridor. No guardian, Priestess' Monk, nor human will stand between us and our Gods-given right to rule."

A knock on the door interrupted Axum's terrifying world domination speech, and Scorch strained his ear as footsteps travelled to answer the caller. He heard the creak of the door, followed by a long-suffering sigh from Axum. "Vivid."

"I need to speak to you in private," came Vivid's irritable drawl.

"We're in the middle of something," Elias spat.

"No," Axum decided, "we're finished here. Leave us."

Scorch held his breath as five sets of footsteps left the room, and when the door shut behind them, his building anxiety lessened. Remaining hidden was a much smaller burden now that Vivid was there. He must have been watching, must have seen everyone enter while Scorch was still inside, and now he had come with a distraction to save him. But for now, Scorch was still hidden behind a chair and his legs were beginning to cramp.

"I assume this is about the Fire," began Axum. "How does his training go?"

"He's improved in his sparring and the control of his element," Vivid answered. "His stealth training has lagged, but I've given him his final test tonight and believe he might survive it with minimal damage."

Scorch's chest would have puffed with pride if he weren't so constrained. Vivid was complimenting him, and he *knew* Scorch could hear. He savored the moment, because he was sure it would never come again.

"Excellent," said Axum. "Then we can give him his first assignment and weigh his true worth to the Hollow."

Scorch couldn't see Vivid's face, but he could picture the storminess of his eyes and the thinning of his lips as he spoke in a grumpy grate. "He won't be agreeable to murder, Axum."

"His assignment will not be yours to dictate. Is that all you have to share?"

Vivid remained silent.

"Then you are excused."

Scorch listened to Vivid's steps as they receded down the tunnel, and when the door closed, it felt like the closing of a tomb. He'd hoped Vivid might lure Axum away from his chamber so he could escape, but no. It seemed his stealth test was doomed to last forever, or at least until Axum went to bed.

It turned out Axum stayed up too late, far too late, reading over scrolls, pacing, whispering to himself, drinking more wine, and when he *finally* snuffed out the torches and left the main room for an adjacent bedchamber, Scorch was about to lose his mind.

Still, he refused to grow reckless with impatience. He waited several minutes longer, listening for signs of activity until he could hear nothing but the silence of sleep, and only then, with stiff legs and an aching back that would never forgive him, did he creep across the room. He stopped at the door and pressed his ear against it. Hearing no sounds from the other side, he eased it open with minimal creaking and slipped through. With equal care, he closed it, and with soft, fast steps, he traversed the Hollow's tunnels.

When he reached the room of cots, Vivid wasn't there. He frowned, gave it a thought, and then headed for the waterfall. Hopes of discovering Vivid taking a dip in the pool were dashed when he spotted him, fully clothed and sitting at the water's edge. Scorch thought of attempting to sneak up on him, but he was sore and tired and couldn't be bothered to keep his feet from their loud, clumsy strut.

Amethyst eyes followed Scorch as he collapsed at Vivid's side. He stretched out on his back and stuffed a hand down his jerkin, pulling out sticky remnants of honey cake. Wordlessly, he dropped the smooshed pieces in Vivid's lap. Vivid glared at a piece that landed on his knee, then picked it up and put it in his mouth. Scorch sat up on his elbows and watched him chew. Vivid licked his lips when he was done, but didn't speak.

Scorch was forced from silence first. "I overheard something when I was hiding."

Vivid picked idly at another crumb.

"Something bad."

Vivid popped the crumb into his mouth and sucked the sweet residue from his fingers.

Scorch tried not to focus on his throat as he swallowed the morsel. "*Vivid*," he pleaded.

At his vehemence, Vivid looked at him impatiently. "What?"

"Axum is planning an elemental domination."

"An elemental domination."

"He talked about assassinating the Queen and enslaving humans."

At first, Vivid looked at Scorch like he was crazy, which wasn't too far off from how he normally looked at him, but then his face began to adopt an unsettling blankness, and he broke eye contact to watch the ripples in the pool.

"You're mistaken," Vivid told him.

"No, I'm not."

"You misheard."

"I did not mishear. Vivid, you didn't know about this, did you?" With Vivid looking straight ahead, Scorch's gaze was free to rove over his profile. He was always startled by the softness he found there, when so much of Vivid was made up of hard, unbending pieces. "The things Axum was saying were crazy. He said elementals were a gift from the Gods. He sounded like the High Priestess. Did you *know*?"

Vivid stood abruptly and Scorch watched the honey cake crumbs rain from his legs. The look he gave Scorch was anything but soft.

"I don't know why you're speaking to me like a confidant, but I have no answers for you."

"Vivid."

"*Scorch*. Stop talking," Vivid ordered. His hair flew from his eyes with a threatening bluster of wind, and then he left.

Scorch watched his sleek climb up the wet stones, until he disappeared behind the waterfall. He had half a mind to follow Vivid and demand explanations, but his other, lazier half of mind wanted to stretch out his stiff body and close his eyes. As usual, his lazier half won. He mulled over the worrisome words exchanged in Axum's chamber and sprawled his limbs.

"Didn't like what you heard?"

His eyes flew open and he jumped to his feet. Standing inches away was Elias, because Scorch couldn't catch a break.

"What?"

In the moonlight, Elias' hair was shining white, ethereal. "Axum's plan," he said. "You didn't like it?"

"What are you talking about?" asked Scorch, but his efforts at playing nonchalant were lost on Elias.

"I know you were in there. It smelled like burning."

Scorch stepped back, taking a deep breath. Elias hadn't caused him to lose control for weeks, but it was best, when dealing with the Fire, to keep him at a distance. Unfortunately, Elias had serious boundary issues. He met Scorch step for step until Scorch was pushed back to the edge of the pool.

"What have humans ever done for you?" Elias asked, his wicked smile firmly in place. The formality of the tone he'd taken with Axum was long gone, and his voice was a taunt.

"Humans took me in when my parents died," Scorch answered defiantly.

"And, so the rumors go, they kicked you out once they realized what you really are. Your guardians sent you on a suicide mission, too afraid to deal with you themselves, too afraid to let you stay. Cowards."

Scorch forced his pulse to stay steady. "It's more complicated than that."

"Was it more complicated than that when humans stuffed you in a cage and forced you to kill for their amusement?"

"How do you know all this?"

"And your trip to the mountaintop, how did the humans there treat you? That's probably complicated, too."

"Not everyone is out to get us, Elias," Scorch said.

"Says the man who was so repressed when he came here, he couldn't even light a candle."

Scorch sighed. He could not deny he'd encountered less than pleasant treatment in the hands of non-elementals, but to be fair, the slavers had never known he was more than human; they were equally awful to everyone.

"Did your parents find it *complicated* when they were murdered?" Elias asked. "You of all people should understand. When given the chance, humans kill our kind. Axum wants to realign the order of the world and make things safe for us again. Don't you want to be safe, Scorch?"

The idea of safety came to his mind in flashes: Etheridge's garden, his tiny room at the Guild, fingers twining through his hair.

Safety was a treasure, but he'd never been fully able to grasp it. Even in the moments he felt safest, it was only an illusion. He figured that must be true for everyone, but as an elemental, maybe it was more so. And yet, he could never imagine gaining safety through the enslavement of others. The Master might have knowingly sent him to his death, but the guardians had instilled in him compassion for those weaker than himself. It was the innocent Scorch had vowed to protect, whether they be elementals or humans. The plan Elias spoke of was no better than the High Priestess' plan to eradicate elementals.

"Axum's plan is madness, and I'll never be a part of it," Scorch declared.

Elias looked him up and down, his face uncomfortably close. "That," he poked his finger into Scorch's chest, "is a mistake."

Scorch knocked Elias' hand away and gave his superior height permission to loom. "The fact that you think so makes me certain it's not." He waited for Elias to move, and when he didn't, he nudged past with his shoulder. The blond hissed as he was knocked to the side, but Scorch didn't look back. He knew exactly what he would see, and he wasn't interested.

Within the Hollow, lying open-eyed on his cot, was Vivid. When Scorch neared, his mouth already forming the first of many questions, Vivid put a finger over his lips and held out his hand. He unfurled his fingers, revealing a white stem at the center of his palm. If Vivid was avoiding conversation, it was nothing new, and whatever questions Scorch had, he could ask tomorrow. He shut his mouth and accepted the Dream Moss, letting his fingers skim the skin it rested on before setting it on his tongue.

Before getting into his cot, Scorch removed his jerkin and shook out the remaining honey cake crumbs. A few pieces stuck to his abdomen and he brushed them off, feeling Vivid's eyes on him. He met them. Vivid allowed the contact for several seconds before closing his eyes and rolling onto his side. Without comment, Scorch settled down for the night.

Safety was an elusive thing, especially in a den of assassins, but somehow, with one lying beside him, he was quick to find sleep.

# *Heartburn*

# *16*

*A*udrey woke Scorch. In her hands was a bundle of dark leather. Scorch eyed it suspiciously, his brain slow moving with sleepiness.

"Your assassin blacks," Audrey informed him, thrusting the clothes into his hands. "Dress and report to Axum. He wants to speak with you."

"Axum?" That did quite a lot towards rousing Scorch's sluggish mind, and he looked to the cot beside him for Vivid, but he was gone. "Where's Vivid?"

"Busy." Audrey slapped her hand over the black leathers. "Dress. Axum doesn't like to be kept waiting."

She left, and suddenly Scorch was the only one among the cots, which was fortunate, because it took him an embarrassingly long time to figure out the workings of his new attire.

It was the same material Vivid wore, but there was considerably less of it. The cuirass was sleeveless, like his jerkin, but much tighter and higher hemmed so that it clung to his waist and cut off beneath his belly button. Mercifully, it didn't buckle up the back like Vivid's or Scorch would have had to roam the Hollow asking the friendly assassins to do him up. There were, however, half a dozen straps at the waist and across the back, which Scorch concluded were places to keep pointy objects.

The trousers were asking for trouble. They sat high on his hips and closed by a series of ties down the outer seam of each leg. He performed a number of squats beside the cot, and beside the form-fitting nature of the leather, it did nothing to impede his flexibility. Utility aside, Scorch had no mirror, but he could tell by touch alone that his backside was flatteringly showcased.

Shiny, knee-high boots were also included in the bundle, but Scorch kicked them under his bed and opted to wear his red boots instead. They were soft and worn in and he liked them. The final addition was his sword belt. He palmed his weapon's handle, making sure it was secure at his side, and then he was ready.

Dressed as an assassin from the shins up was a strange experience, and if Scorch wasn't so consumed by the implications of his meeting with Axum, he might have enjoyed the novelty of it more. As it was, he was walking toward the Leader of the Assassins' chamber, where Elias was probably telling Axum all about Scorch's eavesdropping. If Axum knew he'd overheard his plan, and also knew he was adamantly against the plan, the odds of letting him remain in the Hollow were low. And despite Vivid's annoyance with him the night before, Scorch wasn't ready to leave him yet, and he certainly wasn't ready to leave before he found out more about his parents.

As he traveled through the tunnels, he kept looking for a petite assassin but caught no glimpses, and when he finally reached the outside of Axum's chambers, he remained a solitary presence. He squirmed a bit in his leathers; they were so tight.

Scorch was bent over, pulling at the bunching material at his knees, when the door swung open.

"You're here," greeted Axum. "Come in."

The older man's eyes stalled on Scorch's red boots as he entered. Scorch tried to keep his walk confident, keep his back straight and his chin high. Sure, he had spent three hours curled into a ball behind Axum's chair the night before, but he would not be curling into a ball today. Absolutely not.

"Scorch," Axum began, and Scorch tried to fix his expression into one of a non-eavesdropper. "You have been training in the Hollow for nearly a month now and Vivid tells me you are much improved."

"Erm, yes," Scorch stumbled. "I believe I am. Vivid and Audrey have been excellent teachers." *Excellent, terrifying teachers.*

"They both speak well of you," Axum agreed sagely, and Scorch's brain went haywire imagining Vivid and Audrey saying nice things about him. If he hadn't heard Vivid's words to Axum last night, he wouldn't have believed it. "Elias has spoken to me, also. Of you."

There it was. There was the reason for Scorch's summoning. His fingers twitched anxiously, but he denied himself the comfort of balling them into fists. Fists would only aggravate his nerves, and he needed to stay calm.

"And what are Elias' thoughts?" he asked, holding back a grimace. He knew Elias' thoughts, and they were sick.

Axum moved to lean against his desk, just like Master McClintock used to do, though he never looked so intimidating whilst doing it. "Elias came to me last night to vouch for your skill. He thinks you are ready for your first assignment."

"Oh." Scorch had heard Axum discussing it with Vivid, but he'd never dreamed it would happen with such haste. In retrospect, he should have known when Audrey gave him the clothes. "Elias said that?"

"He did."

Scorch waited for Axum to add something else, to see if Elias had shared more incriminating information, but the man simply stared and said no more.

"That's . . . nice of him," Scorch said.

"Vivid has shared the opinion you would be averse to bloodshed. Was he correct?" When Scorch hesitated, Axum barreled on. "I will be lenient, considering your background, lest you think the assassins heartless. Your first assignment is to collect a name from our client. She is a stable hand in the village of Elanor and will be waiting for you at midnight, on the outskirts of town."

If Scorch was slow to process Axum's words, it was because too much had been given too fast. He was left frowning and picking nervously at his trouser strings. "You want me to collect a name?"

"Just a name and nothing more," Axum confirmed.

"I assume collecting a name from a client is the same as collecting the name of an assassin's next target."

"The name is of no concern to you past its collection," said Axum easily, as if they were discussing the weather and not someone's life. "I can see you are troubled, so before you refuse me, let me make a few things clear." He stood straight from his casual lean on the desk. "If you complete your task, upon your return I will tell you everything I know about your parents. If you refuse, you are to leave the Hollow immediately, never to be welcomed back again. This is not an orphanage. You do your work or you go."

Scorch's decision was made with disconcerting speed, but really, it was simple. If he didn't have to kill anyone, and he didn't have to leave Vivid, he would accept the assignment. Whatever game Elias was playing, it didn't appear to include telling Axum about their poolside conversation, which meant Scorch had time to speak with Vivid about it again. With a grim smile, he said, "I accept the assignment. I'll collect the name."

Axum didn't reveal much of a response, nodding his understanding like he might have done regardless of Scorch's answer. "Elanor is half a day's journey on foot."

"Then I will leave straight away." Scorch moved to leave, eager to be free.

"Scorch." Axum stopped him before his fingers could brush the wood of the door. "You will go alone. Vivid is not to accompany you."

Scorch laughed through the sinking feeling. "That's probably for the best," he said. "I think he's sick of me."

When he left Axum, he did a quick sweep of the Hollow. After finding Vivid in none of his usual locations, he headed outside.

Vivid was standing with his back to Scorch, on the far side of the pool, bare from the waist up. It was evident, as he fitted his arms into the sleeves of his cuirass, that he had very recently finished bathing. He'd already dried himself, but the stone around his feet was dark where water had recently dripped from his body. If Scorch had walked but a little faster, he might have encountered Vivid with no pants.

He didn't doubt that Vivid heard his less than quiet trek down the rocks, but the only indication he gave was a slight stiffening of his back as he approached. By the time Scorch reached him, he was dressed but for the buckles hanging open, and Scorch swallowed roughly at the canvas of his back, pale and painted with silver scars. His eyes fell lower, to the delicate dip above Vivid's waistline, where his back dimpled.

Whether it was the way Vivid hesitated to reach for the buckles, or the way that, when Scorch moved closer, he bowed his head and let out a tiny sigh, the idea became an invitation in Scorch's mind, as extraordinary as it was improbable. He touched a hand to one of the free-hanging buckles, and when the advance went undisputed, he gathered the material together and fastened it closed at the small of Vivid's back. He paused for possible death, but when Vivid did nothing but marginally straighten his back, Scorch continued to the next buckle. He was careful not to touch the skin, knew that would be a step too far. His fingers weren't as deft as Vivid's, but he worked his way up the spine until every buckle was fastened, and then, before he rescinded his touch, he let his fingers brush the tips of Vivid's hair that rested at the nape of his neck.

"Axum is sending me to Elanor with an assignment," he said, breaking the tension before it broke him.

Vivid turned to face him, his eyes darkening as he took in Scorch's black leathers. "I told him it wasn't a good idea."

"Right. Well, Elias told him it was."

Vivid's eyebrow twitched at Elias' name.

"I'm to go alone," Scorch added, studying the ground when he could no longer study Vivid's stormy face. "So." At a loss of what to do next, he smiled and turned away.

"Scorch."

So seldom did Vivid speak his name, the sound of it now in his stony cadence sent a thrill of heat up Scorch's spine. He cast a look over his shoulder at Vivid and waited. For what, exactly, he wasn't sure. It wasn't as if Vivid wanted to wish him luck, or tell him to be careful, or remind him not to be a fool. It wasn't as if he expected Vivid to say anything to him at all. And in the end, he didn't. Vivid just stared at Scorch for a few moments, tucked his hair behind his ear, and that was that.

Scorch watched Vivid head up the stones until he disappeared behind the waterfall, and then he started walking. He had a long way to go before he reached Elanor.

The journey was longer than half a day, but maybe Scorch was walking slower than average on account of his tighter than average trousers. He reached the town at dusk, and because his time was ample before his meeting with the stable hand, and no one was around to tell him no, Scorch let the sound of fiddle music lead him to the local inn.

His track record of visiting inns may have been bothersome, but it was the past's bad luck that made Scorch optimistic. Occasionally, a single drink among simple folk should be possible without inviting disaster.

He entered the inn and found it decently full, with one seat left at the bar. Accepting that as a good sign, he needled through a few dancing couples and plotted himself on the stool. It was no time at all before the barkeep was resting his elbows on the bar and asking for Scorch's order with flirtatious, heavy-lidded eyes.

Scorch ordered a cup of spiced wine and, when he paid the man, their fingers touched in a way that could never be construed as accidental. The barkeep was attractive and well built, with a handsome beard, but Scorch could not have pulled his hand back faster. He smiled kindly to make up for his blatant rejection, and the barkeep shrugged, disappearing for a few minutes, and returning with Scorch's wine.

Bothered by his own reticence, he drank it quickly. He could have had the handsome barkeep bent over in the kitchen by the time the last of the wine ran sweetly down his throat, but he lacked the desire. Almost immediately after finishing his drink, he regretted it. His head began to spin and he leaned his forehead down on the bar.

"Not feeling well?" the barkeep asked, patting Scorch's shoulder.

Scorch mumbled and strained to look up. The barkeep was leaning down, and the lidded eyes Scorch previously took for seductive, now read as ominous.

"It's okay. Why don't you just rest your eyes for a while?" whispered the barkeep in his ear.

Scorch groaned into the sticky wood of the bar, because he was a fool and no one had been there to remind him. He tried to keep his eyes open, tried to move, to cry out, but it was pointless. All he could do was curse himself as the world tipped, and then he was slipping into unconsciousness.

He'd been drugged.

*The leaves rustled under the panicked weight of his breathing, and he was afraid the bush was trembling as badly as he was. He was afraid they were going to find him.*

*He stared through the scant spaces of bare branch, his vision blurred with tears. Amid the struggling, black-outfitted bodies heaved and ripped and burned. His mother's cry was an echo of his father's. Scorch covered his nose and shut his eyes.*

*"Scorch."*

*He opened his eyes and a slight figure stood in the camp clearing, topless, his white and silver back to him, pale and vulnerable as flames crept up his spine.*

*He tried to call his name, but his throat was full of smoke. He tried to escape from the bush, but his feet were frozen with fear. All he could do was watch as dark hair smoldered and curled and turned to ash.*

*The voice called out to him again, and there was nothing he could do. He couldn't save him.*

*He couldn't save him.*

"You do love to talk when you're unconscious."

Scorch flickered to awareness when icy water hit his face and drenched him to the bone. He gasped and opened his eyes. Through a soaking stream of hair, he was not at all surprised to see Elias standing with an empty bucket in his hand and a smile on his face.

"Do you think Vivid will thank me for ridding him of you?" He tossed the bucket and its landing made a muffled noise. Scorch followed its trajectory to a pile of hay, and then scanned the wood-plank walls lined with tools. They were in a barn.

"I take it you're the stable hand I'm supposed to be meeting," Scorch muttered sourly.

"He was the stable hand," Elias said, pointing to a man beside him who Scorch identified as the barkeep. "I'm the one who's supposed to kill you."

Scorch laughed. "If I had a coin every time I heard that." He took stock of his bondage: his wrists were bound and strung above his head with ropes, his ankles were tied together, and his chest was wrapped, adhering him to the barn's loft ladder. He gave his wrists a tug and the rope bit at his skin. "Our conversation last night, it was a test, wasn't it?"

"And you failed." Elias rolled his shoulders and stretched his neck. His flat stomach flexed beneath his open vest. Scorch wondered how he'd ever thought Elias attractive, when everything about him was so repulsively reptilian. "Axum had high hopes, but you bashed them. And now I'll be bashing you." He moved so suddenly that Scorch struggled against his bindings, but Elias only extended a hand to cup his face. He thumbed across Scorch's scar, from temple to jaw, his gaze hot-blue. "With all your scars, I thought you would be wiser." He chuckled, and it was like glass in Scorch's ears. "But you can't always read a man by the scars he bears. Take Vivid, for example."

Scorch rolled his eyes. "I was waiting for you to bring him up."

Elias' fingernails cut into the skin of Scorch's cheek. "You have seen his scars, haven't you? One look at them and he appears unconquerable, strong to have lived long enough for all those pretty wounds to heal. But do you know how Viv got them?" Elias' teeth flashed. He looked entirely too pleased with himself.

"This might surprise you, but Vivid isn't much for sharing," Scorch sneered, but hidden beneath his veneer of disinterest, his curiosity soared.

"It wasn't an epic fight or a heroic turn. He didn't slay a great beast." Elias' fingers pinched at Scorch's chin and gave it a violent shake. "He was just a little boy, unlucky enough to be caught by the Priestess' Monks and taken to the mountain temple. When you see his scars, you might think of bravery and strength, but I think of a crying, pathetic, bloody mess that would have died if Axum hadn't taken him in. The one you follow around like a dog is no more than a broken child with ruined skin."

Scorch's lungs felt constricted. Fire thumped through his veins and made his skin slide against the ropes. He wanted to burn Elias' words, but he also wanted to hear more. He had waited so long to know more about Vivid. Hating himself, he said, "Vivid was the elemental tortured by the High Priestess all those years ago, wasn't he?"

"Apparently, she wanted to see how an elemental reacted to pain when they'd not yet come into their power. How she knew what he was, I don't know. He was only five when Axum brought him home from the Hollow's mission to the temple. Axum could have killed the High Priestess that day if he'd not wasted time and bodies saving that whelp."

"How do you know all this?" Scorch asked. His body was keyed up, taut as a bowstring.

"There are a few benefits to having one's father be the Leader of Assassins," Elias said.

Scorch gaped. "Axum is your father?"

"Shocked?"

Scorch considered the man before him, his cruel eyes and ugly heart. "No," he decided. "It explains why you're so jealous. Your father preferred the whelp to you."

A puff of smoke tendrilled from Elias' nostrils. "Vivid is *nothing* to me. He is," he gave Scorch's hair a tug, "something to you." Scorch tried to turn his head, but Elias yanked at his hair to hold his attention. "He was tortured as a tender, innocent child by human hands. Will you still not join Axum?"

"I'm being tortured by an elemental as we speak," Scorch replied, "but I still don't make the mistake of thinking all your kind is crazy."

Elias slammed Scorch's head against the ladder and it bounced off a wooden rung with a vision-skewing crack. "*Our* kind."

"I'm not like you." Scorch focused the heat in his body and sent it to swelter beneath his rope bindings.

"You are exactly like me," Elias said. The fingers in Scorch's hair were scalding, and he was glad fire couldn't be used as a weapon against him. "We are Fire, you and I. You should have let me teach you. You should have wanted me to teach you."

"I didn't want you. I wanted Vivid." Fire couldn't hurt Elias, but it could damage the ropes that trapped Scorch's body. He pushed against the singed rope, breaking through the binds and surging forward. He knocked Elias to his back and landed on top of him, kicking his ankles free of the rope in time to feel hands clasping his arms. He was hauled off Elias and thrown across the barn, where he landed in a pile of hay beside the bucket. The barkeep was right behind him, swinging at Scorch with a heavy fist. Scorch rolled and shot to his feet, landing a kick in the barkeep's back and sending him face-first into the hay.

A blast of heat hit Scorch between the shoulders and the smell of burning filled the barn. He spun around. Elias' fingers were smoking and Scorch's black leathers were on fire, melting and falling away from his chest in ashy clumps.

The barkeep's hands wrapped around Scorch's neck from behind, and Scorch clutched at the choking grip, letting his power flow from his skin into his attacker. The barkeep screamed and released him, staggering back as his shirtsleeve went up in flames. Scorch snatched the sword hanging from his belt before he scurried through the barn door, his flailing arm setting fire to a hay bale on his way out.

"You cannot beat me with fire," Elias yelled as the barn around them began to blaze.

Scorch's assassin leather fell away completely from his torso and chest, and he was sweating profusely from the heat coiling inside. He felt a prickle at his shoulder blades but ignored the urge to change. Elias was right; no amount of fire would win him this fight. He brandished his blade with a smile. "I don't need fire to beat you."

A plank of wood crashed from the ceiling and landed in a fiery heap between them. Scorch staggered back. A second later, Elias was jumping through the dense smoke, twin daggers shining in his hands. Scorch sidestepped, his sword slicing through the air toward Elias' middle, but the assassin crouched beneath the weapon and swept out his leg, knocking Scorch off balance.

They scrimmaged on the floor of the barn as pillars of fire and smoke raged around them. Soot clogged Scorch's eyes and tears streamed down his face as he struggled to blindly beat back Elias' blades with his sword, but rolling around on the floor wasn't conducive to impressive swordwork, so as soon as he was able to get a foot between them and kick Elias away, Scorch hurried to his feet.

"The best of the guardians is no match for the best of the Hollow," Elias cried.

The ceiling moaned. It wouldn't be long before the entire barn collapsed on top of them, and while the flames couldn't kill Scorch, he was pretty sure a structure collapsing on his head could.

He eyed the barn door, backing up as Elias stalked forward. "Good thing the best of the Hollow isn't here," he said, dropping into a roll to avoid Elias' blades. As soon as his feet were back under him, he rushed through the open door.

The cold night air was a blessing to his lungs. Behind him, the barn lurched, and right before the roof collapsed, Elias escaped, throwing himself at Scorch, his blades spinning and hacking, moving so fast that Scorch could barely breathe from the effort of keeping them at bay.

Elias' white hair glowed golden in the firelight, and the air surrounding them was thick and hazy with smoke. It had been some time since his swordwork was tested so ardently, but his muscle memory protected him, and he proved his worth repeatedly, every time Elias stabbed and Scorch blocked. His body pumped adrenaline into his muscles, and his breath, which had come so quickly in the barn, was steadying as their fight intensified.

Scorch's reach was farther than Elias', and his step larger, and though Elias was smaller and faster, Scorch wasn't slow. He began to gain ground, forcing Elias back, making him struggle to fend off his sword. He could win. He was going to win.

Suddenly, his shoulder flared with pain, and he flinched, not enough to drop his sword, but enough to loosen his grip so Elias could knock it from his hands and kick it toward the burning barn. Scorch ran for it, but the pain in his shoulder sharpened, and he was taken to the ground by the twisting of the blade buried in his shoulder.

"That was my favorite shirt you set on fire," the barkeep bellowed, pulling out the knife he'd stuck in Scorch and kicking him.

Scorch's face hit the grass, and he felt his nose crunch and gush blood. He was on the verge of lifting his head when a shiny black boot planted itself on his neck. He grabbed at Elias' legs, scratching at his ankles, trying to push him off, but the boot crushed harder and Scorch stilled. He knew how vulnerable the neck was, knew how easily Elias could break it whenever he wished with just a bit more pressure.

"Axum will tell Vivid his protégé ran away," Elias announced above him. Scorch knew if he could see his face, it would be wearing a slithery smile. "The assignment was too much for his guardian morals and he disappeared into the Viridorian wilderness, never to be seen or heard from again."

"He won't," Scorch gasped into the blood-soaked grass, "believe you."

"He might not believe me," Elias concurred. "But guess what? He won't *care*."

Scorch shut his eyes and tried to imagine Vivid's face when Axum told him the news. Would it be unmoving? Would his eyes flash? Would his lips thin? Would his nostrils flare? Would he say nothing and simply turn away, accept his next assignment and forget about the idiot guardian he'd met in the Circle? Would he not care at all?

"Does it hurt, Scorch?" Elias asked. Scorch heard him scrape his blades together, metal echoing above the crackling drone of the fire.

Scorch's mind was a disharmony of thoughts: maneuvers to escape Elias' hold, the seconds it would take to change, whether he wanted to escape at all. He saw his parents as they were cut down by the Priestess' Monks, all in black. All in black leather. Wait. *No.*

He laughed and coughed, tasting blood in his mouth. After going so long without his nightmares, what he saw when he'd been unconscious was clearer than ever before, and he knew, he *knew* that his parents hadn't been killed by the High Priestess. The assailants in his memory didn't move like the monks. They moved like assassins.

The wind gusted upon his epiphany, blowing a clean bout of air through the smoky night. It felt cool on the side of his face. It even made the pressure of Elias' boot lighten. It lightened so completely, in fact, it was as if no one held him down at all. A gargling sound from above had Scorch moving, confused as to why he was able to. He rolled over in the grass and looked up. Elias was levitating, his hands clutching at his throat. Scorch staggered to his feet.

First, he saw the barkeep's body drop from high in the air and land with a deadweight thud. Then, he saw Vivid. He was standing in the field, and though the light of the fire hardly reached him, Scorch knew him from the cut of his body and power of his stance. He was but a Vivid-shaped shadow some thirty feet away, with hair blowing wild.

Elias kicked his legs madly in the air and Scorch drew his eyes away from Vivid to watch him squirm. His face was red, but Vivid had not taken all his oxygen yet. He had enough to wheeze and choke and meet Scorch's eye with a mutinous glaze. And then, because Scorch could never stand to look elsewhere for long, he sought Vivid's shadow again. He was walking forward, the wind growing stronger as he came closer, and when he finally stepped into the light, Scorch was stricken by the intensity on his face. He stopped at Scorch's side, but his eyes were for Elias alone.

"I warned you, Elias," he said.

Elias stopped clawing at his throat and lifted his hands in front of him, flames sparking at the tip of each finger.

Vivid stepped closer. "*I told you.*"

Elias' fire flared high in his hands but Vivid's commandment of air was faster, and with clenched fists and a pained grunt, he stole the last of the air from Elias.

It didn't take long.

When the blue fire of Elias' eyes dulled, Vivid lowered his body slowly to the ground. Scorch stood silently beside him, or as silently as he could, breathing with a broken nose. For a few moments, Vivid watched Elias' body as if he expected it to rise again, but when Elias did nothing but lie there dead, he turned to Scorch.

Vivid looked him up and down, distress engraved in his pinched brow and bitten lip. Scorch's bare skin was covered in grime from the smoke, and blood was flowing from his nose, coating his neck and chest. Adrenaline had temporarily numbed the pain in his shoulder, but there was still a wound there, doubtlessly staining his back with more blood. He looked a fright. But Vivid, for the first time since the desert, looked frightened.

"You followed me," Scorch said, hating how stuffy his voice sounded. He scrunched his nose, wincing, and then Vivid's hand darted to his face, closed over his broken bridge, and snapped it back into place.

Scorch doubled over, clapping both hands over his nose. "Ow," he gasped, but the pain was already receding, and he could breathe easier. He straightened and wiped at the blood on his face with a sooty forearm, probably making an even worse mess of himself, but none of that mattered, because Vivid was standing there, staring at him.

"Thank you," Scorch said softly. The words fell heavy between them. They didn't feel like enough. "You saved me again."

Vivid's eyes were brilliant in the glow of the fire and his jaw was clenched so tight that it sent his whole body into a subtle vibration. "I should not have had to," he whispered. "You should have told Elias what he wanted to hear last night."

Scorch frowned, not understanding. "You heard that?" he asked. "Why didn't you tell me to go along with it, then, when I tried to speak to you about Axum's plan?"

"Because Elias was listening to us." Vivid was speaking quietly, but he was furious, and Scorch felt conflicted by his instincts. He wanted to move away from him, and he wanted to touch him.

"And in the cot room?" he asked. Vivid nodded. "So you followed me here, why? Because you knew Axum had ordered my assassination? You couldn't have told me that before I left?"

"I hoped I was wrong." Vivid's eyes swept to Elias' body at their feet.

"You," Scorch began, tight-throated, "you killed him."

"Your observational prowess never ceases to astound me."

"No, Vivid, you *killed* the Leader of the Assassins' son. You can't go back there now." Scorch did try to touch him then, and made it as far as an inch from Vivid's shoulder before his effort was knocked away.

"I know I can't go back," Vivid snapped. "I've buried myself."

"What are we going to do?" Scorch flustered. If they couldn't return to the Hollow, and they couldn't return to the guardians, where were they to go? Frustrated and dirty and exhausted, and probably concussed from hitting his head against the ladder, Scorch asked, "Why did you do it?"

Vivid's reaction was sudden and heart-stopping. "I did it for you!" he yelled, an outburst of feeling so strong that the wind picked up and a shower of embers from the barn swirled around them. "Apparently, I would rather destroy the only future I've ever had than see you dead." The tone of his voice was a contradiction to the words he spoke, thunderous and fuming, and all Scorch could do was listen, his hammering heart a suitable backdrop to the impossibilities he was hearing. "You have," Vivid continued, speaking softer now, but with no less ire, "*burned* everything." Scorch tried to touch him again, and Vivid moved away. "Stop trying to touch me," he growled. "Stop looking at me like you know who I am."

Scorch blinked and saw Vivid as the scared boy Elias described, but that didn't make him broken in Scorch's eyes; it made him even lovelier than he already thought him, and he had to tell him so. "Elias told me how you got your scars," he breathed. Vivid was motionless, hardly breathing. "You were the elemental the High Priestess kept in the temple all those years ago. That's how you knew how to survive the Monk's Path. Because you'd walked it before." When Vivid remained quiet, Scorch tried, one last time, to touch. He reached for the hair hanging loose over Vivid's eye. Vivid let him tuck it carefully behind his ear. "Vivid," Scorch pleaded. For what, he wasn't sure.

Vivid shook his head. "This was the last time."

"No." Scorch didn't know what Vivid meant, but he strongly disliked the sound of it. "I'm sorry about the Hollow, but we can figure it out. Axum is planning to take over Viridor. We have to stop him."

"*We*," Vivid scoffed. He turned his back to Scorch. "Whatever this has been between us, it's done now."

Scorch watched the fine hairs on the nape of Vivid's neck catch the leaping light of the fire. "Why?"

"Because you're dangerous," Vivid answered, his voice almost lost to the howling of the wind. Barely did he turn his head, blessing Scorch with a final view of his sweet profile. "Don't follow me."

He began to walk away, and Scorch called helplessly out to him. "Or what?"

Vivid didn't stop. "Or I'll kill you."

Scorch dropped to his knees and watched Vivid's shadow until it disappeared into the darkness. Every piece that made him whole begged to follow, but he forced himself stay. If Vivid could dismiss him so easily, Scorch had misunderstood everything. He cast a glance at Elias. He didn't want to be like him, forcing his presence where it was unwanted. If Vivid was finally tired of him, Scorch would accept it. It was a miracle he'd tolerated him as long as he had.

Scorch sat in his sadness and grieved among the dead until the barn was only a heap of charred skeleton, and only then did he stand. He looked up and down the field in the dawning light. He had nowhere to go.

So he just started walking.

# *Stealthy*
# **17**

In case more assassins were hiding in the shadows of Elanor, Scorch didn't pass through the town again, nor did he walk the main roads. He kept to the woods, shirtless and filthy, until he found a stream to wash in. The water ran black as he sluiced the grit and grime from his body. He cleaned the wound in his shoulder as best as he could without quite being able to reach it and hoped rinsing it with clean water would be enough to stave off infection. As a slim piece of luck, the knife had not plunged too deep. The barkeep had been a menace, but an unimpressive knife thrower. If he'd been better, Scorch might be dead instead of pattering about in a stream.

He tried not to think about Vivid.

Still shirtless, but clean, Scorch traveled on, unknowing of where, precisely, he was traveling. When he spotted a village near day's end, he almost succumbed to its offer of shelter and food, but as he watched the people light their torches and ready themselves for the night, he found he couldn't be bothered. He would need clothes and a meal and a room, and he would be asked questions, and people would stare. He wasn't in the mood to smile and lie and make nice with strangers. A roof over his head would do nothing for the pit in his stomach. Besides, if he went to an inn, someone would inevitably try to kill him or worse. Better to stay away.

He journeyed deeper into the woods until the trees grew bigger, denser, and he found a decent spot where the roots didn't stick up too much and the grass was soft. He moved quietly, collecting dry brush, and then, without flint or friction, he made a fire. He didn't need the heat, could stay warm through the night all on his own, but he craved the comfort of it, the familiarity. As he sat in its glow, memories shook him. He'd spent so many nights in front of a fire with Vivid and Kio, Julian even. Now, he sat alone, all of them disappeared from his company, through one means or another.

But he tried. He tried really hard not to think about Vivid.

With no Dream Moss to chew, he hardly slept. In part, he was afraid of the dreams he might have, but mostly, his heartbeat was too rebellious for sleep. He tossed and turned in the grass, his sword held tight in his hand, and as soon as it was bright enough to see, he got up for the day.

He was not moved to venture, so he hunted instead. He had no bow, but he fashioned a few traps and caught a rabbit to cook. It tasted good, but it was hard to swallow, and he never felt lonelier than he did in that moment, hunched over his meal in the silence of the forest. Birds seldom chirped, most moved southerly for the cold months, and for the first time, he was paying close attention to the wind. It hardly existed, not even to rustle the leaves.

That first day of solitude passed slowly, Scorch trapping more rabbits and snow finches for cooking as the sun made its lazy progression through the sky. Before night fell, he found a stream a mile off and a shallow cave hidden behind a wall of vines. He saw the choice before him, and it was surprisingly easy to make. He set up a new camp within the cave. He made a bed of leaves and moss and waved a hand before a pit of kindling to make a fire. When he was a child, he had lived in the woods, and he could remember being happy, with his parents. Alone, he could live there again and try not to be so miserable that he couldn't move.

Scorch could take care of himself in all the expected ways. With his skills learned from the Guild, he hunted with a success to keep his stomach full. He abated his thirst with fresh water from the stream. His stealth, meager as it might have been, kept him hidden and unbothered. He was sheltered, fed, and—partially—clothed.

It was his mind he could not make well.

While his body was surviving in the wild, his mind was not, burdened as it was. He worried constantly over Axum's plan, and the guilt of inaction swamped him. Were he a proper guardian, he would have gone to the Master and worked a solution to the assassin's madness. If Vivid had not banished him from his side, they could have discussed a counter plan. Vivid would have reproached him for talking too much, but he would have listened, and he might have helped.

Axum's intentions were an issue of import, no matter whose company Scorch kept, but alone, he couldn't drudge up the courage to act. In the cave, he was neither guardian nor assassin, human nor elemental. What good could he do against Axum, besides get himself killed? He kept close to his cave, kept his blade sharp, and tried not to let his thoughts consume him. In a way, it felt right to be so completely on his own. He had always felt like he was alone at the guild, and now the feeling had manifested into a cave-dwelling reality.

At night, when he wasn't sleeping, he tried not to wonder where Vivid was.

Three weeks passed, long enough to grow accustomed to his new routines, and long enough to grow his beard thick. He scratched mindlessly at it as he made his daily trek to the stream. The air had grown colder and the water icy, but Scorch remained shirtless, clad only in his assassin trousers and red boots. The temperature had no effect on him, and the trees had no complaints of his indecency, so why cover himself?

He knelt at the stream, dipping his hands in the water and running his fingers through his hair. It was as untamed now as it had ever been: messy, falling in golden sweeps over his ears. He should have asked Vivid to cut it for him when he had the chance, though Vivid might have run him through with shears before deigning to groom him with them.

Scorch was smiling sadly when he sensed it, a subtle shift in the air, when space ordinarily unoccupied was suddenly filled with presence. He unsheathed his sword with a whoosh of steel and spun on the bank, water splashing in a dramatic arc around his legs.

When he saw her, he rushed forward, only to be waylaid by a surge of water around his ankles, spinning with a binding force that held him prisoner.

Audrey lifted a hand, her expression fierce. "I'm not here to kill you," she promised, and the familiar scratch of her voice made Scorch ache. He had gone nearly a month without hearing anyone's voice but his own. "Put your sword away and I'll release you."

Scorch stared into her eye in search of a lie. He found none. But he was not the best judge of character. It was with great hesitance that he lowered his weapon, sliding it with a click into its scabbard. Audrey let her hand drop, and the water swirling around his ankles sank back into the stream. He gave his soaked boots a frown.

"If you're not here to kill me, why are you here?"

She looked at him strangely, and he realized his appearance might be appalling. He wished for the first time in weeks that he were wearing more clothes.

"I want answers," she said. "Axum told us you murdered Elias and fled, an easy enough truth to accept. We've all wanted to kill Elias from time to time. But then Vivid never came back." Scorch squeezed his hands into fists to stop their tremor. "Many have the idea you killed him, but I know that's impossible."

"Because I would never hurt him," Scorch said solemnly.

She shrugged. "That. And Vivid's not so easy to kill."

"I'm aware."

"I assumed he'd left with you," Audrey continued. "I assumed you were off together, doing, Gods, I don't know, each other, probably." Scorch blushed. "So imagine my surprise when I found *this* outside the Hollow." She pulled a rolled cloth from beneath her belt.

Dread rose in Scorch's throat like acid as she opened the cloth. At its center was a thick lock of hair, black and shining. He touched it with an unsteady finger, and it was impossibly soft. "Vivid," he whispered.

"Normally, a few strands of hair wouldn't be enough to make me think so," Audrey said. "But look at the cloth it came in."

Scorch had hardly noticed the cloth before, but he examined it now with disbelieving eyes. It was a simple fabric of brown weave,

and Scorch knew it well. "This is cut from the robe of a Priestess'
Monk," he said. Audrey nodded. "That means—"

"They have him." Audrey's one-eyed glare was horrible. "You
really didn't know?"

"Do you think I would be hiding in the woods if I knew Vivid
was in danger?" Scorch asked, the truth of Audrey's news hitting
him so hard that he thought he might collapse. He was sweating,
he was red in the face, and his inner fire was huffing and churning,
begging for release. The idea of Vivid captured had him heaving,
bracing his hands on his knees, and exhaling slow, uneven breaths.
Steam escaped his nostrils and his fingers sparked.

"When was the last time you saw him?" Audrey asked.

Scorch wheezed a hot breath and reminded himself it would do
no good to change yet. He had to save it. Let it fester. Use it when
it counted. "The night Elias died," he answered. "He left. He
didn't—he didn't want me. He left me."

Audrey was not sympathetic, she was angry, and that was okay,
because it was what Scorch deserved. "You should have followed
him."

"He asked me not to."

Her hands found his shoulders and wrenched him straight so
she could better scowl. "When has Vivid ever been honest about
what he wants?" she asked. She released him with a violent shove,
and he fell back into the water. "Now he's been taken, and I have
no idea where he is."

"I'm sorry," Scorch gasped, crawling to his feet, soaked.

"Do you know what the High Priestess and her monks did to
him the last time they had him?" she yelled.

"I'm sorry!"

She stomped toward him, kicking up water, and they stood face to face. "Don't waste your mind feeling sorry. Think, Scorch. You and Vivid were the last ones to see the monks, and Axum says they no longer live on the mountain. Do you know where they might be now?"

Scorch was shaking his head when the memory surfaced. "I overheard Axum the night before my assignment. He mentioned something about a fortress. Elias was supposed to be staking it out, determining a new leader. They might have been talking about the monks."

"Where was the fortress? Do you remember?"

He fought his flustering for the information and jumped when he found it. "Twenty miles east of the Hollow," he said. "Heavily guarded." Audrey pulled them both from the stream, and Scorch stumbled with the weight of water in his boots. "That's where they'll be keeping him. We have to go to him."

Audrey laid a hand on his chest to stop him, for he was trudging forward with blind determination. "Wait a second, before your haste gets all of us killed."

"What?" he asked impatiently. Now that he knew Vivid was in trouble, nothing mattered but reaching him.

"The monks delivered this to the Hollow like a present," she said, handing Scorch the precious, fabric-wrapped hair. "They wanted us to know they had him."

"They have one elemental," Scorch murmured, "and aim to lure more. Did you find this alone, or does the whole Hollow know about it?"

Guilt looked foreign on Audrey's face. "I found it. I know I should have shared it, but if Vivid was involved in Elias' death, I couldn't be sure how Axum would react to news of his capture. So I found my way to you instead."

"How long ago?"

"Two days. Once I had your scent, it wasn't hard to track you."

"That's good, right? It means she's not had Vivid for long."

"She?"

Scorch met her eye and wondered if he looked as fearsome as he felt. "I know who their new leader is."

"You do? Who is it?"

Scorch could still see her face and hear the calming hum of her voice, feel the kindness of her touch. "Kio."

He should have let Vivid kill her.


Audrey, quite expectedly, turned out to be a master thief. The little village Scorch had avoided three weeks earlier fell victim to her skills in the way of two horses and one linen shirt.

"Blue," she said, handing him the shirt she'd nabbed from a clothesline, "to match your eyes."

"My eyes are brown," he told her.

She squinted at him. "Huh."

The two mares she procured were siblings, both with grey manes and white dots speckling their hindquarters. They were lovely, but more importantly, they were fast and able, and Scorch and Audrey kept them at a steady clip, traveling by the main road. Scorch's trek to the town of Elanor had taken close to eight hours on foot from the Hollow, but by horse, they had made up that distance before midday. From there, due east for twenty miles took four hours. By the time the sky turned orange and dusky, Scorch and Audrey had tied their mounts to a tree and were spying on the fortress in the distance.

It stood tall against the colorful sky, a sturdy, stone building with spire-topped towers. It was centered in a woodland clearing and obvious in its abandonment. Wildlife breached its walls and foliage crept through its windows and up its flank. To Scorch, it was a near replica of a drawing he'd seen in one of his Guild tomes of a haunted castle, full of spirits.

Vivid was in there somewhere, beneath the ivy and stone, and Scorch's skin crawled with the need to reach him. But as Elias had reported to Axum, the fortress' perimeter was swarming with monks. Scorch could see the flashing steel of weapons, even in the darkness.

"They'll be expecting us," Scorch whispered to Audrey, who lay beside him in the swath of wild grass. The look she gave him said she was fully aware of that fact. "So how do we go about this? At the Guild, when we were learning rescue tactics, we usually amassed a team and stormed the point of interest from opposing sides."

"Since the team I *would* have amassed consists of people who want to kill you," Audrey whispered back, "we will have to forgo the guardians' approach on this one." Her gaze turned curious. "In your lessons with Vivid, did you ever reach the waterfall?"

Scorch gulped. "I, erm, reached the honey cakes. But . . . they got smashed."

Audrey rolled her eye. "Gods, help us."

To Scorch's dismay, the bulk of Audrey's plan consisted of *stealth*. They were to sneak past the outer guards, scale the western tower, and slip through its midway window. Scorch informed her that climbing vines and craggily old stone was *not* in his training, and that if he were to fall, the drop would most likely kill him. She agreed and suggested he avoid falling.

"Once we've breached the fortress, there is no telling what we might find. The window may lead to a room full of monks, or it may be completely empty."

"I bet I can guess which it'll be."

"If we are seen, our only choice will be to fight," Audrey advised. "But then the fortress will be alerted and our chance of reaching Vivid will plummet."

Resolve hardened inside Scorch. "We'll reach him."

Audrey nodded approvingly. "Hopefully we can remain undetected long enough to find where they're keeping him."

"Then we save him?"

"Then we save him." A smile passed between them. "It will be harder getting out than getting in, especially if Vivid is injured."

His chest burned at the thought of Vivid hurt, and it surprised both himself and Audrey when his next words came out as a growl. "I'm getting him out of there if I have to burn the whole damn place to the ground."

"It might come to that," said Audrey, "so keep your sparks at the ready." He lifted his hand and concentrated his power to the tips of his fingers until they spit little darts of flame. "You know Vivid's not going to thank you for this," Audrey sighed. "He'll call you a fool."

"I *am* a fool," Scorch admitted. "I've come to terms with it, I think." Scorch couldn't wait for Vivid to call him a fool, for him to flare his nostrils and furrow his eyebrows and be pissed off and *safe*. Scorch needed Vivid to be safe.

"Save the moon-eyes for after the heroics," Audrey chided. "Are you ready?"

He tempered the heat swelling in his gut and took a deep breath. "Yes."

"Then let's go." She grabbed his arm before he could move and fixed him with a deadly eye. "Don't smash your honey cake once you have it."

He nodded with fervor, and off they went.

Sneaking up to a fortress was ten times more nerve-wracking than sneaking through a forest. Instead of half-worrying about being caught by Vivid, wherein the punishment was Vivid's hands all over him, Scorch was fully petrified of being spotted by one of the dozen monks guarding the fortress perimeter, wherein his being caught could result, not only in his and Audrey's deaths, but in Vivid's, too.

Every step was a severely monitored challenge, but he kept pace with Audrey through the grass, and he kept Vivid's commanding voice in his head, reminding him how to walk and breathe. His boots fell softly on the ground and his breathing was easy, in and out and soundless. The fortress sat perched at the top of a slope, which gave the guards an easier task of assessing the outlying area, but Scorch and Audrey had the benefit of nighttime, which clung to their sleek-prowling figures and prevented immediate discovery as they inched their way closer.

The Priestess' Monks moved in a pattern as they guarded the fortress, walking back and forth across their designated stretch, often stopping to peer out into the grass. In those moments, Audrey extended her hand and touched Scorch's shoulder, and they knelt together, making themselves small in the shadows. Scorch felt like a predator, stalking toward his unsuspecting prey, only the monks were anything but unsuspecting.

Every new yard claimed felt miraculous and brought him one yard closer to Vivid. When they were thirty feet from the closest guard on the westerly side of the fortress, Audrey squeezed his shoulder and they separated, as agreed. She veered around to approach the tower from the other direction while Scorch kept on as he was; it was under the assumption that should one of them be caught, the other could still have a shot at making it inside. Scorch tried tracking her, but she soon vanished into shadow.

Scorch watched the guard in front of him make their turn and walk in the opposite direction, and then back. He waited, belly to the ground, for what felt like forever, memorizing the movement of the monk, figuring out their timing. He would have to be spot on to slip through the patrol unnoticed. The monk turned their back, their long robe flowing, and Scorch was afraid. Even with his training and elemental power, he didn't trust his odds of going up against a horde of Priestess' Monks. His stealth was imperative. Vivid's life depended on it.

Scorch watched the monk as they turned, walked forward, stopped, turned, walked back. When the monk was turning away again, Scorch took his chance, slinking from the grass and toward the tower. He reached it in seconds, but he only had thirty more seconds in total before the monk would turn back. Praying that his climbing stealth was superior to his puddle-jumping stealth, Scorch reached up and grabbed a jutting piece of stone. His foot found another, and he hoisted himself up, trying not to tangle his limbs in the ivy.

Clinging to the wall, he was exposed, and he had fifteen seconds to move far enough up the tower to *maybe* go unnoticed by the monk. He was pretty sure Audrey was cursing him somewhere in the dark. He was cursing himself as he tried to scamper quietly up the wall. His hands grew hot and he had to pause to breathe, reminding himself that if he set the vines on fire because he couldn't control himself, he would be caught, and then Vivid would remain captured. He searched for another foothold, pushing himself further up the tower.

Five seconds until the monk turned.

He moved upward another few feet, pressed himself against the stone, and held his breath, hoping the heavy vines would help hide him. Footsteps approached from below. They came closer and closer, magnified with chilling clarity. No one had ever walked as slowly as the monk walked. No footfall had ever been so petrifying. No elemental had ever clung so fiercely to the side of a fortress. It was thirty seconds of torture and waiting and being sure that, in the next moment, the alarm would be raised.

But then, extraordinarily, the footsteps began to retreat as the monk made their scheduled turn and marched in the opposite direction. Scorch could have cried with relief, but that would have contradicted the point of being stealthy, so he promised himself a cry later and did all he could do. He carried on, climbing up the side of the tower, and continued in his efforts to not get caught.

He had thought, while examining the fortress from far away, that the intended window was rather far up. It turned out, it *was* rather far up, ridiculously far up, and when he was only halfway there, his whole body was tingling from exertion. Someone with a body like Vivid, small and agile, could probably make quick work of scaling such a height, but Scorch, with his damned muscles and mass, was arguably not made for scaling towers. The fact that he was still climbing was proof of his willpower to reach the windowsill. He maintained his focus on the space above his head, where he could see the ledge, and, careful reach after careful push, it came ever closer to touching.

When he was finally hovering in a jumble of ivy directly beneath the window, he took a moment to re-gather himself. He did not know what waited beyond the windowsill. He strained his ears and heard no signs of movement, but that didn't mean monks were not waiting inside, not if they were being as quiet as Scorch. He looked down to see if Audrey was climbing up behind him. He didn't see her, nor could he wait for her. Sneaky as he was being, if any of the monks dared look up to study the integrity of the spire, he would be spotted. Lingering was not a viable option. With the thought of Vivid in the hands of Kio, he hauled himself over the sill.

He landed softly on a blessedly solid floor. The room was dark save the moonlight seeping through the window. He glanced anxiously at all its corners and saw it was unoccupied. Luck was temporarily on his side, but he wouldn't take it for granted. He crept, moving himself along the dark of the walls, and made for the door that led, hopefully, to the main hall of the fortress.

He was at the door's edge when he heard sounds of life: the faint swish of robes brushing stone, a whisper of murmurs. He stole another glance at the window, hoping to see Audrey climb through. He waited three minutes and then decided he could waste no more time. They'd separated for a reason. Perhaps she'd been captured or found another way inside. Regardless, he had to move on without her and hope for the best.

He rolled his shoulders and rubbed his legs, grimacing at their soreness, but he made an assessment of his body and found he wasn't tired. Adrenaline was coursing through him, loaning him preternatural alertness, and so it was with hyperawareness and soft-stepping boots that Scorch slipped from the room to seek out Vivid.

The main hall of the fortress did not greet him on the other side of the door. Contrarily, the door opened to a narrow, enclosed stairwell, with spiraling steps stretching upwards and downwards. It was lit by torches but filthy with cobwebs, and Scorch was reminded again of the haunted castle.

He had hoped for broader construction, a way to see all around him and determine where Kio might be keeping Vivid, but it wouldn't be so easy. He had to choose whether to head up or down. It felt like the hardest choice of his life, when heading the wrong way could result in his capture and flummox the entire rescue. At least, he acknowledged warily, he had the benefit of knowing Vivid's captor.

He thought of Kio. The last time he'd seen her, she was struggling for breath after Vivid had almost killed her in the temple. Before that, she had shared her Mountain Flower Whiskey in the cave. Scorch closed his eyes and pictured her elevated, high up, in her place beside the High Priestess. If Kio was such a devotee, she would be emulating her deceased Holy One in every way. She would be at the top of the tower. Scorch went up the staircase.

The space was cramped, and he felt trapped as he walked up the stairs. There would be no room to draw his sword if it came to it, but he hoped it would not come to it, not yet, not until he had Vivid. The rustles and whispers he'd heard before decreased as he climbed, making him worry that he'd chosen the wrong direction. He was uncertain, but he kept on.

The stairs ended at a door-less archway. He leaned cautiously around it and peered into the space, seeing no one. The room's ceiling was high and pointed. He was at the topmost point of the western tower, but there was only a large window and no furnishing. Vivid wasn't there. He had chosen wrong. He sighed, and was readying to turn around when a noise stopped him.

Humming.

His insides burned and he scanned the room again, taking a step inside, his hand on his sword. "Kio," he whispered.

"Scorch," a voice answered at his back.

He jolted, spinning around. A cloud of green dust hit him in the face, and he gasped, sucking in a lungful of the strange substance. He coughed violently and dropped to the floor. Somewhere, someone was speaking, but he didn't understand. His vision hazed and his mouth fell slack and everything went dark.

# The Small Sound
# 18

*H*e was in the Hollow, tossing and turning in his cot, and his blankets had fallen to the floor. Someone pulled them over his shoulders and tucked them beneath his chin.

"He's handsome."

"Shut up. He needs to rest."

"Working him hard?"

"Go away."

"You're really not going to share?"

"He's not mine to share."

"He may not be yours, but you're his, aren't you?"

"I wonder why you're still talking to me like I can tolerate the sound of your voice."

"He doesn't see the way you look at him, but I d- Ow! What was that for?"

"I told you to go away."

"Will you punch me in the face when I get your boy bent over for me?"

"He wouldn't."

"If I make him?"

*"I will kill you, Elias, if you hurt him."*

Scorch was wet.

It was such an unexpected sensation that he thought he was still dreaming. In his head, he could hear the remnants of Vivid's voice, and Scorch listened to its threatening rumble, wondering if it had been a dream or a memory. It felt so real.

"What do you think of my nocturne powder? I think it works quite well."

Scorch knew that voice, and he turned his head to the source, opening his eyes. Water lapped at his face.

Kio was sitting cross-legged at the edge of a pool, and he was *in* the pool. It was shallow, very shallow, filled only with enough water to cover his ears. He tried to sit up, but other than being able to turn his head, he couldn't move. He wasn't tied up, but he couldn't move.

"The nocturne powder I made from Peggotty Lush-fern and Starleaf. In larger doses, it can render one paralyzed long after consciousness has returned. I gave you quite a large dose. Sorry about that."

Scorch tried to curse her, but he couldn't speak.

"Muteness is another side effect of the nocturne. I apologize. I know you like to talk." She cocked her head at him, her cattish eyes open and friendly. "But for now, you have to listen."

Scorch could at least roll his eyes, and for that, he was grateful.

"As you can see, I knew you were coming. I made this water chamber especially for you. It's nowhere near as lovely as the temple's, but it should do to keep your fire at bay."

She stood gracefully and smoothed the folds of her monk robe. Her hair was shaved close to her head, bringing out the strong bone structure of her face. If she was closer, he knew he would see the faded burn on her cheek, the one he'd unknowingly left in the cages of the Circle. Objectively, she was beautiful, but when he looked at her, he only saw the friend who had betrayed him.

"It was never personal, Scorch. Not until Vivid killed our Holy One." She watched him watch her. "Her divine work was left unfinished, and I needed test subjects. And why would I capture just any elemental for study, when I already knew of two who deserved punishment?"

He wanted to scream, wanted to, at the very least, splash her, and it galled him that he couldn't.

"Vivid was easier to attain than I anticipated. He seemed distracted. Do you want to know how I snared him?" Scorch prayed for a stare that would kill. "I told him I had captured you. He offered a trade, which I graciously accepted. Of course, you weren't here. Why were you separated, Scorch, when all either of you ever thought of was each other?"

He moved his head defiantly and stared up at the ceiling, the water from the shallow pool lapping at his ears.

Kio walked slowly around the pool's edge. "It took longer for you to get here than I expected," she continued. "And I'm ashamed to say I grew bored waiting. I had tests to run and Vivid was incredibly useful, though I'll admit, I may have been overzealous in my last experiment. Scorch, look at me, please."

He looked.

"Vivid is dead."

No.

*No.*

Scorch's fire flared in his chest and his eyes burned. He thrashed his head and water filled his mouth, making him choke. Lies, lies, lies. She was lying. She was a liar.

"It wasn't my intention to kill him. I misjudged my formula. But now that he's dead, I'm not sorry. And now I have you to help me finish the High Priestess' work, may she rest in eternal light."

Scorch's fingers began to sting, and he formed a weak fist beneath the water, which escaped Kio's notice. He tightened it as hard as he could while his insides seethed with rage. He could feel his blood burning in his veins. The water may have been keeping him from directing his power outward, but his inner fire was cleansing the paralytic powder from his system, and he would soon be able to move. Then he would make Kio tell him the truth.

"I can see in your eyes you don't believe me. You were always so easy to read. Would it help if you saw the body?" She snapped her fingers and a door opened. A monk walked in with something in his arms. "The potion administered was meant to stunt elemental exertion, but Vivid had too strong a dose. Bring him closer. Show him," she told the monk.

The robed figure approached the edge of the water and knelt. And then suddenly, Scorch was looking at Vivid.

His lips were blue and his skin was grey. His eyes were shut, his brow lax. The lock of hair that always fell across his eyes was chopped short. He hardly looked like himself, but Scorch would know him anywhere, in shadow or in death.

He wasn't breathing.

Tears spilled from Scorch's eyes. Kio bid the monk to remove the body.

The body. *Vivid.*

*No.*

"He was hallucinating before he died," Kio informed Scorch, cheery-voiced. Evil. He hated her. He was going to kill her. "He said your name a few times."

He watched the monk carry Vivid from the room. For all its breaking, his heart was a reckoning force in his chest, pumping and painful and spreading untainted blood throughout his body. Within his boots, he wiggled his toes.

"Don't be upset," Kio sighed. "I'll be more careful with you. And I'd like to test the elemental stabilizer on you now, if you don't mind. With the right dose, it should block the access to your core and render your power utterly useless." She snapped her fingers for another monk to enter.

None did.

Kio called out patiently for assistance. When there was no response, she laughed. "Sometimes it can be hard to hear when our hoods are up."

A series of thuds sounded from beyond the door, and a second later, it swung open.

"It's even harder to hear without a head." Audrey stood in the doorway, a bloody dagger in one hand and a monk's head in the other. She threw the head at Kio and it rolled at her feet.

What followed were the longest seconds of Scorch's life, as Kio and Audrey stared one another down. Then, chaos.

Kio jumped as Audrey threw one of her knives. It spiraled and caught Kio in the arm. She lunged, pulling the knife from her arm and colliding with the assassin in a flutter of slicing, spinning steel.

Scorch tested his mobility as they fought. He could tense his shoulders and lift his wrists, and he rolled himself to his side with a splash. He forced his knees to bend, but it was slow work. If only he could get out of the water, he could summon his fire.

"Audrey," he tried to call out, but his voice was still weak from the nocturne powder. "The water!" he rasped. And then, because he could hardly control his body, he tumbled forward and landed face-first in the water.

Only Scorch would find a way to drown himself in six inches of water. He turned his head to suck in air, but he sucked water in, too, and then he was panicking, choking. He splashed his hands desperately and tried to rock himself back over. Then, all at once, the water disappeared.

He gasped in the empty pool and saw Audrey in the corner of his eye, one hand lifted up while the other fended off Kio with her dagger. Scorch coughed up the water he'd breathed in and immediately began to heat up. The hotter his skin became, the more strength he gained in his muscles, until he was able to roll onto his back and sit up.

Audrey had manipulated the pool water, and it was suspended in a million droplets above their heads. Kio's form was as precise and elegant as Scorch remembered, but Audrey was brutal, her attacks merciless, and after Kio managed to cut a slice across her cheek, she roared and slammed her hand down on the ground, and the water droplets in the air formed a wall between herself and Kio. She pushed her hand out and the waterwall rushed forward, hitting Kio with such strength, she went flying back, her head cracking against the wall. She slid to the floor in a daze.

Audrey was at Scorch's side in seconds, pulling him to his feet. He wobbled, but he didn't fall. "I found another way inside," she said. "We can use it to escape once we find Vivid."

Fire sparked from Scorch's fingers. "You didn't see."

"See what?"

"The monk carrying his body." His voice broke, and tears may have been rolling down his cheeks, but he felt nothing but fury.

Audrey's face remained blank as she processed Scorch's words. "We're still getting him back. And we will kill every monk in here on our way out." She looked him up and down. "Are you able?"

He glared at Kio's unconscious body across the room and held up a fist. A burst of flame ignited from his knuckles. "I'm able."

He walked to Kio, the floor beneath his boots wet from the collapsed waterwall. Blood seeped from her temple, where she'd struck her head against the stone.

"Scorch, we have to hurry," Audrey said.

He stared down at the woman who used to be his friend, the woman whose mantle it was to eliminate elementals. The woman who killed Vivid.

"Scorch," Audrey pleaded. He could hear footsteps running toward the door.

Kio's eyes fluttered open, and she looked up at him. "Are you going to kill me?" she whispered.

Maybe a Guardian of the Guild would have let her live, or at least given her a humane death, but Scorch wasn't with the Guild anymore, and she had killed Vivid.

"Yes."

He looked her in the eyes and set her robes on fire.

She didn't scream, and he didn't stick around to watch her burn. He turned to Audrey as Kio was enveloped by flames, power sparking from his fingers. "Let's find him," he growled. Audrey twirled her daggers and let Scorch take the lead.

He strode through the open door as the first of the monks arrived. He didn't stop, just kicked the first of the monks in the chest as he barreled through. Behind him, he heard the hacking of blades into flesh as Audrey finished the job. They were shortly in the main hall Scorch had imagined upon first entering the fortress. Surrounding the wide floor was a plethora of doors and a plethora of monks coming through them, streaming into the hall from a dozen directions. Scorch stationed himself in the center of the hall, Audrey at his side. They were surrounded by thirty monks, the greatest fighters in Viridor. The last time Scorch was confronted with their skill, he'd been running in the opposite direction with Vivid's hand in his. But last time was different. Scorch didn't have any control last time

He had it now.

As the Priestess' Monks charged them, he let loose his element. It was just like lighting a row of candles, just like a torch, just like a campfire. He waved his hand and a dozen hoods combusted. A monk grabbed him around the waist and he turned, laid fiery hands on him, and sent him up in flames. Heat shot from his fingertips and scalded three monks in a row.

Meanwhile, Audrey flowed around him, cutting down the weakened monks. It sent a thrill through Scorch to watch bad people drop beneath the same power they'd tried to stifle. It was satisfying, but it wasn't enough. His heart still ached, still felt like it was being ripped from his chest. He needed to *decimate* them.

"Audrey, I'm changing!" he yelled over the grating violence.

"Don't burn me!" she answered, in the midst of snapping a monk's neck.

Scorch concentrated. He was not thirteen and coming into his power for the first time, he was not saving his friends, he was not jumping off a mountaintop. He was changing, because he wanted to change, and within a heartbeat of making that decision, scales rippled over his skin and his body stretched and bent. His shoulder blades shot through his back and unfurled leathery wings that spanned the hall. He stood, strong and full of vengeful fire, and then he let it out in a spray so hot it was as blue as Elias' eyes.

He was mindful of Audrey's whirring figure, but everyone and everything else, he devastated. The stench of burning bodies filled his nose, but he spared no thoughts for his parents. He thought only of Vivid's closed eyes and grey skin, and he was happy to destroy the monks who had taken his life. They stood no chance.

When the fortress hall was nothing but a chamber of charred bodies, he tucked the heart of his power away and let his body shrink and lessen, until his claws and teeth and skin were human. He sank to the floor amongst the carnage, his boots destroyed, his clothes ripped from his body. With ash on his tongue and clinging to his eyelashes and coating his hair, he sobbed into his hands.

Seconds, or minutes, or a lifetime later, Audrey knelt before him, and he looked at her through sweaty lanks of hair and sooty fingers. She, too, was covered with a film of filth, and her expression was hard. She held out a hand, and he accepted it.

They walked over the blackened monks on light feet, Audrey holding his hand. He wasn't weak like he had been after changing the other times. He felt tired in his bones, but he wasn't overwhelmed with sensation. Tears still streamed from his eyes, but his sobbing had stopped; that, at least, he no longer had the strength for.

When they came to one of the many doors branching off the main hall, Audrey gave it a push and it opened with a squeak. Scorch stared at its innards, wide-eyed. The room was full of stoppered glasses, shelves upon shelves of colorful vials, powders, and potions. A table was the only other furniture in the room, and spread across its surface were drying herbs, pestle and mortars, and a chopping knife. Kio must have done her work at that table. Uninterested in her morbid concoctions, Scorch let go of Audrey's hand and walked to the neighboring door.

Before he opened it, he knew. Grief washed over him, but he made himself open the door. Like a punch to the gut, he saw him there, laid out on a tabletop, small and motionless in the dark. Scorch set the wall torches alight with a flick of his wrist and went to his side. He touched his hair. It was soft and shining, none of its luster lost in death.

Audrey joined him. "I found this for you," she said, slipping a monk's robe over Scorch's naked shoulders.

His breath hitched as he let his fingers trail down Vivid's cheek, barely touching. He stopped his hand over Vivid's heart and closed his eyes.

"We should bury him," Audrey said.

He nodded vaguely, and then he was leaning down and pressing his head against Vivid's chest. It wasn't right. It didn't make sense. Vivid wasn't supposed to die. He'd escaped the Circle and killed a lake monster. Scorch had seen him turn into a *vortex*, and now he was just lying there, gone.

The black leather felt rough beneath his cheek as he nuzzled Vivid's chest with a shuddering sigh, Audrey waiting silently beside him. "We shouldn't bury him," he whispered, his voice ragged. "If we build him a pyre, we can send his ashes into the wind."

Silence.

And then, a sound.

It was a small sound, weak and easy to miss, and maybe Scorch had already missed it, while heaving broken sighs into leather, but he didn't miss it now. His eyes widened, his body stiffened, and he listened, listened, listened.

The same sound, again. Barely there, so faint it hardly registered, but it was there and he heard it.

A heartbeat.

"Audrey." He lifted his head from Vivid's chest, and she was peering down at him worriedly. "He's alive."

"*What*?" Her fingers flew to Vivid's neck, pressing into his pulse points. Scorch watched her and waited, and then her eye met his, wonderstruck. "He's alive."

Scorch, weary and wasted only a moment before, felt like he'd been doused with ice-cold water and struck by lightning. His hands flew to Vivid's face. "He doesn't look alive," he muttered hastily, lifting an eyelid and checking Vivid's pupils. They didn't respond to the light, but neither did his eyes retain the dullness of death. "What's wrong with him?" he asked Audrey, panicked. Vivid was alive, but barely. "What do we do? *What do we do?*"

"I don't know," she exclaimed, wringing her hands.

Scorch picked Vivid gently up from the table, scooping him into his arms. He shoved his nose into Vivid's hair and breathed him in. "Kio told me she was testing something on him," he rambled, heading out of the room and into the main hall, Audrey hurrying after him. "A suppressant for elementals. She told me she used too much on him."

"Did she know he was alive?"

"We'll never know now, and it doesn't matter," Scorch said, rushing through the door Audrey held open for him. The moon was nearly full and the night was bright. Vivid's skin almost resembled its normal shade in the moonglow. "Can we take him to the Hollow? Axum has healed him before."

Audrey shook her head. "Axum began suspecting Vivid when he never returned. If we bring Vivid to the Hollow, he's as good as dead, and so are you."

"*Gods*," Scorch cursed. Vivid's body was feather-light in his arms. They made a quick return to their horses, who were still chomping away at the grass, happy and oblivious. "Do you know any healers? Herbalists?"

"None who aren't under Axum's thumb."

She accepted Vivid into her arms while Scorch mounted his horse, then they worked together to set him in the saddle. Vivid's head fell limply forward and Scorch wrapped an arm around him, holding him against his chest. It wasn't ideal, but it would do for the time. It was a blessing they had the horses at all.

"I know of an herbalist," Scorch admitted, the image of a garden springing forth. "But I don't know for sure if she'll help me."

Audrey mounted her horse and cast him a dangerous gaze. "*Make* her help you."

He nodded.

"I can't go with you," she announced as she picked up her horse's reins. "If I miss my briefing with Axum, he will begin to suspect me."

Scorch couldn't blame her for leaving. She had done so much already. "I can ride faster alone anyway," he said.

"Tell me where you're taking him, so I can contact you again."

He huffed a miserable laugh that ruffled Vivid's hair. "There is a woman named Etheridge that I know," he said, "at the Guardians' Guild."

Audrey maneuvered her horse to his side and clasped his shoulder. "You really are a fool," she said, but there was warmth in her eye. "Ride like the wind." She touched Vivid's cheek fondly. "Save him."

A lump formed in Scorch's throat and all he could do was nod. For Audrey, it was enough. She clicked her tongue at her horse and cantered away, westward, toward the Hollow.

Scorch tightened his grip on Vivid and searched for the pulse at his neck. When he found it, he sighed with temporary relief. Upsettingly temporary. The Guild was south of the Hollow by miles and miles. The journey would take days.

"Don't worry, Vivid. I've got you."

He tutted at his horse and began their trek at a gallop, his robe fluttering out behind them like cloth wings. Vivid jostled in the saddle, despite Scorch's best attempts to keep him sturdy. When they reached the main road, he knew the first thing he would have to do.

Luckily, like so many other things, Vivid had already taught Scorch how to steal.

# *Familiar Faces*
# *19*

Through the night, every time Scorch's paranoia took over, he stopped the horse, pressed his head against Vivid's chest, and waited until he could hear his heartbeat. It remained weak and far between, but it hadn't worsened.

Now, he lay in the middle of the road, clad in a monk's robe, waiting for someone to come along and run him over. He'd hidden Vivid safely among the cover of trees and posed himself as a monk in need of help, like last time. Granted, last time Vivid wasn't unconscious, and they were only stealing a horse, not an entire wagon, but Scorch would make it work.

The hour was early, the sun freshly raised. The southward road was heavily traversed by traders, and it was only a matter of time before Scorch heard hooves clopping and wheels spinning. He shut his eyes and waited.

"Stop! Stop! There's someone in the road!"

A horse whinnied and wood screeched. Scorch smelled the road dust as it was kicked up by hooves.

"Is he dead? We should see if we can help."

"Yeah, alright. Go on and check, then."

"Y-you want *me* to check?"

"Well, I've got to hold the reins, don't I? On you go to play healer, boy."

There was the sound of a distressed sigh, followed by the thud of feet leaping from a wagon. Scorch arranged his face in a way to best earn sympathy. He was covered in soot and looked like a shaggy vagabond, but he hoped the robe would lend him some clout.

He sensed someone nearing and heard a gasp. "Wait a second, Rex. I know this man!" exclaimed the voice, and Scorch cracked open an eye. A young man was leaning over him, studying his face in amazement.

"Since when do you know any monks, Flautist?" scoffed the second voice.

"He is *not* a monk, he is a Guardian of the Guild," the young man insisted, smiling down at Scorch when he saw he was awake. "You probably don't remember me, but Gods, I remember you. I wrote a song about the night you came to the inn."

Scorch blinked up at him. He was pretty and fresh-faced, with big blue eyes and red lips, and Scorch had definitely seen him before. "The flautist from the inn?" he asked uncertainly, scanning his mind for the night he'd tried hard to forget. He saw a young thing sitting across from him at a table. He saw a pretty bar wench kissing his cheek. "Felix?"

"Yes!" the young man laughed. He called over his shoulder to his companion. "He remembers me!"

"Fascinating. Get him out of the damn road."

"Oh, right. Can you walk? Are you hurt?" The flautist took Scorch's elbow and eased him to his feet. "Are you headed back to the Guild? We are going in that very same direction and it would be an honor to travel alongside a guardian. Rex doesn't mind, do you, Rex?"

The older man in the wagon grunted.

Scorch glanced between Felix and the wagon he'd intended on apprehending through thievery. He had not intended, nor would he ever have suspected, that a starry-eyed flautist would be offering him a ride exactly where he needed to go.

"Felix," he said, putting a hand on the flautist's shoulder, "I have never needed help more. I have precious cargo I must deliver to the Guild, and quickly. How fast can your wagon travel?"

Felix whipped his curly head around to his companion. "How fast can we be at the Guild, Rex?"

Rex grunted again. "First light tomorrow if we don't stop, I reckon."

"Is that fast enough?" Felix asked, but Scorch was already running to the trees. He recovered Vivid, checking his pulse before wrapping him up in his arms and returning to the wagon.

"My cargo," Scorch explained, moving around to the back of the wagon so he could settle Vivid. There was a stack of folded blankets beside a box of foodstuffs, and he quickly assembled a pallet and bundled Vivid up. He gave Vivid's hair a pet and poked his head around the wagon. "As I said, he is precious to me. Can you promise me a swift journey?"

Felix traveled around the side of the wagon and peered in curiously. "Rex is good with horses. He can get us to the Guild by sun up tomorrow." He looked like he wanted to ask about Vivid, but hesitated. "I never knew your name," he said. "In the song I wrote, I had to call you the Sun Guardian." He blushed. "Because of your hair, you see."

Scorch allowed himself a small smile. "My name is Scorch."

"Oh?" The flautist made a face. "Hmm."

"Felix?" Scorch asked.

"Yes?"

"Could we get going, please?"

"Yes, yes! All good back here?" When Scorch nodded, Felix patted earnestly at Vivid's shoe and scampered back around the wagon to fuss at Rex. "Onward, onward, Rex! The guardian's cargo is precious!"

The horse neighed and the wagon began to move. Scorch lay down beside Vivid and held his hand, angling his thumb over the pulse point in his wrist. After riding through the night, Scorch's body was beginning to protest wakefulness.

"Please be alive when I wake up," he whispered as his eyes drifted shut, and soon the rock of the wagon lulled him to sleep.

*He was sprawled on the cold floor of the mountain cave, but his body was warm. The Mountain Flower Whiskey had his head cloudy, and he was floating towards sleep.*

*He stretched his arms over his head with a blissful sigh and something shifted against his side. The whiskey had too much claim on him to let his eyes open, so he touched the presence beside him and hooked an arm around it, pulling it closer.*

*Someone mumbled against his chest as he rubbed his hand down rough leather. He sighed contentedly, so much happier with the weight in his arms.*

*His guardianship had been an ordeal, but at that moment, on the floor of a cave, he thought it well worth it. Hands slid across his abdomen and wrapped around his waist, and he heard the mumble again, dreamy.*

*He hoped he would remember that sound when he woke.*

A clap of thunder jerked Scorch awake, and he sat up with a gasp.

"It's okay. Only a little storm. Rex will see us through it in no time." Felix was sitting in the back of the wagon, scrunched up in the corner, chewing on a piece of bread. He offered some to Scorch, who shook his head even as his stomach rumbled.

"I couldn't," he insisted, eyes flashing down to Vivid. He leaned down and pressed his ear to his chest, listening for the weak beat of his heart. At first, he couldn't hear it, the rain pounding the wagon's canvas cover and drowning out heartbeats. He fumbled for Vivid's wrist, his eyes squeezed shut and breath quick, and when he finally heard the *thump,* he sighed. He kept hold of Vivid's wrist as he stared out the wagon's back. Night had already fallen. He'd slept the day away, and Vivid was still hanging on to his scrap of life.

Felix remained an unobtrusive presence, and when he offered Scorch a drink of water, Scorch accepted. He drank a healthful sip and then offered it up to Vivid's lips. It rolled, unswallowed, down his chin, and Scorch wiped it away with the sleeve of his robe.

"Is he a guardian, too?" Felix asked shyly, nodding at Vivid.

Scorch snorted. "No. Definitely not a guardian." He smiled. "You're lucky he's not awake or he'd kill you for even asking." It was fortunate that Felix didn't delve deeper into questions about their association, because Scorch hadn't the slightest idea how to describe his relationship with Vivid. *He's my assassin.*

However, now that the silence was broken, Felix had more to say. His fingers fidgeted in his lap, playing an invisible flute, plainly nervous. "No one blamed you for Flora," he blurted. Scorch had not heard the name in months, and he'd tried not to even think it. Hearing it now shook him, and his grip strengthened around Vivid's wrist.

"I saw you," Felix bit out, in clear discomfort. "That night. I was leaving the inn and saw the slavers dragging you away. I wanted to help you, but I—I only had my flute, and there were three of them, and I was afraid. I'm so sorry."

Scorch couldn't remember being dragged away; he was already unconscious by then. "It's good you didn't try to help, Felix. They would have killed you."

Felix was frowning, like he didn't entirely believe Scorch. "I should have tried," he said, looking out at the rain. "When word came around the next week that the Circle had been taken down by a tall, blond man, I knew it was you. That's w-when I wrote the song." He cleared his throat. "Would you like to hear it?"

"I would love to hear it."

When he'd experienced that terrible night with Flora, he'd never imagined any beauty would come of it, but Felix's song wove a tale so heartrending and inspiring about the Sun Guardian, his barmaid, and vanquishing masked villains, that it almost erased the bloody images from his mind.

Felix's voice was high and crisp and exquisite, and after a verse, he would bring his flute to his lips and play an accompaniment that brought tears to Scorch's eyes. The story was grossly inaccurate and made him sound like a demigod instead of a green guardian, but it was undeniably lovely, and when Felix was finished, Scorch squeezed his shoulder and told him what a talent he was.

"It wasn't your fault, what happened to her," Felix said a few minutes later.

Scorch didn't believe it, but it was nice to hear. He asked if Felix knew any songs about assassins, and it turned out he knew quite a few. They whiled the night away to the trills of black shadows and dangerous folk with stones for hearts and blades for hands. Vivid would have hated them all, but Scorch hung on to every word.

Rex was true as he was fast, and as the sun peeked over the horizon and the world took on the blue tint of early dawn, the road became familiar. High walls stood among the trees and took Scorch's breath away. Before the horses had even stopped, he was gathering Vivid in his arms and jumping from the wagon. He ran to the huge front door of the outer wall of the Guild, wooden and thick, with iron bars protecting it from unwanted guests.

"Help me!" Scorch yelled as loudly as he could, gazing to the top of the wall, where he knew sentry kept a constant post. "Please! I need aid!" His throat burned, and he gathered another deep breath before adding, "It's Scorch! Let me in!"

He knew not what to expect. Had Master McClintock told the others he was an elemental? Would he be greeted with arrows or a welcoming committee?

As usual, the last thing he anticipated was the way of things, and following his yells, the great door unlocked, opened, and a familiar face strode out to meet him. Scorch's vision was filled with deep auburn hair and green eyes.

"Scorch?" Merric asked, walking up to him with his mouth agape. "You're supposed to be dead."

So Master McClintock had just told everyone he'd died. He probably assumed Scorch *had* died.

"Why are you dressed like that? You look terrible. Who is this?" Merric gestured to Vivid.

"I need Etheridge," Scorch begged. "My friend needs healing."

Merric eyed the man in Scorch's arms briefly, and then he said, "Bring him in. Hurry. She's in her tent, as always."

Scorch didn't have time to soak in his surroundings, or relish the feeling of being within the Guild's walls again. He ran for the herbalist's tent, clutching Vivid against his chest. Merric, to his surprise, ran alongside him. Apprentices scattered out of their way and murmurs rose from the grounds in a catching buzz. He could already see the glistening river when a man stepped in front of him and cut off his path.

"Scorch." Master McClintock smelled of smoking weeds and looked almost like home, but his expression was displeased, disconcerted, and disapproving. "I was under the impression you had not survived your guardianship." His words had the air of careful construction, swollen with subtext.

Scorch had no time for it. "Master," he pleaded, holding Vivid tight, "he's dying. You have to let me see Etheridge."

The man he'd always trusted—up until the second he didn't—took a step toward Scorch and spoke to him in a hushed tone. "Your guardianship was a kindness, my boy," he said. "But I think we both know you cannot be here. It pains me to say it, but you are a danger to us all. You must leave."

"This man is dying in my arms," Scorch said, frustrated tears breaking free, "and you want to send me away? What is it you're afraid I'll do? Burn the place to the ground?" He let his voice strengthen with anger. "Because, Master, I will. If you don't let me through to heal him, I will burn the whole Guild down!"

"*Scorch*," Master McClintock whispered, horrified.

"If you were so afraid of an elemental, you should have killed me yourself. Now get out of my way!" Scorch shoved past him and started running for the herbalist tent. Behind him, he heard Merric say, "Father, let him go," and then his own screaming voice filled his ears. "Etheridge! Etheridge!"

She rushed from the tent, her braids lashing at her back as she ran to meet him halfway.

"Etheridge!" he yelled.

"Bring him inside." She held the tent flap open and Scorch hurried through. "Lay him down," she instructed, nodding toward the little cot she kept. When he hesitated, not wanting to let Vivid go, she clapped her hands at him. "Lay him down so I can tend to him, Scorch. Do it now."

He did as she asked, reluctantly placing him on the cot. She put her hands on Vivid immediately, feeling for his pulse and poking at his skin.

"What's happened to him?" she asked.

"Someone gave him something," Scorch explained shakily. "Something bad, to suppress his, his . . ."

"Spit it out."

Scorch took a chance, assuming everyone in the Guild would know about their elemental status before long anyway. "To suppress his powers," he said with an edge of defiance. "He's an elemental, same as me. Someone was experimenting on him, hurting him, and they nearly killed him."

Etheridge showed no reaction to the elemental reveal; she only poked at Vivid some more.

"Can you save him?" Scorch asked, fearful of her answer. "Please."

Etheridge shot him a searching look. "The last time I saw you, my Luna seed was finally ripe for harvesting," she said. Scorch nodded; he remembered. "Hand me that seashell. Over there."

He tripped over himself in his hurry to retrieve the shell from a shelf of dried herbs. "Will this help?" he asked, handing it to her.

She tipped the shell over her carefully cupped palm and out popped a pearly seed. "The Luna seed is said to cure any ailment."

"Give it to him."

"I will, but I should tell you first, the process of expelling poison from a body is a nasty, painful business, and as bad as your friend looks, he could spend hours in agony and die anyway."

"He won't die," Scorch told her. He stared down at Vivid, unmoving and grey and one meager heartbeat away from death. "Do it. Please."

Etheridge popped the seed into Vivid's mouth and massaged his throat until it went down. "It's done. Go clean yourself up and change into some fresh clothes," she ordered. "It'll be about an hour before he reacts."

Scorch lingered. "I don't need to freshen up. I'm fine. I want to stay here."

Etheridge fixed him with a withering glare. "That was my polite way of saying you stink. Go bathe, for the love of Gods. And shave that blasted beard. You look like a mountain bear. Merric, get him out of here."

Realizing Merric had slipped into the tent without his notice was the catalyst for Scorch agreeing to freshen up. If Merric could sneak up on him, it meant his senses were dulled, and a splash of cold water on his face wouldn't go amiss. Scorch was, in a way, in enemy territory, and he would be useless to Vivid if he allowed himself to become sloppy. He indulged in a final glimpse at Vivid, and then, with downcast eyes, followed Merric from the tent.

Master McClintock was waiting for them outside. He and Scorch stared bleakly at one another, until Merric spoke. "Etheridge has sent him to clean up, and then we're reporting back here straight away," he explained to his father.

"I need to speak with you, Scorch." The Master looked older than Scorch remembered, and bone tired.

"It can wait," Merric said, moving so he blocked Scorch's body with his own. "I will stay with him, if it sets your mind at ease, but time is short, and you can speak to him when his ordeal has passed."

Scorch could hardly believe what he was hearing, but he kept his mouth shut and hoped Merric's out of character defense would be enough to let him walk away from Master McClintock. Merric stood straight, his hands relaxed at his sides and his head tipped high, and Scorch had never thought him handsomer.

After an unsettling bout of familial glaring, the Guild Master stepped aside, but as Merric made to pass, he grabbed his arm. "See that you do not leave him alone" he whispered, loudly enough that he may as well have shouted.

Merric's only response was a terse sigh and a rapid progression toward the Guild House, with Scorch on his heels.

He received looks from every direction as they wound their way through the halls and into the bathhouse. Some seemed to know who he was, murmuring his name as they passed, but many didn't recognize him. When he spotted his reflection in the bathhouse looking glass, he was surprised anyone had known it was him, especially Felix the Flautist.

The greatest offense was the layer of soot on his face and in his hair, mixed with days of worried sweat. For once, there was no blood, but that was only because he had burned all the monks before he had a chance to pull his blade. His hair was too long from travel and neglect and his beard had grown thicker while living in the woods. He *did* sort of resemble a mountain bear. When Vivid recovered, he might not recognize him in such a scraggly state.

"I need shears and a razor," Scorch decided, eyes sweeping over Merric as he filled one of the tubs with water heated by the natural springs within the Guild walls.

"They are where they've always been," Merric answered.

Scorch fetched them from the bathhouse's toiletry chest and set to righting himself. He gathered chunks of his hair, dulled and darkened with grime, and clipped it off until it was his usual messy scruff. The beard took longer, because he had to clip it and then shave, but soon that was gone, as well, and his face was smooth. He looked more like himself, but his reflection still instigated unease in his stomach. He was leaner, his jawline sharper, his cheeks gaunter, and his eyes were clouded with weariness.

And he had scars.

"Water's going to get cold," Merric said from the corner of the room. He planted himself on the edge of another tub, his body angled away from Scorch as he disrobed and sank into the hot water.

There was no luxuriating in the bath. He scrubbed his skin and hair perfunctorily, until the water resembled liquid slate, and then he hurried out and wiped himself down with the towel Merric set out for him. Clean and anxious to get back to Vivid, he stood a bit awkwardly with the towel wrapped around his waist, coughing to garner Merric's attention.

Merric faced him, not quite managing to hide the lifting of his eyebrows at the sight of Scorch in a towel.

"Like what you see?" Scorch joked, but his attempt at levity fell in shatters to the floor. He dragged a hand over his newly cut hair. "Sorry, I don't know why I said that." Merric's expression was a puzzle. "I need clothes," he said, trying to ignore the blush in his cheeks. "Can we go to my room?"

"I had some sent down," replied Merric, and sure enough, clean clothes were waiting for Scorch outside the bathhouse. Merric fetched them and handed them over bashfully before turning around to examine the floor tile.

Scorch dressed in the simple clothing, the trousers and shirt given to all incoming apprentices, light brown, soft, and loose. He'd not worn similar for several years. Merric had also thought to have lambskin slippers sent, and Scorch stepped into them gratefully, but with a pang for the red boots he'd lost in the fortress.

Washed, dressed, and yearning to return to Etheridge's tent, Scorch let Merric lead the way. They walked in silence and it was the least antagonistic time the two had ever shared with one another. When Scorch's head had room for thoughts other than Vivid, he would ask Merric why he was being so kind, but for now, his focus was singular, and all that mattered was the man lying on Etheridge's cot.

He'd been gone no longer than half an hour, but Etheridge looked unsurprised to see him back so soon. She motioned to the jugs stacked at the entrance of the tent and ordered him to fill them up. He was eager to help however he could, so he gathered them up and made for the river.

The day was cold and clear, and the river was colder and clearer. He dipped the mouth of a jug beneath the water, staring at the ripples as it slowly filled. Merric helped.

"You're an elemental," Merric said softly, after their jugs were halfway filled. "I didn't know."

"Master McClintock didn't tell you?" Scorch asked.

Merric shook his head, and Scorch noticed, for the first time, a heat in his eyes. "No. He said you died during your guardianship."

Scorch rolled his eyes. He had thought Axum and the Guild Master so different, but in the end, they were largely the same: liars and schemers, the both of them. "Wishful thinking on his part, I suppose."

Merric set his filled jug aside and reached for another. "I didn't know," he said again. "If I had known what he intended when he sent you," he looked up at Scorch with a pained expression, "I would have warned you. I would have spoken with him."

"But you don't like me," Scorch said, perplexed.

"I don't like you," Merric agreed. "But I don't hate you. And I don't believe being an elemental is enough to deserve hate. For what it's worth."

"It's worth a lot."

They finished filling the jugs in silence, Scorch pondering whether he'd ever had the right idea about anyone. When they returned to the tent, balancing the jugs in their arms, Scorch nearly dropped his. Etheridge had removed Vivid's cuirass.

"Wet some cloths with water," Etheridge ordered. "He's already feverish."

Scorch set the jugs down with minimal spillage and dunked a handful of rags in the water, wringing out the excess before rushing to Vivid's side. He tried to keep from staring at the expanse of skin before him, but it was nearly impossible, especially when Etheridge instructed he begin dabbing at his neck and chest with the cool cloths.

Other than the time Vivid had trounced around the inn room topless in order to dress his wounds, Scorch had only ever seen snatches of his skin: his shoulder and collarbone when he'd been injured, the column of his spine at the waterfall. Now, his chest was bared and Scorch had legitimate reasons to touch and look, but it felt wrong. It wasn't the way he wanted to see him.

Vivid's pallor was still a lifeless grey, but his skin, as Etheridge said, was warming. Perspiration shone at his temples and Scorch wiped it away with the cloth. Besides the color and circumstance, his body was very much how Scorch remembered it, all lean muscle and silver scars, his stomach flat and defined. He was beautiful. And he was sweaty. What began as a light perspiration evolved into a profuse sweat.

"This is good," Etheridge said. "His body is purging the poison. The Luna seed is working."

Scorch kept dabbing at his feverish skin while Merric handed him fresh cloths and Etheridge kept track of his pulse. When she announced, an hour later, that his color was beginning to change, Scorch could have wept, because it was true. His cheeks were losing their lifeless tint. Splotches on his chest were fading from grey to chalky white.

After another hour of the same, Etheridge tried to get Vivid to accept a drink of water. Scorch watched closely as she held the cup to his lips. When Vivid's throat bobbed in a swallow, they all sighed in relief, and, for a few moments, Scorch allowed the fire in his chest to flicker with hope.

Then Vivid began to seize.

"Hold him down!" Etheridge yelled.

Scorch and Merric grasped Vivid's shoulders as his body quaked. Etheridge rubbed a black salve over his forehead, the hollow of his throat, and his sternum.

"What's happening to him?" Scorch asked frantically. Vivid's face was flushed and he was gasping and moaning. His hands were clenched into fists.

"This is the dangerous part," Etheridge said, holding Vivid's head in her hands as he shook. "He's expunging the last of the toxins. If he survives the next hour, he should live."

Time seemed to stretch on forever as Vivid fought Kio's poison. His body was in a state of constant jolts, as if he was being electrocuted from the inside out, and it took all Scorch's strength to hold him to the cot. He became nothing more than an anchor for Vivid's storm as he gasped and shook, his body as hot as Scorch's when he was about to combust. It was such an intense series of minutes that Scorch found himself hoping it would never end, because as long as Vivid kept convulsing, he would never die.

He was so hypnotized by the drama of the scene that Etheridge had to peel his hands off Vivid once the seizures finally ebbed. Scorch blinked, and though the world was shaking around him, Vivid had grown peaceful.

"It's over," Etheridge told him. "His pulse is steady." Scorch nodded, numb. "Merric, take him for some fresh air."

Merric took Scorch by the arm and strolled him down the riverbank. They walked for several minutes before he came back to himself. He stopped walking and stared back at the tent.

"Scorch, it's okay," Merric said. "He's resting now. Here." He handed Scorch a canteen with a fixed look on his face, like he'd been offering it for a while.

Scorch accepted the drink and ended up drinking all of it, but Merric didn't seem to mind.

"What happened to you?" he asked when he took back the canteen.

"What do you mean?" Scorch's head was fuzzy. The sun was too bright. He wanted to go back to the tent.

Merric looked at him with those green, green eyes, trying to suss him out. "You're not who I remember." Scorch shrugged, supposing Merric was right, and they both looked back toward the tent. "Who is he to you?"

Scorch inhaled, exhaled. "Vivid."

"Scorch!" called a voice attached to a breathless young flautist. Felix jogged up to them and stopped, panting. The bright sun revealed previously unnoticed freckles dusting the bridge of his nose.

"You stayed?" Scorch asked. He'd never looked back after he leapt from the wagon, not even to thank Felix and Rex for their kindness.

"Of course," Felix breathed with a smile. "Rex had to go on account of his deliveries, but I wanted to make sure you and your cargo were okay." His eyes darted to Merric for a second, then to Scorch, then back to Merric. "Hi," he said bashfully.

Merric returned Felix's slow smile with one of his own, reserved as it was.

"Felix, this is Guardian Merric," Scorch said.

"I'm only an apprentice," Merric was quick to correct, but he took a step forward and extended his hand, which Felix grasped eagerly. "Hello."

"Hi."

"Felix," Scorch interrupted. "You were running. Are you alright?"

"Oh!" Felix jumped, snapping his hand out of Merric's. "Your friend is awake. The herbalist sent me to tell you."

Scorch grabbed Felix and tugged him into a brief, intense hug, and then he was nothing but wind as he ran full speed for the tent. He burst through its white hanging flaps, kicking over the last remaining jug of water. Etheridge cursed him as it spilled all over the floor, but Scorch didn't hear her voice, and he didn't feel the water soaking into his trousers as he knelt beside the cot, because Vivid's eyes were open and clear and looking right at him.

# *Alive and Swell*
# 20

The small assassin looked worn and dehydrated, and his hair was a sweaty tangle, but he was *breathing,* and Scorch reached out and took his hand before he could remind himself how stupid it would make him feel. It did make him feel stupid, but it made him feel other things, too, things that were more encompassing than embarrassment. Vivid's hand felt cool in his, and fragile, and though he glared at the liberties Scorch took in demanding the connection, he didn't pull away.

Scorch had a million things to say, had rehearsed half a million of those things in his head, but now that Vivid's eyes were on him, he couldn't think of a single one, so he didn't speak at all. He looked. He looked at the amethyst gleam of his eyes in their thick frame of lashes, the beads of sweat resting on the soft slope of his nose, the ragged chop of his hair, where Kio had cut the sweep from his eyes.

When Vivid finally spoke, the long-missed sound made Scorch gasp. He realized, with a jab of discontent, he'd not heard Vivid's voice in several weeks, and though it was weak and raspy, it still clapped like thunder in his ears and he found himself levitating closer. The words themselves were predictably venomous. "I told you not to follow me."

Scorch found his voice at the same time he found himself squeezing Vivid's hand. "Audrey made me." It wasn't what he wanted to say. He wanted to tell Vivid how happy he was that he was alive, confess how miserable he'd been when they were separated, how he should have followed him that night, no matter what threats Vivid made. But the way Vivid began pulling back his hand weakened Scorch's resolve. He surrendered his grip and the contact between them was stymied.

A wrinkle formed between Vivid's eyebrows and he crossed his arms over his chest, still exposed. Scorch grabbed a shorn half of Vivid's cuirass, which Etheridge had tossed to the ground hours before, and handed it to Vivid so he could hold it to his chest for privacy. Vivid, apparently disheartened by the gesture, threw the leather back to the ground. He coughed, his lips pale, and stared up at the ceiling, away from Scorch's probing gaze.

"Audrey made you," Vivid said.

"She came to me when—" Scorch looked over his shoulder. Etheridge was watching with a curious expression, and Merric and Felix were lingering by the tent flaps. He turned back to Vivid with a sigh. "We should speak in private. I have so much to tell you."

Vivid's eyes flashed. "You think I want to hear the story of the brave guardian who saved the damsel in distress, but I don't."

"How about the story of a charming, roguish, handsome ex-guardian who rescued an ungrateful, *short* damsel in distress?"

Color painted Vivid's cheeks and sent Scorch's heart into eurhythmics. "You are not charming," he said with a heated rumble. "Or roguish."

"But I'm handsome?"

"I would rather be dead than look at you," Vivid spat, and Scorch laughed.

"Alright, alright," Etheridge intervened, settling a hand on Scorch's shoulder. "Touching as this is, your friend needs to rest."

"He is not my friend," Vivid snapped.

Etheridge smirked at him. Scorch knew that smirk. "That much is obvious," she said. "All the same, get out, Scorch. The boy needs rest."

"I'm not a boy," Vivid protested irritably. He tried to lift up on his elbows, but his arms collapsed beneath him, and he fell back to the cot with a defeated huff.

"Boy, girl, what do I care?" Etheridge said with a pointed finger. "You have been damn near dead for days, and your body needs rest." Scorch grinned down at Vivid, until Etheridge rounded on him and grabbed his ear. "And *you* need to go see the Master and let your boyfriend sleep."

Vivid groaned and Scorch felt his entire body blush. He leaned closer to Etheridge and whispered, "I don't want to leave him."

Etheridge patted Scorch's cheek. "He'll be safe with me." And when he looked doubtful, she patted it again, harder, and joined him in a whisper. "If you think I would let anyone come into this tent and hurt one of my patients, you don't know me very well." She kissed his cheek. "I'll take care of him."

Scorch nodded, blinking away a grateful tear, and then he looked at Vivid. "I'll be back. I promise."

"Stop looking at me like that," Vivid grumbled.

"Scorch?" Felix tapped him on the shoulder. "I can stay with him, if you'd like."

He turned to the flautist. Merric stood beside him. "It's better he not accompany us to see the Master," Merric reasoned.

And since it was obvious that Felix would be remaining in close proximity, one way or another, Scorch shrugged his approval. When he caught Vivid's darkening expression, a brilliant idea came to mind. "Felix, you should play Vivid your song about the Sun Guardian. I think he would really like it."

Felix's excitability was tangible, and he pulled his flute from a fold in his trousers with flourish. "It w-would be an honor to entertain your friend, Scorch."

Etheridge shooed Scorch and Merric from the healing tent, but not before Scorch stole a final glance at Vivid. He looked furious and alive and wonderful.

The feeling of joy sparked in Scorch's chest the entire walk from the tent to Master McClintock's door, but it was abruptly snuffed out when he remembered he was about to either be killed by the Guild Master, sentenced to death by the Guild Master, or thrown out on his ass by the Guild Master. Beside him, Merric's energy was buzzing equally, and Scorch resigned himself to the fact that it would be an interesting meeting, no matter the outcome.

The door opened and the afternoon sun filtered through the stained glass, filling the room with rainbow light. Smoke from the Guild Master's pipe made the air thick and sweet, and Scorch stepped inside with a deep inhale, filling his nose with nostalgia. Master McClintock was pacing the floor in front of his desk. At their entrance, he came to a standstill, his fingers frozen in mid-scratch upon his beard.

"Your friend lives, I hope," he said.

"He's an elemental," Scorch replied. "Do you truly care whether he lives or dies?"

The Guild Master's hand left his beard to reach for the pipe on his desk. Scorch noticed it was freshly packed with purple herb.

The Master patted down his pockets for his flint striker, and then, unsuccessful, his eyes roamed over his messy desk. Scorch couldn't resist. He stepped forward, snapped his fingers, and the herbs within the pipe began to singe and crackle. The Master nearly dropped the pipe.

"Your guardianship proved to be more than a death sentence, Master," Scorch said. "I can control it now." He looked askance at Merric. "And I've not set anyone's underclothes on fire in quite some time. I've set other clothes on fire, of course. But that was on purpose."

Merric and his father never looked more different. It was almost as if their roles had reversed. Usually, it was Merric scowling at Scorch in disapproval while the Guild Master smiled indulgently at the wily apprentice. And though Scorch liked the way Merric was finally smiling at him, he disliked more the Guild Master's sour expression. It made him feel every bit the monster the world supposed him to be, a dangerous *thing* that needed erasing. Once, he might have agreed. But he was no longer the only elemental he knew, and so he could no longer stand for the assault, silent or screaming, of their character. He wasn't a monster. Audrey wasn't. Vivid wasn't.

"You've called me away from the herbalist's tent to speak with me, yet all you do is stare and ignore your pipe. I promise the smoke won't be any worse for you, because it was lit by me." Scorch straightened his shoulders and kept his chin lifted proudly.

Master McClintock returned his pipe to the desk and leaned against it. He did not look, to Scorch, like a man worth respecting. Not anymore. "Merric, wait outside," he ordered, but his son remained at Scorch's side, unflinching.

"I will stay, Guild Master," Merric declared. "I don't believe this conversation should rely solely on your retelling."

The Guild Master sighed and took up his pipe, already forgetting his previous hesitance. He pulled the smoke into his mouth and exhaled through his nose. "There really was a missive from the Queen," he said, eyes glassy. "She had heard rumors that some wished the High Priestess dead. She did not, however, request that the Guild send protection." He paused to suck on his pipe and rub at his temple. "As you know, the High Priestess has her own protection."

"*Had*," Scorch corrected.

The Guild Master choked on a drag of smoke. "Had is correct. Word has spread that the High Priestess is dead."

"Word will spread soon that her leftover monks are dead, too," Scorch provided helpfully. "They seem to have gone up in flames without their Priestess."

The Guild Master stared at Scorch. "I sent you on your guardianship as a mercy, to allow you the chance to die honorably, as a guardian, instead of in shame, as an elemental. And you repay my kindness by—"

"By *living*," Scorch said, anger escaping his body through the heat of his words instead of fire at his fingertips. "As I said before, you should have killed me yourself if you wanted me dead."

"Father." Merric stepped between Scorch and the Guild Master. Scorch's ears perked in interest at the title; he had never heard Merric refer to his father as such. "Is this true? Did you send Scorch on a suicide mission?"

"As a guardian, the risk of death is ever present," Master McClintock defended.

"But to send him down the Monk's Path when his aid was not even requested?" He looked to Scorch with wonder. "It's a miracle he's alive."

"Hey," Scorch said, with a hand to his chest, offended. Then he recalled how many close brushes with death he'd experienced and deflated a bit. "That is true, actually. I would be dead ten times over if it weren't for Vivid."

"Vivid?" asked the Master, handling the name with care, as if it dirtied him to speak it. "I assume that is the name of your elemental?"

"He's not *my* elemental," Scorch said, hating how often he was blushing these days. "But yes. That's his name. And one of the more memorable times he saved my life was when the High Priestess had me tied to a chair with intricate plans to *torture me.*" Scorch let himself enjoy their shock before speaking again. "I take it you were unaware that the High Priestess was insane," he ventured after a suitably dramatic pause. "And that she despised elementals so much that she tortured the few she didn't have murdered, even small children." He grimaced at the thought. "I didn't kill the High Priestess," he admitted, "but good riddance."

More silence, and then Master McClintock asked, "And the Priestess' Monks?"

"Oh, I killed *them*," Scorch answered briskly. "But believe me when I say they started it."

"The High Priestess was going to," Merric's face was screwed up in concentration, "torture you?"

"She was," Scorch said, zeroing in on the Guild Master. "After I risked life and almost all my limbs to save her, she had no qualms about torturing me to death once she found out I was an elemental. Should I be thanking you, Master, for being kind enough to send me straight into her arms instead of doing what she wanted to do yourself? The man who saved my life, who was lying in Etheridge's tent a bit ago, nearly dead, would you see him tortured and killed, as well?"

"Scorch," Master McClintock said calmly.

"I trusted you. And you wanted me dead." Scorch was losing steam as the emotions attached to his words caught up with him. Maybe the Guild had never truly been Scorch's home, and the Guild Master was never his father, but they were all he had for a long time, and he had clung desperately to the idea that Master McClintock took him in because he cared whether or not he lived or died. And he might have, up until the time he discovered who Scorch really was.

"I never wanted you dead." Master McClintock had set his pipe down again and was back to pacing in front of his desk, stirring the smoky air around him. "But I had the entire Guild to protect, and elementals . . . you know how dangerous they are."

"Burning down a forest dangerous?" asked Scorch.

The Master shook his head. "I should have realized the truth back then. Maybe I did and didn't want to believe it."

"Easier to cast out a man of twenty than a boy of thirteen. When did you find me out for sure?"

"It was no moment of absolute epiphany, more an awareness of no other possible conclusion. One too many laundry days where my things were returned to me with . . . scorch marks, if you will. Only on days when you were scheduled to do the folding."

Merric coughed, but it might have been a laugh.

"So setting a forest on fire is fine, but mess with your underclothes and it's a step too far," Scorch said.

"More like a step too many," the Master sighed. "Once I opened my eyes to it, the rest all made sense, and as much as I would have liked to, I couldn't ignore it any longer. I sent you away shortly after. I wasn't proud to do it."

"That doesn't excuse what you did," said Merric.

"It's okay," Scorch said, keeping his eyes on the Guild Master. "I'm thankful you sent me away. I never would have learned to control my powers otherwise, and I never would have—" He paused. Merric was grinning slyly beside him. "I never would have met . . . anyone else like me. If I'd met Vivid sooner, if more elementals had someone to teach them how to control their power, instead of bottling it up until it became *dangerous*, then maybe people wouldn't be so afraid, and maybe elementals wouldn't be hunted down like terrors. But the past is the past, isn't it? The real question is whether or not you're going to send me away again, or raise the alarm that elementals have infiltrated the Guardians' Guild."

Master McClintock walked around his desk and collapsed into his chair, his head falling into his hands. "I never wished you dead, Scorch. And I do not wish it now." His green eyes peered through smoke-stained fingers. "All the same, I cannot allow you to remain a guardian, as it is forbidden by Viridorian law." Scorch nodded. He'd figured as much. "But you may remain here while your friend recovers."

"Housing an elemental is also forbidden by Viridorian law."

"Which is why you will not be allowed inside the Guild House," Master McClintock said. "You can make camp beside the river, well away from any structures. Or trees."

"You're spoiling me," Scorch said drily.

"I will stay close to him," Merric offered.

Scorch narrowed his eyes in suspicion. "Careful, Merric, you'll give me the wrong idea."

"Please. Your boyfriend would murder me."

"Whatever this conversation is, it can be continued elsewhere, far from my ears," pleaded the Guild Master. "Merric, you are to remain at Scorch's side while he remains within the Guild walls. Any unsavory activity is to be reported at once. Understood?"

"Is that your idea of unsavory?" Scorch asked. "Or mine? I have a hunch they're quite different."

The Master tsk-tsked them out of the room and practically slammed the door shut. Scorch was preparing something smart to say when a woman rounded the corner and caught sight of him. She was pretty and tall, with sandy blonde hair, and her name was . . . Gods, her name, her name began with an M, right? Millie. Molly. Missy?

"Mazzy," greeted Merric.

"Mazzy!" Scorch announced as she stopped right in front of him.

"Hi, Scorch. Someone said you were back, but I didn't believe it." She flattened a palm against his chest. "We all thought you were dead."

He backed away from her touch, half-hiding himself behind Merric. "I thought I was dead a few times, myself," he laughed.

She looked at him as if she knew exactly what he looked like without his apprentice clothing on. And she did. "We should get together later and talk. I would love to hear about your guardianship." The way her eyes twinkled when she said "talk" made Scorch doubt she had anything to say to him other than single word commands concerning pace and enthusiasm.

"I can't," Scorch said. "I've got a thing. That is to say, I'm busy later. And forever."

Mazzy didn't look disappointed or insulted, but she did look at Merric with fluttering lashes.

"I'm busy, too," Merric hurried to say, interestingly enough. Scorch remembered Merric being extremely keen to "talk" with Mazzy.

"Okay, then." She was utterly unbothered by their rejections. She squeezed Scorch amiably on the shoulder. "I'm really glad you're alive," she said, and then she sauntered back down the hallway, her hips swishing. When she rounded the corner, Scorch turned to Merric as Merric turned to Scorch.

"You're in love with him," Merric said.

Scorch gasped, then coughed, then crossed his arms defensively across his chest. Far too late, he coolly asked, "With who?"

Merric looked at him like he was stupid, and maybe he was. "Vivid. The elemental you were crying over and refuse to shut up about." Scorch gawked, his mouth hanging open in a way that was probably unattractive, but honestly. *In love with Vivid*? "He's pretty," Merric added thoughtfully.

"I am not in love with Vivid," Scorch insisted as they continued down the hall.

"You didn't even *look* at Mazzy," Merric pointed out unhelpfully. "The Scorch I know would have, you know, definitely looked."

It was true. They passed three more apprentices on their way outside, two boys and another girl, all of whom Scorch had *looked* at prior to his guardianship. But Scorch had been through a lot lately, hadn't he? And he was tired. Too tired to look. "Just because I'm not interested in sleeping around doesn't mean I'm in love with Vivid."

"Of course not," agreed Merric. He held the door open for Scorch and they stepped outside. "Have you slept with anyone since you met him?"

"I'm not sure if you're aware, but I have been extremely busy," answered Scorch. He could already see the white tent in the distance, and the sight of it was instantly soothing.

"Busy being in love with Vivid," Merric mumbled, and Scorch swatted his arm, barely thinking of how strange it was to be talking with Merric and walking with him in camaraderie. He wasn't even compelled to stare at Merric's backside as he trudged ahead of him toward the tent, and he knew from years of admiring that it was an exceptional backside.

But that didn't mean he was in love with Vivid.

Felix poked his head out of the tent as Merric walked up. They smiled sheepishly at each other and Scorch realized why Merric hadn't been interested in Mazzy. He walked past them into the tent, where Etheridge was quietly mixing something mint-scented in a bowl, and where Vivid was lying on the cot asleep, a fat grey cat curled up on his chest.

Scorch went to his side, sinking to his knees and resting his elbows on the cot. The cat blinked sleepily and Scorch watched her lift and fall as she rode the tide of Vivid's breathing.

"He's kept down water and a bite of porridge," Etheridge whispered.

Scorch nodded his thanks, but he couldn't look away from Vivid. He'd fallen asleep with his hand buried in the cat's fur. He liked animals, Scorch knew, and the cat certainly liked him. Her head was resting on his chest and she was purring loudly.

"When was the last time you slept?" Etheridge asked.

Scorch rubbed at his eyes. "Not too long ago," he answered. A yawn crept up on him, and he covered it with his hand.

"I can make a pallet for you," she offered, but Scorch was already lowering his head to rest on the edge of the cot.

"I'm fine here," he insisted. "I like it here."

He did like it there, his head resting an inch from Vivid's body, close enough to touch. He liked it so much that he fell asleep within seconds, the cat's tail curling around his wrist. He liked it so much that, even though his back was bent uncomfortably, and his neck already had a crick in it from the weird angle, and grey fur was irritating his nose, there was nowhere else he would rather be.

But that didn't mean he was in love with Vivid.

# Changes
## 21

Scorch woke up some time during the night. Someone had thrown a blanket over his shoulders and lit a candle, which flickered all alone on Etheridge's worktable. Etheridge herself was absent. The cat had moved from Vivid's chest to his feet, and Scorch's hand had moved from the cot to Vivid's thigh. He let it rest there a moment before realizing that Vivid was just as awake as he was, and then he snapped his hand back, pushing himself so forcefully from the cot that he landed on his backside. It was a relief for his knees, honestly, which had been awkwardly bent for hours while he slept.

Vivid's face was candlelit, and Scorch tried his best to focus on his eyes instead of the tantalizing span of his bare chest. Absently, Vivid's hand moved to brush the lock of hair from his eyes, but it was no longer there. It hurt Scorch to see his fingers fumbling, only to find his hair carelessly clipped to the root. Vivid hid his surprise well, but Scorch still saw it, in the freezing of his fingers and the delicate pursing of his lips. He must have been unconscious when Kio took the lock of hair. Scorch swallowed down the urge to grab onto him and prove to himself he was okay, but he had to settle for watching him in the dark, too many inches away.

"Time for a haircut, I think," Vivid said, tugging on his uneven strands.

"I can give you one in the morning," Scorch proposed, giving his own freshly sheared hair a tug of acknowledgement. He expected a multitude of reactions to such an offer, something sharp thrown at his head, for example, but Vivid, as Scorch should have known by now, was full of surprises.

"Alright," he answered. He flexed his feet beneath the blanket and the cat started purring again, nuzzling against his toes. With no thick lock of hair to hide behind, the way Vivid looked at Scorch was far more distracting, and the route his eyes cut of Scorch's face was far more intimate. When the scrutiny landed on his jawline, Scorch remembered the last time he'd been freshly shaven around Vivid. The memory made him smile.

"I can't tell," Scorch said.

Vivid's eyebrows competed with the rest of his features for the best portrayal of grumpiness. "Can't tell what?"

"Whether you like me better with a beard or not." He rubbed a hand over his smooth cheek.

"I dislike you equally, with or without a beard."

"So I should grow it out?" Scorch asked.

Vivid shrugged noncommittally, but his fingers were tapping a quick rhythm on his leg. "I don't know why you think I care how you wear your facial hair."

"I'll keep it shaved," Scorch decided. Vivid's fingers stilled and his nostrils flared, and Scorch laughed. "See? You do have an opinion."

"No, I don't."

"Tell me what you prefer."

"I prefer not to see your face at all, let alone dictate its state of unkemptness."

They sat in silence until Scorch began to ache from not talking. It had been too long since he'd exchanged words with Vivid; he was craving it. And since he was yet to be thrown from the tent, it seemed Vivid wasn't against it either.

"You should have seen my beard a few hours ago," he said. "Etheridge made me shave it."

"I'll add that to my list of reasons to thank Etheridge," Vivid snarked.

"Thank Felix, too. He brought us here in his wagon."

"And you made it sound as if you carried me in your arms the whole way here."

"Just some of the way," Scorch admitted. He tried to smile, to make light of it, but the memory of holding Vivid was too heavy and too fresh, and he had to duck his head while his eyes misted.

"Stop it," Vivid growled. "Look at me." Scorch's eyes found his in the candlelight. His expression was severe. The cat had moved to his knees and was making biscuits. Scorch waited for Vivid to speak, but he wasn't speaking, only looking.

"What?" Scorch asked self-consciously.

"I went with Kio, because she said she had you. And when I arrived at the fortress, she told me you were dead."

"I wasn't," Scorch whispered.

"I didn't know that until I woke up. Come here."

Scorch's heart fluttered. "Come where?"

"Come *here*," Vivid demanded impatiently, and Scorch scrambled to his knees, scooting closer to the cot. Vivid stared at him intently. "I like it both ways," he said.

Scorch frowned. "What?"

"Your beard. I like it shaved and full. But I like it best in-between." Vivid relayed the admission with annoyance, leaving Scorch blank-faced and speechless. "Now go away. I'm tired."

Somehow, Scorch managed to climb to his feet and stumble from the tent, leaving Vivid to rumble grumpily and roll to his side on the cot, the cat mewing at the disturbance.

The night air was cold, but Scorch was hot, and he walked to the edge of the river, where he dipped his hands into the water and splashed his face. He wasn't surprised when he heard the flautist calling his name. Glancing up, water dripping from his lashes, he saw where Felix and Merric had set up camp a ways down the river. Felix waved his arms, even as Scorch began making his way over. When he collapsed beside the fire, Merric handed him a blanket and a piece of bread.

"Did you get kicked out?" he asked.

"No," Scorch lied. He looked over his shoulder at the white tent standing in the darkness, the tiny glow of the candle within barely visible, like a quiet heartbeat, like a beacon. He couldn't stop rubbing his hand over his chin as he ate and drank, calculating how long it would take for his beard to come in. It suddenly felt dire that he grow out his stubble as soon as possible. It was a silly desire, he knew, but he wished for it nonetheless as he spread out on the grass and gazed at the stars.


In the morning, following dreams filled with soft hair and rough edges, Scorch went to Vivid. Etheridge was anointing him with the same black salve she used the day before, claiming it was good for circulation, and as a result, Vivid had black smudges on his skin and a malcontent expression on his face. He was also,

Scorch noted with a modicum of disappointment, dressed. And though Scorch knew Vivid was relieved he was covered, he also knew he was anything but thrilled to be stuck wearing the clothes Etheridge had given him.

"We match," Scorch said as he bopped into the tent.

Vivid leered at him in his light brown apprentice garb. The soft, loose clothing was a stark contrast to everything else about the assassin, which made Scorch smile.

He tried to stand up from the cot, but he was so weak his knees buckled. Scorch was there in an instant, catching him before he could fall, and then he was pressed up against his chest, his hands seizing Scorch's shoulders for support.

"I told you not to try that yet," Etheridge tutted, and Vivid glared at her. Scorch liked watching him glare at other people, but he didn't have much time to enjoy it before Vivid was pushing away and falling back down to the cot with a frustrated sigh. "You'll feel better with some food in you." Etheridge said. She nudged Scorch. "I'll be in the garden. Make him eat something."

"Right," Scorch answered helplessly, waving at her as she fled the tent. He turned to Vivid, who was drowning in his apprentice clothes, the collar hanging off one of his shoulders. Vivid didn't seem to notice, and Scorch wondered if being topless for so long had skewed his previous need for covering every inch of his skin. Selfishly, he hoped so, because the flash of moon-white shoulder and prominent collarbones was a sight he could get used to seeing. "Hungry?"

Vivid *was* hungry. And thirsty. Ridiculously hungry and thirsty, or maybe not so ridiculous, considering he'd spent the past however many days too almost-dead to eat or drink anything. Scorch rummaged through Etheridge's food stores, picking out the best things, until a pile of options sat in Vivid's lap, mainly cured meats and hunks of bread and blocks of cheese. Some fruit and baked goods. Scorch munched on a cinnamon muffin while Vivid ate his way methodically through the pile, only stopping long enough to drink great gulps of water. Scorch worried he might eat himself sick, but before he exploded from food, he stopped, swallowing another sip of water and sitting back with a groan.

"How does a guardian get clean around here?" Vivid asked. "Or do you even bother?"

"There's no majestic waterfall, but we do have a civilized selection of bathtubs. We even have hot water," Scorch replied with affected haughtiness. "Would you like to hobble there, or shall I carry you?"

Vivid hobbled, but not without Scorch's help. Really, Scorch did most of the work, and Vivid had to keep his side pressed against him and his arm looped over his neck. Scorch thought Vivid would have preferred to skip a bath rather than be forced so close to him, but apparently, he was wrong. He grumbled the entire way to the bathhouse, but he never let go of Scorch, and Scorch held on as tight as he could without crossing the line from helpful to invasive.

The baths were miraculously empty, unlike the hallways, wherein Vivid and Scorch had received a jumble of differing looks, all of which made Scorch smile awkwardly and Vivid tense beneath his hands. He doubted Vivid would have even undressed with a guardian in the room, so it was a blessing they were alone. Scorch was filling up a tub with buckets of hot water when he recalled Merric was supposed to be shadowing them, and they were definitely not supposed to be inside the Guild House. Sure enough, after glancing to the bath doors, he spied a stoic shadow in the hall, accompanied by a trill of musical laughter that could only belong to Felix. Merric, it appeared, had no intention of keeping an elemental from their bath time.

If Vivid was perturbed by Merric's presence, Scorch couldn't tell, because the man was already perturbed by everything else, mainly his hair, which he kept running his fingers through. He let out an irritated little huff.

"We can cut it first," Scorch suggested, already leading Vivid toward a chair in the corner. The razor and shears were where he'd left them, and after lowering Vivid into the seat, he scooped up the shears and snapped them playfully in his hand. "How do you want it?"

Vivid looked unhappy and small in the chair, his hair an uneven, greasy mess. "Just cut it all off," he ordered.

Scorch frowned sympathetically, but he couldn't see another option. Kio had cut the thick front section of Vivid's hair so short that the rest of his hair looked strange in comparison. He would have to cut it as short as his own to even it out. Vivid gave him an impatient look and summoned him closer.

Up until the moment Scorch stepped up to him, he had somehow failed to realize he would need to *touch* Vivid's hair in order to cut it. It was oily from days and days without washing, but it still felt soft between his fingers. The dark strands were longer than he'd initially thought. He let his hand run through the length a few times, getting familiar with its weight and the way it fell. Vivid's part remained a zigzag at the crown of his head and Scorch traced it with a finger. It looked like a lightning bolt. When his fingers felt along the silky wisps at the base of Vivid's neck, Vivid leaned into the touch. Shocked past the point of being able to grip things in his hand, Scorch dropped the shears, and they clattered to the floor.

"Perhaps I should have asked the cat to cut my hair," Vivid said. It took an answering meow for Scorch to notice the cat had followed them from the tent and was lounging beside one of the tubs.

Scorch picked up the shears. "I think I'm more capable than a sleepy cat, thanks."

"Barely."

Scorch began cutting, taking far more care with Vivid's hair than he had taken with his own. He'd never cut anyone else's hair before, and it was harder than he'd anticipated. For a good five minutes, he was certain he'd botched the job and was brainstorming different scenarios of escape, but as he slowly moved around to the back of Vivid's head, things started to even out and look less wonky. His fingers brushed Vivid's skin after he snipped the inches away. It was odd to see his neck so exposed, and his ears, and his jawline. Features he'd never really noticed before revealed themselves with each snip, until Vivid's hair was as short as he dared make it. Their feet were surrounded by black discards, and he picked one up to hand to Vivid.

"Why did she cut it?" Vivid asked, twirling the lock in his fingers.

"She needed a lure," answered Scorch, coming around the chair to check his work. It was an okay job. It wasn't the Vivid he'd grown accustomed to looking at, but he liked seeing pieces of him he'd never seen before. "She sent it to the Hollow. Audrey found it, and then she found me." It felt like years ago when Audrey had handed him the cloth-wrapped hair, but it had only been a few days. "Did she have a lure, when she found you?"

"You," Vivid said. "She only told me she had you." *And that had been enough.* "Where did Audrey find you?"

Scorch fiddled with the shears. "I was living in a cave," he mumbled.

"Pathetic," said Vivid, but when Scorch mustered the nerve to look at him, his face was unreadable. "Leave so I can bathe without you mooning over me."

"You're too weak. I can't leave you."

"The day I'm too weak to get in a tub on my own is the day I kill myself," Vivid retorted. "Get out."

Scorch lingered a moment longer, hesitant to leave Vivid alone. He left only when the cat hissed at him and pawed at his heels. "Holler for me if you need help," Scorch called over his shoulder, to which Vivid replied with a harsh, "I would rather drown."

Merric and Felix were waiting outside the baths, Merric leaning against the wall while Felix smiled shyly in front of him. Scorch coughed to announce his presence.

"Kicked out again?" Merric asked, and Scorch told him to be quiet; he had to be able to hear if Vivid needed him.

Vivid accomplished bathing without incident, emerging from the baths smelling clean and looking healthy. His haircut was jarring, but the more Scorch looked at it, the more he liked it. Vivid's hand kept going to his forehead, though, to tuck hair that wasn't there behind his ear. And he kept pulling at his loose clothing, collarbones flashing.

They walked back to the tent together, Vivid still leaning on Scorch for support, but not nearly as much as before. It seemed the food and bath had done wonders for his strength. When Scorch opened the tent flap for him, he scowled and headed for the riverbank instead. They walked to the camp Merric and Felix had set up, and Vivid sat in the grass by the water. Scorch waved off Merric, who'd been walking several paces behind them, and went to sit by Vivid's side.

His hand was extended over the water, palm up, and he wore a worried crease between his eyes.

"What's wrong?" asked Scorch.

Vivid shook his head.

"Tell me."

"I can't feel it." When Scorch tilted his head in confusion, Vivid clarified. "The air."

"Oh." Amidst the threat of Vivid's death, Scorch had blocked out the rest of it. Kio's words, the burning of the monks, the table full of potions and herbs. He had not considered what would happen, if Vivid survived but his powers did not. "The injections Kio gave you," he said. "Did she tell you what they were for?"

"Yes." Without warning, Vivid's hand reached for Scorch's, linking their fingers. "Fire and air breathe into each other," he said, closing his eyes and squeezing Scorch's hand.

Scorch recalled the night he first made his elemental power work, and how holding Vivid's hand had helped harness his control. Understanding, he closed his eyes and summoned warmth to the palm of his hand, willing his strength into Vivid the only way he knew how. The skin of their touching palms began to sweat. But he felt no wind.

They sat for several minutes, Vivid trying to call to the air while Scorch tried to help, but it was no use. When Vivid finally pulled his hand back, he looked annoyed.

"You're still recovering," Scorch said. "It will come back to you."

"Don't try to placate me."

"I'm not. We don't know if what she did was permanent."

"The last time the monks had me as their prisoner, the damage was permanent," Vivid hissed, and Scorch's eyes slid down to his shoulder, where his scars were shining and prominent in the sunshine. "Thinking otherwise now would do more harm than good." He stood from the bank too quickly and Scorch almost didn't catch him before he fell. "Let go of me," Vivid barked, peeling Scorch's fingers from his waist and pushing him away.

As much as Scorch wished to comfort him, he knew his efforts would be lost to angry ears. He let Vivid stomp past him to the camp, where he sat beside the dead embers and glared. A cool wind made Vivid shiver, so Scorch waved his hand in front of the fire until it crackled to life. Vivid didn't thank him for the warmth, or speak to him at all for several hours, but Scorch hadn't expected him to, and he wasn't offended. He was furious at Kio for all the hurt she'd caused, and he found himself wishing she was alive just so he could kill her again, after he asked her how to reverse what she had done.

A week passed by, fast and slow. Vivid grew physically stronger every day, walking on his own and exercising in the mornings, solitary and vigorous. Scorch would eat breakfast with Felix and Merric and try not to stare too obviously as Vivid stretched and lunged and got sweaty in the cold air. His pallor was healthier, no trace of the scarily grey tones. And he had finally stopped trying to tuck his hair behind his ear, possibly the greatest victory of all.

But mentally, something was off, and the cause was no secret to Scorch. He would watch Vivid daily, sitting beside the river and trying to summon the wind, but it would never come. Every day it didn't return, Vivid lost more faith it ever would. Scorch might have considered it a gift to never need worry about being an elemental, but to Vivid, it was a punishment.

If Vivid was prickly before, now he was impossible. When he wasn't staring morosely into the river, he was brandishing insults like one of his daggers. Merric and Felix kept their distance, trading worried glances as they tracked the assassin from afar, but Scorch refused. He refused to leave Vivid alone with his ill, self-flagellating moods. One day, as Vivid barraged him with one cruelty after another, he finally lost his temper.

"Enough!" he yelled, grabbing Vivid by the collar and hoisting him to his feet.

"Don't touch me," Vivid growled, directing an elbow at his stomach, but Scorch was ready for it. He caught Vivid's wrist and bent low, hefting the smaller man over his shoulder. Vivid kicked wildly and twisted his body, trying to get down, but Scorch had a firm grip, and he couldn't squirm free.

Merric and Felix watched with horrified faces as Scorch stomped past them, Vivid cursing as he struggled over his shoulder. There were a lot of death threats, but Scorch was used to those. When he finally let Vivid go, they were in the empty training ring, where Scorch used to take his sparring lessons. He threw Vivid down, not trying to be gentle. Vivid rolled and landed on his feet.

"Fight me," Scorch demanded needlessly, for Vivid was already attacking, launching himself forward.

It had been a spell since Scorch fought without having his life on the line, but that was assuming Vivid wasn't actually trying to murder him, and, going by the way he was currently strangling him, that was up for debate.

Scorch broke out of Vivid's chokehold and punched, knowing it would be blocked, which it was. Despite being brought back from the brink of death a little over a week ago, Vivid moved like quicksilver, delivering blows and kicks with an efficiency that had Scorch backing up to the edge of the ring. The last time Scorch fought Vivid, they'd been in the Circle, and Vivid's ferocity was even greater now as he jumped, wrapped his legs around Scorch's middle, and toppled them both to the ground. They rolled in the dirt, and within seconds, Vivid had him on his back with a forearm braced against his throat.

"This feels familiar," Scorch wheezed.

"It could end differently this time," Vivid warned, his voice tight.

"It could," Scorch agreed. "You could kill me if you wanted to. Because even without your elemental powers, you're amazing."

Vivid was off him in a second, kicking him angrily in the side before backing away. "What is this? A ruse to make me believe in myself? Are you a child?"

"Are *you*?" Scorch asked, sitting up. "You've been acting like one ever since you lost your power."

"Shut up." Vivid spun around to walk away, but Scorch clamored to his feet and latched onto his shoulder, catching him before he reached the ring fence.

"Stop telling me to shut up," Scorch exclaimed, spinning Vivid around to face him. "Stop acting like your life is over because of what Kio did to you. She wanted to break you, like she wanted to break all elementals, like the High Priestess did, but they couldn't do it. They couldn't break you because you're unbreakable, Vivid.

You don't need to control the air to be the strongest person I know."

Vivid shook off Scorch's hands and tried to get around him. "Who are you to judge my strength?"

"I'd be no one at all if it wasn't for you," Scorch said, blocking Vivid's path.

Vivid kneed him in the gut, tossed him out of his way, and then vaulted over the fence. "That doesn't mean I owe you anything. Leave me alone." He turned his back and walked off.

Scorch slammed his hand on the wooden fence, giving himself a splinter. He called out after Vivid's retreating back. "I don't *want* to leave you alone!"

Vivid kept walking and Scorch stalked off in the other direction, toward the center of the sparring ring. He kicked up angry clouds of dirt and pulled at his hair. Fire roiled inside him and he let a burst of sparks shoot from his fingertips into the air, like livid little fireworks.

His body was a rod of tension, the fight with Vivid unfinished and unsatisfying. It had not been what he wanted. Scorch wanted to lay his hands on him and shake him until he understood. He didn't want to hurt Vivid, didn't want him to hurt at all, ever. He wanted—*Gods*, he just wanted. He let out a pained sigh, head tipped to the sky.

Suddenly, his legs were swept from under him and Scorch fell on his back, all the air whooshing from his lungs. When Vivid crawled over him and grabbed fistfuls of his hair, he could breathe again, but it wasn't a normal breath, it was a gasp, because Vivid's eyes were wild.

Scorch's heart pounded. "What are you doing? The fight's over," he said, his voice ragged.

Vivid's fingers flexed in Scorch's hair. "But I haven't won yet."

And then Vivid kissed him.

It was a soft, careful press of lips, and by the time Scorch regained his senses enough to reciprocate, Vivid was pulling away. Scorch's hands wrapped around the back of his neck to keep him close. They breathed in and out, their noses bumping together, and then Vivid kissed him again.

Scorch heard himself moan pitifully as he returned Vivid's rough affection, but he was too overwhelmed to feel self-conscious, to feel anything at all except Vivid's lips on his and his hands threading greedily through his hair. Vivid was kissing him, and that was the only thought his brain had room for; that and *please, Gods, don't ever let this end.*

Unfortunately, they had to breathe eventually, but when they separated, it was a brief, necessary evil, and Scorch spent it flipping them over so he could better kiss Vivid into the ground. At first, doubt fluttered in his stomach, because Vivid tensed beneath his body, but then his hands were winding around Scorch's shoulders and drawing him in and his doubt vanished. His hand roamed down Vivid's side, and Vivid answered with a needy roll of his hips, so Scorch smoothed his hand down his thigh and hiked up his leg to wrap around his waist.

When Vivid opened his mouth to the kiss, Scorch seriously considered the possibility that Vivid had killed him and he was in the midst of some insanely worthwhile afterlife. It seemed like the only explanation that made sense. Vivid had kissed him, was still kissing him, and showed no sign of ever wanting to stop.

His lips were soft, his tongue was hot and demanding, and his hands were confident, palming over Scorch's biceps and shoulders and backside like he was his to touch and grope as he pleased, and he *was*. Scorch was a malleable thing in Vivid's hands, an element to be commanded, and every kiss and every sigh and every slide of hips made him spark on the inside. He was amazed he'd not set them both on fire yet. When Vivid's mouth migrated to suck a bruising kiss to the underside of his jaw, he nearly did.

"Erm, I hate to interrupt," voiced a sudden addition to the lusty fray of the training ring and/or Scorch's highly enjoyable afterlife, "but Merric says you both need to come straight away."

Scorch and Vivid pulled apart, and Felix coughed uncomfortably as they stood up and brushed the dirt from their clothes.

"What is it, Felix?" asked Scorch, trying not to sound monstrously disappointed that Vivid was now too far away to touch. But his lips were kiss-swollen, and that was because of him, so he couldn't help the swell of pride as he faced the flautist.

"Someone has been caught lurking outside the Guild," Felix reported, casting his eyes down when Scorch adjusted his trousers. "She says she knows you."

Vivid harrumphed grumpily and straightened his apprentice's shirt so it was no longer rucked up in the back from Scorch's wandering hands. "Were you expecting a lady caller?" he asked, glaring at Scorch and giving no indication whatsoever that their bodies had been plastered together only moments before.

Scorch's mind was clogged of all sense. Not only had he not been expecting a lady caller, he could scarcely recall the name of any lady he had ever met his whole life long. There was only Vivid, bright and violent, knocking around in his head and causing an unrivaled ruckus. He tried to voice that fact to Vivid, but the best he could do was shrug his imbecilic shoulders.

"She has an eye patch," Felix added, "if that helps."

Scorch's eyes found Vivid's as a fragment of reality returned to him. "That does help."

"Take us to her," Vivid ordered, already leaping over the training ring fence and staring down Felix.

As soon as Scorch could pry his eyes from the curve of Vivid's back, he hurried after them. His head might have been fuzzy, and his lips might still have felt the press of Vivid's kiss, but if Audrey was at the Guild, it meant bad news. And if Felix had left Merric alone with an assassin, it meant even worse news.

# New Boots
## 22

Audrey's twin daggers were bared, one pressed to Merric's throat while the other pressed against his groin. The edge of Merric's sword was positioned to cut a slice straight through Audrey's belly. They were just beyond the Guild walls, surrounded by the nosy murmurings of a dozen apprentices who'd gathered round as spectators. Vivid shoved them out of his way to get to Merric. He struck him in the nose and kicked behind his knees, collapsing him to the ground.

Scorch grabbed Vivid and pulled him away before he could do more damage. Vivid rolled his eyes, but temporarily refrained from murdering Merric. Felix helped Merric to his feet, and Vivid freed himself from Scorch's grasp to take Audrey's arm, leading her away from the others. Scorch watched him whisper fervently in her ear. She whispered something back and Vivid nodded.

Merric approached Scorch, looking a tad more like the Merric he remembered, the one who'd disliked him immensely. "You're friends with an *assassin*?" he asked, keeping his voice low so the gawking apprentices couldn't overhear.

Scorch winked, because it felt appropriate. "Assassins can't get enough of me."

"I've had enough of you," Vivid said, returning with Audrey. She'd put her blades away.

"Vivid's an assassin, too?" Merric fretted.

Scorch ignored Vivid's jibe and Merric's string of disgruntled noises and grasped Audrey's shoulder. "I didn't think I would be seeing you again so soon."

"Trust me," she returned, "neither did I."

Merric clicked his tongue impatiently behind him.

"Audrey," Scorch said, "I believe you've met Merric. He's—" Scorch stopped, embarrassed by what he'd been about to say. It was stupid of him to even think it.

"I'm Scorch's friend," Merric cut in, "and an apprentice of the Guild. And you are a trespassing assassin." He didn't look like the declaration of friendship had caused him any physical pain, but Scorch was bewildered. He could feel Vivid's eyes on him, assessing his reaction.

"I was not trespassing," Audrey sighed. "I was walking the perimeter."

"You were *thinking* about trespassing, assassin."

Scorch stepped between them when Audrey's hands fell to the handles of her blades. "Maybe we should move this conversation elsewhere, and stop using words like *assassin* in front of all the apprentices before—"

"What is going on here?" a voice boomed from behind the cluster of apprentices. They scattered aside to reveal the Guild Master, who examined the scene with a frown.

Merric stepped forward and managed to sound diplomatic. "We have a visitor, Guild Master," he announced, gesturing to

Audrey. "And if I'm not mistaken, she has brought word from," he glared at her, "an *enemy* camp."

Scorch shrugged apologetically at Audrey before facing the Guild Master. "I know her. She's here to speak to me and Vivid."

Master McClintock took in Audrey slowly. She was a lot to take in: eye patch, tight black leather, tattooed arms, a cornucopia of pointy objects fastened to her body. If Scorch had to guess, he would wager the Master knew exactly what Audrey was, and which enemy camp she hailed from, and the Guardians' Guild was not known for their love of the assassins.

"If she has something to say to you," Master McClintock said, "she can say it to all of us, in my quarters." He crooked a finger at Scorch and the others. "Follow."

Vivid and Audrey looked like they would prefer to do anything but follow the Guild Master, and Scorch didn't feel too excited about the prospect either.

"I think we established a while ago that your precious Master is not to be trusted," Vivid rumbled.

"If he wished you harm," Merric pointed out, "he would not have allowed Etheridge to save your life. Besides, we don't kill people in cold blood at the Guild. Guardians aren't murderers."

"I've had this conversation before, and I don't feel like having it again," Scorch said, clasping his hands together in exasperation. "Audrey, when I came to the Hollow, I had to meet with Axum and trust he wouldn't kill me. Are you willing to show the Guild the same respect?"

The thin line of her mouth revealed her disdain, but the reluctant nod of her head was all Scorch needed. He set off after the Guild Master and knew the others were following him, especially Vivid, because Scorch could sense his extreme disapproval the whole way there.

He had thought it surreal when he first returned to the Guild Master's room after a long time away, but that was nothing compared to the oddity of sitting in front of Master McClintock's desk with two assassins, Merric, and a flautist. The fat grey cat had also joined their party and was twining herself around Vivid's legs. Her purr was the only noise in the room until Master McClintock finished packing his pipe and deemed it time to speak.

"Scorch, I am pleased to see you've finally made a few friends," the Master said, "colorful as they are."

Scorch blushed, but the warmth bundled inside his chest spoke of a pleasantness he'd seldom felt before. The last person he'd considered a friend turned out to be a radical maniac he'd set on fire, and he hoped that the people around him owned a different fate. He certainly had no intention of setting any of them on fire, and he *thought* they mostly felt the same. Well, Vivid was still iffy. Now that they were no longer kissing, he was back to glaring at Scorch as if the power of his eyes alone might force a spontaneous combustion. Scorch met that heated gaze and worried when he felt a stirring below his belt. Was it normal to be aroused by someone possibly attempting to stare at him to death? He squirmed in his seat and forced his attention away, coughing to cover up the embarrassing sigh that went hand in hand with thinking about Vivid.

Master McClintock's eyes swept reservedly around the room. "Does your colorful friend have colorful news to share?"

Audrey—who had refused to sit, and was stalking like a lion behind the chairs—scoffed. Maybe scoffing was part of the assassin training program, in which case, Scorch was sorry he'd missed it. "I would not call my news colorful. Bleak, maybe. Harrowing," Audrey said. At the others' silence, she propped a hand on her hip and delivered her one-eyed stare to Scorch and Vivid, willfully ignoring everyone else. "When I returned to the Hollow, it was in upheaval. Axum is moving his plan forward and taking no chances. They mean to kill the Queen and take Viridor."

Scorch sat ramrod straight in his chair. "What? I thought Axum was going to attempt to sway the Queen first."

"Perhaps he did and already failed," Audrey said. "My insider told me that Axum announced plans for her assassination at their last meeting."

"When is this happening?" asked Scorch.

"As soon as they arrive at the Queen's chamber door, I imagine. They won't be wasting any more time. Whatever restraint Axum had, it disappeared when Elias died."

"Elias didn't die, I *killed* him," Vivid spat venomously, and Felix squeaked somewhere in the back.

"And because you killed him, Axum and his purist elementals are going to kill the Queen," Audrey said. "And then they will do their best to either kill or enslave every non-elemental in Viridor." A piece of hair fell loose from her bun and she blew it out of her face. "I rode for you as soon as I found out."

"Why would an assassin go out of her way to bring news to a guardian?" asked the Guild Master.

"Because I thought he would want to know," she answered bitingly, not even sparing the Master a glance. "Scorch, you helped me without question, and I will help you in return."

"Thank you, but, erm, help me with what?"

"Help you save the Queen and eliminate Axum."

"Scorch will not be aiding the Queen in any capacity," Master McClintock interjected forcefully. "The Guild thanks you for your information, but only guardians can be burdened with such tasks, and Scorch is no longer a guardian."

"Lucky Scorch," Vivid muttered.

Scorch stood abruptly from his seat and Vivid stood with him, as did Merric. Poor Felix had never been offered a chair, but he straightened his posture in solidarity. "I would not consider saving the Queen a burden, Master," Scorch said. "And sorry if I'm mistaken, but since I am no longer affiliated with the Guild, you have no say over the course of my actions."

"The last time you set out to save someone, they ended up dead," said the Master.

"The High Priestess deserved it," Scorch argued. "And if the Queen tortures someone I care about and ties me to a chair, she'll deserve it, too, but until then, I would love to have a go at completing a guardianship that actually *means* something."

Master McClintock shook his head sorrowfully. "There can be no guardianship for your kind, my boy. I'm sorry. You should not even be within Guild walls."

Scorch's throat tightened and he felt something brush against his back. Vivid's hand. A small, fleeting touch.

"If this is a mission worthy of the guardians, let me accept it," said Merric. "You cannot keep me as an apprentice forever."

"You think it a wise decision to send an unseasoned apprentice on a guardianship as important as this one?" asked his father.

Merric didn't back down. "I know you. Before you even consider sending out a guardianship to the Queen, you will check and double check your own sources verifying the assassin's story, and by the time you get around to doing anything, the Queen will already be dead." Father and son glared at one another. "Let me go ahead now. Check and double check to your heart's content, and then send someone more capable after me, by all means. But do not let Viridor suffer because you don't trust an elemental."

Master McClintock's eyes locked on Audrey. "Are you an elemental, too?"

She lifted a hand and the water from a cup on the desk floated in the air. Scorch watched in alarm as she directed it to hover over the Master's head. With a snap, she released it, and his head was soaked, his auburn beard dripping. Vivid snorted. It was the closest thing to a laugh Scorch had ever heard from him, and he wished he had more water to give Audrey so she could coax that sound from him again.

"Scorch," Felix chimed, "I might be wrong, but if you tell the Queen a horde of elementals are out for her blood, it might not go over nicely for the rest of the elementals."

Scorch looked down at Vivid and wordlessly begged for his opinion.

"Things have never gone *nicely* for us," Vivid said.

"Do you think we should do it?" Scorch asked him.

"I think it's a terrible idea," he answered.

"As do I," piped Master McClintock.

Vivid narrowed his eyes at the Guild Master. "We should leave at once if we hope to beat Axum to the Queen."

The Master protested, but his words were lost to Scorch. "You'll come with me?" he asked, surprised.

"Not if you're going to be looking at me like that the whole time."

"I'm coming, too," Felix announced.

"It could be dangerous." Merric's voice was warm when he spoke to Felix. "You should return to your village, where it's safe."

"No!" Felix looked offended by the suggestion.

"Let the little one come along," Audrey voiced, patting Felix hard on the shoulder. "I like his curls."

"This mission will not be Guild sanctioned," the Master called over the chatter.

"Good," Vivid responded. "Then there's a chance something good will come of it." He turned on his heel and headed for the door, the grey cat walking in his shadow.

Scorch and the others streamed after him. They must have looked menacing as they strutted down the Guild hallways, because curious apprentices ducked their heads as they passed. The only person who had enough nerve to call to them was Etheridge.

"Where have you lot been?" she asked as they passed her tent, her hands on her hips. Her knees were dirty from gardening.

"We have a guardianship to embark upon," Merric said, a bit pompously.

"Unsanctioned guardianship," Scorch corrected.

"Well, well," Etheridge sighed, already exasperated. "Best come in and let me have a look at you all."

"It's not an official guardianship, Etheridge," Scorch said. "You don't have to run your usual medical check."

"No one leaves these walls on a mission of any kind without the go-ahead from me," she scolded. "Merric, Scorch, come here."

Chagrined, they left the others. Scorch could hear Felix pulling out his flute and asking Audrey if she knew the song about the princess assassin before they walked through the tent flaps.

Etheridge ushered them both to the table, where they sat awkwardly, side by side. She proceeded through her series of medical checks, proclaiming they each had bright eyes and strong heartbeats, and then she set them up with medicinal pouches.

"How did the last one do you?" Etheridge asked Scorch, eyeing him suspiciously as he fastened the pouch to his belt and stuffed it inside his trousers.

"I'm afraid we suffered an untimely separation," he admitted mournfully.

"Well, I've included more of the same," Etheridge said, patting Scorch's hip where the pouch was hidden. "And extra ointment for your nethers." She wagged a finger. "Trust me, better you have it now and not need it, than need it later and not have it." She lowered her voice conspiratorially. "There's a bit of oil in there, as well."

"Oil?" Merric asked. "What for?"

Scorch groaned and put his face in his hands.

"If you don't know, Merric," Etheridge said sweetly, "then you shouldn't be using it. Now get up and get out. I can't spend the day fussing over you. I have work to do. Wait a moment, Scorch, if you would."

Merric hurried out, but Scorch remained, shuffling his feet. Etheridge smoothed a hand over his hair and lightly slapped his cheek.

"Take care of that boy," she said.

"Merric? I don't think he needs me to take care of him."

"Not Merric."

And Scorch knew she didn't mean Felix. He nodded, and she caught him off guard, pleasantly, by delivering a kiss to his cheek. Her braids tickled his face.

"I'm sorry," she said, and he wrinkled his brow.

"For what?"

"For thinking you were a scoundrel."

"What makes you think I'm not?"

She smiled at him. "Don't lose that pouch," she cautioned, and then she shooed him from the tent.

The fat grey cat's devotion finally reached her limit when Vivid stepped though the large door that led outside the Guild walls. She sat her fluffy bottom down on the grass and meowed until Vivid took a knee. He scratched beneath her chin and said goodbye, then she head-butted his hand and sauntered off to find a patch of sun to sleep in. Scorch tried to keep his face neutral as Vivid stood to rejoin their party. He tried to act like he wouldn't have the image of Vivid snuggling with that cat ingrained in his memory for the rest of his life.

"She doesn't have a name, you know," he said, during the first few minutes of their journey down the main road.

"Of course she has a name," was Vivid's stale response. He'd returned to not looking at Scorch and keeping as much space between them as possible.

"Does she? No one knows it."

"No one knows *your* name, but that doesn't keep you from having one."

"Do you want to know my name?" Scorch asked. The question hung in the air between them. "My real name, I mean."

Vivid hesitated. "No." He rubbed at the smooth patch of skin behind his ear, a new quirk to replace the one he'd lost with the edge of Kio's knife. "You're Scorch. What use would I have for the other?"

Perhaps a sane person would have been insulted, but Vivid's words had the rare ring of fondness to them, so Scorch just smiled. "You should give the cat a nickname, then."

"Why?"

"Because you liked her."

"You may feel the compulsion to assign names to everyone you like, but I don't."

"Whatever you say," Scorch wracked his brain for a befitting nickname, "*Windy*."

"You're operating under the false impression that I won't be killing you in your sleep," Vivid growled.

"I like Windy," Felix said, but a fierce glower from Vivid wiped the smile from his face, and he fell back to walk beside Merric.

Scorch shut up after that, mostly because Vivid walked too far ahead of him to hear anything he might say. In the midst of their trek, however, it was decided they would travel through the first night, as evening was swiftly falling. They would reach the closest village by sunrise and resupply. The thought made Scorch's stomach nervous. That village was where he'd met Felix and Flora, where he was taken by the slavers. The idea of returning didn't sit well with him, but since he and Vivid needed weapons and better armor than flimsy apprentice garb, they would have no choice but to stop. After, they would take the south road and make camp at sunset the following day. That was the plan. Scorch's feet already hurt just thinking about it.

It soon proved that traveling with a flautist had its benefits. His simple tunes kept their pace steady and held back the gloomy mood of traveling at night. Even Vivid didn't seem to mind, or, at least, he didn't threaten to beat Felix over the head with his flute.

Still, Scorch was haunted by the last time he'd walked the same road. He was no longer a smug apprentice, scarless as he was clueless, harboring a horrible secret. He was no longer alone. He was no longer eaten up on the inside with fire he couldn't control and didn't understand. It was a strange sensation, walking the route of a memory.

Often, as they walked, his thoughts returned to Vivid. His eyes returned to Vivid, as well, and his confident stride, the swell of his backside in his apprentice trousers. Scorch found himself missing the black leather, missing Vivid's hands tugging his hair, and Vivid's lips on his neck. He wanted to get him alone again, but his attempts to walk at his side and speak softly with him were thwarted each time. It was unfair that Vivid could walk so much faster when his legs were so much shorter.

But when the daytime finally arrived, and the little village appeared before them, Vivid could ignore him no longer. They both needed clothes, and there was but one tailor to attend them.

They separated from the others with an agreement to meet back in a bit. Scorch kept his head down to avoid looking at the inn, but the tailor's shop turned out to be directly behind it, and he was suddenly face to face with the little room in the back.

He choked on air as the recollection resurged, his body bending to dry-heave in the middle of the road. The dusty ground was bloodstained and his hands were sticky and red. He blinked, and there she was, neck split wide, eyes open and unseeing.

Ebbins grabbed him by the shoulders and pulled him to the side of the road. No, that wasn't right. The hands were too gentle. They were pressing against his forehead, cold.

"Scorch," Vivid said, and it was a command, like he was calling the wind. Scorch surfaced to find him, tearing his eyes from a bloody mattress to a pale face. Dark eyebrows were cutting a line of concern over narrowed slits of amethyst.

Somehow, Scorch had ended up on the ground, and Vivid was crouched beside him. His face flared pink and he breathed out an anguished sigh. "Sorry. I'm sorry."

"You're sweaty," Vivid remarked.

"I sweat a lot," Scorch retorted scratchily.

Vivid took one hand away from his forehead to replace it with his other, cooler hand, and Scorch leaned into it gratefully. "Something bad happened here. The beginning of the flautist's song."

Scorch nodded, looking away.

"Then we won't linger. Get up." He pulled Scorch to his feet. "Are you going to be sick? You can't throw up inside the tailor's."

Scorch assessed the state of his nausea. He'd not had breakfast, and the initial wave of heaving was over, so he shook his head. Vivid thrust a canteen in his hand, and he accepted it gratefully, taking a sip while Vivid steered him away from Flora's room and toward the front door of the tailor.

"Thank you," he said.

Vivid didn't respond, simply pushed open the door and guided him forward with a hand pressed to his back. Once they were inside, he stepped away. When the tailor appeared from the back room, Vivid was cold as ever, but the tailor, Scorch shortly discovered, was even colder.

She wore a scarf wrapped around her hair and a measuring tape hung loose over her shoulders. She looked over her new customers behind thick spectacles, and she did not look impressed. Not that Scorch thought he was impressive at the moment. He was still shaking from the onslaught of memories and had a feeling his face was either too red or too white. Either way, he knew there was an ample sheen of sweat collected on his brow.

"We need clothes," Vivid said, his voice flat. "Something snug, with covered sleeves for myself and a jerkin for him." He nodded to Scorch.

The tailor returned his flatness, straightening her spectacles as she looked them each up and down. "Material?"

"Something hardy," answered Vivid. "Leather. Black, if you have it."

"Does this look like the royal seamstress? I don't have leather in black."

"Something dark then," Vivid amended impatiently.

"Same for you?" she asked Scorch.

"Same for him," Vivid answered.

Scorch, with a slightly shaky voice, looked doubtfully at Vivid. "We don't want to *match*," he protested. "We'll look stupid." He cocked his head at the tailor. "Do you have any leather in red?"

"No."

"Hmm. What color leathers *do* you have?"

"I have brown leather. Dark brown and a slightly darker brown."

Scorch forced a smile. "Dark brown sounds lovely."

Vivid was considerably less enthused, but anything would be better than what they already had on, so they gritted their teeth and agreed to the fitting.

The woman dressed Scorch first. She was quick with her needle, and her selection of leather was a surprisingly pleasant mixture of sturdy and supple, soft to the touch, but thick. It would take some damage. Vivid didn't watch when Scorch undressed and stepped into his new gear. He knew, because he was watching Vivid, and he kept his head turned toward the window, his back to

Scorch, only turning around once the last lace on Scorch's new boots had been laced.

Scorch looked down at the boots and missed the red ones, but there was nothing for it, especially when he knew it was only a matter of time before he destroyed the clothes on his back once again. Eventually, wings and talons and scales would shred his new clothes. Best not to be overly attached.

Vivid, on the other hand, had a fair chance of keeping the tailor's creation for the foreseeable future, and Scorch found himself wanting to watch as the tailor slid her tape up his inseam. He banished himself to the window and resolved to stare outside and give Vivid a semblance of privacy. That's when he realized the window was highly reflective, revealing a near mirror image of the fitting taking place behind him. Scorch smiled. Vivid had been watching him the whole time. It lessened the guilt he felt when Vivid slipped out of his apprentice clothes.

Overall, the whole affair didn't take long. Vivid paid and they left. Scorch no longer had a problem keeping his focus away from Flora's room, because his full attention was on Vivid, and Vivid's new clothes.

The black assassin leather had been skintight, but there had also been a bulk to it, a distraction of buckles and straps and shine that took away from his shape. The tailor's clothes were different: snug, soft leather that clung to every curve of Vivid's body. There was no extra material to mask his physique, just a layer of slightly darker brown leather that hugged him perfectly. The sleeves of his new cuirass were long and fitted, but his neck was no longer hidden by a high collar. Scorch could see him work his neck as he swallowed, could even see the hint of a silver scar racing up the nape of his neck. It was, Scorch decided, a very good look, and

Vivid was kind enough to let Scorch look his fill until they'd walked out of view of the inn. Then, he smacked Scorch across the torso.

"*Stop.*"

"Stop what?" Scorch asked.

Vivid answered with his eyebrows, furrowing them into a threatening V on his forehead.

"We're alone." Scorch reached out to touch Vivid's hand, but it was slapped away. "Vivid," he said, a little hurt, but not surprised. "I want to talk to you about—"

"We need weapons," Vivid snarled, walking ahead of him to the blacksmith.

The blacksmith was more painful than the tailor. Scorch found a sword he liked the weight and balance of relatively quickly, but for Vivid, picking out new blades was a process. A long process. He was unhappy with everything. He tossed daggers in the air and threw them at the practice target, sneering and frowning as he inspected the blades from tip to handle. In the end, he chose what he claimed were the "best of the worst," threw some money down, and stormed off, breezing past Scorch before he could comment.

They found Merric, Felix, and Audrey awaiting them at the end of the road. Felix was holding the reins of three horses and his cheeks were covered in lipstick smudges.

"We went to the inn's tavern for food," he explained.

"The little flautist is quite popular," Audrey smirked. "His lap barely stayed empty. Right, Merric?"

Merric, gloomy-faced, ignored her and stroked one of the horse's flanks.

"The stable master loaned me three horses," Felix continued with a blush.

"In exchange for a date when he returns," Audrey finished.

"Ridiculous," Merric muttered.

"Smart," Vivid declared, taking one of the reins from Felix. "We should get there in half the time now." Felix brightened at the praise.

"Are we not resting here?" asked Audrey. "It's early yet. We could get a room and sleep a few hours."

Scorch fiddled with the handle of his new sword, trying to rummage up an excuse as to why he wouldn't be able to step foot inside that inn. He wasn't sure if Vivid sensed his distress, or whether they were, for once, on the same page, but Vivid spoke up before Scorch needed to, and his word, much like the man, was immoveable.

"We're not sleeping here." He leapt onto the back of one of Felix's horses, a white gelding. "We'll make camp at nightfall, as planned." Scorch tried to flash him a smile of thanks, but Vivid avoided his eye.

"Fine with me," Audrey said, mounting a red-maned mare.

That's when Scorch realized there were three horses and five members of their party. Merric settled into the saddle of the third horse, and then it was only Scorch and Felix left unseated.

"Felix," Merric said politely, holding out a hand. "Would you ride with me?"

The flautist smiled at the invitation and took Merric's hand. He sat in the saddle behind him and wrapped his arms around Merric's waist, pleased.

Scorch, last man standing, wondered if now would be a good time to burst into flames.

"Want to ride with me, Scorch?" Audrey asked, her one eye glinting mischievously.

"He'll ride with me," Vivid said. "We've ridden together before."

Scorch looked up at Vivid, who was staring straight ahead, his knuckles white around the horse's reins. "D-do you want me behind you?" he asked, cursing himself when his voice broke.

"If I recall, that was your preference."

It felt like a conversation they shouldn't be having in front of the others. "I don't have a preference," Scorch said slowly.

Vivid straightened his back in the saddle. He was a stone wall. "I do. Stop wasting time."

Scorch absolutely did not want to waste any time, not in reaching the Queen and certainly not in pressing his chest against Vivid's back. He mounted the horse and settled into the saddle, but hesitated to put his hands on Vivid's waist.

"Hold on to me," Vivid demanded.

Scorch held on, and then they were off.

# Wood and Woolgathering
## 23

Twice, they had shared a horse. The first time was on their way to the Assassins' Hollow, Scorch flustered and self-conscious every time his body jostled against Vivid's. The second time was recently, Scorch clinging desperately to Vivid's limp body, trying to keep them both in the saddle as he rode from the fortress. The third time was a cruel mixture of first and second. Scorch was a flustered mess behind Vivid, trying to keep grinding to a minimum, but he was also desperate to wrap his arms around him and nuzzle into his neck. He kept thinking about Vivid almost dying, and then about Vivid very much alive and on top of him, kissing him, the way his thighs had tightened around his waist. And that—that was not something he should be thinking about whilst sharing a horse.

Vivid sucked an inhale through his teeth and adjusted in the saddle, effectively rubbing his backside against Scorch. Scorch groaned, embarrassed, knowing there was no way Vivid couldn't feel how *enthused* he was by their proximity. He waited to be thrown from the horse, berated, or possibly stabbed, but all Vivid did was grip the reins tighter and roll his shoulders.

Then he leaned back.

It was only a fraction, a minimal movement, but it shifted more of Vivid's weight onto Scorch, and Scorch, in turn, had to wrap his arms tighter around Vivid's waist. Dark hair bristled at his nose, and Scorch breathed in the wintry, green smell. He was undeniably hard, and the pressure of Vivid leaning into him wasn't helping, but he wasn't about to push him away, and Vivid didn't act as if he wanted to be pushed. So Scorch spread his fingers over Vivid's stomach, and he smelled his hair, and he tried to ignore the tightness in his new leather trousers.

The end of the day took forever to reach. They only stopped twice, to rest the horses and take in some food and drink, and only when the sun was beginning to set did Vivid declare it a suitable time to make camp for the night. Scorch could have cried. Pressed against Vivid all day had him frazzled and overstrung. He jumped from the horse and declared he was going to find firewood. Before anyone could shoot him their obnoxiously knowing glances, he darted into the trees and began collecting choice timber. He took his time.

When he returned, Merric and Felix were eating and Audrey was sitting with Vivid, sharpening her blades. She whispered something to Vivid when she saw Scorch and then rushed over to help him with his armload of branches and twigs. He let her pile them up and waved his hand in front of it. The timber sparked and caught fire. Felix gasped.

After everyone had eaten and the sun was gone, there was nothing else to do but sleep. But as the others were settling down and unrolling their packs, Vivid disappeared from the clearing, vanishing into the trees. Scorch busied himself, searching for a prime spot of ground with no rocks, but after a few minutes, his curiosity got the better of him.

He found him on his knees at the base of a tree, using one of his daggers to cut a cluster of ivory vines from where they nestled around the roots. Dream Moss. Scorch watched him for a time, mesmerized by his nimble fingers and the broadness of his leather-clad shoulders. It had been too many hours since the training ring.

"Your stealth is abysmal," Vivid said without turning around.

"I need more practice." It was quiet and calm so deep in the forest, and Scorch spoke softly, reluctant to spoil the peace of the picture he'd entered. "I want to kiss you."

Vivid shoved what Dream Moss he'd collected into a trouser pocket and stood, keeping his back to Scorch. He said nothing.

"Vivid."

He turned. It was dark, but Scorch didn't need much light to detect the tension in his shoulders or the way his fingers curled into his palms. "Go back to camp."

"No." Scorch stepped closer, until Vivid's face began to make sense in the shadows. He was scowling. "Can I kiss you?"

"That was a mistake," Vivid snapped, but it lacked its usual bite, so Scorch stepped closer still.

"I want to," he whispered. "I always want to." They were inches apart and Vivid had to tip his head back to look into Scorch's eyes. Now that they were alone and Vivid wasn't running in the other direction, Scorch couldn't resist the urge to touch. He reached out with a careful hand and brushed his knuckles over Vivid's cheek.

"Kiss someone else," Vivid said.

"I don't want anyone else," Scorch answered, and it was astonishingly, heart-wrenchingly true.

Vivid's hands fell on Scorch's hips, pushing him away before pulling him forward. "This is stupid. You're stupid."

"I missed your compliments when we were apart," Scorch sighed. Vivid's fingers were digging into the flesh of his hips.

"I didn't miss you at all," Vivid insisted, drawing Scorch in until their knees knocked.

"That's understandable. I can be annoying."

Vivid nodded. "You never shut up. Your voice makes my head ache."

"Sorry." He bent down and placed a kiss—gentle, questioning—on Vivid's lips.

When they parted, Vivid's hands skirted up from Scorch's hips to frame his jaw, fingers tracing over stubble. Scorch couldn't believe he was being allowed to touch him again. He moved his hand down Vivid's neck, then back up to thumb the velvety edge of his ear. His nearness was intoxicating, and Scorch swayed forward.

Vivid made a strange noise in the back of his throat and wrapped his arms around Scorch's neck, pulling him down and kissing him hard. His hands were everywhere, threading through Scorch's hair, raking down his back, grabbing his ass and hauling him closer. He deepened the kiss and their lips fitted together in a perfect slide of heat. Scorch was overwhelmed with the sensation of getting everything he'd ever wanted and never known.

"Come here," he whispered as his hands slid down Vivid's thighs. Understanding, Vivid jumped up and wrapped his legs around Scorch's waist. Scorch pushed him up against the tree, and for a while, their affection was frenzied. Vivid nipped at Scorch's lower lip and Scorch pressed against him until they were both breathless, but somewhere in the flow of their embrace, urgency gave way to something else.

Scorch eased his kisses to yielding, slow things, and Vivid's demanding hands began tracing easy, sweet patterns over his chest. They kissed, deep and lazy, until Vivid complained about the bark digging into his back, and then Scorch lowered them to the ground, Vivid in his lap, his legs still wrapped around his waist.

Before, when Scorch had been with someone, kissing had always been a secondary thought. A means to an end. But with Vivid, it was different. Though his weight and warmth felt unfathomably good in his lap, he felt no need to press for more, not when the act of simply kissing was more satisfying than anything he'd ever done with anyone else. Kissing Vivid felt lucky; it felt *right*. And he was afraid to stop.

When a twig snapped, Vivid broke the seal of their lips and looked past his shoulder, his eyes alert. "Someone's coming," he whispered, tilting his head to listen. "The guardian." He kissed Scorch one more time before hopping off his lap and helping him to his feet. They stood, both a bit shaky. Scorch's legs were asleep, and as the tingles worsened, he muttered a string of curses that had Vivid's eyebrows rising.

Merric appeared from behind a bush a moment later, his sword unsheathed. When he spotted them, he put the weapon away with a pissy snuffle. "You've been gone almost an hour," he complained. "I lost the coin toss for who had to come and check on you." Merric did not look happy to be away from the fire on what Scorch was finally realizing was a cold night. He hadn't been cold and neither had Vivid. He must have been keeping him warm, a thought that made him smile.

"We can take care of ourselves," Vivid said. *We.*

"Well, I hope you've," Merric looked between them, "*taken care of yourselves* already, because Felix refuses to sleep until everyone is accounted for, and I'm not going back without you."

Vivid, annoyed, strode past Merric and headed for the camp. Scorch helped himself to the view until he'd disappeared behind a bush, and then he found Merric staring at him, wide-eyed.

"What?" Scorch asked innocently.

"Nothing," Merric said, an amused smirk thawing on his face. The tip of his nose was pink from the cold. "Nothing at all."

They arrived back at the campsite ten minutes later, where Felix was fretfully worrying his thumbnail and Audrey was fast asleep. Scorch gave the fire another pass with his hand, and it revved with sparks. Felix and Merric burrowed down in their blankets, facing the fire and shutting their eyes. They may as well have been sharing a bedroll, they were sleeping so close together.

Instinctively, Scorch sought out where Vivid was unrolling his own blanket. It was on the opposite side of the fire, beside Audrey. That was fine. Scorch hadn't expected them to sleep side by side. That was something they saved for special occasions, like near-death experiences.

Scorch was sitting on his own bedroll, untying his bootlaces, and definitely not feeling sorry for himself, when he felt a tap on his shoulder. He jumped and turned his head to find Vivid standing there.

"Do you ever turn your stealth off?" he asked, his heart beating fast.

Vivid grabbed his wrist and set something light and fuzzy in his palm. His fingers lingered a moment on Scorch's skin, and then he was gone, returned to his bedroll across the fire. Scorch glanced down at his palm where a fresh stem of Dream Moss was lying.

He popped it into his mouth and lay back. His lips were bruised from Vivid's kisses, and his fingers itched to feel Vivid's skin beneath them, but it didn't take long for him to pass into slumber, and when he did, he dreamt about all the things he wanted.

They took the south road in the morning, and by Merric's estimation, would arrive in the Royal Quarter in a little over a week, as long as they didn't idle. The south road was busier than the east, more people traveling back and forth from the Royal Quarter than the Heartlands, so their ability to gallop was largely hampered. Scorch tried to be upset about it, but it was hard to let anything upset him when he got to spend long hours with his arms wrapped around Vivid's waist. Vivid acted annoyed by his presence in the saddle, but every time Scorch worked up the nerve to nuzzle into his neck when no one was looking, Vivid would shiver and lean into the touch.

When the sun set on the second night, they stopped for camp, and after the horses were seen after, Scorch offered to collect timber again. He'd not strayed far and was stooping to collect a prime piece of dry wood, when he heard footsteps behind him.

"Can I help you?" he asked wryly, knowing exactly who had followed him.

"Good question," answered a definitively female voice.

Scorch turned to frown at Audrey. "You're not Vivid."

"Were you expecting him?" she asked, and there was a hint of malice in her voice, a threatening glint in her eye.

"No," he lied. He grabbed for the piece of wood and her boot shot out, pinning his hand to the ground. "Ouch!"

"What are you doing with Vivid?"

"Trying to build him a fire so he won't freeze to death tonight," Scorch answered. He waggled his fingers beneath the crush of her boot. "Do you mind?"

Audrey retracted the boot but intensified her glare. "I know you're in love with him," she said.

Scorch's stomach plummeted. He shook out his hand and fumbled with the wood. "Why does everyone keep saying that?"

"I knew you were before," she continued. "It's why I came to you in the first place, to help me save him. But I didn't know—" She paused. A second later, she had Scorch pressed up against a tree, a dagger to his throat.

"Hey!"

"You give the impression of being trustworthy, but people are inherently deceitful," she said.

"So I've heard," Scorch grunted.

"Consider this your only warning from me. If I find out you're using him, I will slit your throat."

Scorch was torn between terror and bewilderment. "Using him? For what?"

Audrey pushed the edge of the blade into his throat until it made a thin cut in his skin, letting the sting convey her meaning.

"*No*," Scorch said adamantly, anxious for her to believe him. "No, it's not like that."

She looked for a moment like she wanted nothing more than to slit his throat and be done with it. When she finally pulled the dagger away, he sagged against the tree and put a hand over the cut on his neck.

"Was," he asked quietly, hesitantly, "was it like that with Elias?"

Audrey had such fire in her eye that if Scorch had not already known, he would have pegged her for an elemental then and there. "It was like a lot of things with Elias." It was all she offered, and Scorch didn't ask for more. It was enough.

"It won't be like that with me," he promised.

Audrey spun the dagger in her hand and flashed him a terrifying smile. "I hope not."

The remainder of his search for firewood was conducted with trembling hands. When he returned to camp, Vivid eyed the small cut on his neck, but made no comment, which wasn't unusual—he'd said no more than a few words to Scorch all day. Scorch refused to let it bother him.

After they ate, they slept. Vivid's bedroll was as far away from Scorch as possible. That, he could admit, bothered him a little.

The third day was more of the same, up until the point when they passed a village. People were swarming and bells were ringing. Merric slowed his horse as they trotted by, and the others followed suit. A man stood on a makeshift stage in the middle of a crowd, shouting something Scorch couldn't discern.

"They're mourning the High Priestess," Felix said after a minute of straining his ears. "News of her death has just reached them."

Scorch's hands were resting on Vivid's hips unobtrusively, but at Felix's words, and the way Vivid's body stiffened upon hearing them, he commanded himself to be bold and tightened his hold, offering his comfort. Vivid glanced back at him, unimpressed. Scorch wanted so badly to kiss him.

"Should we stop here for supplies?" Merric asked.

"No," Scorch said. "I've had my fill of zealots."

They traveled on, but Vivid remained tense, so Scorch whispered in his ear, "Have I told you how good you smell?" Vivid threatened to make him walk the rest of the way if he talked to him again, but Scorch could feel his body begin to relax, so it was worth it. Besides, Vivid did smell really good.

That night, he was ambushed again while collecting firewood, and not by Audrey. Vivid claimed he was testing his stealth technique and that he'd failed the test, and Scorch complained until Vivid had to kiss him to shut him up, which he thought was pretty stealthy.

On the fourth and fifth night of their journey, Vivid continued to hinder Scorch's attempts at collecting firewood, much to the teeth-chattering dismay of their companions.

But on the day before they were to reach the Queen, Scorch made a mistake.

Vivid had him on his back, lying in a heap of dry branches. He'd caught Scorch as he was bending over, kicking him down and wrapping his hands around his throat in a mock strangle.

"You're dead," Vivid said. "Yet again." Scorch laughed and Vivid glared. "You're not even trying."

"I'm satisfied with my results," Scorch answered, letting his hands rest on Vivid's thighs. "Are you going to kill me now?"

"I should." He gave Scorch's throat a harmless squeeze before sliding his hands into his hair, and then he shifted back so Scorch could sit up.

Vivid's fingers threaded again through his hair, and Scorch smiled. He could feel it stretch happily across his face, could feel his eyes twinkling with pleasure. Vivid didn't smile back. If anything, his face grew darker. "Don't look at me like that."

"How am I looking at you?"

Vivid dropped his hands from Scorch's hair. "Like this means something." He moved, tried to get up from Scorch's lap, but Scorch held his waist, keeping him.

"It does mean something," Scorch told him. *It means everything.*

"It doesn't."

Scorch tempered his smile and let go of Vivid's waist. When he didn't try to get away, Scorch kissed him, and Vivid kissed him back. He should have let it go after that, but he was, as Vivid so accurately and frequently pointed out, a fool. He broke their kiss to mouth along Vivid's jaw, and then he whispered, too familiar, too intimate, "I want to stay with you."

Vivid shoved him back. "Stay with me?"

Despite the fact that Vivid's body was coiled like a snake on the verge of striking, Scorch continued. "When we've warned the Queen and dealt with Axum, I don't want to part ways." Vivid's breath was too rapid and so was Scorch's, but he couldn't stop. "We haven't talked about it, because I know you hate talking, but," he felt himself blushing, "I want you. And I want to stay with you."

It was a mistake to admit it to himself, and a catastrophic mistake to admit it to Vivid. But it was the truth; Scorch felt the weight of it in his chest, even as Vivid stood from his lap. He stood up, as well, tried to take Vivid's hand, but his touch was rejected. He'd ruined it.

"You've confused yourself, I think," Vivid said. He spoke softly, and the back of Scorch's neck prickled, sensing the danger.

"I don't think I'm the one who's confused," said Scorch, and Vivid turned his back. Scorch was tired of Vivid turning his back. "I know you care about me."

Vivid was walking away from him.

"Vivid!" he shouted, but the other man had already disappeared through the trees.

His eyes burned as he piled the forgotten firewood in his arms, hating himself. He'd managed to scare Vivid away in record time. Two minutes ago, they'd been kissing, and now he was unsure if he'd ever be allowed to kiss him again.

He returned to the camp and set up the fire. Merric and Felix tried engaging him in conversation while they ate, but Scorch could manage no more than a few grunts of acknowledgement.

Across the fire, Vivid sharpened his blade, acting as if nothing had happened, and Scorch suddenly stumbled upon a horrible thought, one he'd never before considered. He had always assumed he and Vivid shared a connection. He had thought, like the same egotistical ass he had always been, that Vivid returned his feelings. But what if he didn't? What if Vivid kept pushing him away, not because he was closed-off, but because he wasn't interested? Had Scorch been just as bad as Elias? Forcing his attentions on Vivid when they were unwanted?

The campfire sparked and flared, and everyone looked at him, some with worried expressions, some with no expression at all. Scorch excused himself from the camp and took a walk through the dark. No one followed him.

The next day was uncomfortable, because Scorch spent most of it on a horse with Vivid, whom he was now convinced genuinely disliked him. Vivid did nothing to assuage his fear, ignoring him, not speaking to him, and keeping his back so rigid that his shoulders never even brushed against Scorch's chest as they rode. Scorch felt lecherous placing his fingertips on Vivid's waist. He would have preferred falling off the horse, but then Vivid probably would have complained about him making them late.

Because of their horses, and the quick pace they'd set over the past week, before the end of that seventh day, the south road brought Scorch and the others to a magnificent brick wall that marked the beginning of the Royal Quarter of Viridor.

The Royal Quarter was a city, the largest in Viridor, and at its center stood the palace, where the Queen lived, and where, if Axum had his way, the Queen would die. Scorch had never seen a city before, and when the guards let them through, he gaped at its magnitude. There were so many people in one place, and it was overwhelming. Vivid, unaffected, led the way through the busy, winding streets, cobbled with brightly colored stones and lined with vendors selling sweets and fresh bread and fruit. The air was smoky with pipe weed and chimney plumes, and Scorch couldn't resist lifting his head to follow different scents that wafted by on the breeze. He gawked at the rows upon rows of houses, sturdier and taller than any village home he'd seen. Audrey and Vivid's work must have brought them to the city before, and even Felix looked unbothered, but Merric was as starry-eyed as Scorch. They looked at one another during their clop through the city streets to share a moment of amazement for the culture they'd only ever read about.

Scorch thought the south road had been busy, but the Royal Quarter had enough wagons, horseback riders, and townspeople to slow their progress phenomenally. It took more than thirty minutes to reach the royal stables, and when they did, Vivid dismounted first, handing over the reins to the stable boy. Scorch jumped down after him, brushing the road dust off his clothes and adjusting the sword at his belt. He watched Merric help Felix from their horse with a pang of jealousy, and Audrey cast him a curious glance, as if she could feel the ache in his chest. He gave his head a shake. Now was not the time. He joined the others in a tight circle outside the stables.

"Merric and Scorch have the best chance of gaining an audience with the Queen," Audrey said. "She won't turn away Guardians of the Guild."

"But we're not acting under Guild guardianship," Merric argued. "And Scorch isn't even a guardian anymore."

"Well, he looks more like a guardian than the two of you," Felix said, pointing between Audrey and Vivid. "You look like storybook assassins."

"Scorch will be able to convince her," said Vivid. "He convinced the monks to take him to the High Priestess."

Scorch stared at Vivid. "I thought you were unconscious when that happened." He had counted on Vivid being unconscious when he'd cuddled him in his lap, trying to keep him warm.

"I was more awake than you thought," Vivid said, staring back. "Go with Merric. Try not to get tied to any chairs."

"What about the rest of you?" Merric asked, eyes darting between Felix and the two assassins who would be his only company.

"We'll wait for you," Audrey said. "Don't worry about the flautist." She checked Felix with her hip. "He'll be safe with us." Felix gave Merric a smile.

Scorch nodded, and after Merric squeezed Felix's shoulder and squinted threateningly at the assassins, they turned together for the palace. He refused to glance back at Vivid as they walked away.

"What happened there?" Merric asked as they neared the guards at the palace doors.

"What do you mean?"

"You've been ignoring Vivid all day. You've hardly said a word to him."

"He doesn't want my words. Or anything to do with me," Scorch said grumpily.

"Hmm," Merric hummed. Scorch disliked the tone of that hum.

"He *told* me, Merric. Last night. I don't mean anything to him."

"But he's always saying rude things to you and you're always swooning."

Scorch had no answer to that, but they'd run out of time for answers anyway. Two gruff guards were scanning them from behind their bronze helmets, their spears in a crisscross, blocking the palace entrance.

"Right," said Scorch, standing tall and trying to appear guardianly. There had been a time when he didn't need to try, but it felt a lifetime's distance gone. "We are Guardians of the Guild. We have urgent information for the Queen." Scorch could make out no more of the guards' faces than the slit cut in their helmets for their eyes, but each set narrowed at him in suspicion.

"Do you have an official missive from the Guild?" asked the guard on the right.

Merric looked over at Scorch semi-frantically, but Scorch had expected that line of inquiry. "Our journey to the Queen is of the highest import, and the risk of a missive being stolen from us could not be risked." It's what the Guild Master told him when he'd sent him on his guardianship, and Scorch had believed him well enough.

But Scorch lacked the mistrust of a royal guard. "No missive, no entry," said the guard on the left.

"I am trying to put this as delicately as possible," Scorch continued. "It is vital we see the Queen."

"Do you know how many gutter rats and scum try to worm their way into the palace with that same excuse?" laughed the guard on the right. "At least they put a little effort into their disguises. If you lot are guardians, I'm the princess of assassins."

Merric stepped forward, and the guards clanged their spears together in warning. "I am Merric, the Guild Master's son, and this is Scorch, the Sun Guardian. I demand you let us in to see the Queen. Her life depends on it! If you do not let us in, she will die!"

Scorch groaned. "Oh no. Don't listen to him," he said, but it was too late. The guards slammed down their spears and bellowed out orders as soon as Merric's mention of the Queen's life had been made, and now they were both being seized by a surplus of guards.

"Scorch, what's happening?" Merric yelled in a panic as a huge guard began hauling them toward the barracks.

Scorch sighed, letting the guard manhandle him down a gloomy set of stairs. "You, Merric, have gotten us arrested."

# *Apex*
# 24

The palace dungeon was pretty nice, as far as dungeons went, and Scorch would know, since he'd frequented plenty of them. He wasn't thrown rudely into a cage either. He and Merric were escorted to a roomy cell, complete with a mattress and chamber pot.

With commendable calm, Scorch placed his hands on the bars and pled a final case to the guards. "Please, tell the Queen we have news of Axum." It was all he could think to say that might pique her interest in two arrested gutter rats. "Tell her he's coming, and he will have no compromise. Please."

One of the guards muttered something under his breath and stomped up the stairs, plunging Merric and Scorch into the dim dungeon light. The other guard remained, leaning against the far wall, looking bored.

Merric shuffled close to Scorch and whispered, "I suppose you can't elemental us out of here, can you?"

Scorch rubbed at his neck, thinking about it. "I might could," he admitted. "But let's consider that a last resort."

Merric banged his head against the bars with an aggravated sigh. "Do you think they'll tell her what you said?"

"I don't know. But if they do, even if she refuses to see us, at least she will have gotten a warning." He looked askance at Merric. "We really should have gone over a list of things that shouldn't be said to royal guards."

Merric rattled the bars pathetically. "Did I just play the 'do you know who my father is' card?"

"You absolutely did," Scorch confirmed.

"Oh, Gods, that's humiliating."

"Not as humiliating as it's going to be when we have to share that chamber pot." They glanced uneasily at the ceramic bucket in the corner.

"Is this how your other guardianship went?" Merric asked.

Scorch threw his head back and laughed. "Close enough," he decided. "Usually there's more blood, but it's early yet."

"How long do you think the others will wait for us before they realize something's wrong?"

"They would have seen us getting arrested," Scorch said. He could picture the look on Vivid's face when their flimsy plan fell through, and it made him tighten his fingers around the cell bars. They grew hot beneath his hands and he had to take a few deep breaths to calm himself. "Merric, we shouldn't count on them to get us out of this."

The door from the top of the stairs creaked open and several sets of clunky boots began their descent down the steps.

"What are you talking about?" Merric whispered. "Vivid would never leave you locked up in a palace dungeon."

"What are *you* talking about?" Scorch whispered back. "Vivid has been trying to shake me off since the moment we met and now is the perfect opportunity." Three guards were clanging noisily down the steps and Scorch eyed them warily.

"Look, I don't know Vivid very well, but I know I can believe what I see with my own two eyes, and when I look at him, I see someone who would never leave you locked up in a palace dungeon, just like you wouldn't leave him."

"Well, *he's* not in love with *me*, is he?" Scorch spat. One of the guards dropped their keys while Scorch proceeded to have an inner meltdown, because he had just—in a roundabout way—admitted to Merric that *he* was in love with *Vivid*. Admitted, because it was something to admit, because it was something true. Sometime between being fake-strangled by him in the Circle and kissing him in the forest, that ill-tempered assassin had made Scorch fall in love with him, the stealthy bastard. "Gods," he gasped, stricken by epiphany. "I'm in love with him." He said it aloud, testing the way it sounded. It sounded really nice, if not heartbreakingly inconvenient.

"Obviously," Merric sighed just as the guard who'd dropped his keys moved toward their cell door. "Scorch," he whispered, nodding toward the approaching, armored figure.

Scorch resolved to continue his heart's revelation later, preferably when there was alcohol on hand. "Did you tell the Queen what I said?" Scorch asked the nearest of the guards, but the guard kept his head down and fiddled with the set of keys, deaf to Scorch's question. "Keeping us locked up is a mistake. We must speak with the Queen."

The guard finally settled on a key and inserted it into the cell lock. It clicked and the bars slid open with a loud, grating thrum. A moment later, bronze-gloved hands were grabbing Scorch's arm and leading him up the barrack stairs. The two remaining guards grabbed Merric and pulled him along.

"Scorch, where are they taking us?" Scorch heard Merric's voice echoing as they left the dungeon.

"Either to the Queen or to the stocks," Scorch called to him. "Hope it's the former."

The guards dragged them through the palace courtyard and up the steps. They entered an impressive foyer filled with paintings of plant life, and from there, they ascended a spiraling staircase. It was a beautiful palace, but not so grand it made Scorch feel out of place. There was a hominess to it, warmth that the High Priestess' temple had irrefutably lacked.

They stopped outside a golden door with a rose-crystal knob. One of the guards disappeared through the door, and was gone for—Scorch counted—fifty seconds. At the guard's reappearance, Scorch and Merric were hustled into the room and the golden door was shut. The guards released them, but remained close, their hands on their weapons, ready to draw at any sign of malicious intent. Standing on the far side of the room, staring out a window, was the Queen.

She was glamorous, with dark skin and eyes like honey. Her hair was swept in intricate coils atop her head, a circlet crown resting across her brow and bejeweling her forehead with garnet and amber. Her skin was smooth and belied hardly any signs of aging. Scorch decided she could be no older than thirty-five. Her posture, when she turned to look at the two men brought before her, was perfectly straight, her elegance exaggerated by the slimming cut of her trousers and button-up blouse. Her collar was stiff and embroidered with golden-threaded swirls. Not even the frown on her face could keep Scorch from gaping momentarily at her presence, and she seemed similarly moved by theirs. They stared at one another for a moment before she finally spoke, and, when she did, her voice was strong.

"My guard tells me you bring word of Axum," she said. "Is this true?"

"Yes, Your Majesty," answered Scorch.

Her elbow rested on the windowsill, the late afternoon sun causing her circlet to glow as if on fire. "Do you work for him?"

"No, Your Majesty." It was Merric who spoke now. "We are from the Guardians' Guild."

"Are you?" asked the Queen. "Because the last time I was visited with news of Axum, it was an assassin under the guise of a guardian." Her eyes were sharp. "I did not care for that."

"We are not assassins, Your Majesty," Scorch assured her. "And we don't work for Axum."

"You look rough enough for an assassin," she said.

"I would make a terrible assassin, trust me."

She did not look like she believed him. "You do not have a missive from the Guild Master."

"No," Merric said. "But for the sake of Viridor, you should listen to what we have to say, regardless."

The Queen looked out the window, closing her eyes to the sunshine, and when she opened them again, Scorch could see her resolve. "Axum sent an assassin to me weeks ago," she said, leaving the window and striding across the room to a decanter sitting on a silver tray. She poured a generous amount of amber liquid into a glass, and Scorch instantly recognized it as Guild-brewed whiskey. He jealously watched her take a sip and wondered how she'd gotten it. A gift from Master McClintock? "I had just received word of the High Priestess' death. Not many know this, but the High Priestess had a rather large hand in the last twenty years' ordinances concerning elementals." Scorch fought to keep his face blank. "Axum believes her death was a sign from the Gods that the time for elementals to rule has come. He sent his assassin to gauge my reaction to this proposal."

Merric and Scorch remained silent for a moment, and then, too curious for his own good, Scorch asked, "And what was your reaction, Your Majesty?"

"An assassin was standing in front of me," the Queen responded plainly. "My reaction had to be the one that would let me keep my head. For the time being."

In the meeting at the Hollow Scorch had spied on, the assassin had reported to Axum that the Queen was swayable. "You would let a band of power-mad elementals take over Viridor?"

"Do you fear elementals, Guardian?" the Queen asked.

"Elementals are just people," Scorch pointed out. "I don't fear them. I fear small-mindedness."

"And Axum is small-minded?" She took another sip of her whiskey.

"He's taken hate shown to his kind and molded it into hate for others. Your Majesty, he's coming to kill you and take your throne, and he's coming soon."

The Queen downed the remainder of the whiskey and slammed the glass on the tray. "So you say. But why should I believe you? You come to me with no proof."

"My friend has not lied to you, Your Majesty," Merric said. "He speaks only the truth."

"How would the Guild even know of such a plot? The Guild Master has never been so underhanded. Guardians don't work in the shadows."

"Guardians and assassins can get along as well as humans and elementals," spoke Scorch, losing as much patience as time. "They need only the opportunity to prove they're not a threat to one another."

"For a guardian," the Queen said, a thoughtfully tapping finger on her chin, "you sound rather supportive of elementals."

"All but the mad ones, Your Majesty," Scorch allowed.

Her face was doing something interesting. She had taken on the appearance of someone trying to mask the telltale signs of a mind working overtime. It was similar to looking upon Vivid's face when Scorch pulled away from a kiss. He never minded it on Vivid, but from the Queen, it was wholly unsettling.

"Let me make sure I understand you," she said, taking a few languid steps in his direction. "You come here to warn me elementals are on their way to kill me, and in the next breath you defend elementals. Does this make sense to you?"

Merric stirred uneasily beside him, but Scorch's confidence was flaring in his chest, burning for the Queen to feel. "A group of murderous elementals plotting to assassinate the Queen will do nothing but worsen the relationship between elementals and humans," he said. "It's not what I want."

"What do you want?"

"I want a lot of things," he answered with a trace of bitterness. "But ranking high in my heart is the desire for elementals to live without being hunted and hated."

Perhaps the Queen had not been expecting such straightforwardness, because, for an instant, the cool facade slipped from her face and Scorch saw a flash of something he knew quite well. Guilt. "And the highest ranked desire in your heart?"

Scorch flushed and Merric coughed beside him. "That is personal, Your Majesty."

"You will not tell me? Not even as a sign of trust?" She was baiting him, he knew, and it was almost playful. "Guardians do not support elementals. It is against the law. Who are you really? Why are you here?"

"We are guardians, Your Majesty," Merric insisted at the same time Scorch said, "I'm trying to make things better."

"You are keeping something from me," the Queen said, sucking any air of levity from the room. "Tell me what it is, or I will have my guards throw you in the dungeon."

Scorch heard the guards moving behind him. He glanced at a lost-looking Merric, and an idea came to him, built by desperation and hope and utter idiocy, but they had to make the Queen believe them, they couldn't afford to be locked up when Axum arrived. They may not have had proof the Guild sent them, but Scorch had unquantifiable proof that he not only knew what Axum was capable of, but also had the means to help stop him.

He held out his palm and summoned a sphere of fire.

The Queen staggered back, Merric groaned, and the three guards creaked and clanged as they shuffled, unsure of what action to take. A moment later, more guards burst through the door. Scorch closed his fist and snuffed out the fire before they could see.

"Your Majesty," one reported, out of breath. "Three of your sentinels have been found unconscious and stripped of their armor. Is everything alright in here?"

Scorch held his breath. At his side, Merric was a din of nerves. He waited for the worst to happen, for the Queen to yell for the guards to execute them both. Vivid would be disappointed he'd missed the opportunity to do it himself.

But the Queen did not yell, and the guards were not moving, and the only activity in the room was the absurd pounding of Scorch's heart. He was on the precipice of dying from suspense when the Queen finally said, "Everything is alright. You should find the ruffians who have taken my sentinels' armor and leave me to my business."

"Yes, Your Majesty." The guards who had burst into the room bowed and made a swift exit.

"So," the Queen continued, "an elemental has come to save the Queen while more elementals come to kill her." She waved a hand at the remaining guards. "Take off that armor, please, and show yourselves, or try to kill me and be done with it. I am bored with secrets."

Scorch should not have been as shocked as he was to discover the Queen's royal guard consisted of two assassins and a flautist. He watched, flabbergasted, as Vivid, Audrey, and Felix lifted the bronze helmets from their heads. Merric was at Felix's side in a blink, helping him shrug out of the heavy pauldrons, but Scorch couldn't keep his eyes off Vivid's face. He looked pink in the cheeks, a rarity, and his lips were drawn in a thin line as he stared at Scorch. Scorch's mouth fell open as he recalled what he'd admitted in the dungeon, and the guard who had subsequently dropped his keys.

He was pondering the likelihood of successfully throwing himself out the nearby window when the Queen finally broke the silence. "Needless to say, you are not members of my royal guard."

"Felix, are you okay? What did they make you do?" Merric asked, his fingers grazing over a bruise on the young man's cheek.

Audrey let out a laugh. "Please. It was his idea we knock out the guards and take their uniforms."

Scorch raised his eyebrows at Vivid, who responded with no more than an eye twitch. He wanted to kiss him. Instead, he tore his eyes away in frustration. "Your Majesty," he said, turning toward the Queen, "these are my friends and," he swallowed hard, "we're here to rescue you."

"Rescue me? You're an elemental who has assaulted my guards and infiltrated my palace. I should have you killed."

Vivid was on her before her next breath, slamming her into the wall and holding a dagger to her throat. "Call for your guards and I'll kill you."

"Vivid, that's the opposite result we're aiming for," Scorch sighed.

The Queen trembled beneath Vivid's blade. Sweat broke out on her brow.

"Vivid," Scorch pleaded, walking slowly to him and touching his elbow.

The Queen closed her eyes and her breathing grew unsteady. The crystal decanter began to shake, followed by the tray, followed by the table.

Vivid pulled the dagger away at once, grabbed Scorch's wrist, and hauled him back. "She's an Earth," he growled, and Scorch's eyes widened on the Queen.

She opened her eyes, her hands clasping her throat. When she saw Vivid sheathe his weapon, her trembling ceased and the table stopped shaking.

"No. You're an elemental?" Scorch gawked in disbelief.

"That's impossible," said Merric. "No elemental would pass ordinances allowing the murder of their own kind."

Scorch locked eyes with the Queen. "They might if it was a matter of losing their own head." Vivid still had a hold on his wrist. Scorch yearned to grab his hand, so he took a preventative step away and gestured to the decanter. "Is that Guild-brewed whiskey?" he asked the Queen, and she nodded weakly. He walked to the table and hoisted himself up among a pile of official papers and a perilously sharp letter opener. He picked up the decanter by the neck, swished the whiskey around, and took a swig. It was golden sunshine on his tongue and a delicious burn down his throat. He wiped the back of his hand across his mouth and surveyed the room to find he'd won the attention of all its occupants. "The High Priestess had you under her thumb," he stated.

"She did not know what I was," the Queen answered. "I'm good at hiding it." She glanced at Vivid. "Most of the time."

Scorch looked at her more carefully than before and found familiarity there. There was a peculiar shine in her eyes he'd seen in the looking glass. Her posture, which had seemed regally straight before, now appeared stiff from a lifetime's worth of worry. For so long, he'd lived half a life, petrified of people discovering who he really was. Such a life was hard enough in the Guild. Scorch couldn't imagine surviving it under the close scrutiny of royalty. But it was no excuse.

"I was good at hiding," he said, pouring another shot of whiskey into the Queen's glass. He jumped from the table and walked to her, handing her the glass. "Because I knew people would want me dead if they found out. Because of the ordinances *you* passed."

"I was fifteen when they were passed. I was young and afraid."

"*I'm* young and afraid," Scorch stated. "But as you can see, it's not driven me to complicity in genocide." She looked shocked. "My friends and I will help you deal with Axum, but when this is over, so are your ordinances concerning elementals, or else Viridor's citizens will discover their Queen is one."

"Cheers," said Audrey.

Scorch tapped the decanter against the Queen's glass. "Cheers," he agreed, taking a sip.

The Queen downed her whiskey in two gulps.

"We're wasting time," came Vivid's voice. Scorch turned around to find him at his back, stormy-faced.

"When can we expect Axum to arrive?" asked the Queen, looking past Scorch to his assassin shadow.

The ground trembled again, and Scorch looked from Vivid to the Queen with alarm. "It's alright. He's not actually going to hurt you. He's just grumpy. You need to control yourself."

But the Queen was shaking her head. "That's not me."

The floor beneath them quaked and Scorch stumbled, the decanter slipping from his grip and shattering. Vivid steadied him, his arm winding around Scorch's waist as the shaking worsened. "Axum is here."

"Already?" cried Scorch.

"He'll bring the whole palace down," Audrey cursed, crossing the room and grabbing the Queen. "We need to get her to safety."

"I think we all need to get to safety," piped Merric, who had brandished his sword with one hand and was holding on to Felix with the other.

A loud cracking noise sounded in the room and Vivid yanked Scorch close as a ceiling tile crashed where he'd just been standing. "Go!" Vivid ordered, taking Scorch's hand and running for the door.

The quake intensified as they raced down the staircase. Scorch chanced a glance over his shoulder to make sure the others were following and nearly tripped over a fallen guard. Vivid chided him with an angry "*Scorch*!" as they reached the foyer.

The pretty paintings of plants were falling from the walls and a crack shot through the hardwood. Bits of ceiling and wall were crumbling. The dust was as prevalent as the screaming.

Vivid pushed Scorch through the palace doors, the others tumbling out behind them as the building rumbled and the roof collapsed. As soon as they were clear, catching their breath in the courtyard while guards and servants streamed around them in a panic, the quake stopped.

"What an unexpected turn, finding you all here," Axum's voice reached out to them through the mayhem.

Vivid reacted first, holding up a palm out of instinct to summon his power. When it didn't come, devastation cut deep across his face, a flash of the same horror Scorch had witnessed when the desert took hold of his mind, and he suddenly realized what Vivid had been afraid of. It wasn't the High Priestess' torture. It was the helplessness of it.

Now, even without his powers, Vivid moved in front of Scorch and the others, blocking them from Axum and wielding his twin daggers. But Axum hadn't come alone, and other assassins from the Hollow already had them surrounded.

"Scorch," Vivid whispered, "don't die."

Scorch had no time to answer, or hold him back, or even think, because, like the wind, Vivid flew at Axum with his blades raised high above his head.

Pandemonium unleashed in the courtyard. A tremor knocked Scorch off his feet and he fell to his knees. A black leather boot caught him beneath the chin and sent him to his back, and then an assassin was leaning over him with lips curled into a snarl and a knife twirling in his fingers. Scorch rolled as the blade came down, grabbing the assassin's arm. Heat surged from his core, into his hands. The black leather burned, and the air was perfumed with smoldering skin before the assassin yelped and smashed the heel of his hand toward Scorch's nose. He dodged and jumped to his feet, flames sparking from his fingertips. He unsheathed his sword, waited for the assassin to stand and lift his blade, and then he struck, a wicked plunge that spattered blood on the Queen's courtyard daisies.

Scorch heard a yell and spun, stained sword at the ready. Audrey and the Queen were fending off three more assassins. He held out his arm and shot a jolt of fire toward one of their attackers. The ground shook violently, unsteadying his balance, and he could hear Merric's voice calling from a distance, but a fierce wind skewed his sense of direction. Squinting against the gale, he searched for Vivid. Thunder roared in the sky, and then rain began dropping in sheets so thick he could hardly see. When the rock soared through the air and hit him right above the eye, he never saw it coming.

The pain was searing, and while it did not topple him, blood poured from the gash and blinded his right eye. He wiped at the blood, blinking it from his vision. Through the blur, Axum appeared, rocks floating beside his head. Vivid hadn't killed him, but he'd left marks of his effort: a bright red line across his throat and a steadily bleeding cut on his cheek.

"Is that all you can do?" Scorch yelled through the curtain of rain. "Throw a few rocks?"

Axum sneered and lifted his fists. The earth shifted beneath Scorch's feet and the palace groaned as its walls began to crack. Scorch kept his footing, though a gust of wind pulled at his back and another hale of rocks assaulted his front. He covered his face with his hands and reached for his fire. It sparked and hissed right beneath his skin, but he couldn't release it, not when he was soaking wet. Lightning struck a nearby tree and the sound was deafening. He watched the tree begin to burn, and when he turned back, Axum was gone.

Scorch ran, his sword meeting another assassin's blade after several strides. Swordwork was tricky on a surface quickly slickening with mud, and the assassin escaped a sweep of Scorch's sword and kicked him in the stomach. He windmilled backwards, boots sliding, and the assassin ran at him, blade crimson and ready to slice through skin. It was sheer luck when the assassin caught a flying rock to the shin and his reach lessened just enough to save Scorch from a deathblow. The blade cut across his abdomen, shredding his new leather jerkin and a layer of skin, but sparing his internal organs.

In the next instant, a tide of water surged around the assassin's feet and swept him down the length of the courtyard.

"Scorch!" Audrey ran to his side, her hair flying in the bluster of the storm. "I lost sight of Bellamy!"

"Who's Bellamy?"

"The Queen!" Audrey yelled, fisting Scorch's collar and dragging him to the side as a garden boulder sailed past.

"I'll find her," Scorch promised. He squeezed her shoulder, she gave him a curt nod, and then they parted, Audrey running toward

Merric's voice while Scorch ran where the intense wind blew him. He slipped in the mud and slid a few feet, landing beside a royal guard whose helmet was twisted round the wrong way. Beyond him, more dead guards covered the ground. He was close enough to make out the palace now, or what was left of it, and he scrambled toward it, boots squishing in mud until he reached the steps.

The palace was in shambles, half of it lying in complete decimation. Scorch crawled under a fallen beam and stood in the wreckage. A glimmer on the dusty hardwood caught his eye and he bent to pick up the golden circlet crown. The woman it belonged to was nearby, shaking beside a fallen painting of a willow tree.

"Your Majesty," Scorch said, kneeling at her side. She was unresponsive. "Bellamy?"

Blood streaked across her face. She was soaked, half with rainwater, half with sweat.

"Bellamy?" he said again, touching her hand. Her whole body was thrumming with energy and, at his touch, the building around them shook, displacing more dust and bits of ceiling. Scorch ducked and pulled the Queen toward him to cover her head from falling debris.

"I can't," she quivered. "I can't control it." She couldn't focus her eyes; they stared straight ahead, terrified by an invisible foe. Scorch knew that feeling, had felt his body fight until he was drenched with sweat and thought he might die from the wrongness of it. He didn't know what an Earth elemental was like at their purest form of power, but he didn't want to find out when a ton of palace still loomed over their heads.

"Yes, you can," Scorch told her, taking her face in his hands. "Look at me," he demanded, borrowing the same tone that had calmed him, time and again. "Bellamy, look at me." He gave her head a shake and she gasped, her wide eyes meeting his. Her pupils were small as needlepoints. "If you lose control right now, you will bring the palace down around us, and we will both die."

The Queen let out a panicked squeak and the beam over their heads began to crack. The ground beneath them was vibrating.

"Calm down. *Calm down.*" He remembered the strength of Vivid's hand when he'd talked Scorch down inside the Hollow, and he hoped his own grip was a comfort to the Queen and not a threat. He didn't want to die because a palace fell on him. He didn't want to die not knowing if Vivid was okay. "You *are* strong enough to fight it," Scorch said, praying it was true.

The Queen shut her eyes, her body shaking, until finally, after a brutal spasm, she passed out in his arms. The floor stopped vibrating and Scorch heaved a sigh of relief. But one crisis averted was not a battle won, and so with his next breath, he stood, lifting her from the rubble and toting her back outside, where the rain was still pouring and the courtyard below was a squall of flying rocks, dirt, rain, and wind. He hurried down the steps and hid the Queen's unconscious body in a thick juniper bush. Bushes, he knew from experience, made for excellent life-saving hiding spots. He placed her crown in her hands and ran back into the carnage of the courtyard.

Again, he could barely see besides vague, grey forms moving around him. If only he could find the source of the rainstorm, he could snuff it out and summon his fire. It couldn't be Audrey making it rain so hard; she would never have risked the loss of visibility. No, there was another Water around, making them fight blind. Scorch was just setting off to find them when the ground opened up beneath his feet and a tree root twisted around his ankles.

He tried to kick free, but the roots squeezed him tighter and he lost his balance. His knees sank into the mud as he reached around with his sword to cut himself free, but another root curled from the soggy earth and strangled his wrists. He dropped the sword and blinked away the rain and blood.

"Yours was a grave mistake," Axum said, walking through the veil of rain and appearing before Scorch with a cruel smile. The family resemblance was suddenly all too clear.

"I've made a lot of mistakes," Scorch said, "and a lot of them have been grave. You'll need to be more specific." The ground gave a threatening moan beneath him and the roots tightened painfully. Scorch had a suspicion Axum could make the earth swallow him whole if he wished it, and going by the vicious sparkle in Axum's eyes, he wished for nothing more.

"You should have disappeared," Axum clarified. "Now that you have strayed into my path, I have no choice but to kill my son's murderer."

"You would have hunted me down eventually, though, wouldn't you?" Scorch asked, spitting blood and fifteen years' hatred. "Like you did my parents." Axum's lack of response was verification enough. The memory he'd recovered of black-leathered attackers was real. "Only, you won't be able to blame my death on the High Priestess," Scorch fumed, "or her monks."

"I did hear of the fate of the fortress," Axum said. His hand was spread at his side and a whirl of rocks spun around it like the sun. "You would have been a useful addition to our movement. I'd hoped you would prove more trustworthy than your parents, but the apple and the tree and so on."

"Is that why you killed them? They wanted no part in your madness?"

"Nahla and Rosen Cole were unwilling to do what was needed to save our kind. I returned from my failed mission at the temple to find them gone from the Hollow. Was I to risk them rising up against me, as you do now?"

Scorch struggled in the mud, pulling at his root constraints. "I'm not exactly in the position to be rising. But let me go and I would love to prove my untrustworthiness."

"You killed my son." Axum bellowed through the rain and wind shear. His boots kicked up bouts of mud as he stomped closer.

Scorch hadn't killed Elias, of course, and he looked all around him for the man who had, an insane hope in his heart that Vivid would save him, one more time. It seemed unusually brutal—but also just his luck—that he would finally meet his end at the hand of the man who'd killed his parents.

He tried not to cower as Axum loomed over him, rocks floating, waiting for an order to crush his skull. He would not die begging to live. There was only one name he wanted on his lips before his time was spent. With a petulant grin, Scorch looked up at Axum. "Vivid will kill you."

"Vivid couldn't lift a breeze against me," Axum said, touching the cut at his throat. "Couldn't lift a knife either, after I buried him alive. I think I'll do the same to you."

"What did you say? What have you done?!" Scorch yelled.

"Did you think Vivid could beat me with blades? Your faith has been misplaced from the very beginning."

Dirt rose from the ground and encircled Scorch like a tomb. The roots around his ankles began to pull him down, down. He was up to his knees in mud and rocks, lifting his face to the sky, rain mixing with tears. He couldn't die with Vivid buried beneath the ground. "Vivid!" he screamed. His fingers scratched at the earth piling around him. He tried to summon his fire, but it wouldn't come, not with rain drenching his skin. "Vivid!"

There was another clap of thunder, another scream.

And then the rain stopped.

The rain stopped, but the wind still blew. The raindrops dried on Scorch's skin as the dirt began to fall in heaps on top of his head. The fire under his skin rushed up and burnt the roots away from his wrists and ankles. With his freed limbs, Scorch kicked and clawed, dragging himself out of the dirt. He cast a fiery column from his fingertips, and a furious howl erupted from his lungs. Axum tried to weigh him down, tried to make more roots snare his limbs, but everything that touched Scorch's skin sizzled and turned to ash. He pulled himself to a dizzying stand and directed his fire straight through Axum's heart.

The fire pierced him. Dirt and rocks fell heavily to the ground, and then, so did Axum. Scorch burned him, let a stream of fire engulf him. As the assassin screamed, Scorch's parents screamed in his head, a macabre echo. Fifteen years ago, when the life had left them, they had burned, and now Axum would burn until his life was burned out.

When it was over, Scorch didn't linger by Axum's scorched corpse. "Vivid!" he yelled. "Vivid!" He found his sword in the mud and turned in a circle, eyes widening at the courtyard now that the storm had stopped and he could *see*. He saw Merric first, standing beside the lightning-stricken tree, in a ring of fallen bodies, both in bronze armor and black leather. His face was covered in scratches, and when he stepped forward, it was with a limp.

"Felix!" Merric was shouting.

Scorch saw Audrey next, pushing her hair from her face and wiping her blades on the body of an assassin at her feet. Her eye locked on Scorch as he watched her, then she looked past him, frowning. He knew it was because she didn't see Vivid, and neither did Scorch.

"Vivid!" he yelled again.

"Merric!" Scorch heard Felix a moment before he spotted him. He was lying beneath a pile of dead assassins. Merric stumbled over to him, throwing the bodies off and helping him stand.

"You're alive," he said, hugging Felix tight. "I lost you in the storm. Are you okay?"

"I think so," Felix replied, mystified by his own resilience. "A Water elemental had me. I felt like I was drowning, and then Vivid," he turned his head, searching. "Vivid killed him and saved me. He killed all of them. Where is he?"

"Vivid!" Scorch screamed, running over to the pile of bodies beside Felix. He slipped in the mud, fell. "Vivid!" He turned the bodies over, checking every face. "Vivid!" Fear lodged in his throat and tears streamed from his eyes. He scanned the grimy earth, wondering which patch might contain Vivid buried beneath. He shoved his hands into the muck and began digging, digging—

Fingers threaded through his hair and tugged his head back. "I'm right here." Vivid gazed down at him, covered in mud and blood.

"Vivid!" Scorch yelled again, and Vivid grimaced.

"Stop screaming. You make me want to stab out my eardrums." Vivid released his hair, and Scorch scrambled to his feet, slipping and sliding.

"Axum said he buried you alive," he breathed. He touched Vivid's face reverently, but then he pulled away, afraid to touch him, afraid Vivid didn't want it.

"Only for a second," Vivid conceded. Even covered in dirt he looked fearsome. He reached for Scorch's hand and brought it back to his cheek, holding it there. "You killed him."

Scorch's heart thudded in his chest, more adrenaline rushing through his veins now than when roots had been dragging him into an early grave. Vivid lowered their hands but kept their fingers intertwined. "I killed him," Scorch rasped.

"Good," Vivid answered. He stared at Scorch until Scorch felt the compulsion to do something embarrassing, like faint or propose, but then Vivid finally released him, from his gaze and from his touch. Scorch watched silently as he moved among the others. He nodded at Felix and Merric and accepted Audrey's hand when she reached for him. "Where is the Queen?" he asked her.

"Oh!" yelped Scorch, having forgotten the sole purpose of their guardianship in the wake of Vivid's existence. "I hid her in the bushes."

He ignored Audrey's scoff and Merric's cry of horror and hurried past them. Digging Queen Bellamy out of the shrubbery was a welcomed opportunity to catch his breath and try to mute the riptide of emotions coursing through his body. There was a brief moment when he shook her shoulder and she didn't wake, and he thought *oh Gods, I let the Queen of Viridor die in a bush*, but then her eyes fluttered open and she stared up at him with apprehension.

"What? Where—"

"You are in a bush, Your Majesty," he provided helpfully, extending his hand to her and helping her rise from the green leaves. She had barely straightened her regal shoulders when a horn sounded, startling them both into a crouch.

"Her Majesty the Queen is alive!" announced an errant guard through an amplifying device, bent on scaring Scorch half to death.

Queen Bellamy returned to standing with Scorch at her side, however hesitantly, and a moment later they were being swarmed by dozens of bronze guards. Scorch squeezed through, fighting his way around a fresh gathering of confused townsfolk and those who had fled the palace, until he reached his small group of companions. They lingered in silence beneath the charred tree while the Queen was fussed over and prodded at. For Scorch, it was an anticlimactic end to saving the Queen's life. In the history books, guardians were praised with cheers and adorned with medals when they completed a guardianship for high-ranking citizens. In reality, Scorch and the others waited around for twenty minutes, the drying mud itchy on their skin, before the Queen finally broke away from her adoring subjects and came to speak with her defenders.

"I don't know how to thank you," she began.

"You know exactly how you can thank us," Vivid replied. He cast her a bored glance. "Scorch already told you."

The Queen nodded seriously. "I have not forgotten." She looked Scorch in the eyes. "I will not forget."

"If you're passing out thanks," Audrey said, scratching a layer of mud off her hand, "a bath and a bed wouldn't be refused."

"And some medical supplies, Your Majesty," Felix added. His arm was wrapped around Merric's waist, and Merric was leaning on him, unable to put weight on one of his legs.

"Please, ride with my procession to my secondary residence in the country. I have more I would like to discuss, and there are plenty of baths and beds for everyone." Scorch could already hear the clopping of horse hooves on cobblestone, and when he turned, a slew of royal carriages were lining up beyond the palace walls.

A cold, sick sensation tingled up Scorch's spine in the seconds before he walked for the carriages, because he thought *now is the last time I will see him.* Their task accomplished, Vivid would disappear, any obligation he felt toward Scorch thoroughly obliged, and Scorch would never see him again. That's what he thought. That's what stuck his feet to the ground when Felix, Merric, and Audrey began limping toward the carriages. If Vivid had not given him a push, Scorch might have lingered in suspension forever.

"Scorch," Vivid said impatiently. Scorch blinked at him, admiring the sleek line of his filthy neck as he jerked his head toward the carriages. "Walking is something you might consider."

The moment of separation was being forced upon him before he was ready. He was still trying to think of a fitting farewell when Vivid grabbed his arm and began leading him toward the carriages.

"What's wrong with you? Are you concussed?" Vivid asked, taking Scorch's hand at the open door of a carriage and helping him step in.

Scorch's eyes watered and he touched the gash over his brow. He would have a new scar there. "Possibly concussed," he admitted. They were not the final words he would have chosen, if given the time. Vivid's eyebrows stitched together, and then, with a huff, he pulled himself into the carriage and plopped himself down right beside Scorch.

Scorch froze. He waited for Vivid to call him an idiot, dash out of the carriage, and disappear into the sunset—the sun was setting, and it would have been an enviably dramatic exit—but all Vivid did was scratch at his head and scowl when flakes fell to the carriage floor. Someone coughed and Scorch belatedly noticed the three other passengers sharing the carriage. Audrey was sitting by one window, her single eye fluctuating between studying Scorch and studying Vivid. Merric sat by the other window, his handsome face pinched with discomfort as he prodded his injured leg. Felix sat between them, looking happy and banged up.

Vivid shifted around, and Scorch watched as he tried to make himself comfortable on the plush carriage seat, or maybe he was just trying to rub as much dirt into the Queen's velvet cushions as possible. He was like the fat grey cat at the Guild, making biscuits and walking in circles until she finally settled down for a snooze. Vivid didn't snooze, but neither was he leaving the carriage, so Scorch allowed himself to relax, at least a little.

The horses trotted them through the streets of the Royal Quarter. The city was in uproar. Scorch heard the people shouting, demanding to know what all the noise had been about, whether it was true the palace had been destroyed, who the attackers were. It instilled in him a hearty gladness he wasn't the Queen, though the circlet crown *was* lovely.

The shouting and commotion ended when the Queen's procession exited the city and human voices made way for the silence of a chilly evening. Inside their carriage, it grew dark, and Scorch enjoyed the freeness of not being seen. He admired the silhouette of Vivid's face against the window, outlined by soft moonlight, the slope of his nose and curl of his lashes. Scorch did his best to commit the moment to memory. Surely, once they reached their destination, Vivid would leave.

But he didn't. They rolled up to the Queen's secondary residence an hour later, and all Vivid did was leap from the carriage and offer his hand to help Scorch down, as well as the others. Scorch kept an eye devoted to him as they made their way inside, determined to catch him fleeing, but Vivid didn't flee. He looked worn out, exhausted, and a little sad. Perhaps, he was waiting until morning to sneak away. He would be able to make it further from Scorch after a good night's sleep.

The Queen bid them farewell for the moment and had one of her servants show them to their rooms. Scorch and the others were led to a hallway on the third floor. The servant bustled about anxiously, opening five different doors and proclaiming a hot bath had been prepared for each of them, wine set out, and a plate of food provided. Scorch thanked him and he scuttled off, probably with more work to do than was comprehendible, having to prepare so many rooms for so many unexpected visitors. Everyone displaced by the palace's demise was there.

Merric smiled at Scorch and hobbled for one of the rooms. Unsurprisingly, Felix ignored his own offered room and slipped into Merric's instead. Audrey murmured something in Vivid's ear before vanishing into her own room. That left Scorch and Vivid alone, standing awkwardly in the hallway.

"Don't drink the wine," Vivid warned him. "Or eat the food."

Scorch nodded. "I won't."

Vivid's look was severe. "I'm serious."

"I can resist a few bread rolls, you know." Vivid arched a disbelieving eyebrow. "I *can*." His stomach rumbled and he wondered if there *were* bread rolls. Vivid moved toward one of the empty rooms and Scorch did the same, but he stopped at the doorframe. "In case there are honey cakes in there," he told Vivid, "it was nice. Knowing you."

Vivid's glare sharpened past its usual intensity, and then he stepped inside his room and shut the door.

# *A Conclusion*
# 25

*I*t took multiple baths to get Scorch clean. There was mud in unspeakable crevices, and the gash over his eye began bleeding again at one point, resulting in a literal bloodbath. The poor servants kept a steady stream of hot water coming to his room, and by the end of it, after he'd slipped into the soft trousers and billowy shirt left out for him, it felt like they'd been to war together, the servants and himself. One servant seemed particularly pleased to have aided Scorch's valiant quest for cleanliness, offering to soap him up at one point. Scorch politely refused. He hovered again by Scorch's door, hips jutted to the side, head tilted in invitation. Scorch refused him again, a little less politely the second time, and then he fell face-first onto the gigantic bed.

When there was a knock on his door a few minutes later, he groaned into one of a thousand pillows. He tried to ignore it, but the knocks continued until he was forced from softness. He dragged himself bonelessly to the door and threw it open. A servant stared up at him, looking as exhausted as he felt.

"The Queen wishes to see you," she informed him. "Follow me?"

Scorch sighed and stepped into the slippers the Queen had provided. "Lead the way."

It was a surprisingly short trip to the Queen's room, as she was only one floor above him, and the servant knocked a single time before Bellamy herself opened the door.

"Please, come in," she said.

Scorch entered, declining the glass of wine she offered. He scanned the room and multiple things took him by surprise. For one, it was a bedchamber, and Scorch had been expecting a room with a desk and chairs and no sleeping surfaces. Also, there were no guards or servants present. Scorch and the Queen were entirely alone, and the Queen was wearing *pajamas*.

"Good evening, Your Majesty."

"You may call me Bellamy," she said. "Those to whom I owe my life may call me Bellamy."

"Well, you can call me Scorch."

"Scorch. A prophetic name?"

"A nickname." He was unsure of what to do with his hands so he clasped them behind his back.

"And your real name?"

"Not nearly as prophetic."

She smiled at him. "I have something for you." She turned to rummage through a brassy chest that lay beside a half-empty glass of wine. Scorch soaked in the oddity of the moment. When she turned back to him, she held a thick scroll.

"I didn't get you anything," he said lamely as she handed it over. He unfurled the paper until a spidery cursive revealed unexpected lettering.

"The Royal Ordinances Concerning Elementals," Bellamy told him. "They are all there. Official permission for every act of abhorrence inflicted on them." She cleared her throat. "On *us*, rather."

"And what," Scorch said, eyeing the scroll, "do you want me to do with this?"

"Burn it." There was no doubt in her eyes and no hesitation in Scorch's heart. He let the fire uncoil from deep inside, until a tiny flame sparked from his finger. They watched the scroll burn together, Scorch collecting the ashes in his hands.

"It's done." She directed him to dump the ashes in the fireplace, and when his hands were empty, she filled them again with a fat coin purse. "For your help," she said. "And your discretion, I hope."

She led him to the door.

"I won't tell anyone who you are," he promised. "But you should consider what might happen if Viridor knew you were an elemental, as well as their Queen."

"It could be bad," Bellamy said softly.

"But it could be worth it, too." He left her to mull it over.

It was such a late hour, not even servants were skulking about the halls anymore. Scorch navigated down the stairs, only getting lost once, and then he worried he'd fallen asleep somewhere between his room and the Queen's, because the sight in front of his door was surely a dream. It had to be a dream.

Vivid was sitting on the floor with his back against Scorch's door and his head down, his knees tucked into his chest. Instead of wearing clothes provided by the Queen, like Scorch, he had already laundered his own leather gear.

"Vivid?" Scorch asked, afraid to approach. He stood at the end of the hallway, like roots still had hold of his ankles.

At the sound of his voice, Vivid looked up. "You're not in your room," he accused.

"The Queen wanted to see me," he explained. "Did you," he cocked his head, "want to see me?"

"No," Vivid blustered, rising to his feet. He ran a hand across the clean, short shear of his hair. Scorch could see where he'd missed a spot in the bath, a little smudge on the right angle of his jaw.

"Oh. Right."

"Or, yes," Vivid said. He knocked his knuckles on the door. "I thought you were in there. Ignoring me."

Scorch felt his ears go pink. "I—I was not in there."

"That has been established." Vivid remained a grouchy barrier between Scorch and the door, and Scorch didn't understand why. He decided to take a few steps forward to see what Vivid would do. He did nothing but watch with a carefully constructed expression of indifference.

"Why were you—I mean, I'm here now," Scorch said. "If you still want to—" And that's when it hit him, why Vivid was there. The icy dread was back with a vengeance, prickling the back of his neck and sloshing around in his stomach, making him feel sick. Vivid was leaving. This was his farewell. "You didn't have to say goodbye. I would have understood."

Vivid made a weird noise, a sort of growly whimper, and the anger-fueled crease between his eyes pinched tighter as his scowl intensified.

"But I'm glad you're here, because I wanted you to know that I'm sorry," Scorch continued, trying not to let Vivid's impressive glare dissuade him. "I was too forward in my pursuit of you. It made you uncomfortable. It was a mistake on my part, and I—" Scorch stopped talking, because Vivid had taken hold of his shoulders and pushed him into the door, effectively knocking the words from his mouth.

"I'm not good at this," Vivid said.

Scorch laughed nervously. "At slamming me into walls? I think you're great at it."

"At this," Vivid repeated. "Talking about—" He looked physically pained, and for a long time couldn't finish his sentence, like it was taking away years from his life to even form the thought. "Talking about . . . what I want," he finally choked out, his eyes never wavering from Scorch's, even though his nostrils flared in annoyance and his cheeks filled with a comely shade of pink.

Scorch was breathless, mindless, Vivid pressing him further against the door and making the nerves in his stomach spike. He didn't even notice the doorknob poking him in the back, but he would find a bruise there later. "I know you're bad at it," he said, looking down at Vivid and the way he worried his bottom lip between his teeth. "I don't mind. I just," he dug around in his head for his perfect answer, and he didn't need to dig deep, because it was already at the surface, waiting to be plucked. "I want to know what you want so I can give it to you. It doesn't matter what it is. A goodbye or," he hoped with all his heart, "not a goodbye."

Vivid gravitated closer and the fingers digging into Scorch's shoulders became caresses, up and down his arms. Vehemently, Vivid said, "I want to stay with you."

"Oh. Really? Not a goodbye, then?"

Vivid leaned forward, resting his forehead against Scorch's chest. He breathed in deep as his hands smoothed around Scorch's waist. "Not a goodbye."

Scorch held Vivid for a handful of heartbeats, trying not to fly apart at the seams. His hands were hot where they lay against the cool skin of Vivid's neck, and his pulse was quick. If he wasn't pressed against a door, his knees would buckle and he would be a heap of overwhelming bliss on the floor. As it was, Vivid was holding him steady, and when Scorch exhaled a shuddery breath, he lifted his head, stood on his tiptoes, and kissed him.

Vivid's mouth was perfect, and so was the way he deftly slipped his hand behind Scorch's back and opened the door. They stumbled into the room, kicking the door shut behind them, and then it was Scorch's turn to press Vivid against a hard surface. He picked him up and pinned him against the floral-print wallpaper, Vivid wrapping his legs around his waist. It was the first time they'd kissed inside and the first time no one was expecting them back soon with firewood, so Scorch kissed him as slowly and thoroughly as he wanted.

When his hips thrust forward of their own volition, Vivid broke their kiss to throw his head back with an encouraging moan. They moved against each other, Vivid panting into Scorch's neck, while Scorch gripped his backside with insatiable hands. When Vivid snaked a hand between them and palmed his increasingly tight trousers, Scorch nearly dropped him.

"I don't have the mental capacity for touching you and standing up at the same time," he gasped.

Vivid slid to his feet. "Go lay down," he ordered, shoving Scorch toward the bed. Scorch did as he was told and lay back on the mattress like it was his deathbed. Vivid was going to kill him.

He was finally going to kill him, and he was starting by taking off his clothes.

Scorch got up on his elbows to watch him remove his cuirass. The room was muted and torch lit, but he could still see Vivid's scars streaking silver across his body. Before, in Etheridge's tent, Vivid's exposure had been a guilty attraction, but now, safe in their room, his armor removed of his own free will, Scorch could appreciate him the way he was meant to be appreciated. He was sleek sinew and supple lines, and Scorch wanted to put his mouth on every inch of him, silver and white.

He could tell Vivid was self-conscious, even in the soft light, but apparently the desire to remove his clothes was stronger than the urge to retreat, because he let his thumbs hitch beneath the waistline of his trousers as he walked up to the bed. Scorch opened his legs to let him stand between them, his eyes fastened to the dark trail of hair leading down from Vivid's bellybutton.

Then Vivid stopped.

"Is something wrong?" Scorch asked, arousal making his voice thick.

"Yes," Vivid said, removing his thumbs from his trousers. He gave Scorch a dark look and put his hands on his hips. "I'm doing all the work. Take these off for me."

Scorch couldn't fathom how he was still breathing, but he also didn't hesitate to sit up on the bed and get his hands around Vivid's waist, and that brought his mouth irresistibly close to smooth planes of stomach. He glanced up at Vivid and licked a cautious stripe over his skin. Vivid made a pleased sound, so he continued to kiss a downward trail while his hands found their way to the front of Vivid's trousers. There was a pesky, lace-up front that he struggled with for a moment, but then the laces fell open and he pushed his hands down Vivid's hips. The feeling of warm skin and no underclothes made him smile. He paused to look up at Vivid.

"Is this what you want?" Scorch asked, needing to be sure.

Vivid glared at him, but then he whispered, "Yes."

Scorch slid the trousers down Vivid's thighs, tracing delicate lines down the length of his legs until the fabric rested at his feet.

"You still have your boots on," Scorch laughed, fingering the knee-high leather.

"Did you think I was going to wear the slippers?" Vivid returned snarkily.

"They're very comfortable slippers." Scorch swept him up around the waist, spun them around, and planted Vivid onto the mattress so he could unlace his boots and pull them off, one by one. Next came the trousers from around the ankles. Scorch tossed them over his shoulder, and then, finally, he allowed himself to look his fill at Vivid, naked and spread before him.

His thighs were muscular, his feet finely arched. His entire body was beautiful, but Scorch's eyes were having a difficult time veering away from the cock that lay thick and lovely against Vivid's stomach.

"I'm feeling overdressed," Scorch said, hypnotized by everything, absolutely everything.

"Take off those stupid slippers and come here," Vivid advised, rolling onto his side.

Scorch kicked off the stupid slippers—literally kicked them so they went flying across the room—and joined him on the bed. Vivid melded to him, arms snaring around his neck and drawing him in. Scorch kissed him hard and dragged his hands over his skin, memorizing the way Vivid's breath hitched when he scratched gently down his back, and the way he bit at Scorch's lip when he gave his backside a squeeze.

And Vivid's hands were as inquisitive as Scorch's, tugging off his shirt and tossing it haphazardly to the side. The floor was quickly becoming a graveyard for discarded adornments, and no barrier between their bodies was safe. Scorch lost his trousers next, Vivid yanking them down without pretense. And then Vivid's mouth was on him, his breath hot and damp through the thin cloth of Scorch's underclothes. He felt himself twitch in response, his back arching from the bed. Vivid rubbed a cheek against his painfully hard, painfully clothed erection, until Scorch was practically sobbing. Then he pulled the final impediment down Scorch's hips and placed a single, open-mouthed kiss on the underside of his cock. Vivid reappeared by Scorch's face a moment later, and he was smiling. It was a small smile, but it was real, and it was for him.

"You're going to kill me," Scorch groaned, pushing Vivid onto his back.

"Stop complaining," Vivid answered, letting him.

Skin met skin. Teeth clacked from insistent, desperate kisses. It was immeasurable, the state of them, wrapped around each other like they would never let go. Vivid's eyes were closed, his lips red, and Scorch buried his face against his neck and kissed a path across his collarbone. Every piece of Vivid was presented to him, every inch welcoming his touch, and Scorch touched him everywhere.

Time was broken in the space around them, so when Scorch moved down the bed and his hands firmly grasped Vivid's thighs, he was unsure how long they'd been entwined; he only knew it was nowhere near long enough and never would be. Vivid writhed at the barest touch of Scorch's lips brushing across the soft skin of his inner thigh. He sighed Scorch's name and burrowed his fingers in his hair, and when Scorch teased him with a well-placed exhale, their eyes met across the expanse of his body. Vivid glowered at him crossly, heated, and then Scorch could wait no longer. He gave Vivid everything he wanted.

The taste of him was simple: salt and skin and a clean musk that had Scorch stretching his lips and taking in more and more, as much as he could. Vivid's fingers were soothing against his scalp, pulling gently when Scorch did something he liked. He liked the way Scorch held his hips steady, the way he swallowed him down, but it turned out, what Vivid liked most of all, was Scorch's mouth on his, and it wasn't overly long before he demanded it, yanking on his hair until Scorch found his way back. Vivid kissed him, and when he pulled back, his eyes were shining.

"I have dreams about you," Scorch whispered. He rubbed his stubbled cheek against Vivid's neck. "But I don't think all of them are dreams."

Vivid combed his fingers through Scorch's hair. "What do you think they are?"

"Memories. You, protecting me from Elias, cuddling me in the mountain cave."

Vivid scoffed. "That doesn't sound like me."

"I think it does," said Scorch. And even though he already knew the answer, he had to ask. "Did you hear what I said in the dungeon?"

Vivid stilled beneath him. "Yes." He grabbed Scorch's hand and kissed his fingers, sucking two into his mouth. Then, with a determined gleam in his eyes, Vivid led his fingers down and brought them between his legs.

"Yes," Vivid said again, rocking his hips. "Scorch."

"Hold on. *Gods.*" Scorch unwound Vivid's limbs from his body. His leather trousers were on the other side of the room, folded by the door and forgotten by the servant who'd been too busy flirting to collect Scorch's filthy clothes for the laundry. He blessed that servant for his distractedness, Etheridge for her all-knowingness, and the little pouch of medicinals for not being stolen or lost before he had time to untie it from his belt and tear into it. There, between the nether-cream and the anti-inflammatory tealeaves, was a stoppered vial with a label on it that read, in Etheridge's blocky hand: *for Vivid and Scorch*, followed by a winky face. He snatched it up and hurried back to the bed, where Vivid had turned onto his stomach. Scorch stared. It was a lot to take in.

"Scorch," he said, a summons, and one Scorch was all too happy to indulge, once his brain started working again.

He crawled onto the bed and draped himself over Vivid's back, kissing the nape of his neck and down his spine. He kissed further, too, picking Vivid up by the hips and pressing his mouth over his entrance, attending him with worshipful licks and kisses that had the sweat beading on Vivid's back and his legs trembling. When his knees gave out, Scorch slicked his fingers with the oil and began opening him slowly, biting at the dimple in his lower back when he cursed him for being "too damn slow."

Scorch hushed him and took his time, enjoying the heady warmth of Vivid's body, the way he grew increasingly impatient until he was grinding down on Scorch's fingers and threatening murder. Scorch wondered, overwhelmed, which way it should be, but when Vivid arched his back and braced himself on his elbows, Scorch knew which way Vivid wanted it. He guided himself in, pausing when Vivid clenched around him, waiting for him to relax before inching deeper. Vivid's hand reached around and Scorch held it, folding himself over his back and breathing roughly against his skin. When his hips were flush, they waited, Vivid tilting his head so Scorch could kiss him.

It was Vivid who moved first, rocking back with languid undulations of his hips. It made Scorch's skin burn so hot he might have set the bed on fire if not for the cool breeze from the open window. Awareness was a sluggish, creeping thing, stunted from the tight pleasure of Vivid's body and the quick-building rhythm of Scorch's hips as he moved with faster, less careful thrusts. But when Scorch turned his head to sigh and his eyes landed on the indisputably *closed* window, it hit him.

Vivid grunted in surprise and annoyance when Scorch pulled out, rolled him onto his back, and thrust back in. The breeze ruffled their hair and Scorch leaned down to kiss him, smiling.

Vivid didn't notice until, after an exceptionally deep grind, the wind snuffed out the torchlight and knocked a vase of flowers off the dresser. He started in Scorch's arms and broke their kiss to watch as the wind blew around the curtains, Scorch's hair, and the bed sheets.

"It's you," Scorch said, and Vivid nodded, bright-eyed.

The air swirled around them excitedly when Vivid rolled Scorch onto his back and straddled him with a snarl. He laughed and took Vivid's hands in his, anchoring him as he lifted up and dropped back down. Scorch wanted desperately to watch, to see, but the pleasure was too much and he had to close his eyes as Vivid rode them both to completion. Scorch reached his first, unable to resist after Vivid leaned down and started sucking marks along his neck, and then Vivid came, wrapped in Scorch's fist.

They lay together after, Scorch's head on Vivid's chest, their fingers laced together, a sweet and mild breeze drying the sweat on their skin.

Scorch nearly asked him, once they'd caught their breath, whether or not he was staying the night, but after Vivid turned his head to kiss him with a faint smile on his lips, his eyes fluttering shut with exhaustion, Scorch had his answer. He let his eyes close and slept happily, tucked into the curve of Vivid's arm.

They didn't need Dream Moss to keep them safe anymore.

# A Beginning
## 26

The morning sun woke slowly, stretching its light across Vivid's bare leg, slung around Scorch's thigh like it had always belonged there. It was familiar and new all at once, waking up with Vivid. Familiar, because Scorch was already so accustomed to the way he stretched and yawned in the morning, his eyebrows moodily arched on his pillow-creased face, and new, because Vivid had never stretched and yawned moodily in his arms before. Scorch had certainly never smoothed his thumb over those scowling brows or pressed a kiss on the crease between his eyes, and Vivid had never brought Scorch to gasping wakefulness with his mouth.

By the time the room was golden with sunlight, Scorch was freshly spent and ready to go back to sleep. If not for Vivid's staunch refusal to lie down, he might have.

"Get up," Vivid demanded as he pulled on his snug trousers. Scorch mumbled into the warmth Vivid had left in the sheets, hesitant to move. "You are a mess," was Vivid's assessment, and a moment later Scorch was being bombarded with thrown articles of clothing. "We shouldn't linger here."

Scorch pulled the underclothes from his face. "You don't like the Queen," he said.

"I don't like her, and I don't trust her."

Scorch pried himself from the bed and walked over to Vivid, nuzzling his neck sleepily. "Last night, when I was with her, she had me burn the ordinances against elementals."

Vivid looked back at Scorch dubiously. "The morning changes people's minds."

"Some people," Scorch countered, pointedly placing his hand on the small of Vivid's back.

Vivid rolled his eyes. "She's proven herself an ally only to her own best interests. Burning a piece of paper means nothing compared to the blood that's been shed in her name."

"But she *did* burn the paper. It's a step in the right direction, at least." Scorch closed his eyes when Vivid's fingers reached up to touch the gash on his brow.

"You're a fool."

Scorch opened his eyes. Vivid wasn't smiling, but now that Scorch knew his smile, he could see how close to the surface it had always been. "I think being a fool has worked in my favor, in the long run."

Finally, a few kisses later, Scorch submitted to the idea of clothes. Though Vivid was making a show of righting the knocked over vase, Scorch could tell he was watching, so he pulled his trousers on extra slow, and stretched his arms high above his head before he tugged on his shirt. He also reached down, his back turned suggestively to Vivid, to pick up his slippers.

A gust of wind knocked him down and he definitely deserved it. He looked up from his sprawl on the floor. "Kio's potion was flawed. I knew it."

Vivid's lips still looked slightly swollen from use as he pursed them, and Scorch wondered if he could coax him into joining him on the Queen's soft rug. "You didn't know it," Vivid said.

"I hoped it," Scorch shrugged. "Do you feel back to normal? Do you think the effects have worn off completely?"

Vivid held a hand to his stomach and closed his eyes. "It's not cut off from me anymore." He opened them a moment later. "But there's no predicting the long term effects."

"We will take them as they come," Scorch assured him.

Vivid helped him from the floor. "Yes, we will."

Scorch was enjoying the bursting sensation in his chest when there came a knock on their door. Vivid automatically readied himself to unsheathe his daggers, but Scorch held up a hand to calm him. It wasn't the formal knock of a servant, or the over-confident knock of an assassin. It was an awkward staccato that went on a little too long and was followed by a cough.

Vivid's shoulders relaxed, but he still looked at the door with displeasure. "It's your guardian," he grumbled.

"He's not *my* guardian," Scorch argued, heading toward the door. "And I'll have you know, Merric is the reason Etheridge was allowed to save your life, so you should be nicer to him." Vivid didn't look convinced. "Also, he thinks you're pretty." Vivid snorted as Scorch opened the door.

Merric stood on the other side. Sometime during the night, his leg had been wrapped and he'd obtained the use of a cane. But for all of his injuries, Scorch had never seen him more contented. He guessed it might have something to do with the flautist glued to his side. One of Felix's eyes was swollen and bruised, but he was grinning ear to ear. Scorch moved aside to let them in, grimacing in sympathy as Merric limped over to sit on the unmade bed. Felix sat beside him, but before he did, he plucked something out from the messy covers and held it up to examine in the light.

Vivid's eyes met Scorch's as they both stared at the vial in Felix's hand.

"Whoops. Don't want to lose this," Felix said amiably, tossing it to Vivid. Vivid caught it and stuffed the vial of oil into his trouser pocket, his face coloring.

Scorch stifled a laugh and looked from Felix to Merric, who was as red in the face as Vivid. "Did you have a nice night, Merric?" he asked innocently, suddenly curious whether Merric's morning hobble had anything to do with his injury at all.

"A nice night, yes," Merric replied. "It sounded like you had a nice night, as well."

Scorch refused to be embarrassed. "A very nice night." *The best night of my life.*

Audrey sauntered in next, leaning in the doorway and judging Scorch's fuzzy slippers. She had the look of secrets about her and smelled like flowers.

"How is the Queen this morning?" Vivid asked her. He was propped by the window with his arms crossed. "Your eye patch is crooked."

"Bellamy is in amiable spirits," Audrey said, checking the placement of her patch with a smirk. "And she has sent me to propose an idea to you."

"Why can't she tell us herself?" Scorch asked.

"Because she is in the bath," Audrey answered.

Audrey knowing about the Queen of Viridor's bathtub occupancy was hardly the strangest thing Scorch had ever heard, so he nodded and plopped down on the bed beside Merric. "And what does Queen Bellamy propose?"

"That I remain in the Royal Quarter and help her open a school."

*That* might have been the strangest thing Scorch had ever heard. Vivid looked less shocked, however, and he replied in a bored intonation. "What does that have anything to do with us?"

"Because it will be a school for elementals," Audrey said.

Scorch stood up from the bed. "What did you say?" Vivid crossed from the window to stand at his side, and Scorch had to divide his attention between being stunned by Audrey's announcement and being thoroughly pleased that Vivid was standing beside him, so close their arms brushed together.

"She said she wants to create a place where elementals can hone their craft safely. Like the Hollow."

Scorch harrumphed rudely.

Audrey glared at him with her eye and allotted, "Like the Hollow, but without all the murder."

"But the ordinances," Merric began.

"They've been destroyed," Scorch told him.

"Destroyed or not, Viridor won't change its opinion of elementals overnight," Merric argued. "Even after word spreads that the Queen's stance has changed, most are already ingrained with the idea that elementals are dangerous."

"We *are* dangerous," Vivid growled.

"Only because we are forced to be." Scorch put a hand on Vivid's back, mostly because he could. "If elementals had a place to go, a way to learn control—it could change everything." He looked at Audrey. "Are you going to do it?"

"The Hollow has tainted itself for me," she said. "And the Queen's offer was . . . tempting."

"You'll be putting yourself at risk," warned Vivid.

"Sometimes the right thing to do is the foolish thing," she replied. "But my involvement isn't why Bellamy sent me to speak with you. She's extending an invitation to you both. She requests your aid teaching."

"No," Vivid answered immediately.

"You can't stay here," Merric said, standing from the bed and leaning on his cane, angling towards Scorch. "You have to come back to the Guild."

"I'm not a guardian anymore, Merric," Scorch said, and for the first time, saying it aloud didn't make him sad.

"You *are* a guardian." Felix sprang from the mattress, earnestness plastered on his honest face, and for a horrifying moment, Scorch was afraid he might burst into song. "You will always be a guardian."

"I'm sure my father will come around once word has spread about the ordinances. You can come back, Scorch," said Merric. Merric, with his auburn hair and lovely green eyes. Merric, whom Scorch had always thought hated him and was now pleading for his companionship. "Vivid, you could come, too. You would make a fine guardian, I think."

"Say it again and it will be the last thing you ever say," Vivid snapped.

"I—need to think about it," Scorch sighed.

"Bellamy wants an answer soon," Audrey said.

"Felix and I want to head back tomorrow morning," Merric said. "If you decide by then, we can share a carriage."

"The Queen is loaning us one," Felix chimed. "Though, honestly, I think she's just angling for me to write a song about her."

"We'll think it over," Scorch promised, ushering Merric and Felix towards the door, but before they left, Merric patted his shoulder and smiled warmly.

He leaned in close and said, "I told you he wouldn't leave."

"Yes, yes, you are very wise. I'll see you after I've had ample time to bask in your divine wisdom."

Merric laughed as he disappeared into his room, but Felix turned one last time to look at Scorch. He fixed him with a knowing smile, and Scorch gave him a little wave.

When he turned around, Vivid was trading quiet words with Audrey, and he must have said something funny, because her eye was twinkling with amusement by the time they parted. She strolled out the door, pausing only long enough to twirl a dagger threateningly and whisper to Scorch, "Remember what I said," and then she was gone.

Scorch closed the door and took a deep breath.

Vivid spoke first. "If you need time alone to think about—"

"No," Scorch interrupted, turning to find Vivid right there, right in front of him. "I don't need to think about it. I don't want to go back to the Guild, and I don't want to work for the Queen."

"You don't," Vivid stated plainly, gazing up at Scorch with his amethyst eyes and his fierce, beautiful face.

"It's been tiring work, being alive," Scorch said. Ever since he'd woken up with Vivid in his arms, he'd been mulling over the same thought. "I've had enough of guardians and queens and people who want to kill me."

"You have."

"I want to disappear with you. At least for a little while."

Vivid hooked his fingers in Scorch's trousers and pulled him close. "Where do you want to go?"

"Anywhere," Scorch said, shaking his head. "With you."

Vivid scratched his fingers over the scruff of Scorch's cheek. "You won't know what to do with yourself if you're not busy being idiotically heroic."

"I'm sure I can think of other ways to fill my time that don't involve either of us almost dying. Or actually dying." Vivid's hands were in his hair, on his neck, distracting him. "We could, erm, go east and," Vivid kissed him, "and," Vivid kissed him again, "and do all kinds of non-heroic things." He put his arms around Vivid's waist and tried to convey his seriousness. "If that's what you want."

"I want to disappear with you," Vivid said softly. And then, a little less softly, he added, "And I want you to stop talking." He dragged Scorch back to the bed and did a praise-worthy job of shutting him up.

Later, when the sky had darkened and they'd packed bundles of food nabbed from the kitchen and a flask of Guild-brewed whiskey from the Queen's chamber, and Scorch's pouch from Etheridge was tucked safely in his trousers, Scorch and Vivid used their considerable stealth to sneak away, unnoticed, from the secondary residence.

They unhitched a horse from the stables—only one, because Scorch insisted it would be impolite to steal two—and rode east, Scorch's hands snug on Vivid's waist and Vivid's zigzag part tickling Scorch's nose. And even though they had no idea where they were going, Scorch knew they were headed in the right direction.

# The Sun Guardian

Many a tale has been told of the Gods

And to them all our love we bestow.

For it's in their power to give us the men

Who are heroes to us here below...

And whose real names we often don't know...


Such a man came amongst us a few seasons past,

One whose beauty was bright as the sun.

As tall as a mountain

With muscles of steel,

And with hair as a halo gold-spun

He wooed all the townsfolk,

By his presence alone,

He took one willing lassie to bed,

But when morning came

'Ere he'd said his goodbyes

Villains cut off the dear lady's head.

Aghast and grief-stricken, with powerful rage

He was told by the townspeople then,

Such villains oft came

Seeking people to cage

And to fight to the death for a win.

He took up his sword and began running east,

His feet bare touched the ground as he flew,

'Til he came to the Circle where innocent blood

Was shed for the greed of a few.

Now drawing his sword as an army of one,

He slew fifty men with his might,

And freed from the cages

The captives there held,

And led them all safely in flight.

As the morning was dawning,

He shrugged off their cheers,

Holding tears back, he'd just walked away.

And then set afire,

A villainous pyre,

Of the men who had his lover slayed.

As the flames rose, the sun rose,

And all who were there

Say it shone and made golden his head.

Like a God he thus stood,

A true hero for good

To whom no other man could compare.

And then in the blink of an eye he was gone

As if taken up by the sun,

For now, his battle was done.

For the guardian sent by the sun ...


-- Felix the Flautist

T.S. Cleveland works as an artist, illustrator, and cover designer. She lives in Atlanta, GA. This is her first published novel.

To contact the author, or for
information on buying prints or original art, please visit:
victoriaskyecleveland.com
www.Etsy.com/Shop/ArtbyVictoriaSkye

Made in the USA
Lexington, KY
08 January 2018